TAKEN TO DIE

A DCI DANNY FLINT BOOK

TREVOR NEGUS

PROLOGUE

10.00am, 3 July 1986
HMP Leeds, Gloucester Terrace, Leeds

Sam Jamieson had been awake since five o'clock that morning. Today was the day he would finally be released from his living hell. At eight thirty, he had heard the key turn in the lock of his cell door. He had vowed, there and then, that it would be the last time he would ever have to wait for someone else to unlock a door so he could start his day.

He had spent seven long years rotting inside the walls of the Armley jail. He was that very rare commodity, a genuinely innocent man in prison. He had maintained his innocence throughout his time in custody, even to the detriment of possible early release. Eighteen months ago, he had still refused to admit any involvement in the armed robbery for which he had been convicted. As a result, he had been refused parole.

As far as Sam Jamieson was concerned, the damage had already been done. There was nothing to be gained by being released early now.

Just after he had served three years of his sentence, he had been notified by the prison chaplain that his thirteen-year-old daughter, Vanessa, had passed away. He was coldly informed by the elderly clergyman that she had died at a party with friends after suffering a bad reaction from taking the illegal drug Ecstasy.

He had been allowed out of prison for one morning so he could be present as his only child was buried at the Mansfield Woodhouse cemetery. Standing at the graveside, handcuffed to a prison officer, Sam had been unwilling to even look at his wife, let alone speak to her.

For the six months following his daughter's funeral, Sam had raged against the system. He constantly fought other prisoners and prison officers. He repeatedly smashed everything in his cell and was regularly placed on report.

Sam blamed himself for the death of his daughter.

He knew in his heart that if he had been at home, his daughter would never have been allowed to mix with the people his wife had turned a blind eye to. He had discovered later that his errant wife had been more interested in going out with friends and getting on with her own life to worry about an angsty teenage daughter.

At that most crucial time in her short life, Vanessa had needed both her parents to be there for her.

She had neither.

Eventually, Sam Jamieson stopped blaming himself.

He had come to realise there were other people far more deserving of that blame. There were two people who had been responsible for his conviction, his incarceration and, ultimately, the death of his only child.

One was his cousin. His own flesh and blood. The man

who had said nothing to clear him and allowed him to be sent to prison for something he had played no part in.

The other was Rebecca Whitchurch. She had been counsel for the prosecution at his trial. She had gone out of her way to convince the jury that he had been the getaway driver for the gang that had robbed a sub-post office in Mansfield Woodhouse at gunpoint.

Sam was no angel, but he had never been involved in serious crime and had only one previous dishonesty offence to his name. That was a shoplifting charge from way back when he was still a juvenile.

The only evidence to connect Sam to the armed robbery was a single fingerprint found on the rear-view mirror of the abandoned getaway car. Following his arrest, he had told detectives that he'd borrowed the car from his cousin. The only reason he had used the car was to get medicine for his ten-year-old daughter, who was running a high fever.

Sam had returned the car to his cousin shortly after making a quick visit to the late-night chemist. He had been totally unaware that his relation planned to use the same car during an armed robbery the following day.

Even though detectives quickly established that Sam had been to the chemist the night before, there was no proof he had used his cousin's vehicle to do so. A point that was forcefully made to the jury by the arrogant Rebecca Whitchurch.

She also made capital out of the fact that his own cousin had refused to say, one way or the other, if Sam had been the driver during the robbery. She maintained throughout the trial that if Jamieson had been innocent, then surely his own flesh and blood would have spoken up for him. The fact that his cousin had maintained 'no comment' answers throughout his police interviews and had refused to give verbal evidence during the trial was welcomed by Whitchurch. Consequently, the jury were never given the opportunity to establish what

Sam's cousin would say had he chosen to answer the question of exactly who the getaway driver was.

At the prosecution barrister's insistence, the jury were urged to convict all three men before them for armed robbery. The three men were all subsequently convicted, and each sentenced to seven years imprisonment.

Finally, Sam had come to terms with the death of his daughter. He stopped butting heads with the establishment. He realised that revenge was a dish best served cold, and had used the remaining time of his sentence to prepare for his eventual release. He began working out in the gym every day and studied an Open University course, subsequently gaining a first-class degree in psychology.

During the final four years of his sentence, Sam had transformed himself from violent, troublesome convict to model prisoner. However, he was still refused early release, simply because he refused to accept that he had any involvement in the offence for which he had been convicted. Having served every minute of his sentence, when the time finally came for his release, there was no licence to contend with.

He had served his entire sentence. It was now time for a new start.

Sam Jamieson was being released from prison still holding a burning desire to avenge both the death of his daughter and the loss of seven years of his life. He had decided four years ago that it would be his cousin and Rebecca Whitchurch who would pay the price.

That had changed two years ago, when Sam had learned of his cousin's death. He had hung himself in Lincoln prison while still serving his sentence for the armed robbery. The death of his cousin meant that Sam had polarised all that frustration and hatred against one person, the barrister Rebecca Whitchurch.

On the day of his release, that hadn't changed. The hatred still burned fiercely inside him.

After going through the administrative process of release, he now stood in civilian clothes just inside the last gate, waiting to be released.

The gate officer walked forward with a large bunch of keys and said, 'Is that you away, then, Jamieson?'

'I think I've been here long enough, Mr Armstrong, don't you?'

The experienced prison officer nodded. 'Aye, I reckon you have, lad. Have you got anything lined up on the outside?'

'Not yet. I just want to get out of here. Go home and visit my daughter's grave.'

'That was a bad business, son. A terrible shame that you were in here when it happened. I can't believe that was almost three years ago now.'

Sam shook his head; it was now four years ago. It still felt as raw as though it were yesterday. He knew the fat Geordie screw meant no harm, so he let the man's thoughtless comment wash over him. Four years ago, that same careless utterance would have resulted in Sam beating the middle-aged prison officer to the floor.

Sam Jamieson had changed completely. He was now a very cold, calculating individual, with only one purpose driving his life. The searing violence was still there and capable of being unleashed. He was now a man in total control of his emotions and his actions.

He turned to the prison officer and said, 'How do I get to the railway station from here, boss?'

'When you get outside the gate, turn left and walk along Gloucester Terrace down towards the main road. Use the underpass to get onto Armley Road. There's a bus stop on that road; it'll get you into the city. You'll need to get off the bus at Aire Street. The railway station's signposted from there.'

'Thanks, Mr Armstrong.'

The prison officer stepped forward and unlocked the gate, 'Off you go, then, Jamieson, and good luck. Don't let me see you back here.'

Sam stepped forward, outside, and became a free man once more. He heard the heavy gate slam shut behind him, and heard the bolts being drawn across.

Finally, he was out and alone on the street.

He walked forward, turned, and took one last look at the twin stone turrets that flanked each side of the large wooden gate. He felt a cold shudder that had nothing to do with the freezing temperature.

He tilted his head back, closed his eyes, and drew in a deep lungful of air.

It felt fresh and tasted clean.

He opened his eyes and looked around him. It was still early, and there wasn't another soul on the street outside the jail. As directed by the prison officer, he turned left and began walking towards the main road. As he walked along, he felt uncomfortable. The navy-blue suit he was wearing felt very tight. It pinched under his arms and around his thighs. He was wearing the same suit he'd worn for his trial seven years ago. Four years of working out in the prison gym meant that the jacket and trousers were now a very poor fit.

He would have removed the tight jacket, but the sky was as grey as the twin stone turrets, and the chill breeze made it feel even colder.

He counted the money in his trouser pockets. He had the grand sum of ninety-five pounds and thirty-four pence to his name. The prison officer who had returned his property had sarcastically assured him that it would be more than enough cash to purchase a one-way train ticket to Nottingham.

Sam walked through the underpass as traffic roared overhead on the main A647 road. He stepped back out into the light and found himself on Armley Road. He looked to his right and, in the distance, saw a bus shelter. He pulled up the collar of his jacket and began to walk briskly towards the bus stop. As he got nearer, he could see there was an elderly man sitting alone on the bench, inside the shelter.

Suddenly, the heavens opened, and it began to rain hard.

Sam sprinted for the bus shelter. By the time he had covered the seventy-five yards, the shoulders of his navy-blue suit were several shades darker than the rest. He was soaked.

As Sam dashed out of the rain and under the shelter, he startled the old man. Sam saw that the old man had taken a fright at his sudden appearance. He realised that his shaven head and muscular appearance might make him nervous, so he quickly said, 'Sorry, mate. I didn't mean to make you jump.'

In a broad West Yorkshire accent, the old man replied, 'That's alright, young fella. It's pissing it down out there, and you've got no raincoat.'

He winked, then grinned and said, 'Didn't you have a raincoat when you got sent down, lad?'

Sam smiled back and said, 'Is it that obvious?'

The old man nodded. 'Afraid so, lad. I'm guessing you've served at least a four-year stretch, looking at how that jacket fits. It's either that or they've given you the wrong bloody suit.'

Sam laughed. 'It's a good job I'm not dangerous, the amount of stick you're giving me.'

The old man chuckled and said, 'I don't mean to give you a hard time. I've been a guest at Her Majesty's pleasure a couple of times myself, but that was all a long time ago. Where you headed, lad?'

'I'm hoping I can get a bus into the city centre from this stop. I need to catch a train down to Nottingham.'

'You'll need to get on the number forty-seven bus. There'll be one along soon. Tell the driver you need to get off at Aire Street.'

'Thanks.'

'This is my bus now, son. Don't forget you want the number forty-seven to Aire Street.'

'Cheers.'

The single-decker bus stopped amidst a screech of air brakes. When the doors finally opened, the old man turned. With a knowing grin, he said, 'One last thing, lad: Don't let the bastards grind you down!'

The doors closed; the diesel engine of the bus was revved loudly before the driver pulled the large vehicle away from the kerb. Black clouds of foul-smelling, acrid exhaust fumes billowed out in its wake.

Eventually, silence returned to the bus shelter. Sam was left alone with thoughts of the daughter he no longer had, and seven wasted years.

1

10.30pm, 20 September 1986
Blidworth Bottoms, Nottinghamshire

The bright full moon that had been illuminating the car park at the secluded beauty spot was suddenly covered by thick cloud, and darkness engulfed the only two vehicles there.

The man, standing behind the large tree and watching the two parked vehicles, welcomed the darkness. Dressed entirely in black from head to toe, he was virtually impossible to see.

He had left his small 125cc motorcycle propped against a tree at the edge of the woods after following one of the cars to the beauty spot. He had followed the black Volvo estate at a discreet distance. They had travelled through almost deserted streets, from Nottingham city centre through the districts of Sherwood and Arnold, before finally taking the

A60 road at Redhill roundabout and driving towards Mansfield.

This wasn't the first time he had followed the Volvo. He knew that the second vehicle, a midnight blue Range Rover sport, would already be waiting in the car park.

By the time he had left his motorcycle, replaced his crash helmet with a black woollen ski mask and walked stealthily through the woods, he could see the very attractive, dark-haired woman who had been driving the Volvo was already getting out of her car.

The man in black stood in silence behind the cover of a large tree. He watched as the back door of the Range Rover opened.

He heard a man's voice say, 'What kept you, sweetheart?'

The woman giggled and said, 'The usual thing! My boss is an absolute bastard!'

Hitching up the pencil skirt of her pinstriped business suit and exposing white thighs over black stocking tops, the woman climbed into the rear of the Range Rover. She closed the door behind her.

The man leaned a little further out from behind the tree and continued to observe the Range Rover. Using the deep shadows, he tiptoed closer to the vehicle.

Eventually, he was standing almost directly beside the vehicle. Only the tinted privacy glass prevented him from seeing the activities of the two people inside.

He couldn't see anything, but he could hear the couple's urgent fumblings coming from inside the vehicle. With a growing sense of frustration, he slowly moved back to the tree line, where he continued to stare at the vehicle, which had now begun to rock slowly. He could now hear gasps and moans of pleasure from inside the car. The sounds grew louder as the couple inside raced to a frantic climax.

The rocking motion of the vehicle came to an abrupt stop.

The moans emanating from inside diminished until once again an eerie silence enveloped the car park.

After a few minutes, the back door of the Range Rover opened. Just as the moon emerged from behind the clouds, the woman stepped out of the vehicle.

Now she was bathed in the stark lunar light, the man watching could see that her raven black hair, which had previously been tied back in a ponytail, was now loose and tousled.

From behind the ski mask, his unblinking blue eyes stared as the woman smoothed down her pencil skirt. He was treated to another glimpse of white flesh above black stocking tops. Having smoothed down her skirt, the woman began hurriedly buttoning up her sheer blouse. Very quickly, she covered her full breasts, which had been fleetingly exposed.

The man in black then heard the door on the far side of the Range Rover open and close. He retreated a step deeper into the woods. He observed a man who was fortysomething, short in stature with a small pot belly and collar-length, gelled-back hair walk around the rear of the vehicle and approach the woman.

The man was wearing pinstriped suit trousers and a white shirt that was unbuttoned to the waist. The belt he wore and the top button of his trousers were undone.

As he walked towards the woman, he was swinging her lacy black knickers around the index finger of his right hand. He laughed and said, 'Aren't you forgetting something, darling?'

She giggled before replying, 'You were so quick to take them off me, I thought you wanted to keep them.'

Playfully, she made a grab for the lacy knickers, but he moved them swiftly out of her reach. He grabbed her wrist, pulled her towards him and kissed her hard on the mouth.

The woman responded eagerly, kissing him back. As they kissed, she allowed her hand to slide down to his trousers. She playfully grabbed his crotch, stopped kissing him, and said, 'Don't tell me you're ready to go again already?'

With more urgency now, they kissed again. As they did so, he began to slowly walk her backwards, towards the front of the Volvo.

Still watching from behind the tree, the man in black looked on, mesmerised, as the man with gelled hair lifted the woman onto the bonnet of the Volvo. He then positioned himself between her legs. He stopped kissing her and stood up straight, leaving her draped backwards over the bonnet. He unzipped his trousers, allowing them to slide down his legs to the ground, then pushed the woman's pencil skirt up, once again exposing the white flesh at the top of her stockings.

The sex was fast and furious, lasting just a few minutes before they both climaxed.

The man watching from the woods felt a burning rage building inside him. He struggled inwardly to contain his temper as he watched the lovers get dressed again and enjoy a postcoital cigarette. He listened intently, trying to catch their muffled conversation as they leaned against the side of the Volvo.

Managing to curtail his growing sense of anger and frustration, the man skulked further back into the shadows. He squatted behind a low bush and watched the couple embrace for one last kiss before they got into their respective vehicles.

Watching from the darkness, the man heard the car engines start and saw the lights from both vehicles come on before they were driven slowly out of the car park.

The Range Rover slowly followed the Volvo estate.

With both vehicles now gone, the man in black remained motionless in the woods. From his squatting position, he had slumped forward on to all fours. Feeling suddenly nauseous, he ripped off the ski mask before dry retching. The muscles in his stomach cramped painfully. He could feel tears streaming down his face. His entire body physically convulsed, shaking in a silent, muted rage.

Eventually, he calmed down and got back to his feet. He walked back through the pitch-dark woods to where he had left his motorcycle. He retrieved his full-face crash helmet from the seat and put it on before straddling the bike. He turned the ignition key and stamped down hard on the kickstart.

The small engine fired into life the first time. He selected first gear before steering the motorcycle out of the woods and onto the dark unlit road. As he rode along the shadowy country lanes, towards his house, he vowed to get even.

The tears now streaming down his face had nothing to do with the cold wind biting into his face as he sped away with the visor of his helmet open.

As the cold wind frosted his face, he made a promise to himself. No matter how long it took, he would make them both suffer.

He would ensure they both experienced exactly the same pain he was feeling right now.

2

8.15am, 21 September 1986
Perry Road, Sherwood, Nottingham

Danny Flint glanced down at the photograph once more. The face staring back at him was that of a man who had lived a hard life.

Francis Corrigan was a fiftysomething bricklayer from Cork in Southern Ireland. His face was weather-beaten, and his skin had the ruddy tones of a man who had worked outdoors all his adult life. The face was dominated by a badly broken nose, and there was heavy scarring above both eyebrows. The man was obviously a fighter.

Danny turned to the man sitting in the car next to him and said, 'Are you sure this photo's a good likeness?'

Detective Sergeant Andy Wills said, 'It's the most recent one we have. It was taken when Corrigan was arrested for the ABH in March this year.'

'And what time is he due for release?'

'He'll be released at eight thirty this morning.'

'Does he have any idea what's happening?'

Andy shrugged. 'I don't know, boss. He may have an idea that something like this could be waiting for him. This has all been such a rushed job. When the Garda detective telephoned this morning, he wasn't even sure they had got the right Francis Corrigan. It's quite a common name, apparently.'

'But they're sure now?'

Andy held up a piece of paper and said, 'This is the fax they sent, outlining the details of the offence he's wanted for in Cork. It's a one-punch scenario. Corrigan and another man were having an argument in Flanagan's Bar on Maylor Street, when Corrigan lashed out and punched this other man. When Sean Logan fell, he smashed his head on the kerb edge and died from his head injuries two days later. By that time, Corrigan had already travelled back over to England.'

'So why the urgency now? Why couldn't the Garda have travelled over and dealt with this while Corrigan was still locked up in Nottingham prison?'

'They only found the witness who identified Corrigan two days ago. By the time they found out that Corrigan was serving a custodial sentence here, he was due for release. Initially, they had no idea that he'd been locked up here for another assault.'

Danny was thoughtful.

He hated making gate arrests; they almost always ended in violent confrontations. He totally understood why that was the case. For a convicted criminal to be released, only to then be immediately confronted by police officers wanting to detain him again. Knowing that there was a real prospect of being sent back to prison. Why wouldn't that person be pissed off?

When the fax requesting the gate arrest of Francis Corrigan had arrived at the MCIU office that morning, the only detective in the office had been Andy Wills. Andy was aware that no other staff would be arriving until after nine o'clock that morning. Too late to effect the arrest.

He was just about to go to the local CID office to try to get some staff when Danny had walked in.

Andy had quickly explained the situation, and the two detectives had driven to HMP Nottingham and parked the car outside the imposing gates on Perry Road.

Danny had been confident they would be able to utilise local uniformed officers to provide backup when they made the arrest.

Now, as they sat waiting in their car outside the prison gates, there was no sign of that backup.

Danny said, 'Find out what's happened to the uniforms.'

Andy picked up the radio and said, 'DS Wills to Sherwood Control. Can you tell me what time the two uniform staff you promised will be attending the prison for the gate arrest? The release time is very close now, and there's no sign of your officers yet.'

The reply was terse. 'From Sherwood Control: The two staff who were travelling have had to divert to a serious RTA. We've got no other officers available to assist you at present. Over.'

'From DS Wills. Understood. If any do become available, ask them to travel to the prison as soon as possible. We are anticipating this arrest could turn violent, and there are only two of us here at present. Over.'

'From Control. Understood. Over.'

Danny sighed. 'Bloody marvellous.'

He glanced at his watch; it was now eight twenty. In ten minutes, the smaller gate within the two large wooden gates would open, and Francis Corrigan would step outside for his very short taste of freedom.

Danny looked at the battered face in the photograph and said, 'I think we're going to have our hands full here, Andy. Be ready for anything.'

3

9.00am, 21 September 1986
Nottingham City Centre

After battling through the morning rush hour traffic, Darren Treadgold parked his Suzuki motorcycle in the Broadmarsh Centre car park. He secured it with a bike lock, took off his helmet and made his way down the stairs.

He hated his life.

He knew he looked ridiculous riding his motorcycle. His huge, heavy frame perched precariously on the small machine. It was no wonder people howled with laughter and shouted derisive comments at him as he rode slowly by. He had no choice but to put up with the situation. Apart from stealing his elderly father's car, it was the only way he could get into the city from his father's house at West Bridgford. The car was expensive to run and very risky, as he only had a provisional driving licence. He knew how to drive the car, but had never passed his driving test. It was just one more thing in life he had failed at, in a long list of failures.

He regarded himself as one of life's underachievers and couldn't see how that would ever change.

He knew people regarded him as ugly. With his hooded, piggy eyes, a bulbous, prominent nose, and unkempt, lank, greasy hair, how was anybody ever going to find him attractive?

It didn't help that he was also morbidly obese and waddled when he walked. His personal hygiene was virtually non-existent, and, unsurprisingly, he was still single at forty-five years of age. Worst of all, he still lived at home with his profoundly deaf elderly father.

The only positive in his life was that he had a half-decent job to go to every day.

As supervisor of the McDonald's fast-food restaurant on Angel Row in Nottingham, he could, to a great extent, pick and choose the hours he worked. That wasn't the only perk. He could also help himself to any unsold burgers at the end of a late shift, at two o'clock in the morning.

He adored the taste of the chain's Big Mac burgers. He would often put an extra four or five in to cook just before the end of trading. That way, he was guaranteed a nice free snack when he finished work.

The only other pleasure he had in his pathetic life was smoking cannabis.

He loved the brief high and momentary escape from a dull, boring life that a joint gave him. He smoked weed whenever he could get hold of the banned substance. His main source of supply came from the scruffy hippies who frequented a squat just off the Arboretum. He used leftover burgers to ingratiate himself with the squatters who lived there. In return, they allowed him to visit their squat, buy gear, 'skin up' and smoke it on the premises.

There was no way his father would allow him to smoke 'that filth!' in his house. He might be stone deaf, but there was nothing wrong with the miserable old bastard's sense of smell.

After becoming a regular visitor, Darren had recently attempted to use the squat for a far more sinister purpose.

He was useless around mature, adult women. As a result, he had developed an unhealthy attraction to young, prepubescent schoolgirls. He would often spend time chatting to the young girls from the Nottingham High School who had walked down into town at lunchtime to get a burger from his restaurant. There was something about the cut of the uniform and the way the young girls hitched up their skirts, to make them that bit shorter, that he couldn't resist. Lunchtimes in midweek were always his favourite times to be at work. He would always ensure that he was front of house at these times so he could ogle the young girls as they ate their lunch.

He had befriended one such schoolgirl, who had seemed to be a bit of a loner. The pretty, blonde-haired girl always sat alone and seemed to be a bit of an outcast from her classmates. When he began talking to her, he soon realised why she was sitting on her own. She was completely wild.

As soon as he mentioned smoking dope to her, she was like putty in his hands. She had readily agreed to meet with him, sometime in the future, if she could smoke his drugs.

One afternoon, he had borrowed his father's old Morris Oxford car and picked her up after school. She had been walking with two friends at first. When they had all gone their separate ways, at the junction of Mansfield Road and Forest Road East, he had moved in. She had recognised him immediately. With the promise of smoking a joint, she had readily got into his car. He had then driven her to the squat on The Arboretum, where they had spent hours alone in an upstairs room, talking and smoking dope together.

Eventually, the young girl had become totally out of it. With a growing sense of excitement, Darren had placed his fat, sweaty palm on the bare thigh of the stoned young girl. It felt smooth and cool to his touch. He was about to slide his hand higher up her thigh and beneath her short skirt, when one of the squatters downstairs had shouted that the police were outside.

He couldn't be sure if the police were actively looking for the girl, who was still in her school uniform, and who would have been missing well over five hours by that time. But his instincts told him the police officers were there for exactly that reason. He panicked and didn't hang around to find out. He left the squat, leaving the young, semi-conscious schoolgirl in the room upstairs.

He had made good his escape through the broken-down back door as the two police officers came in through the front.

The whole experience with the young girl had spooked him, but excited him at the same time. It had certainly whetted his appetite; he had desperately wanted to move his hand further up the schoolgirl's leg.

Being a virgin at forty-five years of age was ridiculous. It was something he intended to change, one way or the other, very soon. He planned to get another young girl. Instead of taking her to the squat, this time he would take her back to the privacy of the unused attic room at his father's house.

It wouldn't matter if she screamed the place down. His father was stone deaf, and the property at West Bridgford was positioned well away from any other houses and about fifty yards back from the road. If he planned it right and took the girl back to the house after a late shift, his father would be fast asleep.

With that thought in his mind, he had a broad smile on his fat face as he walked into the fast-food restaurant to start his shift. He eagerly checked the roster to see when his next late shift was. The sooner he picked up another girl, the better. He would start using the car to get to work from now on. He knew he would need it to get the girl back to his house, and you never knew when an opportunity might present itself. He knew it would cost him a lot for petrol every week. Fuck the expense, he thought.

He knew that no girl would go with him voluntarily, and he hated physical violence. Recently, he had visited the local library and read up on the use and properties of stupefying drugs. He learned that the easiest drug to get hold of was chloroform. All he had to do now was go to the chemist and purchase a small bottle of the drug. Everything would then be ready for him to snatch a young girl off the street and start his very first sexual adventure.

For once in his miserable life, he felt in control. With an unusual air of confidence, he breezed past the young waitresses and cooking assistants, through the kitchens and into his office. He ignored their facial expressions and snide comments as they turned their noses up at the stench of body odour he gave off as he walked by.

He knew his staff all referred to him as Fat Daz behind his back. He didn't care anymore. As far as he was concerned, they could all fuck off.

Very soon, he would be the one coming to work every day with a big smile on his face.

4

8.30am, 21 September 1986
Perry Road, Sherwood, Nottingham

Danny stood on one side of the small gate and Andy the other.

They could hear the prison officer on the inside using the heavy keys to unlock the door. They could also hear laughter and a loud voice, full of Irish brogue, from the other side of the door. Francis Corrigan was obviously savouring his moment of release and was enjoying the craic with the prison officer.

Danny turned to look at Andy Wills.

The detective sergeant wore an anxious expression and whispered, 'Where's that bloody uniform backup?'

Danny said, 'Forget it. They're not coming. Have you got your handcuffs ready?'

Andy nodded.

Suddenly, the small door opened, and Francis Corrigan stepped outside the prison walls.

Andy stepped forward and grabbed one of the burly bricklayer's arms. He said, 'Francis Corrigan, I'm arresting you on suspicion of the murder of Sean Logan.'

He had intended to say more to Corrigan, but the punch from the Irishman's free hand landed flush in the detective's mouth, knocking him backwards onto the floor.

Corrigan growled, 'I don't fucking think so!'

Seeing Andy get knocked down, Danny leapt forward to grab Corrigan. As he grabbed at Corrigan's jacket, the man turned and aimed a headbutt towards Danny's face.

Danny saw it coming and managed to avoid the main force of the blow. Corrigan's forehead still landed heavily on Danny's right cheekbone, causing him to lose his grip on the suspect's jacket.

The moment he felt the detective lose his grip, Corrigan started to run away, along Perry Road.

The road the prison stood on was long and straight, flanked by the high prison walls. There was nowhere for Corrigan to go, only in a straight line.

Danny shouted at a slowly recovering Andy Wills, 'Get the car and get on the radio! Tell control we need urgent backup. Now!'

Danny then began to sprint after the lumbering Corrigan. Although Corrigan was a strong man and quick with his fists, he was also short and squat and no runner.

As Danny quickly gained on the fleeing suspect, he could feel an all-too-familiar sharp pain in his right knee. He carried an old football injury that flared up as soon as he tried to run. He ignored the pain in his leg and the throbbing of his bruised cheekbone and closed on Corrigan.

As he got to within a yard of the fleeing suspect, Danny

could hear the high revs from the engine of the CID car as Andy drove it at speed along Perry Road.

As he got to within grabbing distance of Corrigan, Danny shouted, 'Come here, you bastard!'

He half grabbed and half pushed Corrigan. Both men ended up sprawled on the pavement. Danny recovered the quicker of the two and grabbed Corrigan's right arm, twisting it behind his back. He then used all his body weight to force Corrigan's face down into the tarmac.

He could hear running footsteps approaching and was relieved to hear Andy's voice: 'Let me see his wrist, boss.'

Seconds later, the handcuffs were applied to Corrigan's wrists, effectively securing the still-snarling suspect.

As they continued to restrain the suspect, a police patrol car screamed to a halt across the road. Two uniform officers leapt out of the car and sprinted towards them.

Danny stood slowly and said, 'Everything's under control, lads. Thanks for coming. Can you take the prisoner to Central nick? We'll follow you down there.'

The uniformed officer hauled Corrigan to his feet and said, 'Who is he, and what's he under arrest for, boss?'

'His name's Francis Corrigan, and he's been detained on suspicion of murder. DS Wills will give the details of the arrest to the custody sergeant when we get to Central. Thanks, lads.'

With a note of concern in his voice, the young officer said, 'Are you two okay? Your cheek's already swollen, and the sergeant's mouth's a right mess.'

Danny grinned. 'We'll live. What I can tell you is this, I'm getting way too old for all this shit!'

5

11.00am, 21 September 1986
MCIU Offices, Mansfield, Nottinghamshire

Danny had left Andy in Nottingham to prepare the extradition file for Corrigan and had returned to the MCIU office. He was just pressing a cold, damp handkerchief on the livid purple bruise that had appeared on his cheekbone, when there was a very soft, polite knock on the office door. Without removing the cold compress, Danny shouted, 'Come in!'

When he looked up, he was shocked to see a very distressed Chief Superintendent Bill Wainwright.

The granite-tough Scot had been Danny's boss since the inception of the Major Crime Investigation Unit. He couldn't ever remember seeing him look so upset.

Danny stood up and walked over to Bill. 'Christ! Whatever's the matter, Bill? You look terrible. Sit down.'

Bill Wainwright made no comment about the bruising on

Danny's face and just slumped into a chair. After a long pause, he finally said, 'I've just come from King's Mill Hospital. Miles Galton is dead.'

Miles Galton had been the chief constable of Nottinghamshire Police for the last ten years. He had been instrumental in establishing the MCIU almost a year ago.

It was now Danny's turn to be shocked. He sat back down in his chair, stunned into silence.

Eventually, Danny asked, 'How? When?'

Bill replied, 'We were at a meeting at Mansfield District Council this morning, discussing plans for the upcoming visit of the Prime Minister. One minute, Miles was fine, laughing and joking. Then he suddenly clasped his arm across his chest and keeled over at the table.'

Danny muttered, 'Bloody hell.'

Bill remained staring at his hands in his lap. He continued, 'Everyone there suspected it was a heart attack straightaway. Someone called an ambulance, and I tried doing CPR along with a councillor who used to be a nurse. By the time the paramedics arrived, he'd gone. Truth be known, I think he was dead when he slumped at the table. He was only fifty-nine, for Christ's sake, two years younger than me. I've just come from the mortuary at King's Mill. Hope you don't mind me turning up unannounced and dropping this news on you. I needed to take a minute and tell someone else before I drive over to Lowdham and inform his wife, Betty.'

'Do you want me to come with you? Do you want a cup of tea or a coffee first?'

'I wouldn't mind a cup of tea; I'm struggling to get my head round what's just happened.'

Danny walked out of the office and saw DC Fran Jefferies at her desk. He said quietly, 'Fran, if you're not too busy, would you mind making two cups of tea and bringing them into my office, please?'

'No problem. Is everything okay? You look white as a sheet.'

'Thanks, Fran, I'm fine. I'll tell you later.'

Danny walked back into his office. He immediately noticed a distinct change in Bill Wainwright's demeanour. He was sitting straighter, and there was now a determined glint in his grey eyes. The hard exterior was back. The dour Scot inside the man had regained control. He said firmly, 'There's going to be massive changes now.'

Danny sat down and echoed, 'Changes? In what way?'

'Well, for a start, all promotions will be put on hold until a new chief's been appointed. That's always the way.'

Noticing the bruising for the first time, Wainwright continued, 'What the hell's happened to your face?'

Before Danny could explain, there was a knock on the door. He opened it, and Fran Jefferies walked into the office, carrying a tray of hot drinks.

Bill Wainwright said, 'Thanks, Detective, much appreciated.'

Fran left, closing the door softly behind her.

Bill took a long drink of the hot, sweet tea before saying, 'I expect the deputy chief will get the job. I think when he transferred in from Devon and Cornwall last year, it was on the understanding that he would eventually replace Miles when he retired.'

It was a statement rather than an invitation to comment, and Danny remained silent. He was still trying to take in the enormity of what he'd just been told. Now that his brain had processed the initial shock of what had happened, his thoughts turned towards the future of the MCIU.

The specialist investigative team was very much the brainchild of Miles Galton. Would the new chief, whoever that might be, feel the same way?

Bill took another sip of the tea and said, 'Can I take you

up on that offer, Danny? I think I'd like some support when I go over to Lowdham and tell Betty what's happened.'

'Of course. I've met Betty a few times, and I know it's not going to be an easy task, breaking such devastating news to her.'

'Thanks. Delivering a death message never gets any easier. I don't mind telling you, it's made me think this morning. I'm seriously considering bringing my own retirement forward.'

Danny said nothing. He suddenly felt very uneasy about his own future and the future of the MCIU.

6

1.00 pm, 2 October 1986
Mulberry Chambers, The Ropewalk, Nottingham

Sebastien Dawson walked into the plush lounge area of the Mulberry Chambers refreshment rooms. Immediately, the barristers gathered there began to speak in hushed tones. The room was furnished with red leather chesterfield sofas fronted by walnut or mahogany coffee tables. It was the area where barristers would gather to take tea or coffee and discuss upcoming cases. It was also the place where they would congregate to be given new briefs.

Dawson had been the barrister's clerk at Mulberry Chambers for the last fifteen years; it was part of his role to select individual barristers for briefs that had been presented to Mulberry Chambers by solicitors wanting expert representation for their clients in the Crown Court.

He was a large man in every sense of the word. He stood over six feet four inches and weighed well above twenty stone. The charcoal grey pinstriped trousers strained against an ever-expanding waistline; the gap between the trousers and black waistcoat was getting wider every month. He habitually wore garish-coloured bow ties that struggled to remain in place against the rolls of fat on his oversized neck.

Sebastien Dawson's downfall was a love of good food, red wine and malt whisky. Now in his early fifties, his brown eyes were becoming bloodshot, hidden by heavy lids above and deep bags below. His large nose had developed a distinctive red tinge at the end, with miniscule thread veins crisscrossing the very tip. Those veins on the end of his nose, in turn, drew attention to his permanently moist, fleshy red lips. His once-thick blonde hair was rapidly turning grey and becoming sparse.

Although his appearance was generally dishevelled, beneath that ramshackle exterior was a mind that remained as sharp as a tack.

He knew he wielded a lot of power in chambers and very adroitly played office politics to ensure it stayed that way.

The brightest legal minds in Mulberry Chambers undoubtedly belonged to Dominic and Rebecca Whitchurch.

The two barristers had met and fallen in love at Oxford University. They had married while both were completing their articles at a London-based law firm. As soon as they had been accepted to the bar, they had moved north and joined Mulberry Chambers on the Ropewalk in Nottingham. The reasons behind this move had all been carefully thought through by the astute young barristers.

Rebecca had been heavily pregnant with their daughter, Emily, at the time of the move. The couple believed it would be much easier to become the leading lights in a provincial chambers rather than begin swimming with bigger fish in a London-based legal firm. They also believed that Nottingham would be a healthier place to raise their daughter.

Their tactics had reaped immediate and tangible dividends. This had continued apace after the birth of Emily. Dominic and Rebecca had both been able to forge burgeoning reputations around the circuit in which they operated.

Initially, Rebecca had concentrated on prosecution work. For the last six years, both barristers had achieved a deserved reputation as supreme defence advocates. There was definitely a race between the two of them to determine which one of the Whitchurch family would achieve silk first.

Now in their early forties, the husband and wife team were both extremely smart in appearance and very career-minded. The tall, elegant Rebecca had always been proud of her natural beauty. She understood, and revelled in the fact, that she was a woman who was getting better with age. She took great care in everything about her appearance. She maintained her slim figure with regular yoga sessions, and her ash blonde hair was always cut in the latest style. Her fingernails were perfectly manicured and her makeup applied impeccably.

For her to achieve everything she had wanted from her career, she had always employed nannies and au pairs to help look after her only child, Emily. From the time of her daughter's birth, there had always been someone else on hand to help raise and care for the girl.

She had always been career-driven, and becoming a mother hadn't changed her outlook.

Her husband, Dominic, despite his diminutive stature, had genuine presence. He wore beautifully cut suits that helped disguise the slight paunch he had developed over recent years. His collar-length dark hair was always gelled and slicked back off his face. He changed his dress wig twice a year because of the damage caused to the hairpiece by the gel.

Along with their ever-growing reputations as brilliant defence barristers, Dominic and Rebecca were also known for being arrogant, aloof and downright nasty to the staff and junior members of Mulberry Chambers. On more than one occasion the head of chambers, Anthony Conway QC, had been asked to resolve complaints of harassment and bullying by the two senior barristers.

The resolution of these complaints was always achieved in the same way. The matter would initially be swept under the carpet; then the junior barrister would be asked to leave Mulberry Chambers shortly afterwards.

Anthony Conway could not afford to lose his two leading barristers. Dominic and Rebecca Whitchurch were the sole reason Mulberry Chambers had grown from fifteen to forty barristers within the past six years.

Sebastien Dawson was fully aware of this and, as a result, always ensured that Dominic and Rebecca were offered the pick of cases coming into chambers – much to the chagrin of many of the younger, equally talented barristers.

Today would be no different.

Dawson had walked in, clutching four new briefs to allocate to the gathered barristers. He was delighted to see Dominic and Rebecca enjoying a pot of Earl Grey tea together. He had two very lucrative briefs that would be perfect for them. He totally disregarded the six other barristers all eagerly awaiting a brief, and walked directly over to the red leather sofa occupied by the Whitchurches.

Standing in front of them, he said imperiously, 'Good afternoon. I've new briefs here for each of you, your timetables permitting.'

Dominic replied, 'I'm fairly free at the moment. What have you got for me, Seb?'

'I've a rape case that's due to be heard in a week's time at Leicester Crown Court. The trial's expected to last for at least one week, maybe two. The instructing solicitors are Wahab and Patel, from Leicester. Their solicitor, Imran Patak, has done some sterling work preparing the brief. There are some very big holes in the Crown's case that he's highlighted. It's most definitely a winnable case.'

'Toss it here, Seb, I'll take it. It will be good experience for one of the juniors to second chair on this one.'

Dominic's comment had made one of the young barristers, sitting on the next sofa, suddenly pay much more attention.

Freddie Fletcher had been at Mulberry for less than a year, but was already growing increasingly frustrated at the poor-quality briefs coming his way. A second chair role alongside the great Dominic Whitchurch would do his fledgling career no harm at all.

Never one to hide his light under a bushel, Fletcher said loudly, 'Dominic, I'm also free for the next few weeks. I'd be delighted to work alongside you so I could learn from you.'

With a distinct air of disdain in his voice, Dominic Whitchurch said, 'Thanks, but no thanks, Freddie. I'd already got wind this brief might be heading my way, and I've provisionally arranged for our learned friend Angela Temple to assist me. It's always helpful for a jury to see a female barrister helping to defend a man charged with rape. Surely you can see that?'

'Of course, I understand. No problem. Perhaps you would consider me in the future at another trial?'

A smirking Whitchurch replied, 'I'll definitely bear you in mind.'

Fletcher allowed a thin smile to pass his lips, but inside, he was raging. He couldn't believe how he had been dismissed in such a condescending manner. Dominic Whitchurch was a complete bastard, and so was his snooty cow of a wife, who was now grinning at him like a Cheshire cat. She was revelling in her husband's acerbic put-down of the young barrister.

Rebecca Whitchurch might not have been so happy and smug had she known the real motives behind Dominic's wish to have Angela Temple assisting him at the Leicester trial.

Sebastien Dawson now turned his attention to Rebecca Whitchurch. 'This brief is perfect for you, Rebecca. It's an armed robbery case that's due to be heard at Manchester Crown Court in the next couple of weeks. Again, the evidence being presented for the Crown is sketchy at best. Almost all of it is only circumstantial.'

With a haughty air, she said, 'I'll have a look at it. I'm pretty free at the moment. I'll read the brief and decide later if I need a junior with me. How long's the trial expected to last?'

'There are only two defendants, so two weeks at the most, I'd say. Our client's accused of waiting outside the post office and acting as lookout for the robber inside. He claims he wasn't involved at all and that the police have got it all wrong. It's all in the brief.'

'So let me get this straight. You want me to defend a lookout? Why is this high-profile?'

'This is the case that's been all over the news, Rebecca. The postmaster was beaten with a lump hammer. He almost died. It's the Denton Post Office robbery. You must have heard about it?'

She had indeed heard of the horrendous case. This was most definitely the kind of high-profile, media-enriched trial that she craved. Without further hesitation, she said, 'I'll take it. Pass me the brief, Sebastien.'

With a greasy smile, the portly clerk handed over the bundle of documents, tied with the traditional dark pink ribbon, to Rebecca Whitchurch.

He then handed out the remaining two briefs, again overlooking a seething Freddie Fletcher.

The young barrister huffed, stood up and stormed out of the lounge.

Rebecca chuckled and said, 'Somebody's not a happy bunny.'

Dominic grinned and took another sip of Earl Grey tea.

Sebastien Dawson had noted the reaction of Freddie Fletcher. He would seek him out later and make sure he was promised the next available brief. He knew Fletcher was a bright and capable young man who would eventually become a brilliant barrister. He didn't want to field yet another complaint made by a junior, and he didn't want to lose a barrister of the calibre of Fletcher to another chambers.

For now, at least, he would have to toe the line and ensure that Dominic and Rebecca Whitchurch continued to get the pick of briefs.

7

3.45pm, 2 October 1986
North Sherwood Street, Nottingham

It was rapidly getting dark now, the nights had been closing in for a while, and the black rainclouds overhead made it appear even darker. It had been raining hard for the last ten minutes, and she had kept the Mini's engine running, with the windscreen wipers on intermittent, as she waited. It was the only way to stop the windscreen misting over.

Sitting alone in her car, Alina Moraru was beginning to get very worried.

She had arrived at the arranged meeting place at the junction of North Sherwood Street and Alpha Terrace ten minutes later than normal.

The arrangement made with the girl's mother had been for Alina to pick her daughter up directly outside the gates of the Nottingham High School for Girls, not a couple of streets away.

Alina had been employed by Rebecca Whitchurch for three months now. The twenty-two-year-old Romanian had been delighted to land the role of au pair at the Mapperley Park home Rebecca Whitchurch shared with her husband, Dominic, and fourteen-year-old daughter, Emily. Rebecca Whitchurch had been impressed by the standard of Alina's spoken English and had not hesitated to employ the young Romanian.

It was a wonderful job that Alina loved and desperately wanted to keep. The money was excellent, and the work wasn't very taxing. Rebecca's husband, Dominic, treated her with respect, and her room at the top of the large house was comfortable and beautifully furnished. Most importantly, the Whitchurch house was very near the bedsit owned by her Romanian boyfriend, Florin Chirilov. Elm Bank, in the nearby Sherwood Rise area, was only a fifteen-minute walk away.

The only downside to the job was the behaviour of the Whitchurches' daughter, Emily.

She was nothing short of a precocious brat who ridiculed Alina at every opportunity. Even though she was still only a teenager, Emily constantly spoke down to her and ordered her about. The young girl constantly made insulting comments about Alina's plump figure. Alina had always been self-conscious about her weight. She wasn't overweight but had a curvy figure accentuated by her short stature. The young au pair had to bite her tongue on many occasions for fear of upsetting the young brat's parents. She knew if she spoke out of turn, she would lose her job.

It was the daughter's fault that Alina was now waiting on North Sherwood Street and not at the school gates as instructed. Emily had complained incessantly, saying that it was an embarrassment having the hired help pick her up in her tatty little car in front of the entire school.

Emily had subsequently ordered Alina to wait two streets away. That way only her two best friends, Rosie and Polly, would see the atrocious, battered old Mini that she was collected in every day.

Alina knew it had been wrong to cave in to the daughter's demands, but she desperately wanted to keep her job. She couldn't risk upsetting Emily and consequently her parents. Everything had gone without a hitch up to this point, as she had always been waiting at the junction of North Sherwood Street and Alpha Terrace in plenty of time.

Today had been different. Alina had arrived at the meeting point ten minutes late. She knew it had been a mistake to go to Florin's flat in the afternoon. As soon as he had started kissing her neck in that special way, she had been powerless to resist, and they had ended up in bed.

Making love with Florin at his flat was the reason she had arrived late and was now worried sick.

Where was the stupid girl?

She peered through the windscreen. As the wipers shifted the excess water from the glass, she finally saw the girl walking towards the car.

A wave of relief washed over her as she recognised the navy-blue blazer and blue check skirt of the school uniform. As she got closer, Alina could also see the distinctive long blonde hair, which was soaking wet and stuck to the girl's face and shoulders.

A joyful Alina jumped out of the Mini and shouted, 'Where have you been, Emily? Hurry up and get in the car. You're soaked!'

The girl was now much closer.

A huge sense of panic coursed through Alina's body as

she suddenly realised that the young, blonde schoolgirl in front of her wasn't Emily.

The young schoolgirl looked worriedly across the road, glancing nervously at the woman who had shouted to her.

Seeing the worried expression on the girl's face, Alina said quickly, 'I'm so sorry, I thought you were somebody else. Do you know Emily Whitchurch?'

The young girl laughed and said, 'Everyone at school knows Emily Whitchurch.'

'Have you seen her? Is she walking far behind you?'

'She's not behind me. Emily left school ages ago.'

Alina was panicking big style now; she didn't care what the precocious brat would say, she was driving to the school right now.

She jumped back in the Mini and started the engine. Within a couple of minutes, she was parking the small car outside the main entrance to the Nottingham High School for Girls. She got out, locked the car and, ignoring the torrential rain, raced inside the school.

Alina saw a female teacher in the main corridor and said, 'I'm here to collect Emily Whitchurch. Is she here?'

The teacher could see the panic in the young woman's face and said calmly, 'Wait here, my dear. I'll find out where Emily is.'

The teacher then left Alina alone in the corridor.

Alina was worried sick now. Questions and recriminations raced through her mind. *Why did I arrive late? Where is Emily? What will her parents say? Why did Florin kiss my neck like that?*

The return of the teacher, with an older woman, dragged Alina back from her thoughts.

With an air of authority in her voice, the older woman said, 'I'm Mrs Henson, the deputy head. May I ask who you are, young lady?'

'My name is Alina Moraru. I'm the au pair employed by the Whitchurch family. It's part of my job to collect Emily from school every day. She hasn't walked to my car today, and I'm very worried. Is she still here?'

'I'm afraid not, Miss Moraru. Emily left at three thirty. I watched her walk out the school gates myself.'

'Who was she with?'

'Nobody. She was alone.'

'That's not right. You couldn't have seen Emily; she always walks with her friends Rosie and Polly.'

'You must mean Rosie Penwarden and Polly Garrett. Rosie and Polly are still here in school. They're doing rehearsals for the school play this evening. I'm sorry, but it was definitely Emily I saw leaving at three thirty. Is there anything we can do?'

'No, thank you. I need to go.'

Alina's heart was racing as she ran out of the school and back to her car. *What should I do now? Where can I look? Where is the stupid brat?*

She started the car and began driving slowly around the desolate, dark streets, searching for Emily. The rain was torrential, and as her warm body reacted to her soaking wet clothes, the windows in the small car began to steam up, making it almost impossible to see anything outside.

After fifteen minutes of aimless driving around, Alina made the decision to make her way back to the Whitchurch residence at Mapperley Park. She needed to find out if, somehow, Emily had got home by herself.

She drove her car slowly along Mansfield Road, aggravating other road users with her dawdling pace. Disgruntled motorists noisily sounded their car horns as they passed the crawling Mini. Alina didn't care about the other cars. She desperately wanted to see a soaking wet, angry Emily. She would put up with any amount of foul language and name-calling just to see her walking along the road.

There was no sign of the blonde teenager.

Eventually, Alina found herself outside the Whitchurch residence on Richmond Drive, Mapperley Park. She drove her car onto the driveway. The large, detached house was still completely in darkness. Neither of the cars owned by Dominic and Rebecca Whitchurch were on the drive. More importantly, there was no sign of a soaking wet Emily waiting outside the front door.

Alina parked the Mini, got out and walked to the front door. Using her key, she let herself in and shouted, 'Emily! Are you home already?'

There was no school bag dumped in the hall, and no wet coat or blazer hanging on the bannister post.

The girl hadn't made her own way home.

Alina slumped onto the bottom stair and began to sob. Through teary eyes, she glanced at her wristwatch. It was now almost five o'clock. An ice-cold fear descended upon her and gripped her heart, making her shudder involuntarily.

She stood up and walked down the hallway to the telephone.

She needed to call the girl's mother.

Alina subconsciously made the decision not to tell Mrs Whitchurch about being late, or that she had arranged with Emily to meet her away from the school gates. That damning information could come later.

Right now, she needed to tell a mother that her daughter was missing. That was bad enough.

8

6.30pm, 2 October 1986
De Montfort House, Richmond Drive, Mapperley Park, Nottingham

Rebecca Whitchurch stormed into the house, closely followed by her husband. As soon as she saw Alina sitting on the bottom stair in the hallway, she shouted, 'What the hell's going on?'

The young au pair was already close to tears. She sobbed, 'I don't know where Emily is.'

'Explain yourself, girl. What do you mean, you don't know where she is?'

'I mean, I went to the school and waited outside the gates as usual, but she never came out. I waited and waited, and eventually I went into the school and spoke to a teacher, who told me that Emily had already left. I've been driving round the streets looking for her, but I can't find her. I'm so sorry.'

Dominic muttered under his breath, 'Not again.'

Rebecca rounded on him and hissed, 'Not now, Dom, and definitely not in front of her!'

Dominic put his hands up, palms facing out in mock surrender, and turned away.

Rebecca turned back to the au pair and said angrily, 'Exactly what time did you get to the school?'

Alina knew there were cameras on the gates of the house, which would have logged the time she left earlier. She also knew that Rebecca Whitchurch did not approve of her boyfriend, Florin.

She hated lying to her boss, but she felt she was left with no alternative if she wanted to keep her job, so she said, 'I left the house at one o'clock to go to the shops. I needed to buy cleaning products for the house. I went into town to fetch them first; then I went to the school. I got there at three fifteen, in plenty of time. I sat there and watched as all the girls came out, but there was no sign of Emily. I started to get panicky, so I went inside to try to find her.'

'Didn't you see any of her friends?'

Alina didn't like to say that Emily only had two friends, so she just said, 'No, I was concentrating on looking for Emily.'

'You said you've been driving round looking for her; where exactly have you looked?'

'Everywhere. I've been driving round for ages. I'm sorry; I don't know all the names of the streets yet.'

Dominic said quietly, 'This is getting us nowhere. We need to call the police and report her missing. It's already been dark for over an hour, and our daughter's out there somewhere.'

Rebecca put her head in her hands and nodded, acknowledging her husband. She removed her hands and stared hard at Alina. Fixing her with an unblinking gaze, she said menacingly, 'Are you telling the truth, Alina? Were you outside the school on time?'

Unable to bear Rebecca's eyes boring into her, Alina looked down at the floor. When she replied, her voice was barely a whisper, 'Of course, Mrs Whitchurch. I'm sorry.'

With a disgusted look on her face, Rebecca hissed, 'Go to your room. The police will want to talk to you when they get here.'

Alina nodded, turned and ran upstairs. She just couldn't face her angry employer anymore, and she was terrified that the police would soon find out the truth.

Dominic waited until the au pair was out of earshot before picking up the telephone in the hallway. He dialled the number for the local police station and said softly, 'Hello. I want to report my fourteen-year-old daughter missing. She hasn't arrived home from school.'

There was a long pause; then Dominic said, 'Her name's Emily Whitchurch, and yes, she's been missing before. Our home address is De Montfort House, Richmond Drive, Mapperley Park.'

There was another, shorter pause before he said, 'Okay, ten minutes. See you soon. Thanks, Sergeant.'

He put the phone down, turned to Rebecca, and said, 'The police are on their way.'

9

6.45pm, 2 October 1986
De Montfort House, Richmond Drive, Mapperley Park, Nottingham

There was a loud knock on the front door. Dominic walked from the lounge and opened the door to a uniformed policewoman.

'Come in, please. My wife's in the lounge.'

PC Sandra Tyler had been told by her sergeant to get to the property as quickly as possible. He had informed the experienced policewoman that Dominic and Rebecca Whitchurch were high-flying defence barristers, who would cause a shitstorm if everything wasn't done quickly and by the book.

This instruction had irritated Sandra Tyler. She liked to think that she always did her duty expeditiously and to the best of her ability. There would never be any favouritism shown to anyone, as far as she was concerned. She had just bitten her lip and told the sergeant that she was on her way.

Dominic showed PC Tyler into the spacious, beautifully decorated lounge and said, 'Please, take a seat.' He remained standing near the door.

PC Tyler sat down opposite Rebecca Whitchurch and said, 'My sergeant, who took your call, has informed me your daughter's been missing before, Mrs Whitchurch. When was that?'

Rebecca answered, 'Yes, she has. Only on one previous occasion, though, she isn't constantly running off. That was just over three months ago.'

'Where was she found last time?'

It was the question Rebecca had been dreading, and this policewoman was straight into it.

Rebecca leaned forward in the armchair, resting her elbows on her knees, and said quietly, 'Emily was found in some dreadful squat, on Arboretum Street. She was on her own when the police found her. It seems she had been smoking cannabis and was quite out of it.'

'I see. Did Emily tell you how she'd got to the squat?'

'She told us, at the time, that she had been met outside the school by a man in a dark green car. She isn't very good on cars. She told us that she didn't know this man, but that he'd offered her the chance to try smoking cannabis. Like an idiot, she went along with him. She hasn't spoken about it since and gets angry if we mention it. She did swear to us that she would never do it again.'

'And this all happened outside the Nottingham High School for Girls, on Forest Road East?'

'Yes, it did.'

'Is she still at the same school?'

'Yes, of course. It's the most prestigious school in this city.'

'I've got to ask this question, Mrs Whitchurch. Have either

of you seen any evidence around your home that Emily still indulges in substance abuse?'

'Of course we haven't! We're not stupid.'

'I'm not saying you are. I know that some kids can be very resourceful in the way they hide things, especially from their parents.'

A disgruntled Dominic said, 'We've seen no evidence of substance abuse here, Officer. Does that answer your bloody question?'

Registering the note of anger in his voice, PC Tyler looked across at Dominic and said flatly, 'Yes, it does. Thank you.'

Turning back to face Rebecca, she said, 'You said that the last time Emily went missing, she was picked up outside the school by this mystery man. Was he ever traced?'

'Not as far as we know. The police never contacted us to say he'd been traced.'

'Since she went missing back then, have you put anything in place to prevent anything similar happening again?'

'Alina, our au pair, picks her up from school every day. She waits outside the school gates, collects her and drives her home.'

'But not today?'

'I've already spoken at length with Alina. She has told me that she was there in plenty of time, but didn't see Emily come out of the school.'

'Is Alina around? I'd like to speak to her, if I may?'

'She's upstairs in her room. I'll go and get her. Rather than talking to the hired help, shouldn't you be out there looking for my daughter?'

'Mrs Whitchurch, your daughter's details and description have already been circulated to every officer on duty. We used the details from her previous missing person report. Officers have been actively looking for her since your husband made the report.'

Somewhat chastened by the policewoman's curt reply, Rebecca said quietly, 'I'll go and get Alina.'

As soon as his wife left the room, Dominic said quietly, 'Our daughter can be very headstrong. She's also extremely naïve and trusting, not very streetwise. After what happened last time, I'm very concerned.'

'Try not to worry, Mr Whitchurch. I'm sure we'll find her very soon. While I'm talking to your au pair, would you find me a recent photograph of Emily and a list of her best friends at school, please?'

'I'm sorry, I don't know any of her friends' names. My wife will probably be able to help you better with that. I'll go and find a recent photograph.'

Briefly left on her own in the lounge, PC Tyler wondered exactly what sort of father Dominic was, if he had no idea who his daughter's best friends were.

The return of Rebecca Whitchurch with a very nervous-looking au pair brought PC Tyler back from her thoughts.

She looked at an obviously anxious Alina and said, 'Please don't be worried. You're not in any trouble. I just need to ask you a few questions. Okay?'

Alina nodded.

The policewoman said gently, 'What time did you arrive at the school today?'

'I got there at three fifteen, as usual.'

'Where did you park your car?'

'Outside the school gates.'

'Did you find a parking space okay?'

'Yes. I always park in the same place. I only have a Mini, so it's easy to park.'

'What time does Emily usually come out of school?'

'Usually around three thirty.'

'Does she have any close friends she walks with?'

Alina hesitated, and the hesitation was noted by the experienced policewoman.

Eventually, the young au pair said, 'Emily only has a couple of friends at the school.'

Rebecca interrupted and said, 'That's ridiculous! Emily has lots of friends.'

Alina said, 'No. Only two really, Rosie and Polly.'

'Do you know their last names?'

'No, I don't. Sorry.'

'Did you see Rosie or Polly today while you were waiting for Emily?'

'No, I didn't. When I went into the school to look for Emily, the teacher I spoke to told me that Rosie and Polly were rehearsing or something, and that they were both still in school.'

'Okay, Alina. Thank you.'

'Is that it?'

'That's all for now.'

Rebecca said, 'Go to your room, Alina.'

As soon as the au pair left the lounge, PC Tyler said, 'How long has she been working for you?'

'Just over three months. We set her on just after Emily went missing last time. My husband and I are very busy people. We often have to work away from home. I wanted someone to be here for Emily. I wanted her to be met outside the school by someone every day. Up until today, everything had worked perfectly.'

'Where did you find Alina?'

'From a very reputable agency.'

'I'll need the details of the agency so I can check her background.'

'They'll be in the study; I'll find them for you.'

'Thanks.'

As Rebecca left, Dominic walked back into the lounge and said, 'Here's that photograph.'

PC Tyler looked at the fresh-faced girl in the photograph, with her long blonde hair and large blue eyes. She said, 'Is this recent?'

'Yes. It was taken a couple of months ago. We all managed to get away for a couple of days, skiing in France.'

Rebecca returned with the au pair agency documentation. She handed the paperwork to PC Tyler and asked, 'Is there anything else you need?'

'I think I've got everything I need for now, thanks. I would like to have a quick look at Emily's bedroom before I go.'

Rebecca turned to her husband and said wearily, 'Dom, can you show her where it is, please? I've got one of my headaches coming on.'

Dominic nodded and said, 'This way, Officer.'

PC Tyler followed him upstairs.

The bedroom was unremarkable. It was like any other fourteen-year-old girl's bedroom. There were posters of pop stars on the walls, cuddly toys, a pink duvet cover and cushions.

PC Tyler said, 'Does your daughter keep a diary?'

'If she does, I've never seen it. My wife has certainly never mentioned seeing one to me.'

'I'd like to have a quick look through her things, to see if I can find anything.'

'Please, look wherever you like.'

After a brief search, PC Tyler had found nothing. She followed Dominic back down the stairs, to the front door of the house. She said, 'Thank you, Mr Whitchurch. As I said to you earlier, please try not to worry. I'm sure we'll find Emily soon.'

'Thanks, we'll try.'

As she walked down the long driveway, PC Tyler was troubled.

There was no obvious reason for this young girl to go missing. There was something about the young au pair that didn't feel right. The experienced policewoman knew when she was being lied to. Then there was the general air of apathy shown by the girl's parents.

PC Tyler knew that if it had been her own fourteen-year-old daughter who was missing, out on the streets in such foul weather, she would have been going out of her mind, frantic with worry.

They both said the right things and made the right gestures of despair, but there was no raw emotion or fear being shown by either parent.

She ran to the patrol car, jumped inside out of the heavy rain and headed for the police station. She needed to run her thoughts past her sergeant.

Something about this whole thing just didn't feel right.

PC Sandra Tyler had learned a long time ago to always trust her instincts.

10

9.00am, 3 October 1986
Mansfield Woodhouse Cemetery

Sam Jamieson stared down at the shiny black marble headstone that bore his daughter's name in gold letters. The rain, which was now falling heavily, cascaded down over the visor of his crash helmet and onto his black leather jacket.

In his gloved hands, he held a bunch of red and white carnations. Bending forward, he placed the flowers at the base of the headstone. He closed his eyes and whispered a silent prayer before standing upright.

Having placed the flowers and confided in God, he glanced around to make sure he was alone. Satisfied that no one was within earshot, he began a conversation with his daughter. He spoke out loud: 'I'm going away for a little while, sweetheart, but I'll be back soon.'

He paused, then said, 'I hope you're proud of your old

dad. I've got a place at Nottingham University to study for my master's degree. How about that, eh? Not bad for a Woodhouse lad!'

He paused again, as though waiting to hear the answer that would never come from his daughter, before continuing, 'So, I'm going to be living in digs in Nottingham at a place called Forest Fields. It's not far from where I took you to that big funfair, the Goose Fair. Do you remember that? That was a fun night, wasn't it?'

Once again, the delay.

'I'm going to be gone for a couple of years, but I'll come back and visit you whenever I can. I'll bring more flowers and tell you how I'm getting on at university. I'm also going to take time off from my studies, to meet the person responsible for you being here, sweetheart. You know who I mean, don't you?'

No pause now.

'While I'm living in Nottingham, I'm going to track the bitch down and make her pay for what she's done to us. What do you think of that?'

No pause.

'I knew that would put a smile on your face and make you happy, gorgeous girl. I'll be back to talk to you again soon. Don't ever forget, Vanessa, your daddy loves you.'

He turned and walked briskly away from the grave.

He had parked his motorcycle next to the chapel of rest. The red-brick building stood at the top of the small hill that led down to black wrought-iron gates that guarded the entrance into Leeming Lane cemetery.

Without once looking back at the headstone, he strode through the deserted graveyard until he reached his motorcycle. He started it up and rode away. He had made a vow to his dead daughter a long time ago. It was now time to carry that promise through.

He owed it to Vanessa to ensure that justice was done.

As far as Sam Jamieson was concerned, his only daughter was lying dead in the ground because he had been wrongfully incarcerated and left to rot in prison for seven long years.

As he sped along the wet streets, the same question he had asked himself many times before came rushing back into his brain.

Why did that bitch Whitchurch go out of her way to put me behind bars?

This time, the answer came smashing through.

Rebecca Whitchurch had put him behind bars to further her career, nothing more, nothing less. She had known that he hadn't been involved in the offence, but had still prosecuted him.

Where is the justice in that?

The time for her to pay for all that greed, all that ambition, all that arrogance and indifference to true justice, was fast approaching.

11

4.15pm, 3 October 1986
Nottingham

The young girl sat up and tried to look around.
Her head was pounding, and her wrists hurt so badly, she felt like crying. She was in a very dark place and strained her eyes to see. Try as she might, she couldn't make anything out. It was pitch black. There didn't appear to be any light anywhere.

She began to rack her brains, trying to find the answers to so many questions. *How did I come to be here? What happened? Why am I here?* The most worrying question of all overwhelmed the others: *What is going to happen next?*

When no obvious answers came to her, she began to try to take stock of her situation. She knew she was cold, but she was still wearing her clothes. Her hands were bound tightly together, and that was why her wrists were aching so much. She was sitting on some sort of scruffy mattress in a small dark room. Now that her eyes had fully adjusted to the darkness, she could see that there were no windows. She could just make out the single door in one wall.

There was a strange, repetitive noise coming from above her, one that she couldn't quite recognise.

The young girl started to shout for help. There was no response to her shouts except for a sudden fluttering noise above her head. She now realised that the repetitive noise she had heard was the sound of pigeons cooing. Her shouts had scared the birds, and the fluttering sound was them flying away.

Her throat was parched, and her repeated shouts for help became more and more croaky.

Suddenly, there was a scraping noise coming from the direction of the door. In the darkness, she heard a man's voice: 'Be quiet, and I'll bring you water. If you keep shouting, you'll get fuck all.'

She shouted back, 'Please, I'm so thirsty. I promise I'll be quiet.'

The door slowly opened.

Instinctively, the young girl recoiled in horror from the black-clad figure who stepped into the room. The half-light that filtered in through the open door meant she now got a better look at the room she was being held in. It was a roof space. That was why she had heard pigeons above her.

It was a dusty old attic; rubbish had been piled at one end, and her mattress placed at the other. There was an all-pervading musky smell that told of damp and decay.

Staring at the figure who had walked into the attic room, she was horrified to see he was wearing a hood that covered the top half of his face. Through eyeholes that had been cut out, she could see small piggy eyes. Only his mouth was visible below the mask. She could clearly see his thick, glutinous lips, which looked wet and sticky.

She tried to back up on the mattress, but the figure approached her, getting closer and closer.

Finally, he knelt beside her on the mattress. For the first time, she saw that he was carrying a plastic bowl and a large bottle of water.

He held out the bowl and grunted the word, 'Toilet.' He then held up the water bottle and mumbled, 'Water.'

He placed both items on the floor next to the mattress. He was about to stand up when the girl found the courage to speak. She said quietly, 'Where am I?'

The figure grabbed a handful of the girl's long blonde hair, pulled her face close to his, and said menacingly, 'You're with me, darling. That's where you are.'

He drew his moist tongue along her cheek, licking her alabaster skin once. As he did so, he placed one of his fat, sweaty hands on her bare leg. She instinctively drew her legs up to her chest, so his hand fell away. He pushed her backwards onto the mattress, stood up and said quietly, 'You're mine now. You'll do what I tell you, when I tell you to do it. Don't piss me off by resisting me. If you want food to eat and water to drink, you'll do exactly what I say. Do you understand me?'

The terrified girl nodded and said, 'Please don't hurt me. I'm only fourteen.'

'I know exactly how old you are, and I don't care. Do what I tell you, and I won't hurt you. It's your choice. One more thing. There's to be no more shouting. No one can hear you. Understand?'

The terrified girl nodded.

The man stepped back through the door and closed it behind him. As the door slammed shut, it plunged the attic back into darkness.

As she listened to the sound of a padlock closing on the other side of the door, the girl shivered with fear and sobbed.

12

9.00pm, 3 October 1986
Mansfield, Nottinghamshire

Danny and Sue Flint were watching an old black-and-white film on the television. They were snuggling together on one of the large sofas in the living room of their four-bedroom detached house.

Danny held a half-full whiskey tumbler in his right hand. He was repeatedly swirling the ice around the glass.

Sue reached over and gripped the glass, stopping the annoying, repetitive movement. She looked at Danny and said, 'Come on, spill the beans. You've got something on your mind, and it's definitely not Gregory Peck and this movie. What's going on?'

Danny placed the tumbler on the coffee table and said, 'I'm sorry, sweetheart.'

'Don't apologise; just tell me what's on your mind.'

'The new chief constable will be announced tomorrow. I think it's going to be Jack Renshaw who gets the job.'

'The deputy chief who transferred in from Devon?'

'Yeah.'

'You've always said he was a good man. So what's the problem?'

Danny looked at his beautiful wife and placed a hand on her ever-growing bump. Sue was now five months pregnant and was starting to bloom, like most expectant mothers in their second trimester.

He said, 'I don't know if it will be a problem, but one thing's for sure, one way or another, it will mean change. The promotion to superintendent I was promised may not happen now.'

'If it doesn't happen now, I'm sure it will one day in the not-too-distant future.'

'Maybe so. I have to admit that part of me was looking forward to being able to spend more time at home when the little one arrives.'

'Time off would have been lovely, but I think it's more important that you're happy every day. Look me in the eye and tell me you would have been happy sitting behind a desk at headquarters every day.'

Danny smiled again. 'Sometimes, I think you should've been the detective in this house, Mrs Flint.'

'I don't know about that, but I know my husband. You're never happier than when you've got a difficult case to work on. I just think that you would miss that everyday interaction too much. That may not be the case forever, and one day, you may be ready to take a back seat. That's not how I see things currently.'

'There's an element of truth in what you say. I can't say I was relishing the move to headquarters. I think the politics of the place alone might drive me mad. I do think it would be too quiet for me at the moment, however hard Bill tried to sell that to me as a positive. There's something else I haven't mentioned to you. I think Bill Wainwright's going to hand in his resignation sooner rather than later.'

'Now that does surprise me. I thought Bill loved his job. Why now?'

'I think it's a combination of things. He's never really been the same since he lost his wife, and now, being there when Miles Galton died really shook him up. Don't forget, the chief was a few years younger than Bill. I think he just wants to enjoy his retirement and not keel over at his desk.'

'Well, I can't say I blame him for that.'

'The thing is, sweetheart, if Bill does retire, there would need to be a new head of CID appointed, as well as a new chief constable. I've always had a brilliant working relationship with Bill. That may not be the case with somebody new.'

'That's true, but the chief was always very pro MCIU. You told me it was his idea to set it up after the Jimmy Wade enquiry.'

'The MCIU was very much Miles Galton's idea. He's gone now, and if Bill goes too, I really don't know what will happen to the MCIU.'

Sue snuggled in a little closer. 'Let's just wait and see what tomorrow brings, shall we? It's no good worrying about something you have no control over.'

'You're right, sweetheart.'

Sue sighed and said, 'Can we get back to the movie now? This is my favourite bit, where the kids see Boo Radley for the first time.'

Danny said nothing. He picked up his glass and took a long drink, feeling the fiery liquid hit the back of his throat hard.

There was no chance that Gregory Peck, Boo Radley or anyone else could drag him away from his thoughts.

13

8.45am, 4 October 1986
Nottingham City Centre

The Volvo being driven by Angela Temple was crawling along at a snail's pace. The traffic heading towards Nottingham city centre at this time of day was always heaviest on this stretch of Mansfield Road.

She hated this journey.

The fact that she had to drop her husband off, at the Newton Building of the Trent Polytechnic on Goldsmith Street, would mean that after negotiating the heavy traffic in the city centre, she would be late for work at Mulberry Chambers on the Ropewalk.

Once again, the traffic came to a dead stop. She threw her head back, causing her long, raven black hair to be swept back off her face. With a cry born out of exasperation and frustration, she shouted, 'For God's sake! This fucking traffic!'

Her husband, Brandon, who was sitting quietly in the

passenger seat, cringed. He could already feel the tension coming from his beautiful wife and didn't want to upset her further by saying the wrong thing.

As far as most of their friends were concerned, Brandon and Angela were polar opposites. Apart from both being in their early thirties, the only thing they really had in common was that they had both graduated from Cambridge University with spectacular degrees.

It had been the picturesque university, on the banks of the River Cam, where they had met, fallen in love and got married. Both had been brilliant scholars in their very different fields.

After graduating, Brandon had gone on to do his master's. He subsequently landed his dream job, working as a professor of Geological Studies at Nottingham Trent University.

As a direct result of Brandon being offered that post, Angela had been forced to abandon her plans of furthering her career as a barrister at a prestigious London-based chambers. She was fortunate, though, to be offered a post as a junior at Mulberry Chambers in Nottingham.

The pair of them together seemed to be a very odd couple to most who knew them.

Angela was extremely glamourous. She was tall, with a slim figure; she always dressed impeccably, taking great pride in her appearance. Brandon, on the other hand, was quite short and slightly overweight, with tousled dark brown hair. He always appeared as though he had got dressed in a hurry, throwing on the nearest garments that came to hand. It was this quirky eccentricity that had first attracted Angela to him. That and his razor-sharp mind.

Angela had felt a growing sense of anticipation all morning. Her sense of excitement had stemmed from the telephone call she'd received late last night from Dominic

Whitchurch. He had asked her to be his second at an upcoming rape trial. She knew it would be a major opportunity for her to shine, working alongside such a well-respected barrister. Everyone who worked at the law firm knew that it was Dominic and his arrogant wife who were the real powers at Mulberry Chambers.

That feeling of excitement had been somewhat dimmed by the knowledge that she was now going to be late for her meeting with Dominic. She wasn't unduly worried about that; she knew he wouldn't mind.

It was just the bloody inconvenience of dropping her husband off every day that was grinding her down.

Sensing his wife's growing annoyance, Brandon said quietly, 'Don't worry about dropping me off for the rest of the week. I'll take my motorcycle.'

She snapped back, 'How can you take the bike? The weather forecast has predicted heavy rain all bloody week!'

'I'm going to buy a set of waterproofs today. I don't think it's fair dragging you through this traffic every day.'

'Well, hallelujah!' she said sarcastically.

The rest of the journey was made in stony silence.

Finally, they arrived outside the iconic Newton Building. She flicked on the indicator and steered the Volvo to the side of the road.

Brandon grabbed his briefcase, leaned over and pecked his glamourous wife on the cheek. Angela did not reciprocate the tender moment. He got out of the car, turned and said through the open door, 'Thanks, sweetheart. Will you be home on time tonight? I thought I'd cook us something. What do you fancy?'

With a disinterested air, she replied, 'Anything, I really don't mind. Hopefully, I'll be home on time. It all depends how work on this new brief with Dominic goes today. Bye, darling. Close the door; I'm late enough already.'

He closed the door and stepped back from the car just as she sped away from the kerb edge.

He stood in the rain, watching as the Volvo once more became engulfed in the heavy traffic.

As the car went out of sight, he muttered under his breath, 'Bloody Dominic.'

14

9.30am, 4 October 1986
MCIU Offices, Mansfield, Nottinghamshire

Danny Flint sat in his office, poring over the briefing reports from the previous night. His concentration was interrupted by the sound of raised voices coming from the main office.

He put the report down, stood up and walked over to the window that separated his office from the main office. Peering through the venetian blinds, he could see and hear Detective Inspector Brian Hopkirk laying into DC Nigel Singleton. Both men had lost their tempers and were shouting at each other.

Danny opened his office door, stepped into the main office and shouted, 'That's enough!'

Both men immediately fell silent.

Danny said, 'In my office, both of you. Now!'

The two detectives walked into Danny's office, heads down.

Danny kept them standing and said quietly, 'What the hell was all that about? DC Singleton, you first.'

Nigel Singleton was starting to get red blotches around his neck at the embarrassment of having to explain his outburst. He looked Danny squarely in the eye and said, 'I was trying to explain to the DI that I would need a bit longer to complete the enquiry he's asked me to do. I apologise for raising my voice, but I wasn't being listened to, sir.'

'What's the enquiry?'

'It's for the Bowker murder, sir. DI Hopkirk asked me to check all manufacturers of crossbow bolts in the UK that make the type of bolt recovered from Andrew Bowker's body. I was trying to explain how many manufacturers there are, that's all.'

'How much longer do you need?'

'Working on my own? At least three more days. If I had someone to help me, we could get it done in half that time, sir.'

'Okay, give Fran Jefferies my apologies and ask her to abandon her office manager's tasks for today. She can help you with this enquiry. I know how important it is that we have that information. That will be all.'

As the young detective started to turn away, Danny said, 'Nigel, if I ever hear you showing that level of disrespect to a senior officer again, you'll be off this Unit. Is that understood?'

'Yes, sir.'

The young detective turned to Brian Hopkirk, held out his hand and said, 'Sorry, boss.'

The burly detective inspector took his detective's hand, shook it and said, 'No. I'm sorry, lad. I should have listened to what you were telling me. Go on, crack on with your work.'

DC Singleton left the office, and Danny said, 'Sit down, Brian.'

As soon as the detective inspector had sat down, a still-seething Danny said quietly, 'What the fuck was all that about?'

'I'm sorry, sir. I know how important getting that data together is, that's all.'

'Bollocks! That's not what I'm talking about, and you know it. What's wrong? The Brian Hopkirk I value and trust would never talk to his staff like that. What's going on?'

'It's personal.'

Danny bit his lip. Holding onto his temper, he said, 'It might have been personal once, but you've just brought it into work. So, I'll ask you again. What the fuck's going on?'

Brian slumped in his chair and said, in barely a whisper, 'My ex-wife's getting married again.'

'For Christ's sake! You've been divorced for seven years. I really don't see what the problem is.'

'I'm not bothered about her getting married again. The man she intends to marry currently lives and works in Florida, that's the bloody problem. They plan on living out there after they're wed. That means they'll be taking my daughter, Laura, with them. That's what I'm struggling to come to terms with. Laura's only thirteen years old. She's still my baby girl.'

'Bloody hell, Brian. When's all this happening?'

'In the next couple of months. It's all been pretty sudden.'

'Do you have any concerns about the new husband?'

'None at all. I've met Graham a few times, and he is a hard-working, stand-up bloke. He's got a responsible, well-paid job, and it's obvious he really cares for Maggie and Laura. It's just the distances involved. I've always had a brilliant relationship with Laura, and I desperately want that to continue. At the moment, I can see her regularly, and we do lots of things together. That will all stop when she moves to the States. I don't mind telling you, I'm sick to my guts worrying about it.'

'Do you need to take some time off work?'

'If I'm being honest, I don't think that would help. It's going to happen. Me moping around at home isn't going to stop it.'

'Have you spoken to Maggie and told her how you're feeling?'

'Yes, we've talked things through. She has assured me everything will be fine, and that they will be coming back over to the UK on a regular basis. She's also said that I'll always be welcome to travel over to Florida and stay with them.'

'That all sounds very positive.'

'I know it could be a lot worse. The bottom line is, I love Laura with all my heart. It's killing me, knowing I won't be there for her anymore.'

'Brian, that's just plain wrong. I know you'll always be there for her, and more importantly, so does Laura. Things will turn out okay, trust me.'

Brian nodded and stood up.

He stopped at the door, turned and said, 'Thanks for listening, Danny. I'll come to terms with things, and don't worry about the job. I won't be having any more tantrums. I'll square things with young Nigel. He's a bloody good detective who was just standing his ground. I was the one who was out of order.'

Danny said, 'Anytime you feel you need some time off, just ask. Okay? My door's always open if you need to talk some more.'

'Thanks. One more thing, can this conversation be kept between the two of us?'

'Of course, that goes without saying. Take it easy.'

15

10.30am, 4 October 1986
Foxhall Road, Forest Fields, Nottingham

Sam Jamieson had planned to spend the day working from home. The weather outside was so abysmal, that now seemed like a very good decision. The rain was incessant and heavy. It had done nothing but rain for well over a week. Typical, when his only mode of transport was a bloody motorcycle. He should have known better. It was the start of Goose Fair this week, and traditionally, the famous fair was always plagued by foul and inclement weather.

He was enjoying studying for his master's degree in psychology, but the daily commute was becoming a drag. It was taking him an extra hour each day to get home and get dry after riding his motorcycle through the rain-soaked streets. A day spent at home, in his small, cosy flat, would be a welcome relief.

The one-bedroomed flat in the large house in the Forest

Fields area wasn't the best. It was still a huge improvement on the small cell he had shared at the Armley jail for the last seven years.

Sitting on the threadbare settee, nursing a mug of hot coffee, he looked at the work he had spread all over the floor. There were piles of reference books he had borrowed from the college library, as well as copious amounts of handwritten notes. He planned to write a paper on miscarriages of justice in the modern penal system. He felt uniquely qualified to write such a piece.

He took another sip of the strong black coffee, then looked at the pinboard on the wall opposite. The board was full of photographs of Rebecca and Dominic Whitchurch. The images had been captured outside Mulberry Chambers on the Ropewalk, and in front of the beautiful detached house they owned on Richmond Drive in Mapperley Park.

There was also a Polaroid photograph of the two of them standing beside a young, blonde-haired girl outside the Debenhams store on Long Row in the city centre. The three of them caught in a carefree smiling moment.

There was a myriad of newspaper and magazine articles that chronicled the growing success of Mulberry Chambers. At the centre of the board was a close-up image of Rebecca Whitchurch. She was wearing her full Crown Court regalia, but with wig and brief in hand. He had taken the photograph covertly as she dashed between courtrooms at Nottingham Crown Court.

Taking the photograph had been risky, but it had been worth it. One look at the self-importance and arrogance etched upon her smug face provided all the motivation he needed to remain on track.

It was the first thing he saw every morning and the last thing he saw at night.

Every time he stared at that one image, the urge for

revenge grew even stronger. Just looking at the authoritarian bearing of the woman made him think of the daughter he had lost. The feeling it engendered inside him was a strange mixture of rage, sadness and peace.

He had known for years what his destiny was going to be.

Now he was finally able to carry that destiny through to its conclusion. That thought made him feel at peace with the retribution he was planning.

The weeks since his release from prison had been a blur. After finding out there was an opportunity to study for his master's degree, he had applied for and been accepted at Nottingham Trent University.

He had enjoyed his psychology studies while incarcerated in the Armley jail and wanted to carry on with the subject now he was once again a free man.

He had taken the decision to sever all ties with his hometown of Mansfield Woodhouse. There was nothing left for him there. He wanted nothing to do with his ex-wife or his family and old friends. He felt badly let down by all of them.

The only time he would go back to the small mining village would be to visit Vanessa's grave at the Leeming Lane cemetery.

As soon as he had found the flat on Foxhall Road, he transported everything he owned from Mansfield Woodhouse to Nottingham. It hadn't taken long; he didn't own many possessions. Seven years of imprisonment had seen to that.

Any spare time he had, between lectures at college and his studies at home, was spent keeping fit, running up and down the hills of Mapperley Park.

He used the time he spent running to plan and prepare. It was the perfect opportunity to imagine different scenarios. While jogging through the deserted streets, he could mentally explore the pitfalls and problems various plans threw up. It afforded him the time to develop strategies to overcome those problems. All his thinking, as he ran, was geared to one purpose: how to exact the perfect revenge on Rebecca Whitchurch.

He was pleased with how his preparations had gone so far. He felt ready to take it to the next level and actually make contact with the bitch.

It was time.

16

12.30pm, 4 October 1986
Elm Bank, Sherwood Rise, Nottingham

Alina Moraru was close to tears.
It was now two days since Emily Whitchurch had gone missing, and there was still no information from the police. The tension in the Whitchurch house was almost unbearable. As soon as she had finished her work for the day, Alina had taken the opportunity to get away from the house on Richmond Drive.

She had made the short walk through the leafy streets of Mapperley Park to the Sherwood Rise area of the city. She needed to spend some time with her boyfriend, Florin.

As she walked up the garden path towards Florin's small flat on Elm Bank, Alina was worried sick. She could think of nothing but the missing girl.

It was raining hard, and by the time she arrived at Elm Bank, she was soaking wet. She had quickly dried off in the bathroom and put on the towelling robe she kept at the flat. She was moody and sullen. Since her arrival at the flat, she had hardly spoken a word to her boyfriend.

Florin had noticed the strange mood Alina was in, and said brusquely, 'I don't know why you come here if all you're going to do is sulk like a child.'

Her voice cracking with emotion, tears not very far away, she replied, 'Don't you even want to know what's wrong?'

'Not really. If you want to tell me, you will.'

Some days she wondered why she even bothered to be his girlfriend. Today was rapidly becoming one of those days.

Alina had first met Florin Chirilov on a night out, drinking with friends at the Royal Children pub on Maid Marian Way, in the city. She had been instantly taken by the handsome stranger's athletic build and the lustrous black hair that he wore tied back in a ponytail. Most of all, she loved his dark brown, soulful eyes. As soon as he had met her gaze and smiled, Alina had been smitten. One of her girlfriends had warned her that Florin was a charmer and bad to the bone.

He had a reputation as a petty criminal and a womaniser. Alina was having none of it. She had readily accepted Florin's advances over the rest of that evening.

They had been together for almost four months now. Ever since she had landed the job as au pair for the Whitchurch family, things had become a little more serious. It had meant she could spend much more time with Florin. He had been very interested in her job at first and regularly asked about the family she was au pair for. He had laughed when she had told him what a brat the young girl was. He had said brusquely that if he were the girl's father, he would soon straighten her out. He always became more attentive when Alina described the luxurious house on Richmond Drive. He was always interested in how wealthy her employers were.

She had, on a few occasions, seen glimpses of his criminal ways. With no explanation from Florin, strange property would suddenly appear in his flat. Then, just as quickly, it would disappear. She also noticed that money always seemed to be an issue for him. Some days he would be rich and spend freely, and other times he would complain that he had no money at all.

He had no job that she knew of, and she often wondered where his money came from.

She wondered, but she never asked.

Florin could be very moody and aggressive. He would shout and lose his temper quickly, but he had never laid a finger on her. The reason for this was because Alina had made it clear to him, from the start of their relationship, that she wouldn't tolerate any type of physical abuse.

As though mirroring her own mood, he was being especially distant and moody today.

Alina made the decision to tell him about the girl anyway.

She blurted out, 'The brat's missing.'

He looked disinterested, but asked, 'What do you mean, Alina? Who is missing?'

'Emily. The little brat I look after. She didn't arrive home from school two days ago and hasn't been seen since. Now the police are involved. They even questioned me the other day. Their questions made me feel awful, and Mrs Whitchurch keeps giving me strange looks.'

Florin quickly became indignant. 'Why were you questioned by the police? It's not your fault she's missing, is it?'

'No, of course it's not my fault. When I left you the other day, I went straight to the road where I meet her. I was there in plenty of time, but she never showed up. I went to the school to find her, but she'd already left.'

Florin sat down beside her on the settee. He put his arm around her shoulders, stroked her damp hair and said, 'I don't care about the stupid brat. Her parents have more money than sense. Why don't we go somewhere more comfortable so I can take your mind off things?'

He leaned in and kissed her neck, just below her ear.

She wasn't really in the mood for his amorous advances; she felt too worried and upset. Initially, she pushed him away, but he just smiled at her and began kissing her neck again.

Eventually, she stopped resisting and kissed him back.

When they finally stopped kissing, he stared at her and said, 'Come. Let's go to bed. You need to forget about this silly girl. She's not your problem. I'm sure she'll turn up soon enough. Don't worry.'

Looking into Florin's beautiful, brown eyes, Alina quickly forgot all about Emily Whitchurch. Smiling, she followed him into the bedroom.

17

11.30am, 4 October 1986
MCIU Offices, Mansfield Police Station, Nottinghamshire

Danny Flint sat alone in his office; he was deep in thought. He hadn't moved from his desk since he'd arrived at work that morning.

He felt consumed by a feeling of dread at what the immediate future held, for both him and the Major Crime Investigation Unit.

It was now official.

It had been announced earlier in the day that a new chief constable had been appointed by the police authority. Unsurprisingly, the person chosen for the role was Jack Renshaw. He had previously held the rank of deputy chief constable.

It was a logical appointment. One that spelt continuity for the Nottinghamshire force. The knowledge of that continuity didn't ease the gnawing anxiety now felt by Danny.

Suddenly, he was torn from his thoughts by the strident ringing of the telephone on his desk.

Danny snatched up the telephone. 'Major Crime Unit, Detective Chief Inspector Flint speaking.'

'Danny, I'm pleased you're in the office. It's Jack Renshaw.'

As soon as he had heard the distinctive accent, Danny had known instantly who it was. He took a moment, then said, 'Good morning, sir. Congratulations on your appointment.'

'Thanks. Obviously, I've got to hit the ground running, so I'm trying to speak to the heads of each department. I want to see for myself their current workloads. I need to be aware of what resources they have and what they may need, that sort of thing. I already have a good idea of what your department are currently involved with. I was still hoping to pencil in a meeting with you on the eighth of this month if that suits you as well?'

Danny already knew that he had no prior commitments in four days' time, but he allowed a brief pause before he said, 'My diary's clear at the moment, sir.'

'Excellent. Shall we say ten o'clock on the morning of the eighth? Here at headquarters?'

'That's fine, sir.'

'As I said, I've already got a good idea of your current workload, Danny. Just bring with you an up-to-date résumé of the cases the MCIU are currently working on. I'll need to know your capabilities for any new cases that may come in, as well as staff numbers. That would all be very helpful. Thanks.'

'No problem, sir. See you on the eighth.'

'Thanks.'

The line went dead.

Danny sat quietly; he twirled his pen between his fingers as questions raced through his mind. *What changes will be made? He didn't mention anything about my planned promotion. Is that even still on the table?*

Danny had always enjoyed a good working relationship with Jack Renshaw when he'd been the deputy. The uncertainty of change made him feel nauseous.

He suddenly felt the need for some fresh air.

Grabbing his raincoat, he stepped out of the office and said to his office manager, 'Fran, I'm popping out for ten minutes. I need some air; won't be long.'

Fran said, 'Better take your umbrella. It's chucking it down out there.'

Danny smiled and nodded, but his mind was already elsewhere.

18

10.30am, 5 October 1986
Richmond Drive, Mapperley Park, Nottinghamshire

Three days had passed since Emily Whitchurch had failed to arrive home from school. Her mother, Rebecca, was going out of her mind with worry. The telephone call she had received the night before had disturbed her greatly. It had been quite late when Jacquie Garrett called.

Rebecca had known Jacquie for three years; her daughter Polly was probably Emily's best friend at the Nottingham High School for Girls.

Rebecca had always thought that something about the narrative given by her au pair hadn't been right. The late-night telephone call from Jacquie Garrett had confirmed those instincts.

She planned to confront Alina as soon as she arrived back

at the house this morning. The young au pair had stayed out all night again, something else Rebecca wasn't happy about.

Before Alina arrived home, Rebecca needed to make a telephone call of her own. She picked up the phone in the lounge and dialled the number from memory.

The telephone at Mulberry Chambers was answered on the second ring by one of the secretaries on the reception desk.

Rebecca said tersely, 'It's Rebecca Whitchurch. Put me through to Sebastien Dawson.'

The call was put through instantly. The next voice she heard was Sebastien Dawson. In his usual lisping, clipped tones, he said, 'Good morning, Rebecca. How are you bearing up?'

'It's a complete bloody nightmare. There's no way I can even consider travelling up to Manchester for the robbery trial. I'm sorry.'

'To be perfectly honest, Rebecca, I was going to call you this morning and suggest we put someone else in. It would be impossible for you to concentrate on the intricacies of a robbery trial under these circumstances. I really don't know how Dominic's going to cope with the impending rape trial at Leicester Crown Court.'

'Dominic will be fine. We both know he's got a swinging brick where his heart should be. We've already had words about his misguided priorities this morning before he left for work. Personally, I don't think he should be going to Leicester or anywhere else until we've got Emily back safe and sound. He obviously has other ideas.'

She let out an ironic chuckle, and with sarcasm heavy in her voice, she said, 'But then again, I don't suppose he has my maternal instincts, does he?'

Sebastien Dawson was far too experienced and wily to get

drawn into the complexities of the relationship between a man and wife. With no emotion or inflection in his voice, he said simply, 'Don't worry about work. You've enough on your plate already. I'll arrange for another barrister to take on the Manchester brief. I'll probably give it to Freddie Fletcher. He is desperate for a good, high-profile case, to really cut his teeth.'

'Seb, I really don't care who you give it to. Talk to you soon.'

Rebecca slammed the telephone down; she was angry at having to give away such a high-profile trial.

Where was that bloody au pair? It was now almost a quarter to eleven. The wretched girl should have been here, ready to start work, at ten o'clock.

Just then, she heard the key turn in the lock of the front door and heard footsteps in the hallway. From the lounge, Rebecca shouted, 'Alina, come in here for a minute, please!'

The young Romanian looked flustered as she walked into the lounge. She hadn't been expecting this. She knew her employer didn't like her to be out all night, but it wasn't like she stayed out all the time.

Alina saw the angry expression on Rebecca's face and said, 'I'm sorry for being late back this morning, Mrs Whitchurch. I didn't hear the alarm go off at Florin's flat.'

Rebecca stood up and said angrily, 'I really don't give a toss about Florin or his bloody alarm clock in his stupid flat! Young lady, you've got some questions to answer, and I want the bloody truth this time!'

A stunned Alina grew red in the face and said, 'I don't understand? What questions?'

With her voice raised higher than normal, Rebecca asked, 'Where did you wait to pick up Emily?'

'Outside the school gates, as always. Why?'

'As always? Really? Why are you bloody lying to me?'

Alina could feel her face reddening more and more by the second.

She blustered, 'I'm not lying, Mrs Whitchurch. I met Emily at the same place every day after school.'

'Yes, I'm sure you did. But it wasn't outside the bloody school gates, was it? Before you say anything else – any other lies – you need to know that I've been speaking to Polly's mother.'

Alina knew, at that exact moment, that her employer already knew everything.

She could feel tears starting to sting her eyes as she blurted out, 'Emily didn't like me waiting right outside the school for her. She was ashamed of my car. She ordered me to wait for her a few streets away. I didn't think it would be a problem, because she always walked to the car with Polly and Rosie.'

'And now what do you think? Do you think it's a problem now? You stupid girl!'

Alina could no longer fight back the tears. 'I'm sorry. I didn't know this would happen. It's not my fault.'

'I told you to meet my daughter outside the school gates for a reason. Emily's only fourteen years old, for Christ's sake. Why did you let her dictate to you where you should pick her up?'

Suddenly, Alina could feel herself becoming angry. How dare this woman take it out on her because she was a bad parent? She rounded on Rebecca, pointed an accusing index finger at her and shouted, 'Because your beloved daughter's a nasty little bitch! She's rude and aggressive; that's why she has no real friends. You should try being her parents instead of big-shot lawyers for a change!'

Rebecca was outraged. She wasn't having the hired help talk to her like that. She shouted back, 'Pack your bags! You're fired! Give me your door keys and get out. I'll forward any money we owe you to the agency. Get out of my sight, you wretched girl!'

Alina ran from the lounge and up the stairs, to her room.

Immediately, she began throwing her clothes and belongings into two large suitcases. She was upset about losing her job, but also, in some ways, relieved. She wouldn't have to tiptoe around the brat any longer. As she packed, she thought, *Who cares where the stupid girl is?* Whatever happened to her, it would serve her right. It would also serve her arrogant, selfish parents right as well.

Having packed her bags, she stomped, heavy-footed, back down the stairs. In a fit of temper, she threw her set of door keys on the small table in the hallway and slammed the front door behind her.

She didn't see or hear Rebecca Whitchurch sobbing quietly in the lounge. Even if she had, right at that moment, she wouldn't have cared.

19

11.30am, 5 October 1986
Mulberry Chambers, The Ropewalk, Nottingham

Angela Temple knocked lightly on Dominic Whitchurch's office door. Without waiting for an invitation, she walked in.

Dominic was sitting at his desk, sifting through reams of statements and documents. He looked up, removed his reading glasses and smiled. 'Where have you been, sweetheart? I've been waiting for you to arrive all morning.'

She smiled back and said, 'The traffic was horrendous. There's been a nasty accident on Mansfield Road. The tailbacks it caused went right back through Sherwood. It's this bloody incessant rain. It doesn't look like stopping anytime soon.'

He stood and walked round his desk, to help her remove her wet raincoat. As he took the coat from her shoulders, he leaned in and kissed her neck. She said, 'Stop it, Dom. We've got too much work to do. We'll have plenty of time for that when we get down to Leicester tomorrow. Right now, we need to prep for this trial.'

He laughed as he hung her damp coat on the coat stand. 'There certainly will. I've booked us two double rooms at the Belmont Hotel on Winterburn Street. It's beautiful there and only a short walk to the Crown Court building.'

She winked at him and said seductively, 'Which one of the two rooms will we be using?'

He laughed. 'I think we should christen them both, don't you?'

'That sounds like a wonderful plan,' she purred.

Suddenly, she looked serious and said, 'Are you sure you still want to go? All this business with your daughter, it's bound to affect you. Are you going to be okay?'

'Everything will be fine. Rebecca's going to stay at home now.'

'What? I don't believe she's turned down the Manchester brief.'

'She contacted Sebastien this morning and told him to put someone else in. She wanted me to cancel my commitment in Leicester as well. I told her straight, not a chance.'

'Are you sure, Dom?'

He put his arms around her slim waist and pulled her in close. Feeling her breasts against his chest, he kissed her full lips. When they finally stopped kissing, he looked into her sultry brown eyes and said, 'I'm one hundred percent sure. It's only a matter of time before the police find Emily. There's absolutely no point in me waiting around at home. I know exactly where I'd rather be, and that's lying next to you in a warm bed.'

They kissed again.

This time, it was Angela who stopped first. She said,

'Dom, we really do need to start work, or we won't stand a chance of winning this trial.'

'You're right. I'll phone down to the girls on reception and arrange for coffee and sandwiches to be brought up. That way, we can work through. Is that okay with you?'

'Perfect. The more work we do here, the more time we'll have for play in the Belmont Hotel.'

20

7.30pm, 5 October 1986
Nottingham

The young girl thought she had been held captive in the attic for two days and two nights. There was a tiny gap between the rafters and the wall in one corner, which allowed a splinter of light in during the daytime. She had focussed on that small shaft of light to try to stay sane.

She was starving hungry, and her throat felt parched and dry. She desperately needed food and water. Only once had she used the bowl the monster had left her. Her stomach had ached before she succumbed to the indignity of urinating into the bowl. Afterwards, she wondered why she had waited so long. The relief she had felt, emptying her full bladder, had been wonderful.

She knew the monster would be returning soon.

Like last time, he would have food and water with him. As

desperate as she was for something to eat and drink, she knew she would fight him off again. There was no way she was going to allow him to take her without a fight.

Sitting in the darkness, she had asked herself the same questions repeatedly. *How long could she continue to fight him off? How long would it be before she caved in to her body's need for sustenance and allowed him to do what he wanted to do?*

Maybe she could allow him to do certain things, which didn't amount to full sex, in exchange for food and drink?

After hours of soul-searching, she had made up her mind. When the monster came, she would stay strong and put her own proposition to him.

It must be night-time now. There was no light shining through the small crack. In the distance, she heard a familiar noise that filled her with dread. Stairs were creaking somewhere else in the old house.

He was on his way.

The noise of the padlock being removed and the bolt being drawn back on the door seemed amplified in the darkness.

Suddenly, the door opened, and light streamed into the dark room. He was wearing the same terrifying mask. She could clearly see saliva glistening on his fat lips as his tongue darted between them.

He was carrying a bottle of water and a pack of sandwiches.

He held them out and snarled two words: 'Hungry? Thirsty?'

She nodded.

'If you want to eat and drink ...' He paused before continuing, 'You know what I want.'

The girl summoned all her courage and said, 'I'm so nervous. If I give you what you want, can you take it slowly? The last thing I want is to keep pushing you away. I know how much it upsets you. How about you just touch me tonight? In exchange for the food and drink.'

There was a long silence.

Finally, the monster said, 'Okay. I say when to stop, though.'

The girl nodded and said, 'Alright, but not too long the first time. I'm not used to doing anything like this. I don't want you to hurt me.'

Saying nothing, he put the food and drink down next to the mattress and knelt beside the terrified girl.

Once again, he placed a fat, sweaty hand on her bare thigh. This time, she didn't fight him off like a wildcat. As he slowly moved his hand along her thigh, she gritted her teeth and didn't move.

His hand remained at the top of her thigh, feeling her, exploring her. His hand was inside her panties for less than a minute before she noticed his breathing change. He let out a small gasp, then quickly withdrew his hand.

No words were spoken. The silence between them terrified the girl even more.

She couldn't bear to look at him and had screwed her eyes tightly shut. All she could hear was his rasping breath as he had become aroused.

As he withdrew his hand, she felt him lean forward as he tried to kiss her. She turned her head, allowing his fat lips to brush her cheek. Once again, she could smell stale, fried onions on his rancid breath. Then, without saying a word, he stood up and walked out of the room.

A massive wave of relief washed over her as she heard the door close. The bolt screeched across, and the padlock clicked as it was closed.

She tried to put the horror of what had just happened to the back of her mind. Even with her eyes screwed tightly shut, she could still feel his fat fingers inside her. She bent double, dry-retched and began to sob.

Eventually, she stopped sobbing and felt the hunger pangs again. Now that her prison cell had been plunged back into darkness, she fumbled around the floor, trying to locate the food and drink.

As soon as she found it, she undid the water bottle and gulped down two mouthfuls of cool water. She replaced the screwcap, intending to save some water for later.

She unwrapped the packet of sandwiches and took a bite of the first one.

Cheese and pickle on white bread had never tasted so good.

The food in her stomach energised her. She knew she would need to keep her strength up if she was to successfully fight him off.

Sitting in the darkness, she vowed to herself that the monster would not touch her again.

Thoughts now raced through her mind: *Is anyone looking for me? Surely my parents would have called the police when I didn't arrive home from school? Did anyone see me being snatched off the street?*

One thought soared above all the others: She was now prepared to do whatever it took to stop her captor abusing her again.

21

9.30pm, 5 October 1986
Honeysuckle Cottage, Papplewick, Nottinghamshire

Angela Temple remained sitting in her Volvo long after she had parked the car on the driveway of Honeysuckle Cottage. The stone cottage looked stunning during the daytime and was just as beautiful at night. Soon after buying the cottage, the Temples had invested heavily in subtle mood lighting that accentuated the beauty of the stone structure.

She loved the cottage, but wasn't sure she could say the same about her husband anymore.

The only sound disturbing her brief moment of tranquillity was the heavy rain falling incessantly onto the metal roof of her car. She had remained in the vehicle, trying to work out exactly what she was going to say to Brandon.

She had stared at the leaded light windows illuminated from within. She had an image of her husband half asleep on the sofa in the living room. She had left him a message on the answerphone earlier in the day, letting him know that she would be working late.

He was obviously still up and was waiting for her to arrive home.

The problem she now faced was that ever since they had been married, she had never spent a night away from home. To compound the issue, this trial would necessitate her being away for an entire week.

She had already spent hours carefully considering the best way to break the news; she knew Brandon wasn't going to like it.

The thought of him being so disapproving of the situation suddenly renewed her own self confidence. Who was he to dictate to her what she could and couldn't do? She was her own woman. A powerful woman, with a brilliant career ahead of her. She would not allow it to become the subject of a debate. She would be away for a week, in Leicester, working a high-profile trial. It was just what her career needed.

He would just have to accept it.

It was his problem, not hers.

She grabbed her briefcase off the front passenger seat, opened the car door and ran the few yards to the front door.

The heavy wooden door was unlocked. She quickly ducked into the hallway, keen to get out of the inclement weather.

As she hung her raincoat on the coat rack, she shouted, 'I'm home, sweetheart. I've got some really exciting news.'

Brandon shouted from the living room, 'I'm in here, sweetheart. Do you want a drink fixing?'

'A large G and T would be perfect, thanks.'

She walked into the living room and placed her briefcase at the side of one of the leather armchairs. Brandon was standing next to the ornately carved welsh dresser. He was busily pouring tonic water into a tumbler already half full of gin.

He turned and asked, 'Ice and a slice?'

'No, don't bother going to the kitchen. I just need a drink. It's been a very busy day.'

He handed her the tumbler and lay down on the comfortable leather settee. He picked up his own half-full whiskey glass from the floor. Took a huge gulp and said, 'So, what's your exciting news?'

Angela flopped into the armchair and took a long drink of her gin and tonic. As she felt the warmth from the alcohol coursing through her body, she said, 'I've landed the position of second chair in a very important rape trial.'

In a voice that betrayed his lack of enthusiasm, he said, 'That's great. When does the trial start?'

'We're travelling down to Leicester Crown Court tomorrow morning.'

'That's going to be an awful lot of commuting, sweetheart.'

'No, it's too far. We're stopping in Leicester for the duration of the trial. It would be totally impractical to commute there and back every day. We'll need to work every night, prepping for the trial.'

She watched his face closely. She was looking for a reaction as he began to come to terms with what he was being told. She could almost hear the cogs of his brain turning as he took another sip from his cut-glass tumbler.

Finally, in clipped tones, he said, 'That's wonderful, darling. How long, and who with?'

She smiled confidently and said, 'The trial should only last a couple of weeks, maybe less. It's a fantastic opportunity for me and will definitely push me up the pecking order at Mulberry.'

'You still haven't told me who's going to lead?'

'I've been fortunate enough to be selected by Dominic Whitchurch.'

Brandon said mockingly, 'Selected by Dominic Whitchurch? The main man himself. Fortunate indeed.'

She chose not to acknowledge the blatant sarcasm.

She gushed, 'I know. Dominic always likes a female barrister to second chair a rape trial. He says if there's a woman helping to defend the alleged rapist, it makes it easier to convince a jury the defendant's not guilty.'

Brandon didn't give a toss about the tactics of a trial. He said quietly, 'And where will you be staying while you're working on this trial?'

'Rooms have been booked for us at the Belmont Hotel on Winterburn Street in Leicester. Everyone at work says it's a beautiful hotel and very expensive. Mulberry Chambers have agreed to foot the bill, on expenses.'

'Chambers have?'

'Yes. One of the secretaries booked the rooms earlier today.'

With the same heavy sarcasm in his voice, he said, 'That's wonderful, sweetheart. I hope the trial goes really well, and you get the scumbag rapist off.'

She ignored his sarcasm, laughed and exclaimed, 'Brandon! How many times do I have to tell you? They're not scumbags, they're innocent people. How many of those have you had tonight?'

He took another drink from his glass, laughed and said, 'Whatever. I've had a few, why?'

She turned serious and said, 'So, are you okay with me going?'

'Don't be silly, darling. Of course I am. It's your career. I'm sure you'll be brilliant.'

Brandon smiled, but inside he was seething.

He felt sick to his stomach.

He knew exactly why Dominic Whitchurch had selected his wife to accompany him, and it had fuck all to do with trial tactics.

He finished his drink and said, 'If you're going to be away for a whole week, I think we should have an early night, don't you?'

She said, 'That does sound a lovely idea, but I've still got quite a bit of work to do before I turn in.'

He put his empty tumbler down on the coffee table a little harder than he had intended, and said, 'Okay, sweetheart, no problem. Don't stay up all night.'

As he walked up the stairs of the small cottage alone, Brandon Temple tried to work something out: Exactly when had he lost his wife?

22

9.00am, 6 October 1986
Elm Bank, Sherwood Rise, Nottingham

Alina Moraru stretched lazily before snuggling in closer to her boyfriend. Feeling his girlfriend's movement beside him, Florin stirred sleepily. He looked at the clock on the bedside table and said, 'Come on, Alina, you need to get up now. You're going to be late for work again.'

She put her hand on his flat muscular stomach and said, 'I won't be late today. I won't be late ever.'

He sat up, half awake, reached for his cigarette packet and said, 'What are you talking about? Come on, get up!'

Lazily, she also sat up in the warm bed. 'There's no work for me today. I got fired yesterday.'

'What?'

'The crazy bitch fired me. Her bloody daughter goes

missing because she's a little cow, and somehow, it's all my fault.'

'Why is it your bloody fault?'

'She spoke to the mother of one of her daughter's friends yesterday and found out that I used to wait for her daughter a couple of streets away from the school. I was supposed to pick her up right outside the school gates. She wouldn't listen when I told her that I only waited for her there because her brat of a daughter insisted on it.'

He lit a cigarette, took a long drag and said, 'I still don't understand, baby. If the daughter made you park there, why is it your fault that this stupid, bloody girl has run off?'

'That's just it, none of this is my fault. The bitch is blaming me because she doesn't want to admit that they're both shit parents.'

Florin stroked his chin thoughtfully. He took another long pull on his cigarette and exhaled the smoke in rings, up towards the ceiling.

Finally, he stubbed out the cigarette and said, 'How long has the girl been missing?'

'This will be the fourth day unless she's come home by now.'

'Have they called the police?'

'Yes. I told you the other day, the policewoman questioned me.'

'Okay, okay.'

'Why are you asking all these questions?'

'I'm just angry that this bitch has fired you when you've done nothing wrong. I'll make this big-shot lawyer pay for disrespecting you, sweetheart.'

'What are you talking about?'

He ignored her question and said, 'There's one good thing about you being fired.'

She looked at him quizzically.

He laughed out loud and lunged across the bed, towards her. 'We get to spend all day in bed together.'

He began kissing her throat, his hands caressing her breasts. His mind was elsewhere. He was already planning his next criminal enterprise.

Very soon, he would be a rich man.

23

10.00am, 8 October 1986
Nottinghamshire Police Headquarters

Danny Flint was feeling apprehensive. He was in the seating area outside the chief constable's, waiting for his appointment time. He had been contacted the day before by Caroline Mee, the chief's secretary, confirming that an appointment had been made for him to see Chief Constable Jack Renshaw. She had told him matter-of-factly that he would need to be outside his office at headquarters at ten o'clock sharp.

Danny had arrived with fifteen minutes to spare. He had exchanged pleasantries with Caroline Mee before sitting down to wait.

As he waited, all kinds of thoughts were racing through his mind.

Has Bill Wainwright handed in his resignation yet? Will Jack

Renshaw envision a different role for the MCIU? What does the future hold for me personally?

The voice of Caroline Mee snapped him back from his troubling thoughts. 'The chief will see you now, sir.'

Danny stood and said, 'Thanks, Caroline.'

He walked down the corridor and knocked politely on the chief's door.

His knock was answered by a shout from within: 'Come in.'

Danny walked in and was met by Jack Renshaw. 'Danny, it's good to see you. Take a seat. Do you want a tea or coffee?'

Danny sat down and said, 'No, thank you, sir.'

'Bill Wainwright told me you were always straight down to business. I like that. I can't stand all that small-talk bollocks.'

Renshaw sat down and said, 'So, straight down to business, then. The reason I've asked to see you this morning is to let you know that Bill Wainwright has decided to call it a day. I think he's got a few personal reasons for wanting to go now. I think the death of Miles Galton finally made his mind up for him. Obviously, I'm very sorry to see him go, but I've wished him well in his retirement.'

Here comes the bombshell, Danny thought.

Renshaw continued, 'Anyway, his unexpected decision has left me needing a new head of CID to fill the void. It's probably the one appointment that I couldn't afford to take my time over. It's a vital role and one that needed to be filled quickly. With that in mind, yesterday I approached Detective Chief Superintendent Adrian Potter, from my old force in Devon and Cornwall, and I'm pleased to say that he's accepted the job.'

'I'm sorry, sir, but what has this appointment got to do with me, specifically?'

'Danny, I'm fully aware that Miles Galton and Bill Wainwright had promised you a promotion to the rank of superintendent, to undertake an assistant role to the head of CID here at headquarters. Adrian Potter's a much younger man than Bill Wainwright, and he's of the opinion that he doesn't need an assistant. I've got to say, I'm inclined to agree with him. I don't want to bad-mouth a decision by my predecessor, but I don't see the value of an assistant to the head of CID. Your promotion to superintendent, in this role, isn't going to happen. I'm sorry.'

Danny felt like a ton weight had been lifted from his shoulders.

The promotion would have been great for him financially, as well as working less antisocial hours. It had never been what Danny really wanted. He was happiest being a hands-on detective. Being in command of the MCIU, that was his passion.

Surprised by the lack of a reaction from Danny, Jack Renshaw repeated, 'I'm sorry, Danny.'

'That's fine, sir. I completely understand the logic of your decision.'

Renshaw said, 'What I do want is for you to continue the brilliant job you're currently doing, heading the Major Crime Investigation Unit. I see the MCIU as an extremely valuable resource. This force's ability to clear up serious crime has never been better. I know that an awful lot of that is down to your leadership. Is that okay with you?'

Danny allowed the faintest smile to cross his features. 'That's fine by me, sir. I firmly believe that the MCIU has a pivotal role in modern policing. A dedicated team of detectives being used to their maximum abilities, to detect the most serious crimes that impact on the community the greatest. That's got to be a great asset.'

'I couldn't agree more. I'm sure that Adrian will think the same. He'll no doubt want to schedule a meeting with you as soon as he's settled in. He takes up his new post tomorrow, so you can expect a phone call from him. He'll obviously need you to bring him up to speed on the Unit's current commitments and capabilities.'

'I'll make sure I've got everything ready for him, sir.'

'That's it, then, Danny. I hope you're not too disappointed about the promotion. I'm sure you'll achieve that crown sometime in the very near future.'

'Nothing was ever set in stone, sir. Thank you.'

Danny stood up and left the office.

He was smiling broadly when he walked past the chief's secretary. She looked at Danny's grin and said, 'Well, that obviously went well, Chief Inspector.'

'As far as I'm concerned, it couldn't have gone any better.'

As he walked back to his car, Danny felt relieved. He had always known running the MCIU was where he truly belonged. He couldn't wait to get home and share the good news with Sue.

24

11.00am, 6 October 1986
Mulberry Chambers, The Ropewalk, Nottingham

Sebastien Dawson was looking forward to his next meeting.

He always enjoyed pouring oil on troubled waters, and today he would definitely be doing that. He was about to make someone's day, and he felt good about it.

As he heard the polite knock on his office door, he leaned back in the red leather captain's chair. He coughed once and shouted, 'Come in!'

The door opened a fraction. The fresh, young face of Freddie Fletcher peeked inside the office. Freddie was still a little in awe of the barrister's clerk, and he had no idea why he had been summoned to his office.

With a confidence that belied his feelings of trepidation, the young barrister said, 'You wanted to see me, Sebastien?'

Sebastien waved him inside and said, with his usual bluster, 'Yes, I did, Freddie. Come inside and take a seat.'

Freddie Fletcher did as he was asked. He sat down in one of the two chairs on the other side of Dawson's enormous desk.

He had only been at Mulberry Chambers for ten months and was still very much the new boy around the place. He knew his worth, though. He had graduated with a brilliant law degree from Oxford University and had completed his articles at one of the most prestigious law firms in York. Soon after finishing his articles in York, he had felt like he needed a change of scenery and direction. He had applied for and got the job at Mulberry Chambers. He knew that Mulberry was fast becoming one of the top law firms in the country. More importantly, he knew about their penchant for defending celebrity clients.

This was where Freddie Fletcher saw his future.

Ten years from now, he wanted to be the 'go-to barrister' for any so-called celebrity in trouble with the law. Be it an actor, pop star or footballer, they would all be asking for Freddie Fletcher to defend them in their moment of crisis.

That was all for the future. Right now, Freddie was only concerned about the reason he had been summoned, so urgently, to Dawson's office.

The fat barrister's clerk steepled his fingers over his ample stomach and said, 'Now then, Freddie. How are you settling into Mulberry Chambers?'

'I'm enjoying it so far. Nottingham's a beautiful city, and my apartment in The Park is splendid. If I'm being brutally honest, the work could be a little more challenging. I had expected to be undertaking far more substantial briefs than the ones I've been allocated so far.'

Dawson allowed a huge smile to spread across his face.

He said, 'Well, if that's the case, I hope you're going to be pleasantly surprised with the news I've got for you this morning.'

He paused, observing the young barrister's reaction.

Always very quick on the uptake, Freddie said swiftly, 'Do you have a new brief for me?'

Sebastien nodded. 'I know it's short notice, but I'd like you to take on the Denton Post Office robbery trial, in Manchester.'

'I thought Rebecca Whitchurch was defending that client?'

'Unfortunately, her current circumstances dictate she cannot be away from home and therefore can't travel to Manchester.'

Freddie was starting to enjoy this meeting. He said with a smirk, 'Ah, because of her errant teenage daughter doing another disappearing trick, I suppose?'

'Yes, exactly that, Freddie. This is a very worrying time for Dominic and Rebecca. She feels unable to prepare properly for such a high-profile trial.'

Every cloud, thought Freddie.

He looked at Sebastien Dawson, gave his best look of concern and said, 'As you say, it is very short notice, but I'd be more than happy to step into the breach. Where's the brief and the rest of the trial documents?'

'I've got the brief here.'

Hampered by his bulky frame, with a great deal of effort and struggle, Dawson leaned over the side of his chair. From the floor at the side of his desk, he retrieved a stack of papers tied with a dark pink ribbon.

He placed the heavy brief on his desk and said, 'I'll have all the other documentation sent to your office so you can start prepping. You'll need to be in Manchester by tomorrow evening. That gives you all of today and most of tomorrow to do your prep. Is that going to be long enough?'

'Yes, that'll be fine. I'll only prep for the first two days of the trial here. When I get to Manchester, I'll prep at night as the trial develops. I prefer to work a trial that way anyway. You never know what's going to turn up during the presentation of evidence by witnesses. Thank you so much, Sebastien. This is exactly the reason I came to Mulberry, good-quality case work.'

'I thought you'd be pleased. Do a good job on this trial, and it will stand you in very good stead for future quality briefs. Make sure you grasp this opportunity, Freddie.'

'Don't worry, I intend to.' He smirked slyly, winked and continued. 'I do hope the young Whitchurch girl decides to extend her vacation.'

Sebastien's avuncular mood changed instantly. He scowled from behind his glasses. 'There's no need for indelicate remarks like that. As I said before, this is an extremely worrying time for Dominic and Rebecca. Wait until you're a father; maybe you'll understand then. Comments like that are uncalled for and not in any way humorous.'

Realising he had overstepped the mark, Fletcher said quickly, 'I do apologise, Sebastien; I was only being playful. Probably vulgar, and in poor taste, as you say. I'm sure the police will find the poor girl very soon. Meanwhile, I'd better make a start with all this prep.'

Sebastien had instantly changed his opinion of the bright young lawyer sitting in front of him. He could now see there was something distinctly unpleasant and rather nasty about Freddie Fletcher.

Trying to hide the scowl that had replaced his earlier smile, he said, 'I'll get one of the secretaries to book you a hotel in Manchester for the duration of the trial.'

'Thanks. Would you mind asking them to book me a first-class rail ticket as well? Driving into Manchester these days is a bloody nightmare.'

'Consider it done. I'll also arrange for a courier to make sure all the documents you'll need for the trial arrive safe and sound. We don't need anything to go missing on a bloody train.'

Freddie stood up, picked the heavy brief up from the desk, and said, 'Thank you so much for considering me, Sebastien. I won't let you down.'

Dawson replied curtly, 'I'm sure you won't. Good luck.'

Fletcher closed the door behind him and walked down the hallway, towards his own office.

He was beaming from ear to ear.

He had noticed the mood change in Dawson after his quip about the girl being missing. He chastised himself for being careless with his comments. He told himself that he needed to take more care when making such acerbic remarks.

He chuckled and said quietly to himself, 'Thank you so much, Emily darling. I'm begging you, please don't stay away from home too long.'

He planned to prep for the rest of the day, then go into Nottingham that evening to celebrate his good fortune properly.

He planned on asking Felicity, the gorgeous brunette who worked in admin, if she fancied helping him celebrate his good fortune. He had been told, by another of the younger barristers in Chambers, that Felicity was always up for a night on the town, drinking copious amounts of champagne.

He closed the door of his small windowless office, sat down at his desk and pulled at the dark pink ribbon on the brief. He smiled as he began reading the documents.

He loved it when a plan came together.

25

12.30pm, 6 October 1986
The Arboretum, Nottingham

Darren Treadgold slumped onto the wooden park bench.
He had caught the bus from Maid Marian Way to Clarendon Street. He hadn't realised that the walk from the bus stop on Clarendon Street, alongside the old cemetery and into The Arboretum, was a gradual uphill incline.

He was now sweating profusely and badly out of breath.

He placed the brown paper bag containing his three Big Mac burgers and paper cup full of hot latte coffee onto the bench beside him. He would need to get his breath back properly before he could enjoy his lunch.

It was a bit of a pain to get here during his lunch hour. He needed the greenery and the peace and quiet today.

He had some serious thinking to do about his situation.

Things weren't going the way he had envisioned. He was now seriously worried about what to do next.

He still couldn't quite believe how easy it had been to carry out the first part of his plan. It had been a foul, inclement afternoon when he had gone stalking the streets after finishing his shift at the fast-food restaurant.

He had only been driving around for about ten minutes when he had spotted the girl in her school uniform. She was walking alone on Mount Hooton Road, alongside the Forest Recreation Ground. She had been soaking wet and looked totally miserable. Her long blonde hair was wet and sticking to her school blazer. She had no raincoat. He had driven alongside her and stopped the car. He had then wound the window down a little and asked if he could give her a lift, out of the rain.

He had never in a million years expected her to get in the car. But she had leapt at the chance to get out of the driving rain. The girl had immediately apologised to him, saying, 'Sorry for making your car seats wet. Could you drop me off near the bus stops on Mansfield Road, please?'

Not quite able to believe his luck, he had quickly said, 'No problem. Don't worry about the seats. They'll soon dry. I need you to fasten your seatbelt, though.'

As the girl had turned to fasten the seatbelt, he grabbed the chloroform-soaked cloth from the compartment in the driver's door. Before she could turn back to face him, he had clamped the damp cloth across her nose and mouth.

She had let out a small squeal, then quickly fell unconscious. He held the cloth over her face for a full minute before risking driving off. Satisfied that she was totally unconscious, he had used plastic tie wraps to bind her wrists and ankles. He had then forced her down into the passenger footwell so she was out of sight.

Now, as he sat on the park bench, he shuddered at the thought of his hands touching the bare skin on her wet legs.

He leaned back on the bench and closed his eyes, relishing that delicious thought.

As he thought back to that night, he remembered how nervous he had felt when he arrived at his father's house in West Bridgford. He had been so relieved to find the old man was already in bed, asleep.

It had been an arduous task to carry the still unconscious girl up two flights of stairs, to the third floor of the house. He had been out of breath and had to stop twice to get his breath back. Finally, he had carefully laid her down onto the old mattress in the attic.

In his mind's eye, he could still see her lying on her back on the mattress. Her short skirt had ridden up on her wet thighs, exposing the merest flash of white panties.

He had resisted the temptation to touch the girl and had simply turned her onto her side. The last thing he had wanted was for her to choke before she came around. He had stood in the darkness staring at her for over an hour before she had started to stir. He had then quickly cut the tie wraps from around her ankles but had left her wrists bound. He then left the attic, securing the door with a padlock.

The sound of two children laughing as they ran past snapped him from his reverie.

He opened his eyes and stared after the squealing children as they ran by. His breathing had returned to normal, so he reached down for the brown paper bag.

A mouth-watering smell of fried onions, relish and pickles wafted from the bag as he opened it. He quickly devoured two of the Big Mac burgers before greedily gulping down most of the warm coffee. He smacked his lips, belched loudly and then demolished the third of the burgers before finishing the coffee.

He wiped his greasy hands on the brown paper bag before screwing it up and hurling that, and the empty paper cup, into the waste bin.

Feeling satisfied, he leaned back on the hard wooden bench. Having eaten, he needed time to think now. There had been some encouragement, a glimmer of hope, the night before. When the girl had finally allowed him to touch her.

Even then, it hadn't been as wonderful as he had imagined it would be. She had sat there, unmoving, paralysed with fear. As he groped her, he could feel her trembling. That wasn't what he had planned, what he wanted.

He needed the girl to participate, to enjoy it as well, or it was no good. Maybe he should try smoking a little weed in the attic with her and see if that relaxed her as much as it had done in the squat. He discounted that idea, as his father would be downstairs. The old man was bound to smell it and create a fuss.

Suddenly, an idea burst into his brain.

It was such a simple notion that he wondered why he hadn't thought of it before. In just five days' time, his father was due to go on a day trip to Matlock. The trip had been organised by the local Age Concern group. The old man would be away from the house all day.

Darren Treadgold was smiling broadly now. As soon as he got back to work, he would alter the duty roster to make sure he was off work that day.

In his mind, he was already planning the day's events.

As soon as his father had been picked up by the Age Concern volunteers, he would spend the morning with the girl in the attic, smoking dope. If it had the same effect as it had in the squat, the drug would relax the girl enough to let her enjoy him touching her. If she were totally relaxed, who knows where it would end.

In Darren's mind, he was already making love to the girl on the mattress.

He now had a huge grin on his face.

He continued smiling as he stood up from the park bench and waddled his way back towards Clarendon Street, to catch the bus back into town.

He would keep the girl fed and watered without making any further attempts at touching her. He hoped that by doing that, she would get used to him and not fear him so much.

He could wait another five days, no problem.

The young girl with the long, blonde hair would soon be his to enjoy in that very special way.

26

10.30pm, 6 October 1986
Nottingham City Centre

The champagne had been flowing steadily, and Freddie Fletcher was more than a little tipsy. He'd met Felicity Spencer, as arranged, in Champagne Charlie's Bar in the fashionable Hockley area of the city, at eight o'clock. He had ordered bottle after bottle of Bollinger, Grande Annee, ever since.

As the third bottle was drained, Freddie declared loudly, 'Same again!'

Felicity was also starting to feel the effects of the alcohol. She shook her head at Freddie. 'No more for me, darling. If I have one more glass of bubbly, I'll be totally pissed!'

'Oh, come on, Fliss! I thought you were a sport. You've got to help me celebrate getting this brief. What could be a more appropriate celebration than drinking vintage champagne in the company of a very beautiful woman?'

Felicity was flattered by the compliment from the slim, blonde-haired, handsome barrister. She giggled and said, 'Why, thank you, kind sir!'

'Does that mean yes to another bottle of bubbly?'

'Oh, go on then, Freddie! But you'd better make sure I get home okay.'

'Don't worry about that, darling. You can always crash at my apartment in The Park. I don't mind sleeping on the sofa; it's very comfortable.'

He winked and smiled at the young secretary.

She grinned and said seductively, 'That sounds like a plan. So long as you promise to stay on that sofa and behave yourself. I'm not that kind of girl.'

Freddie held up three fingers of his right hand and declared loudly, 'Scout's honour! Trust me, Fliss, after another bottle of bubbly, I won't be capable of stealing your virtue even if I wanted to.'

He roared with laughter and shouted above the din, 'Bartender! Another bottle of Bolly over here! Quick as you can!'

They were sitting in a private booth, just away from the main bar. Now that it was getting later, the clientele had thinned out a little. The lights were low and the music soft. It was the perfect place for young professionals to unwind and relax. There were two huge bouncers working the door of Champagne Charlie's, and admission was strictly controlled. The management only wanted clientele who would spend big and conduct themselves properly. A couple of times during the evening, when Freddie had got a little too boisterous and loud, one of the doormen had come over and had a quiet word with the overexuberant barrister.

Freddie was enjoying himself. He wasn't going to let being bollocked by some gorilla in a dinner jacket spoil his night. He was pleased he had asked Felicity to join him. She was an extremely pretty girl. The tight black leather trousers and clinging peppermint green mohair jumper she wore for the night out accentuated what a fabulous body she had.

Freddie knew she wasn't the brightest, but she had a fabulous sense of humour and was great fun. His ego was also relishing the envious looks he was getting from other punters in the bar. He knew every other man in the bar would have loved to have been in her company.

While they waited for the next bottle to arrive at their table, Freddie leaned in close and whispered conspiratorially, 'You do know why I'm celebrating, don't you, Fliss?'

'Yes, Freddie. Old man Dawson gave you the brief for the Manchester robbery.'

His speech became slightly slurred as he whispered back, 'That's only partly right, sweet girl. The real reason is not so much that I'm doing it; it's more because that bitch Rebecca Whitchurch isn't doing it.'

He rocked his head back and roared with laughter.

Felicity shook her head and said, 'Yeah, but if her daughter hadn't run off somewhere, Rebecca would still be doing it.'

'That's so very true, Fliss darling. Sad, but very true.'

He smirked slyly and continued. 'So, it's a bloody good job the brat's gone missing, then, isn't it?'

'That's a horrible thing to say, Freddie! God knows where that poor girl is. Rebecca must be going out of her mind with worry.'

Freddie fixed the young secretary with a wild-eyed, alcohol-induced stare and whispered, 'Oh, I don't think God has the first clue where that girl is now.'

A frown came over the young secretary's face, and she said seriously, 'What do you mean?'

Just then the waiter arrived carrying a bucket full of ice, with a bottle of Bollinger sitting in it, and two lead-crystal champagne flutes. He placed the ice bucket and flutes on the table, took the bottle from the bucket and, with a theatrical flourish, loudly popped the cork.

Ignoring the question asked by Felicity, Freddie roared his approval and said loudly, 'Wonderful! Do the honours, my man.'

The waiter carefully poured the effervescent drink into the flutes.

As she watched her glass fill, Felicity wondered what Freddie had meant by his remark. As soon as the waiter had filled both glasses and left them alone, she leaned in close and whispered, 'Freddie, what did you mean?'

Brushing off her concern, he replied, 'Oh, I didn't mean anything, you silly thing. I'm just glad that, for the time being, the bitch's daughter is nowhere to be found. Personally, I hope she fucking well stays missing if it means more nights like this. Every cloud and all that.'

He raised his glass high in the air and said, 'I propose a toast!'

Felicity raised her glass and clinked her crystal flute alongside Freddie's.

In a booming voice, he said, 'Here's to the wonderful, absent Emily!' Then in a much quieter voice, he added seriously, 'May she stay hidden in the shadows forever.'

The smile vanished from Felicity's face, and she pulled her glass away.

She pouted and said, 'I can't drink to that. That's a horrible thing to say.'

'Oh, come on, Fliss, I'm just teasing.'

He could feel her mood change; she wasn't impressed. So he said quickly, 'Don't take me seriously. I'm just having a bit of fun. Look, I know I can be a twat at times, but I'm only joking with you. You should see your pouty, little face. It's really quite endearing.'

'Fuck off, Freddie! You're not funny, and if you don't

change the subject in the next thirty seconds, I'm going home.'

Freddie swept his blonde hair back with his fingers, fluttered his eyelashes and beamed his most charming smile at her. 'Felicity, darling, I hear that the weather forecast is predicting even heavier rain all day tomorrow.'

She tried hard not to, but in the end, she laughed at his little joke and the pathetic, hangdog expression he had put on his face.

As she laughed, she said, 'Bloody hell, Freddie, you can be such an idiot.'

He grinned and topped up his own glass. 'Come on, Fliss. You're starting to lag behind.'

She picked up her crystal flute and took two gulps of the Bollinger. Immediately, she felt the alcohol rush as the bubbles exploded in her throat. Felicity knew she would be suffering in the morning, but right now, she didn't care. She was having a good night; Freddie was very generous and great fun to be with.

She smiled at Freddie and raised her glass.

Behind her smile, and even though she was feeling the effects of the alcohol, there was something troubling her.

When he had proposed his drunken toast to Emily Whitchurch, why had Freddie used the word *hidden* instead of *missing*?

27

7.30am, 7 October 1986
Richmond Drive, Mapperley Park, Nottingham

Sam Jamieson was coming towards the end of his morning run. He loved the challenge that Mapperley Park offered. The steep hills and long gradients were just what he needed to start his day. He tried to make time to run every morning. He had discovered that after being locked up in a small cell for years, just the feeling of being able to move freely around the streets was very therapeutic.

His circuit around the Mapperley Park area always included a couple of passes along Richmond Drive. That way, he could jog slowly by the house owned by Dominic and Rebecca Whitchurch.

Soon after moving to the Forest Fields area of the city, he had followed the barrister from Mulberry Chambers on the Ropewalk to her home address.

Over the last few days, he'd noticed that her car hadn't moved on the driveway. On a couple of occasions, he'd seen police officers at the house. He had planned on leaving the letter at the house two mornings ago, just to get her thinking. The police car parked outside the house had thwarted him from dropping the letter through the letterbox on that occasion.

It wasn't a threatening letter, as such. He just wanted her to know that somebody wasn't happy with her, and that they were watching her every move. He knew it would unnerve her, maybe even frighten her. That was all he wanted to achieve at the moment.

Simple revenge wasn't going to be enough for Sam Jamieson.

He needed Rebecca Whitchurch to suffer an excruciating, drawn-out agony over a long period of time. Only then would his need for payback be sated.

He slowed down as he jogged past the house, peering through the wrought-iron gates and up the driveway. Her car was still in the same place. It hadn't moved since yesterday.

He quickened his pace.

Soon the bitch would know what real loss, real fear, real helplessness felt like. For now, he was happy to let her fret at home, wondering what was going to happen next.

He wiped the sweat from his brow and began the final part of the morning run. He always gradually increased his pace on the way back to Forest Fields. It would only take him ten minutes from here to reach his small flat. He needed to have a hot shower and eat breakfast, ready for another day of lectures at university.

He felt a little frustrated about the letter. One thing prison had taught him, though, was that patience was a virtue. He'd waited years to even the score. A few more days, weeks or months wouldn't hurt him. He knew he was already well on the way to achieving the ultimate revenge.

He could afford to be patient, for as long as it took. He had the upper hand. Rebecca Whitchurch wasn't going anywhere.

28

7.30pm, 8 October 1986
The Belmont Hotel, Winterburn Street, Leicester

Angela Temple finished drying her hair and slipped into the soft towelling robe that bore the logo of the Belmont Hotel. She felt relaxed and was looking forward to spending the entire week with her lover.

Dominic Whitchurch was in the bedroom. He was studying all the police statements for the rape charge they would be defending at Leicester Crown Court in the morning.

Angela knew she would be able to distract him from his work any time she felt like it. Allowing her robe to open, exposing her naked, tanned body, she smiled at her reflection in the steamy mirror. She was confident that as soon as he saw her naked, Dominic would be unable to resist.

From the moment she had started work at Mulberry Chambers, there had been a chemistry between the two of them. It had taken just over three months for that subtle chemistry to turn into a full-blown affair.

Until this week, intimate moments had to be snatched when their respective workloads allowed. Making love with Dominic in the back of his Range Rover was not ideal. It was better, however, than nothing. This was the first time they had been away together, and Angela could feel butterflies fluttering low down in her stomach.

Dominic was completely different to her husband; he always took the time to ensure she was pleasured. Unlike her husband, he was a very gentle and considerate lover.

Angela had waited for an opportunity like this for a long time. She was determined to make Dominic realise what he could have all the time if he would only see sense and leave his domineering wife, Rebecca.

She brushed her long, silky hair and applied bright red lipstick to her full lips. The vivid red contrasted with her jet-black hair and dark brown eyes perfectly.

With the bathrobe hanging loosely from her shoulders, she walked into the bedroom. Dominic was sitting on the bed with papers strewn all around him. Without looking up, he said, 'I'll only be a few more minutes, sweetheart.'

Angela said nothing.

She knelt on the bed in front of him and allowed the robe to slip from her shoulders, totally exposing her slender body.

Finally, Dominic looked up from the paperwork and saw her kneeling naked before him. Very slowly, he removed his glasses and said, 'You look absolutely stunning.'

She moved closer, put her arms around his neck and drew him in close. She whispered seductively, 'That's enough work for tonight.'

They kissed passionately, and Angela could feel the fire rising in her stomach.

Suddenly, Dominic broke away from the smouldering,

sexy embrace and said, 'Bloody hell! Room service is going to be here any minute!'

Angela laughed, pushed him backwards onto the bed, straddled him and said, 'You must have ordered something wonderful if it's better than this, darling?'

She laughed again, climbed off him and continued, 'It's a bloody good job we've got all night, Dom.'

Right on cue, there was a loud knock on the door. A voice shouted, 'Room service!'

Angela quickly slipped the towelling robe back on and walked to the door. Dominic quickly cleared the crumpled paperwork from the top of the bed. He desperately tried to smooth the sheets of paper before putting them back inside the folder.

Angela opened the door, and the room service waiter walked in. He placed the large tray onto the table and removed the metal tureens covering the hot food. He left the room, returning immediately with an ice bucket containing a bottle of Moet champagne.

Dominic followed the waiter to the door, handed him a ten-pound note and said, 'Thanks.'

The grateful waiter replied, 'That's very generous of you, sir. If there's anything else you need, just call down, and I'll bring it straight up.'

'There won't be anything else, but thank you.'

Angela looked at the two plates of creamy carbonara linguini and said, 'Mmm, pasta and ice-cold champagne. Two of my favourites.'

She picked up a fork and began eating while Dominic popped the cork and poured two glasses of champagne.

Passing her a glass of chilled champagne, he said, 'I know my timing sucks, but I was starving.'

'Don't worry, sweetheart. I hadn't realised how hungry I was. Just make sure you leave room for your dessert.'

She winked at him and raised her champagne glass. He clinked her glass with his own and said, 'Don't you worry about that. Dessert is always my favourite course.'

Staring at each other as they ate the pasta, their sense of anticipation was growing.

Having finished the food, they got undressed in a hurry and fell onto the bed.

Their lovemaking was as slow and sensual as they could make it. They had both wanted this first time together in a warm, comfortable bed to be special.

Two hours later, feeling spent, they sat up in bed, cuddling each other in a way that had previously been denied to them. Both were relishing that wonderful feeling of quiet intimacy enjoyed by lovers.

It was Dominic who finally broke the silence. 'More champagne?'

'Mmm, yes, please, darling. That would be lovely.'

He walked over to the table and refilled the glasses. He handed one to Angela and got back into bed. Feeling the warmth from each other's bodies as they sipped the ice-cold champagne felt delicious.

After a few minutes, Angela whispered, 'Don't you want this all the time, Dom?'

'You know I do, sweetheart.'

She put her glass down on the bedside table, looked into his eyes and said firmly, 'When?'

He placed his glass down as well. 'Very soon. It's just so bloody difficult right now.'

'It's always going to be difficult. I'm so ready to leave; every day at home feels like a nightmare. We barely speak anymore. I thought you were ready to leave, as well.'

'I am, sweetheart, but you know what's going on at home. There's no way I could walk out now.'

With just a hint of annoyance in her voice, Angela said, 'What's that got to do with anything?'

Staring into her brown eyes, he replied firmly, 'How can I leave Rebecca now? In case it had slipped your mind, my fourteen-year-old daughter's missing, for Christ's sake!'

She sat back, leaning against the quilted headboard. After a minute, she let out a long sigh and said softly, 'I'm sorry, Dom. I shouldn't have said that. It was selfish and crass. I'm so sorry. It's just that I want to be with you so badly. Every day we're apart hurts like crazy. I feel like I'm just treading water at home. I don't love my husband. I'm in love with you.'

He also leaned back against the headboard. He put his arm around her shoulders, pulled her in close, and said, 'Trust me, sweetheart, it's what I want too. I promise you, just as soon as Emily's found, I'll make the break. Things haven't been good between me and Rebecca for years. It took meeting you to make me realise what I was missing in my life. I just hope you're ready for the massive shitstorm that's going to follow our actions?'

'I'm more than ready. It's what I wish for every day. I really hope Emily's found sooner rather than later.'

'I've already asked Richard Conway to write a strongly worded letter to the new chief constable to gee his men up. I'm sure she'll be found soon, sweetheart.'

'Do you really think a letter from the head of chambers will have any impact on the police, darling?'

As he reached over for his glass of champagne, he said, 'It can't hurt, can it? The cops need rousting every now and then.'

He raised the champagne flute and said, 'Now, why don't we drink some more of this champagne and get comfortable again? Let's try to forget about what's happening back in Nottingham, and make the most of this week, shall we?'

After drinking more champagne, they snuggled down

under the duvet again. Angela whispered seductively, 'Oh, I intend to make the most of you, darling. Come here.'

As they kissed and caressed, Dominic's mind was in turmoil. He loved being with Angela, but there was no way he was ready to leave his wife and daughter for her. Leaving his wife would almost certainly be the end of his career at Mulberry Chambers. It would definitely scupper any chances he would have of making silk. That was something he couldn't let happen.

For now, he would continue to enjoy the weeks and months ahead with Angela. There really was no need to rush anything. He would end it with her when it suited him and not before. It wasn't time yet; he would cross that bridge when he came to it.

While ever his daughter remained missing, there was no pressure on him to leave his wife. Angela would have to understand that there was no way he could leave while that was still the situation.

As Angela's head disappeared beneath the duvet and she began kissing his stomach, his mind was suddenly yanked away from thoughts about his dysfunctional marriage and his missing daughter.

The only thought going through his mind at that moment was that the beautiful, sexy woman in bed with him was insatiable.

29

9.00pm, 8 October 1986
Mansfield, Nottinghamshire

Danny Flint was sitting on the sofa, quietly reading the newspaper, when Sue came into the living room. She looked at her husband and said, 'You're very quiet tonight. Is there anything on the television worth watching?'

Danny put the paper down, looked at Sue and said, 'I haven't looked, to be honest; I was just relaxing.'

'Sorry, I didn't mean to disturb you.'

Danny patted the cushion on the settee next to him. 'Don't be daft. Come here.'

Sue sat down beside him on the comfortable sofa and cuddled in.

She said quietly, 'How did your meeting with the new chief go?'

'It was fine. What I'd expected, to be honest. No promotion to superintendent, but he wants me to continue running the MCIU.'

'How do you feel about that?'

'I'm a little disappointed about missing out on the promotion. That's the bad news, but it's not the end of the world. I'm just happy he sounded so positive about the MCIU. That's eased a lot of the worries I've been feeling lately.'

'If you ask me, it's all good news. I think working at headquarters every day would have slowly driven you mad. You're a detective; that's what you do best.'

Danny said nothing and just squeezed her gently.

They sat quietly, just enjoying the feeling of closeness.

After a few minutes, Danny broke the silence. 'The chief also confirmed to me that Bill Wainwright's retiring, effective immediately. He's owed that much annual leave and time off; he's got no notice to work.'

'Oh. That was all very quick. Any idea who'll be taking his place?'

'Yes. Jack Renshaw has promoted a superintendent from his old force into the job.'

Sue laughed. 'Another Cornishman? You'll need to take a Cornish pasty every time you go to headquarters soon.'

Danny laughed and said, 'Very funny, but I don't think so. Apparently, the new guy's originally from West Yorkshire. As soon as I found out who was being appointed, I asked Rob to check him out. It would appear that Detective Chief Superintendent Adrian Potter is a bit of a butterfly.'

'A butterfly?'

'Yeah, it's what we call someone who flits from one force to the next in order to climb the promotion ladder. This will be the third time he's moved forces, all on promotion.'

'I see. So, what else did your spy tell you about Adrian Potter?'

'Rob's not my spy. It's just sometimes forewarned is forearmed, that's all. Potter was the superintendent in charge of the Administration and Finance Department in Devon and Cornwall. He was responsible for overseeing all the drastic budget cuts and changes within that force. Rob called a few people he knows from that force. Adrian Potter was far from being a popular figure. Seems like Devon and Cornwall are glad to see the back of him.'

'That doesn't sound very encouraging.'

'Quite.'

'So, he's going from an admin role in Cornwall straight in as the head of CID in Notts? That's a bit of a quantum leap, isn't it?'

'Possibly so. Jack Renshaw spoke very highly of him today. My only worry is that he hasn't got much of a CID background. He worked as a detective sergeant in Bradford for six months as part of his accelerated promotion. That's the only time he's ever spent working on the CID. All his other postings have been in uniform. He's another Bramshill flyer.'

Sue frowned. 'Just because he's been on the accelerated promotion scheme doesn't mean he's not up to the job, though.'

'You're right. I just can't help thinking about that pervert Maurice Dennington, another Bramshill product who ran the Sexual Offences Unit.'

'You mustn't do that. You can't compare Dennington with this new man. Dennington was an abusive criminal who should never have been a police officer, let alone a superintendent. He was an accomplished liar who managed to hide his past and slip through the net. All candidates for accelerated promotion aren't like him. Look at that young woman who came to work on your department; I can't remember her name, but you said she was highly intelligent and extremely competent.'

'Tina Prowse.'

'Yes, that's her. I'm sure the majority are like her. Hard-working, highly motivated and intelligent.'

'You're probably right. I shouldn't let one person cloud my judgement about the scheme.'

'I know you, Danny. I'm sure you'll get on just as well with Adrian Potter as you did with Bill Wainwright.'

'Well, I'll soon find out. I've got a meeting with him tomorrow morning.'

'I'm sure everything will be fine. Now what do you want to watch?'

He placed his hand on her baby bump and said, 'Shall we just have an early night? A cuddle would be lovely.'

She leaned over and kissed him, saying, 'That sounds wonderful, sweetheart.'

30

10.00am, 9 October 1986
Nottinghamshire Police Headquarters

Danny had arrived at police headquarters fifteen minutes before his scheduled appointment with Detective Chief Superintendent Adrian Potter. He had waited patiently outside the office that had been occupied by Bill Wainwright for as long as he could remember.

For reasons he couldn't quite explain, Danny found himself wishing today's meeting were still going to be with the dour Scot he'd become such firm friends with.

As he waited, he became consumed by a feeling of dread. It was an irrational anxiety, one that he couldn't fathom.

Finally, he was called into the office.

He walked in and stood in front of the desk. There were no pleasantries exchanged. For a full two minutes, Adrian Potter continued to read a report. Not once did he even acknowledge Danny's presence in the office.

Danny took the time he was kept waiting to study his new boss. The first thing that struck him about Adrian Potter was how physically small he was. Everything about him seemed diminutive. Even his head, topped with crew-cut blonde hair, seemed small. The only large thing about him were the bulging, unblinking blue eyes, which flicked infrequently from the report to Danny.

Even though he remained seated, he was still wearing his suit jacket. It smothered him, giving the appearance of being a couple of sizes too big. The crisp, white shirt he wore gaped at the neck, with the Windsor knot in his tie pushed firmly up. It looked like a size sixteen collar around a size fifteen neck.

Eventually, and without speaking a word, Potter raised a hand and motioned for Danny to sit down.

The arrogance of the gesture was not lost on Danny. He felt himself biting down hard on his lower lip. He was being made to feel like a probationary constable standing in front of a disciplinary hearing. Not at all like the chief inspector in charge of the Major Crime Investigation Unit.

An increasingly annoyed Danny broke the silence, saying curtly, 'Sir, you wanted to see me?'

'I'll be with you in a second, Chief Inspector.'

Even the man's voice was small. He spoke in a reedy, almost effeminate voice.

This meeting wasn't going well.

Finally, Potter looked directly at Danny, his bright blue eyes unblinking. He said quietly, 'So, Chief Inspector, let's talk about this Major Crime Investigation Unit, shall we? Do you think it offers good value for the taxpayers' money?'

Danny couldn't quite believe what he had just heard. Was this really the first question?

'I'm positive it does, sir.'

The 'sir' came out very begrudgingly. Danny realised he

had to check his emotions. He could feel himself becoming angrier by the second, and that would not do.

In a more measured tone, he continued, 'Prior to the Major Crime Investigation Unit being set up, all murders and other serious crimes were investigated by divisional CID officers. This protocol inevitably led to two things. Firstly, murder enquiries took longer to complete, because there was a lack of skill and expertise in investigating such crimes. Secondly, it caused a massive headache for the divisional CID officers who were not seconded onto the murder enquiry. In effect, run-of-the-mill crime investigation was suffering, and major crime wasn't being detected. It was a lose-lose situation. Following the inception of the MCIU, we now have a dedicated team of officers who know exactly what is required to investigate major crime. As a direct result, detection rates and clear-up times have improved beyond all recognition. We currently have no unsolved murder enquiries on our books. The other plus is that when a murder is first reported, there's very little impact on the overall investigation of crime on the divisions. Both the previous chief constable and the head of CID were big advocates for the creation and implementation of the MCIU, sir.'

'Be that as it may, I'm not convinced at all, Chief Inspector. Your Unit comprises fourteen highly skilled detectives. Fifteen, if you include yourself within that number. At your disposal, you have two detective inspectors, two detective sergeants and ten detective constables. I think there's a genuine financial argument that these resources could be better utilised back on the divisional CID strength. The additional manpower would undoubtedly raise detection rates for all crime, right across the force.'

'Having worked in this force area under both systems, I can assure you that isn't the case. The MCIU is an extremely valuable resource that has always been looked upon favourably, not only by Command at headquarters, but also by the detective chief inspectors on the divisions. They value the fact that incoming major enquiries do not impact on the running and management of divisional CID offices. The Nottinghamshire MCIU model is now being copied by other provincial forces.'

Potter appeared to totally ignore what Danny had just said, dismissing his argument in an instant. He simply moved the meeting on, saying, 'What enquiries are your officers currently investigating?'

'We're currently carrying out three separate murder enquiries. Two in Nottingham city and one in Worksop.'

'Do you have suspects already charged for these three offences?'

Danny could see he was being set up; Potter obviously knew the answer to his own question.

Danny sighed heavily and said, 'We've charged an offender for each of the current murders. As an experienced detective yourself, you'll appreciate that between charge and conviction at the Crown Court, there's always a mountain of work to do.'

Danny had deliberately emphasised the word 'experienced' in his reply. He could see by the pinched reaction on Potter's face that he'd struck a nerve.

Ignoring the substance of Danny's reply, Potter said haughtily, 'As I'm sure you're already aware, Chief Inspector, my experience within the CID is somewhat limited.'

Danny made no comment, choosing to allow the silence to hang heavy in the room.

Potter eventually continued, saying brusquely, 'I want a full breakdown of every enquiry your team has undertaken since its inception. Only when I've seen for myself the productivity, or otherwise, of the MCIU will I be able to decide on its future. My gut feeling is that there's no real need for such a specialist department. This is Nottingham, not the Bronx in New York, or South LA.'

Now, Danny was extremely angry.

In a voice trembling with pent-up rage and frustration, he growled, 'Ah, yes. Sleepy little Nottingham, that you, of course, know so well. The provincial city that last year, apart from London West, had the highest rate of violent crime in the UK. You might do well to have a look at the city, the county and all its problems before you pass judgement, sir. Everything isn't always about pounds and pence!'

'Chief Inspector Flint, I want that report on my desk in seven days' time, is that clear?'

Not once throughout the meeting had Potter ever referred to Danny by his Christian name. The differences between this small, arrogant Yorkshireman and the granite-tough giant that had been Bill Wainwright were both astounding and total.

Once again, Danny bit his lip and stifled the response he wanted to give. He just growled, 'Will that be all, sir?'

'No, Chief Inspector, there's one more thing before you leave. The chief constable has received a letter from Anthony Conway. He's the head of chambers at the prestigious Mulberry Chambers law practice in the city. The fourteen-year-old daughter of their two star barristers has been missing for a week. Obviously, the chief's very concerned about this and has suggested that your team take on the investigation.'

Danny was incredulous. Inside, he was raging. He tried to remain calm and said in a measured tone, 'Is there any suggestion this girl has been kidnapped? Or is this simply a missing person enquiry?'

'I don't have all the details, but I believe it's a missing-from-home enquiry.'

'As you are no doubt fully aware, MFH enquiries are definitely not in the remit of the MCIU. I have also just informed you that we're currently running three separate murder investigations already. I haven't got any staff spare to look for a missing girl, whoever her parents may or may not be.'

'I think you misunderstood me, Chief Inspector Flint. This wasn't a request. This was a direct order from your chief constable; he wants you to find this girl. In fact, I see it as the perfect opportunity for you to demonstrate to me what a talented, hard-working group of specialist detectives you have in your team. Find the girl, Chief Inspector! That will be all!'

Danny didn't answer. He shook his head, stood up and walked out of the office, resisting the urge to slam the door on his way out.

As he walked back to the car park, his mind was spinning with unanswered questions.

Could that meeting have gone any worse?

Could Adrian Potter be any more of an arrogant, insufferable, incompetent prick?

How on earth was he ever going to forge any kind of working relationship with this egotistical Yorkshireman?

Having reached the car park, he sat in his car, closed his eyes and said aloud, 'Bloody hell, Bill! What have you done to me?'

31

12.30pm, 9 October 1986
MCIU Offices, Mansfield, Nottinghamshire

It wasn't exactly a council of war, but it was the closest Danny would ever get to one. As soon as he arrived back at Mansfield Police Station after his disastrous meeting with Adrian Potter, Danny had called his two detective inspectors back to the office. He needed an urgent meeting to discuss the ramifications of Potter's plans for the MCIU.

Both men had listened carefully as Danny outlined exactly what had been proposed by the new head of CID.

Breaking the heavy silence in the room, it was the ever-abrasive Rob Buxton who spoke first: 'He simply can't do that, boss! Surely the chief constable will have the final say on the future of this, or any other, specialist department?'

Danny replied, 'Of course the chief has the final say.

We've got to accept Potter was appointed by Jack Renshaw to be in command of the CID. I'm pretty damn sure he'll want to back him.'

Brian Hopkirk said, 'That's spot-on. Of course he will. How bad would it look if he didn't back him on his first major policy decision? What we've got to do is try to sideline Potter. We need to concentrate on convincing Jack Renshaw of the merits of this department.'

Rob said, 'And how exactly do we do that?'

'We have to show him that we're good value for money. That investigating major crime this way is not only financially sound, but also causes far less upheaval to everyday life in a divisional CID office.'

Danny sat back, deep in thought.

After a few minutes, he said, 'Brian's right. All our efforts need to be aimed at proving that the MCIU is not only effective, but that it's also cost-effective. It's obvious that all Adrian Potter's interested in is the pounds and pence, the cost of everything. With him, it's all about the money. Potter's never been a detective, the man couldn't detect a Catholic at the Vatican. He's strictly admin, a bean counter through and through.'

Rob said, 'Well, we've always kept the Unit's costs down to a minimum as regards overtime, so that's a good start.'

Brian said quietly, 'Boss, you need to contact all the divisional detective chief inspectors. You'll need them to outline to the new chief exactly how much disruption is caused to the successful running of a divisional CID office by sudden major crime investigations.'

Danny nodded. 'I'll get onto that straight away.'

Rob asked, 'What do we say to the team?'

Danny was quiet for a moment, then said, 'I don't want you to say anything yet. Let me get this report prepared first, and we'll take it from there. How are we doing on the current murder enquiries?'

Brian said, 'The murder of Sammy Pagett in Worksop is just about done and dusted. All the paperwork's complete, and we're ready for Crown Court.'

'That's good to hear; good work. Rob, how are the two murder enquiries in the city progressing?'

'We're nowhere near ready on either. Yes, we've charged a suspect for each of the murders, but we still have a ton of statements to get. The witness list alone at the Bodega Bar stabbing is massive. The place was packed, and it seems like everyone in there saw or heard something.'

Danny turned to Brian and said, 'Can we use some of your staff to give Rob's team a dig out on that enquiry?'

'Of course. I'll need to keep two detectives back, to dot the I's and cross the T's on the Worksop job, that's all.'

'How's your own workload?'

A puzzled Brian Hopkirk said, 'It's manageable. Why?'

'Because the other little bombshell Potter dropped on me, just as I was leaving the meeting, was that the new chief wants the MCIU to look at an outstanding missing-from-home enquiry.'

Brian was incredulous. 'He wants what?'

'You heard me right. The chief has received a letter from the head of Mulberry Chambers in Nottingham, complaining that the police are being negligent in investigating the disappearance of the fourteen-year-old daughter of two barristers at his law practice. The misper is Emily Whitchurch. She's the daughter of Rebecca and Dominic Whitchurch, whom I'm sure you both know.'

Brian said, 'I know them two, alright. I've clashed with them both at court before now. He isn't too bad, but she's an arrogant bitch. Not a very nice person at all.'

Danny said, 'I've got no choice, so I want you to have a

look at this misper enquiry, Brian. I've already spoken to Detective Inspector Gail Cooper at Canning Circus CID, and she's expecting you later today. She'll bring you up to speed on the enquiries her staff have done so far to trace the girl.'

Brian replied, 'Okay, boss, I understand. I know Gail; she's extremely capable. I can guarantee that "negligent" isn't in her vocabulary. There's no way she would have been dragging her heels on a case like this.'

Rob said, 'Had you forgotten that Rachel's starting back today? This misper enquiry might be just what she needs. It will help get her back into the swing of things after her time off sick.'

Brian chimed in, 'That's fine by me. I might need some help, and Rachel's a cracking detective.'

Danny said, 'Bloody hell! Now I feel awful. I'd completely forgotten she was back today. All this business with Potter has made me lose track a little.'

He paused for a moment, then continued, 'I think you're right, Rob. After everything that happened with Jimmy Wade, it might just be the perfect way for her to get back into things.'

Rob nodded.

Danny continued, 'I think that's everything for now. Rob, keep me posted on the progress of your two murder enquiries; I need to know everything that's happening, now more than ever. I won't let that penny-pinching, pen-pushing, arrogant sod close us down without a fight. Brian, will you ask Rachel to come in and see me, please?'

Brian nodded, and the two detective inspectors left the office, leaving Danny alone with his thoughts. He had a mountain of work to do, if he was going to be able to prepare a blueprint in the coming week for the very survival of the MCIU.

There was a nervous tap on his door, and he shouted,

'Come in!'

The door opened, and Rachel Moore stepped inside.

The young detective had been off sick since early August after having a breakdown following an incident with a violent psychopath. She had courageously lured the escaped prisoner Jimmy Wade out into the open, where the maniac had been shot dead by a sniper team from the Special Operations Unit. But not until seconds before he attacked her with a ball-peen hammer.

Rachel had been inches away from becoming the serial killer's seventh victim. During her absence from work, the Home Secretary had confirmed that she was to be awarded the Queen's Police Medal for Gallantry.

She looked very different from the last time Danny had seen her. She had lost a little weight, but looked physically strong. She had obviously spent a lot of time working out in the gym in preparation to return to work. Her once-long chestnut brown hair had now been cut short in a neat pixie style. It was also dyed an ash blonde colour.

As always, Rachel was impeccably smart, dressed in a navy-blue business suit and white blouse.

Danny smiled and said, 'Rachel, it's great to have you back. I apologise for not seeing you first thing this morning, but I had an urgent meeting at headquarters. I'm afraid it's been a bit manic ever since I got back. Anyway, never mind all that. It's good to see you looking so well, and congratulations on your award. How are you feeling about being back at work?'

Rachel smiled. *Still the same Danny Flint,* she thought. Concerned about everybody else.

She said, 'I'm good, sir, thank you. I'm feeling extremely fit and ready to get back to work.'

'Are you still having counselling?'

'I'm at the stage now where if I need to see Wendy, my

counsellor, I can just phone for a chat. Really, I'm all good and raring to go.'

'I'm so pleased to hear that, Rachel; we were all very worried about you.'

'I just want to get stuck into some work, boss.'

'That's good, because I've got a very important job for you.'

'That sounds intriguing.'

'I want you to work alongside DI Hopkirk to trace a missing fourteen-year-old girl.'

'Wow! I wasn't expecting that. A detective inspector and staff from the MCIU to trace a misper? Who is this girl, royalty?'

'Her name's Emily Whitchurch. She's the daughter of two high-powered barristers who work out of Mulberry Chambers in the city. If we can't trace her quickly, the political fallout could be huge.'

'Whitchurch? Is she the daughter of Rebecca Whitchurch, the snide barrister who specialises in defending the scum of the earth?'

'The very same. Rachel, I can't stress to you how important it is that we find this girl. There have been major changes while you've been off. We now have a new chief constable and a new detective chief superintendent in charge of the CID. They both need to see, for themselves, how effective the MCIU can be.'

Always astute and lightning-fast on the uptake, Rachel said, 'I think I'm seeing the bigger picture, sir. When do we start?'

'I've already briefed DI Hopkirk. You've got a meeting scheduled with Detective Inspector Cooper at Canning this afternoon.'

'If Gail Cooper's had this enquiry, it will have been done properly. Are you sure we're going to be able to find something she's missed? Personally speaking, I very much doubt it.'

'I need you to try, okay?'

'No problem, sir.'

Rachel stood to leave. Danny smiled and said, 'Welcome back, Rachel. It really is great to have you back.'

32

3.30pm, 9 October 1986
Canning Circus Police Station, Nottingham

Detective Inspector Gail Cooper sighed and said, 'Here's the Emily Whitchurch file. It's a real mystery; this young girl seems to have vanished in mid-air. She left the Nottingham High School for Girls on Forest Road East as usual, and within the space of three or four streets, she disappeared. The problem is, even though it was broad daylight, we haven't found any CCTV that helps us, or witnesses who saw anything suspicious.'

Brian took the folder and said, 'Thanks, Gail. Tell me what you know about the girl.'

'From the enquiries made at the school, it would appear she isn't at all popular. She's been described as precocious, nasty and bitchy. One girl described her as fourteen going on twenty-four. You get the picture?'

Rachel said, 'Does she have any friends?'

'There are two girls in her class, Rosie Penwarden and Polly Garrett. I wouldn't say they were close friends, but Emily usually walked with them along Forest Road East until she got to the street where her lift home would be waiting.'

'Where were her friends on the afternoon she went missing?'

'They were both rehearsing for the school play. Polly saw Emily walking through the school gates on her own about fifteen minutes after everyone else had left.'

'Did Polly have any idea why Emily was so late leaving school that afternoon?'

'She didn't. I've checked with staff at the school, and she hadn't been given a detention or anything. The only thing anyone could think of was that maybe she'd spent a little longer in the library than the other girls. Her last lesson that day was a free period. Like most girls at the school, Emily always used the free period to get her homework done in the library. This is all supposition, Brian. The only thing we know for certain is that Emily Whitchurch walked through the school gates, on her own, at approximately three forty-five that day. A full fifteen minutes after everyone else had left.'

Brian said, 'Has she been missing before?'

'Yes, she has. She was found the same day, last time. Three hours after she'd been reported missing, a uniform patrol found her in a squat near the Arboretum. The kid was completely stoned. She was out of her face after smoking a joint.'

'Any witnesses at the squat?'

'None who would talk to the police. As you can imagine, we aren't the most popular people down there. All the details from that previous missing-from-home report are in the file.'

Rachel said, 'You mentioned her getting a lift home every day. Who was that with?'

'The Whitchurch family have an au pair, a Romanian girl called Alina Moraru. One of her duties was to meet Emily from school every afternoon, to drive her straight home. I think this was put in place by the parents in response to her going missing previously. Anyway, it turns out that Rebecca Whitchurch believed her daughter was getting picked up directly outside the school gates, but this wasn't actually the case. Emily had made her own arrangement with the au pair. She had instructed her to pick her up away from the school gates. She was to wait a few streets away.'

'How do you know this?'

'This has come from Polly Garrett. It seems that Emily was embarrassed at being picked up in front of everyone, so she kicked up a fuss until the au pair agreed to pick her up somewhere else.'

'And her mother had no idea?'

'None.'

Brian said, 'I take it you've already spoken to both her parents?'

'Of course I have. To say they aren't very helpful is an understatement. I just don't get it. Whatever your opinion of the police may be, if your daughter's missing, you'd bend over backwards to help find her, wouldn't you?'

'Well, I would. I think we need to speak to the parents first and take it from there.'

'Anything else you think we should know, Gail?'

'Everything's in the file. My gut feeling is there's more going off at home than we currently know. I don't know if this girl's been abducted or just doesn't want to be found. I've got four other teenagers all reported missing from the same area. Do you think the MCIU could look for them as well, please?'

'I think we both know the answer to that question.'

'Oh well, it was worth a try. Good luck; I hope you find her.'

Brian stood and nodded. 'Thanks.'

As they walked slowly back to their car, both Brian and Rachel were deep in thought.

Brian broke the silence. 'First impressions?'

Rachel replied quickly, 'First impressions? I think we need to find this girl and fast. People don't just disappear; my instinct is that someone's got her and is holding her somewhere. I don't know why. That's just what I feel.'

'Me too. I've got a bad feeling about this; I don't think it's going to have a happy ending. Let's get back to Mansfield and go through this file. You can fire a call in to Mrs Whitchurch and make arrangements for us to see her and her husband first thing tomorrow morning.'

'Sounds like a plan, boss.'

33

9.00am, 10 October 1986
Richmond Drive, Mapperley Park, Nottinghamshire

Rebecca Whitchurch stepped out of the shower and reached for her robe. Slipping the cool, silken cloth around her hot, moist body felt good. She sat at the dressing table, picked up her hairdryer and began to blow-dry her hair. She didn't bother to style it; she wasn't going anywhere.

She brushed on a light foundation powder and the barest hint of eye shadow before applying lipstick. She stared hard at her reflection and saw that tears weren't far from her eyes.

Where is my daughter?

Rebecca felt nauseous. Her mind was in overdrive, thinking of terrible scenarios. Each new image that burst into her brain was more terrifying than the last.

Trying to push the awful thoughts to the back of her

mind, she grabbed a pair of comfortable jogging pants and a loose-fitting Reebok sweatshirt. She quickly got dressed.

Would today be the day Emily came back to her?

She walked downstairs, feeling lonely in the vast, empty house, and wandered aimlessly into the luxurious kitchen. Without really thinking about what she was doing, she filled the kettle with fresh water. She switched it on, then reached for an earthenware mug in the cupboard. She placed a heaped spoonful of instant coffee and a splash of milk in the mug, followed by hot water from the kettle.

Just as she was about to take a first sip of the piping hot coffee, she heard the letterbox rattle in the front door.

At first, the sound didn't really register. Then, as she thought about it, she suddenly felt worried.

She hadn't opened the wrought-iron gates that morning. That meant the postman would have left any mail in the letterbox that formed part of the stone pillars supporting the electric gates.

Had someone climbed the gates and walked up the driveway to the house?

Splashing hot coffee all over the kitchen table as she slammed down her mug, she raced through the house to the front door.

On the doormat, beneath the letterbox of the front door, there was a cream-coloured envelope.

Quickly unlocking and unbolting the heavy oak door, she flung it wide open.

There was nobody to be seen.

Feeling suddenly scared, she slammed the door shut, quickly locking and bolting it again.

With a growing sense of foreboding, she bent down and retrieved the unmarked envelope from the doormat.

The first thing she noticed was that the envelope hadn't been stuck down. The flap was just tucked inside.

She held it on the very corner, between forefinger and thumb. She carried it into the lounge and placed it carefully on the coffee table. She stood staring down at it for at least five minutes before she plucked up the courage to open it.

She bent down and snatched it up before quickly ripping it open.

Placing the envelope back on the coffee table, she then unfolded the single sheet of paper that had been inside. As she started to read the note, her legs buckled. She allowed herself to flop down onto the settee, where she sat and stared at the note.

She could feel tears starting to sting her eyes as she read the words that had been composed using letters individually cut from newspaper articles.

The message in the note was as brief as it was graphic:

If you want to see your brat bitch daughter alive again I want £250,000. No Police.

Rebecca gasped and threw the note onto the floor as though continuing to hold it would scald her flesh.

Her brain was now in near-meltdown as thoughts raced into her mind.

What should I do?

The note stated quite clearly she was not to contact the police, but the police were already coming this morning. The female detective had called her last night to arrange everything. They would be here in an hour's time. She began to panic, and her breathing became hurried and shallow.

Battling against the anxiety attack, she scolded herself to remain calm.

The officer who had phoned the night before had introduced herself as Detective Constable Rachel Moore from the Major Crime Investigation Unit. She was a female detective.

She wouldn't be wearing a uniform. It would be okay. She could show her the note when she arrived.

Still in a daze, Rebecca walked upstairs and into the ornate bathroom. She grabbed a packet of drugs from the medicine cabinet and popped two Valium tablets from the blister pack. She filled the tumbler at the side of the sink with cold water and quickly swallowed the tranquilisers.

They would help her calm down. She needed to be calm and rational by the time the detective arrived.

As soon as she felt steadier, Rebecca walked back down the stairs and into the lounge.

She picked the note up off the floor and placed it carefully onto the coffee table next to the envelope.

As she sat motionless, staring at the note, the same questions kept burning into her brain.

Why isn't Dominic here with me? Why am I having to deal with this alone? I cancelled my trial; why couldn't my husband have done the same?

In a trancelike state, she walked through to the hallway and picked up the fob that controlled the electronic gates. She opened the gates and went into the lounge, to wait for the detective to arrive.

34

10.10am, 10 October 1986
Richmond Drive, Mapperley Park, Nottinghamshire

Rachel and Brian rang the doorbell on the front door. They could immediately hear the scraping of bolts and the sound of a mortice key turning in the lock. The heavy wooden door was opened slowly and stopped after two inches. As it opened a fraction more, both detectives held their warrant cards out towards the frightened woman who peeked around it.

Rachel recognised Rebecca Whitchurch, but only just. There was no sign of the confident, arrogant swagger that she usually displayed when dressed in her black robes and white wig at the Crown Court.

The woman standing before them looked troubled and very frightened.

Rachel said softly, 'Mrs Whitchurch, I'm Detective

Constable Rachel Moore. I spoke to you last night. This is my colleague Detective Inspector Hopkirk. May we come in?'

With a faraway look in her eyes, Rebecca Whitchurch asked, 'What type of car have you come in?'

Brian replied, 'We've come in my car. It's a red Ford Sierra. Are you okay?'

She replied, 'Get inside quickly. They mustn't see you.'

Both detectives stepped inside the house, and Rebecca locked the door behind them.

Brian said, 'What's going on, Mrs Whitchurch?'

She walked off down the hallway and said, 'This way, follow me. It's in here.'

They followed her into the lounge. She pointed towards the note on the coffee table, saying, 'This came this morning. Someone climbed the gates, walked up the drive and posted it through the front door.'

Rachel asked, 'Did you see them?'

Rebecca shook her head and slumped wearily into an armchair.

'Do you have any CCTV?'

'We've just had cameras installed, but they're not connected yet. So no, we don't have CCTV.'

Brian took two evidence bags from his jacket pocket and placed them next to the ransom letter and the envelope. He put on a pair of blue plastic gloves, then carefully placed the note inside the bag.

He repeated the process, placing the envelope in a separate evidence bag, noting that it hadn't been stuck down.

'Have you handled the note much?'

'Only when I took it from the envelope.'

'Okay.'

Rachel asked, 'Where's Mr Whitchurch?'

'Dominic's defending a client at Leicester Crown Court all

this week. He's staying at a hotel in Leicester rather than commuting every day.'

'Have you told him about the note?'

'No. He'll be in court by now. I can't disturb him. I won't be able to contact him until this evening.'

Rachel sat down opposite the frightened woman and said, 'I think you need to call your husband and get him to come home as soon as you can. Don't you?'

Suddenly, there was a glimpse of the real Rebecca Whitchurch as she snapped, 'I know what I need to do, Detective. I don't need you to tell me.'

Brian said, 'Rachel, stay here with Mrs Whitchurch. I need to contact Danny and let him know what's happening here.'

Rachel nodded. Brian turned to Rebecca and said, 'Do you have a telephone I can use?'

She said, 'There's a telephone on the table in the hallway. You're welcome to use that one.'

Brian stepped out into the hallway, picked up the telephone and dialled the direct number for Danny's office.

The telephone was answered on the second ring. 'MCIU, Danny Flint speaking.'

Brian said, 'Boss, it's Brian. I'm with Rachel at Richmond Drive, talking to Rebecca Whitchurch. This missing person enquiry has just ramped up a few notches. A ransom note, demanding a quarter of a million pounds, has been hand-delivered at the Whitchurch home this morning.'

Danny was stunned. He took a few seconds' thinking time, then said, 'Exactly what does the note say?'

Brian read the note in the bag: 'It says, "If you want to see your brat bitch daughter alive again, I want £250,000. No police".'

'Okay. I want you to stay at the house with Rachel. I need to get things organised here. We need to get recording devices attached to the telephones in case the kidnappers make contact that way. I also want to get covert surveillance organised on the house. As soon as I've done that, I'll drive over with Helen Bailey. She can act as the liaison officer for Mr and Mrs Whitchurch. I'll make sure the technical support guys are discreet when they arrive to install the recording devices. I'll see you in about an hour.'

Danny put the phone down.

The report for Potter could wait. This had to take precedence.

He quickly made a list of things he needed to put into place.

As he did so, an all-too-familiar sense of trepidation began creeping over him.

He had never dealt with a genuine kidnap enquiry before. He was struggling to remember all the protocols.

Suddenly, he had an idea. Grabbing the telephone on his desk, he dialled the number for the Regional Crime Squad.

The phone was answered immediately, and Danny said, 'Good morning, it's Chief Inspector Danny Flint at the MCIU. Can you put me through to Chief Inspector Carlisle, please?'

After a brief pause, a familiar voice came on the line. 'Danny Flint, it's good to hear from you. Have you got another surveillance job that needs doing?'

'No, Mattie. What I've got is a full-blown kidnap, and I need your expertise.'

'Bloody hell! What are the details?'

Danny quickly outlined the circumstances.

After listening carefully, Mattie Carlisle said, 'Listen, Danny, I'm free this morning. Why don't I drive over to your office; then we can get our heads together and talk this through properly?'

'Thanks. That would be a massive help. Can you meet me

at Radford Road nick in an hour, and we'll go and see the victim's parents together?'

'That sounds like a plan. Don't worry, Danny. I know this type of crime is as rare as rocking-horse shit, but we'll soon get things organised.'

Danny suddenly felt much happier. Mattie Carlisle was an old friend. Somebody he knew he could trust.

35

3.00pm, 10 October 1986
MCIU Offices, Mansfield, Nottinghamshire

Rob Buxton knocked on Danny Flint's office door. He opened it quickly and said, 'Everyone's here.'
'Thanks, Rob, we'll be out in a minute.'
Rob nodded and closed the door.
DCI Mattie Carlisle turned to Danny and said, 'Are you happy you've got everything covered now?'
'I think so. It's helped massively, having you here. Did you pick up on anything else from Rebecca Whitchurch when we were at the house?'
'Nothing. The only vibe I got from her was that of an extremely worried mother. I didn't pick up anything remotely sinister.'
'Me neither. Right, let's go and brief the teams.'
Danny walked into the large briefing room, flanked by Mattie Carlisle.

There was a general murmur in the office as the assembled detectives speculated as to why the briefing had been called. Unless a new murder case had broken, it was unusual for the entire MCIU to be called to a briefing.

Danny shouted above the din: 'Alright, everyone, settle down!'

There was instant silence.

Danny said, 'Thank you. We've now got an active kidnapping to investigate. A fourteen-year-old girl, by the name of Emily Whitchurch, was reported missing eight days ago. This morning, a ransom note has been delivered to her parents' address, at Richmond Drive in Mapperley Park. The note states that the parents of this young girl will not see their daughter alive unless they pay a ransom of a quarter of a million pounds.'

Danny paused to let that information sink in before continuing. 'The MCIU haven't previously investigated a kidnapping offence. I've spent the morning in close liaison with Detective Chief Inspector Carlisle from the Regional Crime Squad, and together we've determined the tactics we're going to use to investigate this crime. Our number-one priority will always be the safe return of the victim. Is that understood?'

There was a murmur around the room.

'I've already spoken with our press liaison officer to arrange for a total media blackout on this case. The ransom note demanded that the girl's parents were not to contact the police in any way. Therefore, all our enquiries must be carried out discreetly. Are there any questions?'

The room remained silent, so Danny continued, 'DC Helen Bailey is currently at the victim's home address, on Richmond Drive. She'll remain at that location for the duration of the enquiry and will act as the liaison officer with the family. I don't want anybody going to the home address, under any circumstances, without contacting her first.'

Again, Danny paused.

'Our technical support unit has installed a recording device that will monitor all calls into the property. Any calls made, both in and out of the property, will be recorded. I want DC Singleton and DC Ball to monitor all calls into the address. I'm relying on you two to ensure that as soon as the kidnappers make contact, we're onto it straight away. Are you both okay with that?'

The two detectives nodded, and Danny continued, 'I want you to sort out your own shifts. I want one of you on duty, listening to the phone, at all times. Can you sort that out?'

Mike Ball said, 'No problem for me, boss.'

Nigel Singleton said, 'Or me. I'll let the DI have a copy of the roster we work out to cover it.'

Danny smiled and said, 'Thanks, gents. I think you're both going to be working some very long hours.'

Both men nodded.

Danny then turned to DC Martin Harper. 'Martin, I want you to undertake a complete survey of the streets between the Nottingham High School for Girls and the junction of North Sherwood Street and Alpha Terrace. Alpha Terrace is where the girl was supposed to have been met by the family au pair after school. I'm aware that divisional CID have already looked for CCTV along this route and found nothing. There's always a slim possibility they have missed something, so I want you to do a thorough check for me. Okay?'

Martin scribbled down the locations. 'Okay, sir.'

Danny continued, 'As from five o'clock this evening, the Special Operations Unit will be conducting covert observations on the victim's home address. This will be a twenty-four-hour commitment by them, and they will be updating me twice a day with any information. Their brief is that should anyone be seen approaching the premises after dark, they are to be placed under surveillance and followed to their home addresses. Under no circumstances are they to make an arrest. As I said earlier, our number-one priority has always got to be the safety of the girl.'

Danny then turned to DC Fran Jefferies and said, 'Fran, I want you to undertake the role of exhibits officer, okay?'

Fran nodded.

Danny continued, 'Start by fast-tracking the ransom note and envelope through forensics. I want to know, as soon as possible, if there are any marks of value on that note. You will need a set of elimination fingerprints from the girl's mother, as she handled the note when it was first received. You'll need to liaise with Helen Bailey to obtain the mother's prints.'

Fran Jefferies said, 'I'll get onto Helen straight after the briefing.'

Danny said, 'Thanks, Fran. You never know, we may get lucky and get a worthwhile print.'

Danny paused before saying, 'The parents of the missing girl are Rebecca and Dominic Whitchurch. Both are extremely successful barristers, who have spent their working lives undertaking both prosecution and defence work at the Crown Court. DI Buxton, I want you to sort the remaining staff into pairs and start making discreet enquiries into the backgrounds of both parents. I know the ransom note has intimated there's a financial motive for the kidnapping, but that could be a smokescreen to hide a grudge. I'm sure that, over the years, both parents will have made quite a few enemies.'

Rob replied, 'Okay.'

'Rob, the most difficult enquiry will be at Mulberry Chambers. Earlier today I had a conversation with Anthony Conway; he's the head of chambers. He suggested that all our enquiries are directed through Sebastien Dawson, the barrister's clerk. He's the man responsible for the distribution of briefs. Mr Conway tells me that Dawson has an encyclopaedic knowledge of all previous cases undertaken by the law firm. He can recall details of defendants, results of cases, any threats made, etc. I want you to contact Sebastien Dawson and arrange for two detectives to go to Mulberry Chambers and trawl through old case files involving either Dominic or Rebecca Whitchurch.'

'No problem.'

'Right, everyone. There isn't much more we can do for now. If you've already been allocated a task, crack on with that. If not, speak with DI Buxton to be given one. Let's get going – and remember, discretion is of paramount importance. There will be an updated briefing tomorrow morning at eight o'clock. Thanks, everyone.'

There was a crescendo of noise as chairs were pushed back, and everyone started talking at once.

Mattie followed Danny back into his office.

There was a knock on the door, and Brian Hopkirk walked in. He said, 'You haven't allocated me an enquiry.'

Danny said, 'No, I haven't. I've never been one to put all my eggs in one basket. I want you and Rachel to continue making enquiries as though this was still just a missing person situation. Do you know what I mean?'

Brian was thoughtful for a second, then said, 'I understand. We'll start by reinterviewing the au pair. We can then follow up where young Emily was found the last time she went missing.'

Danny smiled. 'That's it. For all we know, this ransom note could be a load of bollocks. I've got to try to keep an open mind as to exactly what may have happened to this girl.'

Brian nodded and walked out.

Mattie said, 'You seem to have things well under control. I'll shove off.'

'Thanks for all your help, Mattie.'

'No problem. If there are any further developments and you need more advice, you know where I am.'

Danny was then left alone in the office, with just his thoughts for company. For the first time all afternoon, he allowed those thoughts to turn to Adrian Potter. At some stage, he would need to update his new boss that the misper case had now potentially turned into a full-blown kidnapping.

Potter could wait. Right now, he had too much to organise.

36

7.00pm, 10 October 1986
The Belmont Hotel, Winterburn Street, Leicester

The sound of lead-crystal wine glasses clinking together was followed by Dominic Whitchurch saying softly, 'Here's to us. What a formidable team we are.'

Angela Temple took a sip of the velvety red wine and smiled.

The first day of the trial had been slow going as the jury was selected and sworn in. That whole process seemed to take an interminable amount of time. Dominic had just concluded his opening statement to the jury when the judge had called time on proceedings.

She had watched the jurors intently as Dominic painstakingly set out the numerous reasons why their client should be found not guilty. How he was, in fact, the subject of a malicious and unsubstantiated allegation by a woman who was clearly working to her own agenda. That agenda was simply one of revenge. He had explained at great length how the alleged victim had been scorned by the defendant. He went into great detail outlining the false allegation and how it was all an elaborate plan for revenge, fuelled by that hurtful rejection.

The signs were encouraging, especially from the female members of the jury. She had noted head-shaking and tutting as Dominic had laid into the character of the alleged victim. If the female members of the jury were set against the victim already, the men would surely follow their lead.

After arriving back at the hotel, Angela had taken her time getting ready. Wearing a tight-fitting black cocktail dress and black stockings, she looked amazing.

Dominic couldn't take his eyes off her as they sat in the bar of the hotel, enjoying an aperitif before dinner.

The table had been booked for six thirty. In the thirty minutes they had been waiting in the bar, Dominic had drunk three large whiskies. He was in an avuncular mood and enjoying himself. A concerned Angela had told him to slow down a little.

She had winked and said, 'Take it easy, darling. I don't want you too drunk for later.'

He had smiled and told the barman to cancel his fourth whisky.

Eventually, they had walked through to the Michelin star restaurant that formed part of the hotel's magnificent reputation. The waiter had shown them to a table set for two, in a private alcove.

The starter had been delicious.

After the waiter had cleared the table and as they waited for their main course to arrive, Angela slipped one stiletto-heeled shoe off. She ran her stocking-clad foot slowly up Dominic's leg until she reached his crotch. She made full eye contact, and as her foot caressed him, she said seductively, 'Shall we take dessert in the room?'

Dominic's eyes lit up. He placed his wine glass on the table and spluttered, 'I think we'd better, sweetheart.'

Angela hastily removed her foot from the top of Dominic's thigh as she saw a waiter approaching their table.

The waiter wasn't carrying food.

He was carrying a telephone, which he plugged into a socket at the side of the table. He checked that it was working, and said, 'Mr Whitchurch, I'm very sorry, but we have your wife waiting on this line. She said to stress to you that this is urgent. There's been a development regarding your daughter.'

As Angela tutted loudly, all the colour drained from Dominic's face.

He snatched the telephone from the waiter and said sharply, 'I'll take the call. Put her through.'

The waiter signalled over to the reception desk, then moved away from the table to afford privacy. Seconds later, Dominic heard his wife's voice, 'Dominic, thank God. You need to come home, now. The police are here at the house.'

'What do you mean, the police are at the house? What's happening, Rebecca? Have they found Emily?'

'No, they haven't found her, but it's really bad, Dom. I need you here. Come home, please.'

With his wife starting to cry, Dominic said, 'Okay. I'll drive back now. Is there a police officer there I can speak to?'

Rebecca didn't answer.

Dominic raised his voice slightly. 'Rebecca?'

A woman's voice came on the line: 'Mr Whitchurch?'

'Yes. Who's this?'

'Sir, my name's Detective Constable Helen Bailey. Your wife needs you back here now. There's been a serious development that I can't discuss with you over the phone, but you are needed here.'

'Okay, Officer. I'm on my way.'

Dominic hung up the phone and looked across the table to Angela.

She was sitting with her arms folded across her chest, and an angry look on her face. 'What the fuck's happening, Dom? What did that arrogant bitch want?'

'Sweetheart, it's my daughter.'

Angela rolled her eyes. 'For fuck's sake, Dom. Don't you get it? She'll say anything to make you go home.'

'You're wrong. It's not like that. There's a detective in my house, for Christ's sake. I need to get back tonight. There's something dreadful happening; I can sense it.'

'How can you get back? You've already had way too much to drink.'

'I know it's asking a lot, and I'll make it up to you, I promise, but I need you to drive me home right now. You'll have to come back and take over the trial tomorrow. I need to know what's happening with my daughter.'

Angela leaned forward and put her head in her hands.

'Please, Angela, I need you to do this for me. If you won't drive me, I'll get a fucking taxi.'

With an exasperated expression, she said, 'Alright, alright. Come on, let's go back to the room and grab your stuff.'

As they hastily left the restaurant, Angela was raging.

She had made her mind up right then. If Dominic didn't tell his wife about the two of them very soon, she would.

37

10.30pm, 10 October 1986
Richmond Drive, Mapperley Park, Nottinghamshire

The white streetlights, spaced well apart, cast a myriad of dark shadows throughout the Nottingham suburb of Mapperley Park. It was an affluent area where all the roads were flanked with tall well-established trees, and the large houses were detached and set back from the roads.

Angela Temple drove her Volvo slowly along Mapperley Hall Drive, towards Richmond Drive.

Just before the car reached the junction, Dominic Whitchurch said, 'Pull in as soon as you turn into Richmond Drive, sweetheart.'

Angela said through gritted teeth, 'Yes, of course. God forbid your wife's waiting outside the house for you, at this time of night.'

As the car came to a stop in dark shadows, he said, 'Please

don't be like this. I had to come back; can't you see that? If it had been anything other than my daughter, I promise you we would still be in Leicester.'

With a more conciliatory tone in her voice, she said, 'I understand, Dom. I'm just so disappointed. I've wanted to share this special time with you for so long, I'm bound to be a little upset. I need us to be together now. Can't you understand that?'

'Of course I understand. It's what I want too, more than anything. I promise you we'll be together very soon.'

He leaned over, took her in his arms and kissed her passionately.

They embraced and kissed each other for several minutes, unaware their every move was being observed from the shadows.

Finally, Dominic stopped and pulled away from her. He said in a hoarse whisper, 'I need to get inside and find out what's happening, and you've got a long drive back to Leicester. I'll call you first thing in the morning, as soon as I know what's happening here. Good luck with the trial. I love you, sweetheart.'

'I love you too. I hope Emily's okay.'

38

10.30pm, 10 October 1986
Richmond Drive, Mapperley Park, Nottinghamshire

Sam Jamieson was enjoying his late-night run through Mapperley Park.
 The incessant rain that had fallen steadily all day had finally eased. The roads were quiet and still. There wasn't a soul about. He had run his usual route, which took him along Richmond Drive and up the hill towards Mapperley Plains. He had then turned back, running down the hill, along Mapperley Hall Drive. He always ran along Richmond Drive on the way back as well. He liked to keep an eye on the house owned by Rebecca Whitchurch.

As he jogged steadily down Mapperley Hall Drive, he could see a vehicle approaching, coming up the hill. The vehicle was a dark-coloured Volvo, and it was being driven very slowly.

At first, he wondered if it was an unmarked police car. He

slowed his pace a little and saw the vehicle being driven onto Richmond Drive. As the vehicle turned into Richmond Drive, he could see the occupants. The driver was a dark-haired woman. The front-seat passenger was male. There was something about this man that he thought he recognised. He watched as the Volvo came to a stop in the black shadows.

He slowed to a walk and crept towards the parked car.

The couple inside were locked in a steamy embrace, kissing passionately. They broke away from each other for a second, and Sam suddenly realised why the passenger looked familiar. It was Dominic Whitchurch.

It was Whitchurch alright, and the woman he was kissing so passionately was definitely not his wife, Rebecca.

He bent down, pretending to tie the shoelace of one of his training shoes, and said under his breath, 'Well, well, well, who's a naughty boy, then?'

He made a mental note of the make and registration number of the car, then stood up and began jogging back down Mapperley Hall Drive. He decided not to run along Richmond Drive towards the Whitchurch house, as he didn't want to be seen by the lovers in the car.

It was just as well. His presence, and a detailed description of him, had already been noted once that night, by the team of Special Operations Unit officers hidden in the dense bushes in the garden opposite the Whitchurch house.

From their position, the officers carrying out the observations hadn't got a clear view of the vehicle that had dropped off Dominic Whitchurch. All they noted was that the vehicle was a dark-coloured estate.

39

9.30am, 11 October 1986
Nottinghamshire Police Headquarters

Danny Flint remained in the main car park at headquarters.

He had contacted Detective Chief Superintendent Potter, by telephone, at nine o'clock that morning and requested an urgent meeting. He wanted to update Potter, in person, that there had been major developments surrounding the missing schoolgirl, Emily Whitchurch.

Now that he was at headquarters, he felt a growing sense of unease. He'd never felt comfortable attending briefings at the command level. At least when he was here to speak to Bill Wainwright, he knew he would be received well and treated with respect.

With Adrian Potter in charge, he knew that would no longer be the case.

He steeled himself, got out of his car, and walked into the main headquarters building.

He walked straight upstairs and stood outside Potter's office.

He paused for a moment before politely knocking on the door.

A voice shouted, 'Enter!'

Danny walked in, closed the door behind him and stood in front of Potter's desk.

'Sit down, Chief Inspector.'

As soon as Danny had taken a seat, Potter said abruptly, 'Well? What was so important and sensitive that it couldn't be dealt with on the telephone?'

Danny took a deep breath to control his already-rising temper. He said evenly, 'There's been a major development in the missing schoolgirl case you ordered the MCIU to look at, sir.'

A mocking smirk passed over Potter's face. 'Don't tell me: Those amazing detectives on the MCIU have found her already.'

Ignoring the senior officer's derisory tone, Danny said, 'No, sir, the girl hasn't been found. What you need to know is this: Yesterday a ransom note was hand-delivered to Emily Whitchurch's home address. A demand has been made for a quarter of a million pounds for her safe return. The note intimated that if the ransom wasn't paid, the girl would be killed.'

The sly smirk on Potter's face instantly disappeared as he realised the seriousness of the situation.

'I see. What have you done about it?'

Now it was Danny's turn to stifle a half smile.

He recognised the look on Potter's face. It was fear. The man was obviously a long way from his comfort zone and was terrified.

Danny quickly ran through what the MCIU had been doing since the ransom note was received. He outlined his plan, which he hoped would achieve the safe return of the girl and the capture of the kidnapper or kidnappers.

At the conclusion of his briefing, and to test his theory about Potter, Danny asked, 'Can you think of anything we haven't covered, sir?'

Potter blustered: 'No, I don't think so. You seem to have everything in hand. Have you spoken to the chief constable about this yet?'

'No, sir, not yet.'

Potter's eyes lit up. 'Good. I'll brief him personally. I know he always likes to hear bad news immediately. I don't see any reason to detain you here any longer, Chief Inspector. From what you've just told me, I'm sure you've got plenty to be getting on with.'

Danny stood up to leave. As he reached the door, Potter said, 'By the way, Chief Inspector, I'm still waiting for those breakdowns I asked you for. Don't let this little enquiry get in the way of preparing those. It's in your department's best interests that I see the financial viability of the MCIU at the earliest opportunity. Personally, I'm still of the opinion that the detectives on the Unit should be integrated back in to the divisional CID strength. After all, serious crime only ever accounts for one percent of all reported crime.'

Danny turned to face Potter. With a voice full of suppressed anger and frustration, he said, 'I don't believe this. In case you weren't listening, I'm rather preoccupied at the moment, sir. There's a missing girl out there somewhere, whose life may well be in danger, and all you're concerned about is the most cost-effective way to utilise resources. What sort of a police officer are you?'

'I appreciate that you're under a little pressure, so I'll pretend I didn't hear that little outburst, Chief Inspector. I think the clock's ticking on the existence of the MCIU. I suggest you find this girl.'

Danny slammed the door behind him and stalked out of the building, back to the car park. He wasn't stupid; he realised that Adrian Potter had totally outflanked him.

He knew that by the time Detective Chief Superintendent Potter had finished briefing the chief constable, all the plans and enquiries Danny had instigated would have suddenly become Potter's ideas.

Whatever happened in the future, Danny seriously doubted that he could ever have a meaningful working relationship with the arrogant little Yorkshireman.

40

10.00am, 11 October 1986
Elm Bank, Sherwood Rise, Nottingham

'It's that one, Rachel.'
Brian Hopkirk pointed to the large Victorian house, set back from the road, on Elm Bank.
Rachel parked the car outside the house and switched off the engine. 'What's the number of the flat?'
Brian looked at his notepad and replied, 'Number two. It's a ground-floor flat, rented by Florin Chirilov. It looks more like a bedsit than a flat to me. Let's go.'
The two detectives walked up the garden path to the front door of the property. Like most houses of multi-occupancy, this one had a large intercom system that showed individual flat numbers. There were twelve flats in the building. Brian ran his finger down the board until he came to Flat Two.
He pressed the button and waited.

There was a crackling noise from the speaker; then a woman's voice said, 'Hello?'

Rachel spoke into the intercom. 'Alina Moraru?'

'Yes.'

'My name's Detective Constable Moore. I need to ask you a few questions about Emily Whitchurch.'

The woman's voice sounded worried. 'I've already spoken to the police about that.'

Rachel persisted, 'This won't take long, Alina. Don't worry, you're not in any trouble.'

There was a loud buzzing sound as the automatic door lock opened. Brian pushed on the door, and it opened.

The two detectives walked into a spacious hallway. There were four flats on the ground floor. One of the doors on the right of the hallway opened slightly. A young woman, wearing a coffee-coloured robe, stood in the doorway.

Rachel said, 'Alina?'

The woman nodded.

'Can we step inside, please? This will only take a few minutes, and I don't want your neighbours to hear us talking.'

Alina nodded again and said, in a voice that was barely a whisper, 'This is my boyfriend's flat. He's still in bed.'

Rachel and Brian followed Alina, stepping inside a large room. It was a bedsit, not a flat. There was a large double bed in one corner of the room. A double settee in front of a coffee table, facing a small television on a stand. One end of the room had a table, two chairs, a microwave oven and a fridge. The room stank of cigarettes, dirty clothes and fried food. There were piles of unwashed clothes on the floor, and dirty pots in the small sink.

Alina started to gather up the clothes and said apologetically, 'Please excuse the mess. I'm going to the launderette later today.'

Rachel smiled and said kindly, 'Don't worry about the clothes, Alina.'

She flashed a nervous smile back and said, 'Please, sit down.'

As the two detectives sat down on the wooden chairs next to the table, there was a stirring in the double bed, and a man with long black hair sat up.

As he looked, open-mouthed, at the strangers in his bedsit, Alina said, 'Don't be angry, Florin; they're detectives. They want to ask me about the Whitchurch girl.'

Florin snarled, 'Why did you let them in? Idiot!'

Rachel said, 'Florin Chirilov, I presume? This won't take long. It's just a few questions.'

Florin Chirilov stared at Rachel, then said, 'Ask what you want. Alina's done nothing wrong. She's a good girl.'

He reached over to the small bedside table, grabbed his cigarette packet, took one out and lit up. Inhaling the first drag deeply, he leaned back against the headboard and blew smoke towards the ceiling. He looked totally disinterested, a sullen expression on his face.

Alina sat on the edge of the settee with her body turned towards the detectives.

Rachel said, 'How long were you working for the Whitchurch family?'

'Not long. About three months.'

'Did you enjoy your job?'

'I loved my job.'

'Tell me what happened the day Emily went missing?'

'It was like every other day. After dropping Emily off at her school, I returned to Richmond Drive and did all the washing and cleaning at the house. Once I had finished all my work, I drove here to see my boyfriend. After spending time here, I drove back to the school to pick her up. She never arrived.'

'We know you weren't at the school. Where had you arranged to meet Emily?'

'I always met her at the same place, Alpha Terrace.'

'Why didn't you meet her outside the school gates, as arranged?'

'Emily refused to meet me there. She complained that my car was too scruffy. It's not my fault the car is small and scruffy. It's all I can afford.'

From the bed, Florin said under his breath, 'The girl's a spoilt brat, with no manners!'

Picking up on the expression used by Florin to describe Emily, Brian said quietly to Alina, 'I noticed you didn't refer to Emily by name earlier. Didn't you like her?'

Alina was close to tears. 'I tried my best to like her, but Emily's a horrible girl. She was always very rude to me, calling me names and being nasty. She made me park away from the school, ridiculing me in front of her two friends. I had to do what she said if I wanted to keep my job. None of this is my fault, Detective. I was always pleasant to Emily.'

Florin snarled angrily, 'That's enough! I won't have Alina upset like this. No more questions. None of this is her fault. You should be talking to the brat's big-shot lawyer parents. They're the ones who raised a devil child. I want you to leave my flat. Now!'

Brian said, 'You need to calm down, Mr Chirilov. Nobody's accusing Alina of anything. We need to find this young girl, and anything she can tell us is going to help. Okay?'

Florin grunted something unintelligible and resumed smoking.

Rachel carried on, 'Alina, what can you tell us about Emily? Did she have a boyfriend?'

'I don't think she had a regular boyfriend. She was always talking about sex though. She's still a child, but she always wanted to act like a grown woman. She always said to me that she liked older men and would never go out with a schoolboy.'

'Did she have many friends at school?'

'None.'

'What about the girls you mentioned earlier? The ones you say she ridiculed you in front of?'

'You mean Polly and Rosie. They aren't real friends. I can see they only tolerate Emily. She's just too nasty with everyone.'

'Okay. Is there anything else you think we should know?'

Alina looked troubled and glanced at Florin.

Florin said tersely, 'Tell them!'

Alina said quietly, 'She was always talking about drugs. Bragging about how she loved getting high. She even asked me if Florin could get her some cannabis to smoke.'

Florin said indignantly, 'I have never done drugs. I hate drugs.'

Alina continued, 'I should have told her parents, but I was too scared of them.'

Brian asked, 'Why were you scared of them?'

'I was scared because they're powerful people. Don't misunderstand me; they were always civil towards me. I could always tell that they didn't really want me in their house, even though I did everything for them. I couldn't tell them about their only daughter wanting to smoke drugs. They would have dismissed me straight away.'

Rachel said, 'Just one last question, Alina. What do you think has happened to Emily?'

Tears began to fall down the Romanian woman's cheeks. She said tearfully, 'I honestly don't know. I'm so scared for Emily. She's still a child, but wants to be a woman so badly. She's her own worst enemy; she knows nothing of the world.'

'Okay, thanks. Try not to get upset. If you think of

anything else, will you call me, please?' Rachel fished inside her handbag and handed a card to her.

Alina nodded.

Florin said angrily, 'Is that it? Are you done? I want you to leave now, please.'

Alina opened the door to the flat, and as the two detectives walked out, Florin shouted, 'You should be looking at the brat's fucking parents! This is all their fault, and they blame my girl. They are big-shot bastards!'

The door to the bedsit closed behind them, and the detectives could hear continued raised voices from inside.

Rachel said, 'Do you think we should go back in there?'

Brian listened to the raised voices and said, 'No, it's okay. He's venting against us, not her. He's very protective of Alina, but he's got a bit of a temper on him. I think I'll do a little more digging into Florin Chirilov. I'm guessing he's no fan of the police.'

41

12.30pm, 11 October 1986
Mulberry Chambers, The Ropewalk, Nottingham

Sebastien Dawson was waiting for the two detectives at the rear entrance of Mulberry Chambers.

Detective Sergeant Andy Wills and Detective Constable Simon Paine had been sent to check through all the previous cases handled by Rebecca and Dominic Whitchurch. Their job was to read through the files and ascertain if there were any possible leads within them that might identify the person or persons responsible for the disappearance of Emily Whitchurch.

The overweight barrister's clerk shifted uncomfortably from foot to foot, trying to distribute his enormous bulk evenly. He wasn't used to standing still for long periods, but he didn't want to risk the two detectives being seen by any of the legal staff.

He had prepared one of the meeting rooms, nearest to the

back door, to accommodate them while they trawled through the old files.

Finally, the two detectives walked into the rear car park. They had parked their vehicle, as instructed, two streets away.

Dawson acknowledged them: 'Wills and Paine?'

Andy Wills said, 'I'm DS Wills, and this is DC Paine. Mr Dawson, is it?'

'Sebastien, please.'

He held the rear door open and said, 'I've organised a room just inside, so you won't be disturbed. I've put all the files in the room. I've placed them in order, so the most recent cases are at the top of the respective piles. I've also made a third pile that I consider to be the most promising for the type of thing you might be looking for. Cases that were particularly nasty, where threats were made towards Rebecca or Dominic, and where the subjects have recently been released from a custodial sentence.'

'That's very thorough, Sebastien, thank you. Hopefully, we won't be here too long.'

'I need to ask you a big favour, Sergeant. Could I ask that you remain in the room provided, please? I don't want to answer any awkward questions from the staff as to why we have two detectives trawling through our old case files.'

Andy could see the discomfort that question had caused the barrister's clerk, so he smiled benignly and said, 'Of course, no problem.'

Feeling happier about the whole situation, Dawson said, 'I've provided a kettle and coffee-making facilities, and there's a disabled toilet you can use across the hallway. None of the staff ever come down this end of the building, so you shouldn't be disturbed.'

'That's great, thank you.'

'Have there been any developments in the case, Sergeant?'

'Please, call me Andy. None that I can discuss with you now, I'm afraid. Suffice to say, we're treating the disappearance of young Emily as a priority, and we hope to locate her very soon.'

Dawson was long enough in the tooth to know when he was being fobbed off.

Not in the least put out by the rebuff, he simply said, 'In that case, I'll leave you to it. I've marked the three columns of files accordingly. I'll come back down in a couple of hours and see how you're getting on.'

'Thanks.'

Andy Wills closed the door, turned to Simon Paine and said, 'These piles are big enough, but I've got to be honest, I thought there'd be a lot more paperwork than this to wade through.'

'Me too.'

Andy said, 'I'll start on Rebecca's old cases. You can get cracking on Sebastien's special recommendation pile.'

'Cheers. I think this is going to be a long day.'

42

1.00pm, 11 October 1986
The Arboretum, Nottingham

The building was an ancient three-storey tenement block that had stood empty for years. None of the doors or windows were still intact, and weeds grew between the bricks. Most of the roof tiles were missing, exposing the bare wooden trusses of the roof.

Rachel turned to Brian and said, 'Are you sure this is the place? It looks too bad to even be used as a squat.'

'According to the misper file, this is where Emily was found last time she was missing. Let's see if anyone's home, shall we?'

The detectives walked through the open doorway and into a large room. It was dark apart from the light filtering through the open doorway and the single window. Someone had attempted to tie a sheet of red plastic over the window space, so everywhere was cast in a strange red light. The walls were full of graffiti, and there was an overpowering stench of urine and faeces.

There was ample evidence of drug use. Dirty needles and foil wraps were strewn amongst the rubble and the empty fast-food cartons that had been discarded all over the floor.

In one corner of the room was a dirty, single mattress covered by a pile of old dust sheets and cardboard boxes.

One of the dust sheets moved a fraction.

Brian turned and whispered to Rachel, 'We're in luck. I think someone's home.'

As he stepped towards the covered mattress, Brian turned and said, 'Watch where you're putting your feet. There's all sorts of crap on the floor over here.'

After negotiating a path through the mess, Brian kicked the base of the mattress, hard.

From beneath the dust sheets and cardboard, a voice shouted, 'Fuck off!'

Brian kicked the mattress again.

This time, the top dust sheet was flung back. Brian was surprised to see two people under the covers. One man and one woman.

The woman appeared to be totally out of it. Her face was ashen and gaunt. Her eyes had rolled back in her sockets, and her lips were black and drawn back across her teeth. The eerie red light that filled the room made her appearance look even more macabre.

Rachel said, 'For fuck's sake! Is she okay?'

The man sat up and said angrily, 'She's okay. Who the fuck wants to know, anyway?'

Brian said tersely, 'We're the police, shithead! What's wrong with her?'

'Nothing's wrong with her, man. She's just coming down, that's all. She only scored half an hour ago.'

Rachel said, 'I'm calling an ambulance, boss. She doesn't look good.'

The man sitting next to the semi-conscious woman said, 'There's no need for that. She won't thank you for it, and neither will the ambulance crew. You'll see; in five minutes, she'll start coming round.'

Brian ripped down the red plastic sheeting covering the window and had a good look at the man doing the talking. He was obviously a drug abuser as well. He was painfully thin, with a skeletal face hidden behind matted dreadlocks. There was a strange, jaundiced colour to the parchment-like skin stretched across his cheekbones.

The clothes he wore were little more than a collection of assembled rags.

Brian said, 'What's your name?'

The man curled his lip and said, 'Don't get all heavy, man! We ain't doing anything wrong.'

'You just told me she's high. Last time I checked, using controlled drugs was still illegal.'

'There's no drugs here now, though, is there?'

The addict grinned a brown-stained, toothy grin.

Brian chuckled, smiled back and said, 'Fair enough. You've beat me this time, kid. Just tell me your first names so I know who I'm talking to.'

'My name's Breezy, and my girl's called Heart.'

As he said her name, the woman stirred and blinked. As soon as she opened her eyes, she started coughing violently. By the time her rasping coughing fit had stopped, some colour had returned to her face. She muttered in a croaky voice, 'What's happening, Breezy?'

He turned to her and said, 'Chill, sweetness. It's the filth, but they're cool.'

The woman, who looked like a female version of Breezy, but with more piercings in her face than Rachel had ever seen on a single person, began coughing again. It was a hacking, rough cough, and Rachel asked, 'Are you sure you're okay? I was just about to call you an ambulance.'

The woman stopped coughing long enough to say, 'I'm fine, sweetheart, never better.'

Breezy smiled the same toothy grin and said triumphantly, 'Told ya!'

Brian said, 'I'm glad your lady's feeling better, Breezy. I need some help from you.'

He chuckled and said, 'Like that's ever going to happen. Breezy don't talk to no Babylon policeman. Ever.'

Brian said patiently, 'All I want you to do is look at a photograph of a young girl and tell me if you've ever seen her here before. That's not grassing, is it?'

'Ain't gonna happen, man. Ain't looking at no snapshot of anybody.'

Brian reached inside his jacket pocket and came out with a ten-pound note.

He held the banknote in front of the addict's face and said, 'Not even one with the Queen's head on?'

As soon as Heart saw the cash, she said, 'Breezy, are you seeing that, man?'

'I'm seeing it, lover.'

Brian said, 'Want to see the photo now?'

Both the addicts nodded vigorously.

Brian took the photo of Emily from his jacket pocket and held it in front of Breezy and Heart.

Heart said, 'That's the chick who was here with Fat Daz.'

Breezy said, 'Yeah. Bang on, girl. That's deffo who it is. I remember her being with Fat Daz that time. They were smoking dope upstairs until the feds arrived, and he scarpered.'

Brian retrieved a second ten-pound note from his pocket.

He held out the banknote and said, 'I'll make it twenty if you tell me who Fat Daz is.'

Heart said, 'That's the only name I've got, lover. That's what everyone calls him. He comes here sometimes to sit and smoke weed. He always brings loads of free burgers, fries and shit like that.'

Breezy said, 'He works at Maccy Dee's in town. He brings us the stuff they can't sell. Everyone knows Fat Daz. He's a blinding geezer.'

Rachel said, 'Which McDonald's?'

Breezy said, 'I think it's the one on Angel Row. He's some sort of gaffer in there.'

Brian handed over the two crisp, ten-pound notes to Breezy and said, 'You are going to buy food with this cash, aren't you?'

Breezy grinned and said, 'Sweet, man. Yeah. Food, right. Of course.'

Brian turned to Rachel and said, 'Come on, Rachel. I fancy a Big Mac.'

43

2.30pm, 11 October 1986
Mulberry Chambers, The Ropewalk, Nottingham

DC Paine turned another page of the thick file he was reading. 'This one looks interesting, Sarge.'
'What have you got?'
'It's a bloke called Sam Jamieson. He's just been released from the Armley jail in Leeds after doing a seven-year stretch for an armed robbery.'
'What's the connection?'
'Rebecca Whitchurch prosecuted the case. Jamieson was the getaway driver. He never got out of the car, but he still got seven and a half years.'
Andy Wills sighed. 'Sounds a steep sentence, but pretty run-of-the-mill stuff for a prosecutor.'
'There's a lot more to it, though. This bloke, Jamieson, has always maintained his innocence. Throughout the trial and afterwards, while he was serving his time.'

'Yeah, him and every other con who's inside the nick.'

'He even refused early release rather than admit any guilt.'

'Now *that* has got my interest. You don't see that very often. Go on.'

'Jamieson has also made numerous threats against Rebecca Whitchurch; he blames her for being found guilty and getting sent down.'

'Again, that's not unusual.'

'No, but this is, Sarge. There's a note in the file that says Jamieson also blames Whitchurch for the death of his thirteen-year-old daughter, Vanessa.'

Andy Wills put down the file he was reading. 'Now you've got my full attention. What's the circumstances around the girl's death?'

Before the young detective could answer, there was a knock on the door.

The door opened, and Sebastien Dawson stepped inside. He closed the door behind him and said, 'How's it going, gents?'

Andy Wills said, 'Great timing. What can you tell me about Sam Jamieson?'

Dawson sat down before saying, 'I'm not surprised you've picked him out. It wouldn't surprise me one bit if he was involved in this business with Rebecca and her daughter.'

Simon Paine said, 'What can you tell us, Mr Dawson? The information in the file is quite scant. It just says Jamieson blames Rebecca Whitchurch for his own daughter's death.'

Dawson stroked his chin thoughtfully, then said, 'This was a very tragic case. Obviously, out of professional courtesy, I'm not going to get into the minutiae of the trial with you. It's not for us to discuss whether or not it was a sound conviction.'

Andy Wills said, 'I sense a "but" coming.'

'The fact of the matter is this: Sam Jamieson was serving time in prison for an offence he's always maintained he had nothing to do with, when his teenage daughter died from a drugs overdose. For a long period after that tragic event, Jamieson railed against the system inside. He was involved in countless assaults, against prison officers and fellow inmates. He became an extremely dangerous individual.'

'And that violence is the reason you think he could be involved in Emily's disappearance?'

'No, Sergeant. It's what happened next that has me worried.'

'Go on.'

'Suddenly, for no apparent reason, Jamieson changed. I mean *really* changed, in every way. Almost overnight, he became polite; he became compliant; he even enrolled on a psychology degree course. Which, by the way, he subsequently graduated from, with a first. Jamieson isn't stupid at all.'

Andy was puzzled. 'Why does that make you worried? It sounds to me like he's tried very hard to reform.'

'Sergeant, I've spent many years studying the human psyche. It's my theory that Jamieson only changed because he no longer blamed the system. I believe he found a new target to focus all his anger upon.'

'Rebecca Whitchurch?'

'Precisely.'

'Has there been any contact between Jamieson and Rebecca Whitchurch?'

Dawson hesitated and glanced away.

In that split second, Andy Wills knew there had been some sort of contact. He said, 'When?'

Dawson looked a little flushed around his collar. 'Three years ago, a letter was received in chambers. It was from Jamieson. In the letter, he made veiled threats. Basically, he wrote that he didn't care how long it took him, he would get even with Rebecca.'

'And you've never showed that letter to Rebecca, have you?'

'I made a qualified decision at the time, Sergeant. I thought it best not to show her the letter back then, and I still do. After all, at that time, Jamieson still had many years to serve in prison. I thought it would just die a death, so to speak. I must admit, ever since Emily disappeared, that letter's been at the back of my mind.'

'Have you still got the letter?'

Dawson looked down at the floor and shook his head. 'I destroyed the letter over a year ago. When nothing followed the first correspondence, I thought it was an empty threat.'

Andy Wills muttered, 'Jesus, what a mess.'

He paused a moment, then said, 'With your permission, I'd like to take this file with us so we can delve a little deeper into Sam Jamieson. I think we need to identify his current whereabouts. Is that okay with you?'

'It's the least I can do, Sergeant. I would prefer the entire file to be photocopied so we can keep the original in chambers.'

'That's fine. I think we're done for the day. DC Paine will be back tomorrow morning. I still want him to go through the remaining files.'

'No problem. I'll meet him the same as today. Pass me over the file, and I'll get it photocopied.'

'Please don't omit anything. I want the whole file. We both know you should have disclosed that letter to Rebecca Whitchurch.'

Sebastien Dawson wrinkled his bulbous nose and sniffed. 'You'll get the whole file, Sergeant. There really is no need for your clumsy veiled threat. Don't forget, I didn't have to mention that letter in the first place. Like you, all I want is for Rebecca's daughter to be found.'

Andy smiled. 'I'm glad we understand each other.'

Dawson snatched up the file and left the room in a huff.

Simon Paine asked, 'Do you think Sam Jamieson has something to do with the girl's disappearance, Sarge?'

'I've no idea, but it sounds like he has genuine cause to hold a serious grudge. As soon as Dawson brings the file back, we'll call it a day. I want to get back to Mansfield. I've got some digging to do.'

44

2.30pm, 11 October 1986
McDonald's Restaurant, Angel Row, Nottingham

Brian and Rachel walked into the fast-food restaurant and sat down. From their seats, they scanned the wall-mounted menu. Brian said, 'What do you fancy? My treat.'

Rachel replied, 'I'll have a cheeseburger, small fries and a Fanta orange drink, please. Thanks, boss.'

'Don't worry, Rach, it'll be going on expenses. I'm not made of money.'

The detective inspector was still laughing as he made his way to the counter to order the food. Rachel looked around the restaurant. It was half empty; the lunchtime rush had obviously finished.

A young girl, wearing one of the fast-food chain's uniforms, came over and began wiping the table where Rachel sat.

Rachel smiled. 'Worked here long?'

The girl smiled back and said, 'Been here a couple of months now. The money's helping me to get through uni.'

'Cool. What are you studying?'

Happy to talk to a friendly customer, the young girl said, 'I'm in my first year at Nottingham Trent, studying for a biology degree.'

'That's amazing. I hope it goes well. That's not a Nottingham accent, is it? Where are you from?'

The girl had finished cleaning the table and nervously looked at the front counter.

Rachel quickly said, 'Sorry, I don't want to get you in any bother.'

'Nah, it's okay. The boss is out at the minute. He's not back until three o'clock, and he'll be leaving for home again at half past four. It's okay for him to skive off, but he doesn't like us chatting to customers. Bristol, that's where I'm from, by the way.'

'Enjoying life in Nottingham?'

'Yeah, it's great. I'm really enjoying it.'

'You don't sound too impressed by your boss, though. What's he like?'

She leaned forward and pretended to wipe the table again before saying in a conspiratorial whisper, 'Mr Treadgold's a bit of a pig. Everyone here calls him Fat Daz. He must eat four or five Big Macs every shift.'

Rachel pulled a face and said, 'Eww, gross! Is that why he's called Fat Daz?'

The girl shrugged, laughed and walked off.

Brian returned with a tray of food and drinks. He placed the tray on the table, sat down and said, 'I wonder if Fat Daz does work here.'

Rachel took a bite of cheeseburger and said, 'He does, and he'll be in at three o'clock.'

'And precisely how do you know that?'

Rachel laughed and said in a whisper, 'Trust me, I'm a detective.'

Twenty minutes later, Rachel was just finishing her Fanta orange when the door to the restaurant opened and an extremely overweight man walked in. He waddled past the two detectives and made his way slowly over to the counter. He opened the door marked 'Private' at the side of the counter and walked in.

A few seconds later, the fat man emerged on the other side of the counter. He began pointing angrily and talking to the staff.

Brian said, 'I'm guessing that's Fat Daz.'

'I don't think it could be anyone else, boss.'

'I think we should watch him and follow him when he leaves work. I want to see where he takes us. Have you got any plans tonight?'

'Nothing planned tonight. My little bird also told me that Fat Daz will be leaving work around four thirty. Why don't I fetch the car and park outside while you order us a coffee to go?'

'Good idea. There's parking on the street outside.'

'I'll make sure the staff car park doesn't have a separate entrance; we want to be able to drop on him when he comes out.'

Brian smiled. He was enjoying working with Rachel.

He said, 'How do you take your coffee?'

'White, no sugar, thanks. See you in a minute or two.'

45

4.00pm, 11 October 1986
MCIU Offices, Mansfield, Nottinghamshire

Andy Wills had spent the last hour and a half trying to find out everything he could about Sam Jamieson. He walked across the MCIU office, carrying his briefing pad, and knocked on Danny Flint's office door.

Danny shouted, 'Come in.'

Andy stepped inside and said, 'Have you got a minute?'

'Of course, grab a seat ... How are you getting on at Mulberry Chambers? Have you finished down there?'

'Not quite. Simon's going back first thing in the morning to go through the remaining files for Dominic Chambers. We've found a promising lead today though. That's what I want to talk to you about.'

'Fire away.'

Andy glanced down at his briefing pad as he spoke. 'In

the late seventies, Rebecca Whitchurch was doing a lot of prosecution work. One of the cases she prosecuted at Nottingham Crown Court around that time was an armed robbery at a sub-post office in Mansfield Woodhouse. There were three defendants, who all got seven years apiece. The getaway driver on that robbery was a man called Sam Jamieson. He was released this July from Armley Prison in Leeds.'

'The timing's right, but what's so special about Jamieson?'

'Throughout the police interviews and the trial, he maintained his innocence. I know what you're going to say: They all do. I thought exactly the same. I've spent the afternoon doing a bit of digging into the original investigation of that Mansfield Woodhouse post office robbery. Turns out, the only evidence against Jamieson was a single fingerprint found on the rear-view mirror of the getaway car. That car belonged to one of his co-accused, a cousin, who refused to say anything when interviewed by the police. This cousin also utilised his right to silence during the subsequent trial. Jamieson maintained throughout his interviews and the trial that he had borrowed the car the night before. This was to get an emergency prescription from a late-night chemist, as his daughter was sick. The time of this trip to the chemist's by Jamieson was confirmed by staff who worked there.'

'Go on.'

'When Jamieson had served three years of the seven-year sentence, his thirteen-year-old daughter died of a drugs overdose. Jamieson stated at the time that if he hadn't been locked up, he could have prevented her death. He stated that he could have stopped her getting involved with the people who got her into drugs.'

'It sounds a very tragic story. I still don't see why this makes Jamieson of interest to this enquiry.'

'There's more. For twelve months after the death of his

daughter, Jamieson raged against the system. I've checked his prison record, and for that period, he was totally out of control. Constantly involved in fights with other prisoners and assaults against prison staff. Jamieson's a big, strong man who had suddenly found a propensity for violence. He became an extremely dangerous individual. Then suddenly, he changed. His prison record bears this out. He went from being like a caged animal, to being totally compliant. His behaviour from that moment on was impeccable. He even enrolled in further education and achieved a degree in psychology while at Armley. All the penalties that had been added to his sentence for his violent behaviour were wiped out by his good behaviour. There's one last thing about his prison record that you need to know. Jamieson was offered early release eighteen months ago but turned it down because it would have meant him admitting his part in the robbery.'

'So the question you're asking is, what caused the change in him?'

'And I think the answer to that question is that he found a different target for all his anger and hate.'

'What target?'

'Not what, sir, who. I believe he channelled all that pent-up anger and frustration against the one person he blamed for getting him sent down, Rebecca Whitchurch.'

'It wasn't one person, though. What about the cousin who refused to speak up? If I were Jamieson, I'd be raging more against him than Whitchurch.'

'The cousin's dead. Suicide, apparently.'

'I see what you're driving at, Andy. I still think it's a stretch of the imagination to say that's what he's done.'

'Just before this change of Jamieson's personality manifested itself at Armley, a letter was received at Mulberry Chambers addressed to Rebecca Whitchurch. The letter was written by Jamieson and somehow got past the prison censors. It was intercepted at chambers by Sebastien Dawson. For reasons best known to him, he decided not to show it to the barrister. I think he believed it was just a convicted prisoner letting off steam and wasn't to be taken seriously. The content of that letter was explicitly threatening. In it, Jamieson stated that he had come to realise that the only person responsible for his daughter's death was Rebecca Whitchurch. He made threats that he would gain his revenge no matter how long it took him.'

Danny was deep in thought. 'Have you got the letter?'

Andy shook his head. 'No. Sebastien Dawson destroyed it when there was no other follow-up. He didn't think it was important.'

'Bloody hell! What does he think now?'

'He knows he's fucked up. He did tell us about the letter in the first place, which he didn't have to do.'

'That's true, I suppose. So, where's Sam Jamieson now?'

'Here's where we have a problem. I checked with the Armley jail for his release address. This was his previous address in Mansfield Woodhouse. I've done a quick basic check, and it appears that he's no longer at that address. He moved out shortly after returning home from Leeds. He left no forwarding address.'

'So he's in the wind?'

'Yes, sir.'

'Had he left the Mansfield Woodhouse address before Emily Whitchurch went missing?'

'It looks that way.'

'Can you think of a better way to get revenge for the death of your own teenage daughter than to abduct – and do God knows what to – the daughter of the woman you hold responsible? We need to locate Sam Jamieson as quickly as we can. I want you to stay on this enquiry, Andy. Let Simon check the rest of the files at Mulberry tomorrow morning on his own. Providing there are no other urgent enquiries overnight, I want all your energy placed into tracking this man down. He might have absolutely nothing to do with the Whitchurch girl's disappearance, but we won't know until we've traced him. Before you go off duty tonight, I want you to get over to Mansfield Woodhouse. Make some discreet enquiries with the people who live near his release address. Someone in the village might know where he's moved to. This is great work, Andy.'

'It was Simon who found the link, boss.'

'Pass on my compliments to him. I'll have a chat with him myself next time I see him. Let me know how you get on at Mansfield Woodhouse this evening. I want Sam Jamieson located. We need to eliminate him from this enquiry as soon as we can.'

46

5.00pm, 11 October 1986
Endsleigh Gardens, Edwalton, Nottingham

Darren Treadgold had left work, clutching a brown paper bag full of Big Mac burgers, at exactly four thirty. Brian had watched him walk through the staff room door, then out through the front door of the restaurant. He had then waddled around to the side of the building where the staff car park was located.

Treadgold had walked straight to a dark green Morris Oxford car. Brian had waited until he saw him getting into the vehicle before sprinting back to the front of the McDonald's restaurant on Angel Row.

Jumping into the CID car, he had shouted to Rachel, 'Green Morris Oxford, get ready.'

The detective had started the car and waited for the Morris Oxford to emerge from the car park. As Treadgold's car was driven left out of the car park and onto Angel Row, she had driven the unmarked police vehicle directly behind it.

Twenty minutes later, they had travelled out of the city centre, over Trent Bridge, and out through West Bridgford to the leafy suburb of Edwalton. It was obvious to the two experienced detectives that Treadgold had no idea he was being followed. Rachel kept a discreet distance. It was an easy task to keep the old Morris in sight, driving through the last of the slow-moving rush hour traffic.

The detectives had followed Treadgold along Melton Road, hanging back as they saw the right-hand indicator of the vehicle come on.

Brian had said, 'Careful, Rachel. Stop the car just short of the junction. I'll jump out and see where he's going. The road he's turning into is a dead end.'

The CID car had barely come to a stop before Brian opened the door. He jumped out and sprinted round the corner, into Endsleigh Gardens.

He returned two minutes later and said, 'He's parked up on the driveway of a house about fifty yards down the road. The house is bloody huge and set way back from the road. It's all in darkness and looks like the Norman Bates motel in *Psycho*.'

Rachel slipped the car into first gear and drove slowly onto Endsleigh Gardens. Brian said, 'Stop here. That's the house.'

Rachel switched the engine off and looked down the driveway, towards the house. As Brian had said, it did appear to be in total darkness. She said, 'What do we do now?'

'I think we go and ask Fat Daz about smoking dope with young girls in a city centre squat. What do you think?'

Rachel said, 'My thoughts exactly, boss.'

The two detectives got out of the car and walked through the rusting, wrought-iron gates. They had been left open, hanging on rotten hinges. They walked along the long, dark driveway that led through the overgrown garden to the dilapidated house.

Rachel whispered, 'At one time, this house must have been amazing.'

Brian snorted. 'It hasn't been that for a long time, lass.'

There was a small flight of stone steps that led up to an open porch covering the double front doors.

Peering through the frosted glass of the two front doors, Brian could see there was a dim light emanating from the back of the house. He knocked loudly on the front door.

After knocking, he continued peering through the glass and saw the kitchen door open slowly. He saw a huge, hulking figure lumbering towards the front door, still taking large bites from the burger he was holding as he approached.

As the huge figure reached the door, Brian stepped back. He could hear bolts being drawn back and a key turning. Eventually, the door was opened.

Brian asked, 'Mr Treadgold?'

Quickly swallowing the last mouthful of burger, Darren Treadgold nodded nervously.

Brian held out his warrant card, smiled and said, 'Mr Treadgold, my name's Detective Inspector Hopkirk, and this is Detective Constable Moore. There's nothing for you to worry about; we just want to ask you a few questions. Can we come in? It's bloody freezing out here.'

The last thing Darren wanted to do was to invite the police into his house. However, there was something ingrained in his psyche that prohibited him from ever appearing to be rude. He blithely said, 'Yes, of course. Please come in out of the cold. Will this take long? I was just having my evening meal.'

As they followed him down the hallway, past the wide flight of stairs leading to the first floor, Rachel said, 'No, not at all. Five minutes, tops. Do you live here alone, Mr Treadgold? It's a big place for one person to look after.'

'Yeah, there's just me. It's a nightmare to keep straight.'

Darren walked into the spacious lounge and switched the light on. The room was crammed from floor to ceiling with years of collected, and subsequently abandoned, junk. There was a threadbare three-seater settee and a single armchair. That was the only furniture that could be seen. Every inch of available space was being used to store everything from old newspapers to ancient gas lamps. It looked as though Darren Treadgold never threw anything away.

He allowed himself to collapse into the big armchair, which subsequently strained under his enormous weight. He then gestured for the two detectives to sit on the settee.

He said, 'You said you wanted to ask me some questions?'

Brian said, 'It's all rather strange, really. I've received a complaint from a concerned member of the public that you've been engaged in smoking illegal substances. Is that true?'

He feigned a shocked look and parroted, 'Illegal substances?'

'Yes, Mr Treadgold, illegal substances. Cannabis to be exact. I'm told that you like to smoke dope.'

With an indignant air, Treadgold replied, 'That's outrageous. I've got a very responsible job in Nottingham. There's no way I'd ever smoke dope.'

Brian said, 'How about I tell you that we've been talking to a couple of friends of yours. They live in a squat on the Arboretum. Would that help your memory at all?'

A sly look passed over Treadgold's face. 'You mean Breezy and Heart the tart, don't you?'

Brian said nothing, letting the silence do the work.

Inevitably, Treadgold continued talking. 'Out of the goodness of my heart, I take that pair of ingrates food from the restaurant. It's just a little something I do to help them out, that's all.'

'Isn't it fairer to say that you take them leftover food you haven't been able to sell at McDonald's? Hoping that they'll turn a blind eye to you smoking the odd joint in the squat?'

'That's a ridiculous thing to say.'

Brian continued, 'They also told us that you like to take young schoolgirls there, to smoke dope with you. Is that ridiculous, too?'

The colour drained from Treadgold's fat, bloated face. He began to sweat heavily.

Brian raised his voice slightly. 'How many times have you taken young girls to the squat, Darren?'

Hearing the detective use his first name startled Treadgold. He blustered, 'I think you both need to leave. You can't come into my house and make these vile allegations. It's disgusting.'

Brian took the photograph of Emily Whitchurch from his jacket pocket and shouted, 'When was the last time you saw this girl?'

Treadgold merely glanced at the photograph of the pretty, young, blonde-haired girl before he stood up and shouted back, 'That's it! I've had enough. This is outrageous! I've done nothing wrong, and I want you to get out of my house, right now.'

As the two detectives stood, there was a loud bang from upstairs. It sounded like it had come from the room directly above them.

Darren's eyes flashed toward the ceiling, and Rachel said, 'Mr Treadgold, I thought you said you lived here on your own. Who's up there?'

'It's just my dad. He lives with me, but he's very old, stone deaf and bedridden.'

Rachel pressed, 'Why did you lie? Who's really up there?'

'Honestly, it's my dad. Truth is, I'm embarrassed that I still live with my dad at my age. I'm a grown man, for Christ's sake.'

Rachel scowled at him and said, 'I'm sorry, Mr Treadgold. I don't believe a word you're telling me. I think I'd better go and see for myself who's up there.'

Starting to get annoyed, Darren said, 'Please yourself, Detective. I'm telling you the truth. The only person up there is my bedridden, incontinent old dad. You'd better not frighten him.'

'If it's your dad up there, I won't frighten him.'

'I've been out all day and haven't had time to go and clean him up yet. I hope you've got a strong stomach, Detective.'

Brian said, 'Go and check, Rachel.' He then turned to Treadgold and said, 'Darren, why don't you sit back down?'

'I'm not sitting down anywhere. As soon as you've checked on my dad, I want you both out of this bloody house. I'll be contacting my solicitor in the morning to make an official complaint. This is outrageous!'

Brian could see through Treadgold's bluster. Something was terrifying the overweight fast-food restaurant manager. He was sweating even more, and his breathing was getting wheezier and shorter by the second.

Brian hoped Treadgold didn't suffer a heart attack while Rachel checked upstairs.

47

5.10pm, 11 October 1986
Endsleigh Gardens, Edwalton, Nottingham

Rachel climbed the creaking stairs and found the door that led into the room immediately above the downstairs lounge.

As she opened the door, the smell coming from inside almost rocked her back on her heels. It was a rancid mixture of stale urine, faeces and sweat. The heavy curtains were still closed, and the room was dimly lit. There was just a dull bedside lamp on a stand next to the double bed.

As her eyes became accustomed to the gloom, Rachel could see an old man sitting up in the bed. He looked startled to see a woman standing there, and he shouted, 'Who are you?'

Rachel started to explain who she was, but the old man interrupted her, saying again, 'Who are you?'

Without waiting for her to reply, he shouted, 'I can't hear

you. Where's my son?'

Rachel remembered what Treadgold had said about his father being profoundly deaf. It was pointless trying to say anything, so she left the room and closed the door behind her.

As she started to walk back down the stairs, the old man started to shout repeatedly, 'Darren!'

In between the shouts, Rachel thought she heard another sound. This sound was coming from above her. Looking over her shoulder, she saw there was another, much narrower flight of stairs that led up to an attic room.

Ignoring the shouts from Treadgold's father, she made her way up the steep flight of stairs to the small landing. There was only one door off the landing, and it was secured by a brand-new padlock.

Rachel tried the door, but the padlock held firm. She placed her ear to the door and listened, trying to drown out the howls of protest from Mr Treadgold senior.

Suddenly, she heard what sounded like a whimper from behind the padlocked door.

She shouted, 'Who's in there?'

The whimpering sound again.

Rachel turned and ran down the stairs, back to the lounge.

Bursting into the lounge, she said, 'Boss, someone's up there.'

Brian said, 'I know. We can hear him. His dad, right?'

Rachel said, 'No. I'm not talking about the old man. There's an attic room above the bedrooms. Someone's inside, but the door's secured with a brand-new padlock on the outside.'

In Darren Treadgold's mind, he tried to make a sprint for the door.

In reality, Fat Daz managed to take one waddling step

towards the door.

Brian grabbed his arm and said, 'Who's up there?'

Panicking, Treadgold spluttered, 'There's nobody up there! Only my dad.'

'Where's the key for the padlock?'

Treadgold shrugged.

Brian took a set of handcuffs from his pocket and said, 'Darren Treadgold, I'm arresting you on suspicion of abducting Emily Whitchurch. Now sit down!'

As the steel handcuffs were tightened around Treadgold's fat wrists, he began pleading with the detective. 'You're hurting me. These are too tight. I want a lawyer. Now.'

Brian said, 'Rachel, pass me your cuffs.' Rachel handed over her handcuffs. He used Rachel's cuffs to secure Treadgold to a radiator, preventing him from waddling off anywhere. He then said, 'Show me the attic.'

The two detectives made their way up both flights of stairs until they were standing on the small landing in front of the padlocked door.

Brian shouted, 'If there's anybody in there, stand back from the door!'

He then kicked the door near the padlock, splintering the wood around the hasp. The door flew open, and Rachel stepped inside the small attic room. In the half-light, she could see a mattress at one end of the room. On the mattress was a young girl sitting with her arms folded across her knees, which were drawn up to her chest. She had pulled the single blanket on the bed up to her face.

All Rachel could see of the girl was her long blonde hair and blue eyes. The detective walked slowly towards the girl and said, 'Don't worry, Emily. I'm a police officer.'

The girl lowered the blanket from her face, and in a voice little more than a croaky whisper, she said, 'Thank God you're here. Where's the monster? And who's Emily?'

48

8.00pm, 11 October 1986
West Bridgford Police Station, Nottingham

It had been three hours since Rachel and Brian had found the young girl in the attic room of Darren Treadgold's house at Edwalton.

The two detectives had called for urgent assistance at the house on Endsleigh Gardens. Within minutes, officers started to arrive. The first uniform officers on scene had transported Treadgold to West Bridgford Police Station. As other uniform staff attended, Brian had organised them with the local sergeant. Arrangements were made for the social services to attend and care for Treadgold's elderly father. There was no way the old man could be left to care for himself at the house. Although Darren Treadgold left him to go to work, he was on hand to care for his basic needs at different times of the day. Without that care, the old man wouldn't survive.

Brian had also arranged for Scenes of Crime to attend

and carry out a full forensic examination of the attic. A full search of the premises and Treadgold's car would also be carried out later that night.

Finally, Brian had contacted Danny Flint at the MCIU offices. He had informed him of the arrest of Treadgold and where he was now being held. Danny had immediately set off for West Bridgford Police Station to liaise with his detectives and to fully assess the development.

During their telephone conversation, Brian had been adamant that he wanted to continue enquiries into the abduction and false imprisonment of the young girl they had rescued. Danny had insisted the enquiry should be carried out by divisional CID officers, as it was not within the remit of offences covered by the MCIU.

Before setting off for West Bridgford, Danny had contacted Detective Inspector Gail Cooper and informed her of the arrest. First accounts from the girl suggested that the original offence of abduction had occurred on Mount Hooton Road, Hyson Green, which was within Cooper's area.

She had agreed with Danny that the offence should be investigated by detectives from divisional CID. She had then travelled to West Bridgford Police Station, along with two of her senior detectives, to commence enquiries.

In the small office usually occupied by the uniform inspector at West Bridgford nick, Danny was in animated conversation with Brian and Gail Cooper.

Brian said, 'I still think we should carry on with the investigation, boss. There's something really nasty about Treadgold; he's so cold and calculating. I just wonder how many times he's done this.'

Gail responded testily, 'Brian, I've known you for a long time, and I know you're not intending to disrespect me. But can't you see that's exactly what you're doing? My officers are more than capable of dealing with Treadgold in a thoroughly professional and diligent manner.'

Brian flushed a little and said, 'That's not what I meant, Gail, and you know it. I just think with all the resources on the MCIU, we could look into him that much deeper, that's all.'

Danny poured oil on troubled waters. 'The decision's already been made. Gail's team will take on the Treadgold enquiries.'

He then turned to Gail, saying, 'That said, Gail, if you find that you need extra resources for anything, just call me, okay?'

'Thank you, sir.'

Danny turned back to Brian and said, 'So who is the girl in the attic?'

Brian said, 'Her name's Theresa Stanhope. She's just fourteen.'

Danny said, 'I know Rachel's travelled with her to the hospital, but what's the early disclosure from Theresa?'

'As soon as uniform backup arrived at the house, we brought the girl back here to the police station to wait for the ambulance. I thought it was better to do that than keep her at that house of horrors for one second longer. She was very talkative as we drove from Edwalton back to the nick. I'm positive she'll have carried on chatting to Rachel at the hospital.'

Gail Cooper interjected, 'I've sent DC Jenny Hirst to meet Rachel and the girl at the hospital. That way, we can ensure there's continuity of any disclosure the girl may make. Jenny's an extremely competent detective, who's dealt with numerous child abuse cases. Theresa Stanhope will be in good hands.'

Danny nodded towards Brian. 'Go on.'

'Theresa has no idea how long she's been missing. From

comments she made to us about the weather and what lessons she had on the day she was taken, it sounds like she was probably abducted on the same afternoon as Emily Whitchurch.'

Gail Cooper said, 'Did she say anything about the actual abduction?'

'She said that she was a little late getting out of school, so she was on her own. I forgot to say, she attends the Manning School for Girls on Gregory Boulevard, not the high school. Anyway, she was late leaving school, and as she began walking over the Forest Recreation Ground, the heavens opened, and in no time at all she was soaking wet. She walked onto Mount Hooton Road and was walking up the hill towards Forest Road East when a big green car pulled up beside her. Theresa says she thought she recognised the man in the car. So when he asked if she wanted a lift, she readily accepted and jumped in the car, to get out of the rain. She remembers putting her seat belt on, but that's it. Her next memory is waking up in that bloody attic.'

There was a knock on the office door, and Rachel Moore walked in.

Danny said, 'How's the girl?'

'I think the enormity of what's happened is hitting her now. DC Hirst is still with her at the hospital. Theresa's made disclosure to us that she's been sexually assaulted by Treadgold. It happened while she was being held prisoner in the attic. The poor girl's now undergoing the full sexual offences examination by the police surgeon, to ascertain the extent of the assault. Theresa's intimated to us that it was touching only. Her parents have arrived at the hospital and are with her now.'

'How's mum and dad?'

'Relieved that their daughter's now safe and well. They're

also extremely angry and upset. Everything you would expect them to be, boss.'

Danny said, 'Brian, Rachel, I want you to find DI Cooper's team and talk everything through with them thoroughly. I want them to have the full picture about Treadgold; this monster needs putting away. There's a further briefing on the Whitchurch enquiry at Mansfield, nine o'clock tomorrow morning. Make sure you're there. Great work today, both of you.'

Brian and Rachel stood up and walked out, closing the door behind them.

As soon as the two detectives had left the room, Gail said, 'Brian hasn't changed one bit. Always wanting to hammer down the bad guy, never quite seeing the big picture.'

Danny replied, 'I wouldn't have him any other way. Don't forget it was those very instincts that enabled him to find that poor girl in the first place.'

'I didn't mean it as a criticism. He's just a force of nature sometimes. Do you know what's really disconcerting about all this? If there hadn't been such a fuss made about Emily Whitchurch going missing, it's almost certain that Theresa Stanhope would still be in that bloody attic, enduring God knows what at Treadgold's hands.'

'Don't think that thought hadn't crossed my mind too. I'm just glad she's been found and that she's now safe.'

'Emily Whitchurch is still out there somewhere, though.'

Danny grimaced. 'I know, Gail. I'm going straight back to Mansfield nick; I've still got a lot of work to do before I go home. Do me a favour?'

'What's that?'

'Make sure this bastard Treadgold gets potted!'

'From where I'm sitting, looks like abduction, false imprisonment, assault and indecency offences. I think he'll be going away for a long time.'

As Danny made his way back to the car park, his mind was in turmoil. He was overjoyed that Theresa Stanhope had been rescued, but part of him dearly wished that Brian had found Emily Whitchurch in that attic room.

He felt empty.

All he could do now was wait and hope that the writer of the ransom note got in touch with Rebecca Whitchurch again soon.

49

9.00am, 12 October 1986
MCIU Offices, Mansfield, Nottinghamshire

Danny sat in his office, sipping a hot coffee. He had managed a few hours' sleep and felt refreshed. His mood had changed from the gut-wrenching disappointment he had felt the night before to one of optimism.

He had to take the positives from yesterday. It was a massive bonus that his team had been responsible for finding Theresa Stanhope and arresting Darren Treadgold. He would make sure that the chief constable knew exactly who had found Theresa Stanhope and how they had done it.

He had worked late last night, preparing the report for Detective Chief Superintendent Potter. The figures in the report were impressive. He felt optimistic about being able to convince the new chief constable that the MCIU were still very much a worthwhile and cost-effective resource.

If he could just locate Emily Whitchurch and return her safely to her parents, that would be the icing on the cake.

He took another sip of coffee and mentally chastised himself for starting to think like Potter. The most important thing was finding the missing girl, safe and well. Nothing else really mattered.

He picked up his briefing book in one hand and half-full coffee mug in the other and walked into the briefing room.

Rob Buxton and Brian Hopkirk were already seated at the front of the assembled MCIU.

Danny took the seat between them, looked across to Andy Wills and said, 'Did you have any joy at Mansfield Woodhouse last night?'

Andy Wills stood up and said, 'I'm afraid not. If anybody does know where Sam Jamieson has moved to, they didn't want to tell me.'

'Doesn't he have a probation officer?'

'No, sir. He served his full sentence. There's no probation order or licence involved with his release. Like I told you yesterday, for the last few years at Armley, he was a model prisoner.'

'Okay. I want you to go back to Mulberry, with DC Paine, this morning and get through the remaining files as quick as you can. Then I want both of you to concentrate fully on tracking down Sam Jamieson. How long will you need at Mulberry?'

'Two of us will get it done in a couple of hours.'

'Right. Get that enquiry bottomed out, and then concentrate on Jamieson. This is a top priority. I want this man located as soon as possible, okay?'

'Yes, boss.'

Danny then said, 'Who's been tasked with finding any possible CCTV?'

DC Martin Harper stood up and said, 'I made a start on that yesterday, sir.'

'Okay, Martin. What can you tell us?'

'I spent all day yesterday walking the streets around the area Emily Whitchurch went missing. I've checked every route she could have taken between Nottingham High School for Girls and Alpha Terrace. There are several possible ways she could have walked to Alpha Terrace. I've walked them all twice and, unfortunately, I haven't located a single camera.'

Danny shook his head; this was a blow.

He looked at Martin. 'Is there anywhere else left to look?'

'The only other place left is the bus station. I'm checking what buses, if any, run along Forest Road East. Sometimes the drivers have small security cameras fitted in the cabs.'

'Let me know if you find anything. Thanks for your efforts.'

'Sir, there is one more thing.'

'Go on.'

'Yesterday, while I was walking the routes, I also concentrated on the most likely spots for an abduction. There's one spot on Forest Road East, opposite the cemetery, where there's a row of derelict garages. Some have doors on, but most have the doors open or hanging off the hinges. That stretch is almost seventy yards long. There are no streetlights at all in that area, so at night it would be pitch black. Is it worth setting up a witness trawl one evening around the same time as the girl went missing?'

'Normally, it would be a very good idea. This case is under a media blackout, though, so our hands are tied for now. I'm not doubting your word for one second, Martin, but I want you to recheck all the routes again today. I know it's tedious, but anything you can find from CCTV could be vital.'

'No problem, sir. I'll get straight on it.'

Danny said, 'I've already been on the phone with Chief Inspector Chambers from the Special Operations Unit this morning. There's nothing to report from the observations team on Richmond Drive.'

Danny then said, 'Brian, can you let the team know about the information you obtained from the au pair yesterday, please?'

Brian coughed once to clear his throat, then said, 'Myself and Rachel reinterviewed Alina Moraru at her boyfriend's flat. From what she told us, it seems Emily was very much a loner. Unpopular at school, somebody with no real friends. Alina also told us that Emily was keen to experiment with drugs. She said that on a couple of occasions, Emily had asked if her boyfriend could score some cannabis for her.'

Danny said, 'Any reason she didn't let Emily's parents know about this drug issue?'

'Alina said that Rebecca Whitchurch is very aloof and unapproachable. Basically, she feared that if she'd said anything about drugs, she would have been sacked.'

'Did you speak to the boyfriend as well?'

'Alina's boyfriend is another Romanian national, Florin Chirilov. He has a record here, for petty theft and handling. He's very protective of Alina and does have some anger issues. He seemed totally disinterested in our questions about the missing girl. He was listening, though, because he became angry very quickly when he thought Alina was being blamed for her disappearance. He dislikes Rebecca Whitchurch intensely.'

Danny turned to the assembled detectives and said, 'There has been no further contact from the kidnapper overnight, so unless anyone else has anything else to add, that's it for now.'

He paused, but nobody said a word.

After waiting for a few seconds, Danny said, 'Before you

all get on with your allocated tasks, I just want to tell you about the outstanding work by DI Hopkirk and DC Moore yesterday. As a direct result of their diligent enquiries on this case, a young fourteen-year-old girl reported as missing from home was rescued from an attic in Edwalton, where she was being held captive by a sex offender. This was great work and reflects well on this department. That's it, everybody. Crack on and let's see if we can locate Emily Whitchurch today.'

Danny stood and walked back into his office, followed by his two detective inspectors.

As soon as they closed the door, Brian grinned and said, 'Bloody hell, boss, that was a bit embarrassing.'

Danny said, 'It *was* great work, Brian. You and Rachel both deserve credit. It also served as a kick up the arse for any detectives out there who don't think they should be dealing with a missing-from-home case.'

Rob said, 'Nobody out there's thinking like that.'

'Rob, I can't stress how important it is that we, the MCIU, find this girl. I feel like a piece of crap to keep harping on it. I know that our survival shouldn't be my driving force, but I've just got a gnawing feeling in my gut that if we don't find her, this department's days are numbered." He paused. Then said, 'Have you heard me? I'm even starting to sound like that prick Potter.'

Rob said, 'We'll find her, Danny. I'm sure the kidnapper will make contact again soon. That's when we'll get them and return the girl to her parents.'

'I hope you're right; I really do.'

Danny then said to Brian, 'I want you to carry on working with Rachel. I'm giving you free rein. I want you to try to look at things from every conceivable angle. Just follow your instincts, okay?'

Brian nodded, stood up and left the office.

Danny said, 'Hang on a minute, Rob.'

Rob sat back down. 'What's wrong?'

'This is for your ears only, okay?'

Danny then quietly outlined to Rob the personal problems his fellow detective inspector was experiencing concerning his wife's remarriage and plan to take his daughter to America.

Rob said, 'So your idea is to keep him involved on the periphery of the enquiry rather than be worrying alone at home?'

'Don't get me wrong. I still have every confidence in Brian. He's still a great detective, as he showed last night. I just don't want him to have the added pressure of running this enquiry at the moment. That's why I've given him free rein.'

'Makes perfect sense to me. I can run things on the ground as the enquiry develops, and you're already running the day-to-day liaison with the Special Operations Unit and the Regional Crime Squad. I'm sure we'll be fine.'

The telephone began to ring. Danny snatched the receiver up and said, 'Chief Inspector Flint.'

'Sir, it's DC Bailey. Another letter has just arrived at the house. This one was delivered by the postman. Rebecca Whitchurch opened it; it's composed in the same way as the first note, with letters cut from a newspaper. It's full of details about the ransom drop, sir.'

'Okay, Helen. I'm on my way with DI Buxton. I'll want to speak with Rebecca and Dominic when I get there. Are they both at home?'

'Yes, sir.'

50

11.30am, 12 October 1986
Richmond Drive, Mapperley Park, Nottinghamshire

Rob Buxton drove his nondescript Volkswagen Golf straight on to the driveway of De Montfort House. The rusting car looked very odd outside the million-pound property owned by Dominic and Rebecca Whitchurch.

As soon as the car came to a stop, Danny got out and walked briskly to the front door, followed by Rob. The door was opened by DC Helen Bailey as the two senior detectives approached.

As the two detectives stepped inside, Helen said, 'They're both in the lounge, sir.'

Danny said, 'Thanks, Helen. Where's the letter?'

'It's on the coffee table in there. I've placed the letter and the envelope it came in into separate exhibit bags.'

'That's great. We'll follow you in.'

. . .

As they walked into the lounge, Dominic Whitchurch stood up and said, 'Thanks for coming so promptly, Chief Inspector.'

From behind him, Rebecca said, 'What car have you come in?'

Rob Buxton said, 'I'm Detective Inspector Buxton. We've not met. We came in my private car. It's a small Volkswagen.'

Rebecca didn't acknowledge Rob. She directed her next remark at Danny. 'Did anybody see you pull on to the driveway?'

There was a real element of panic in her voice, so Danny replied soothingly, 'There's nobody on the street, Mrs Whitchurch. We were very careful.'

Rebecca sighed heavily and leaned back on the settee.

Dominic pointed to the coffee table and said, 'This arrived in the post this morning.'

Danny looked down at the kidnapper's demands. The message had been made up of letters cut out from a newspaper and stuck on plain paper.

The note was short and had very explicit instructions.

Danny read it several times.

Dominic Whitchurch
If you want to see your daughter again
You must place a black bag containing £250,000 in used notes next to the grave of Benjamin Fosdyke in Forest Road cemetery
This must be done at midnight on the 14th
No police

Dominic waited for Danny to look up, indicating that he had finished reading the note. In a panicky voice, he asked,

'What do we do now, Detective? I'm so scared. I haven't got that sort of cash.'

'What we don't do is panic, Mr Whitchurch. We've got two days to put everything in place. I want to intercept the kidnapper as he moves in for the bag of cash, then place him under full surveillance. If we get everything right, he'll lead us to your daughter. Don't worry about the money; we'll arrange for marked notes to be used. Are you prepared to do as the note instructs, and take the bag of cash into the cemetery?'

'I'll do whatever it takes to get my daughter back safely.'

Rebecca said coldly, 'And what happens to our daughter if you *don't* get everything right, Chief Inspector?'

Danny couldn't answer that question, so he simply said, 'We need to make sure that we do. I'll keep you both involved throughout the planning. That way, you'll know exactly what's happening every step of the way.'

Dominic sat down next to his wife and said, 'Try not to worry, darling. I'm sure they know what they're doing.'

Danny looked at Dominic and mouthed silently, 'Thank you' before saying out loud, 'I need to get back to the office. There's a lot to arrange in a short space of time. We need to be ready for the fourteenth. I'll leave you in the capable hands of DC Bailey. If there's anything you need or want to know, just ask her. Okay?'

Dominic replied, 'Thanks.'

Danny and Rob walked out of the house and got straight into Rob's car. As Rob drove the car off the driveway, he said, 'What's the plan?'

Danny remained silent. He was thoughtful for a long time, and it was only as the car was driven along Mansfield Road through Sherwood that he replied to Rob's question.

He said, 'The plan is this. I'm going to arrange for a team of Special Ops lads to get in that cemetery and stay hidden in there. I want them in position from tonight. They'll be our eyes and ears on the ground. I want maps of the cemetery. I want to know all the exits and entrances; I want to know exactly where Benjamin Fosdyke's grave is. I'm going to arrange with Mattie Carlisle to have the Regional Crime Squad surveillance team ready and in position to follow anyone who picks the ransom up. I want the kidnapper to lead us to the young girl before we move in and nick the evil bastard.'

Rob said, 'Where are we going to get a quarter of a million quid in marked notes?'

'That particular headache is one for Chief Superintendent Potter to sort out. I was reading up on the policies for ransom demands yesterday. The head of CID has the contacts in place to provide marked banknotes for any ransom demand. He will have to sign for the cash. It's his problem.'

'Are you happy about Dominic Whitchurch delivering the ransom?'

'Not really. It's never ideal to involve a civilian, but we must follow the note's instructions. If he's properly briefed about all the dos and don'ts, he'll be fine. I don't suppose for one second the kidnapper will make any attempt to come straight in for the pickup. He's bound to spend time watching the cash first. That's why I want our Special Ops guys in there tonight. I want them *in situ* so they don't have to move. Put your foot down, Rob. The clock's ticking, mate.'

As he drove his car away from the Redhill traffic island, along the A60 towards Mansfield, Rob did just that. He gunned the engine and accelerated quickly along the wide road.

Danny stared out the passenger-door window at the vegetation flashing by. His mind was in overdrive. He knew his plan had serious flaws, but all he could do was to try to minimise the risk.

His number-one priority had always been the safety of the girl. That hadn't changed. In addition to that, he now also had the identification and arrest of the kidnapper, the safety of Dominic Whitchurch and the security of a quarter of a million pounds to worry about.

His head was beginning to ache, and he could feel the pulse in his temple beginning to throb.

Rob safely negotiated another bend at speed and said, 'Ten more minutes.'

51

1.00pm, 12 October 1986
MCIU Offices, Mansfield, Nottinghamshire

Danny put the telephone back on its cradle, leaned back in his chair and took a deep breath. Since arriving back at Mansfield, he'd made telephone call after telephone call, trying to get everything organised.

His first call had been to the Regional Crime Squad office so he could update Chief Inspector Mattie Carlisle on the developments in the Emily Whitchurch kidnap case.

Arrangements had been put in place for the crime squad to provide their skills in covert surveillance at the time of the ransom drop. This was a huge weight off Danny's mind. The skill and experience Mattie Carlisle could provide was going to be invaluable.

The next call was to Chief Inspector Chambers at the Special Operations Unit. This call had yielded four two-man teams who would deploy into the Forest Road cemetery that evening under the cover of darkness. These eight men had all been trained in the secret art of covert rural observations. They would build hides within the area around the main entrances of the cemetery. They would also observe the grave of Benjamin Fosdyke, as specified in the kidnapper's demands. These eight men would remain in position, undetected, for the duration of the enquiry.

Danny had arranged to brief the chief inspector and his men at four thirty that afternoon.

The final call had been to the curator of the Forest Road cemetery, to arrange a face-to-face meeting later in the day. He would need to be informed of the police activity in and around the cemetery, even if he couldn't be told the reason for it.

He glanced at his wristwatch and picked up the telephone again. This was the call he'd been dreading. The telephone was answered by the chief constable's secretary on the second ring.

Danny said, 'Hello, Caroline, it's Chief Inspector Flint. I need a meeting with the chief and Adrian Potter as a matter of urgency, this afternoon.'

Caroline said, 'Hi, Danny. Give me a second. I'll just check his diary.'

Danny could hear her flicking through the pages of the diary; then she said, 'The only time he's got today is between three o'clock and three thirty. Will that be long enough?'

'That will be fine, thanks. I need you to ensure that Detective Chief Superintendent Potter is also there. He will need to hear what I've got to discuss with the chief.'

'No problem. Adrian's in his office all day today. I'll make sure he's there for the meeting this afternoon.'

'Thanks, Caroline; see you at three o'clock.'

Danny put the phone down and whispered to himself, 'I wonder if Adrian Potter ever leaves that office.'

Danny walked into the main office. He was relieved to see Rob Buxton still there.

Danny said, 'Have you got anything on at three o'clock this afternoon?'

Rob looked up from his desk and said, 'Nothing that won't keep. What's up?'

'We're going to see the chief constable and tell him we need a quarter of a million quid in used notes by the fourteenth.'

Rob grinned and said, 'I've got the maps of Forest Road cemetery that you wanted. I was just marking the location of Benjamin Fosdyke's grave on them.'

Danny said, 'That's great. Grab a couple of coffees and bring them in with the maps. We need to discuss strategy for this meeting.'

Rob stood up and said, 'Two coffees coming up, boss.'

52

3.00pm, 12 October 1986
Nottinghamshire Police Headquarters

When Danny and Rob walked into the chief's office, Jack Renshaw was sitting behind his large desk. Adrian Potter was sitting to the right of the desk, with a notepad opened on his lap.

Jack Renshaw said, 'Take a seat, Detectives,' indicating the two chairs in front of his desk.

Danny and Rob sat down. Rob placed the folder, containing the new demands from the kidnapper and the maps of Forest Road cemetery, on his knees.

Renshaw leaned forward and placed his elbows on the desk, interlocking his fingers as he did so. 'What's so urgent, Danny?'

Danny said, 'Sir, there's been a major development in the Whitchurch kidnapping. This morning, the family received new correspondence from the kidnapper. It contained detailed instructions for a ransom drop.'

Rob opened the folder and placed the letter from the kidnapper, still in its clear plastic exhibit bag, in front of the chief.

Renshaw picked up the exhibit bag and read the note before passing it to Potter.

Potter read it quickly and handed it back to the chief, who placed it on his desk in front of him.

He stared hard at the note, then said abruptly, 'Plan?'

Danny said, 'Dominic Whitchurch is prepared to deliver the ransom. I need Chief Superintendent Potter to arrange for the funds to be available by no later than nine pm on the fourteenth ...'

Potter spluttered, but before he could speak, Danny carried on, 'As you're no doubt aware, sir, the responsibility to raise the cash for any ransom demand falls to the head of the CID. He will have already established liaisons with banks and building societies for such a set of circumstances.'

Jack Renshaw glared at Danny and said with a growl, 'I don't need you to remind me of policy, Chief Inspector Flint. Now, what's your plan for the fourteenth? I assume you've got one.'

Danny glanced at Adrian Potter and relished the uncomfortable look on his face before saying, 'I've arranged with the Regional Crime Squad to provide a full covert surveillance capability on the night of the ransom drop. I've also arranged for members of the Special Operations Unit to provide covert observations within the grounds of Forest Road cemetery. Specifically, all the entrances, as well as the grave of Benjamin Fosdyke.'

Rob reached into his folder and passed the marked maps of the cemetery to the chief constable and to Potter.

Danny said, 'You will see the grave of Fosdyke marked on

the map. It's very close to the catacombs, within the cemetery grounds. So, the covert observations teams should be able to observe it and remain undetected. My plan is for Dominic Whitchurch to deliver the ransom, as instructed. He'll be observed every step of the way. Once the ransom has been delivered, the bag containing the cash will be kept under observation. The person who subsequently picks up the ransom will then be placed under covert surveillance by the crime squad. Hopefully, the kidnapper will then lead us to the girl. We can then arrest the offender or offenders and recover the cash.'

Jack Renshaw was tight-lipped. He remained silent, taking in the enormity of the operation Danny had just described.

When he finally spoke, it was in a voice barely more than a whisper. 'How confident are you this will work?'

'Chief Inspector Carlisle and his team are highly skilled in covert surveillance, and with the Special Ops observations teams as our eyes and ears on the ground, I'm very confident, sir.'

Potter said sarcastically, 'I'm not sure I liked the word "hopefully" when you described the chances of getting the girl back, Chief Inspector.'

Danny replied, 'If you have any recommendations or alterations to the plans you'd like to suggest, sir, I'm more than happy to be guided by your expertise.'

Potter shifted uncomfortably in his seat and said nothing.

Danny turned back to Renshaw and said, 'Of course there are risks involved, sir. Nothing about police work is ever an exact science. This is the moment we've been waiting for. We'll only get this opportunity to find the girl and get her back unharmed once. We've simply got to respond to the kidnapper's demands. Anything else could cost the girl her life.'

Renshaw stroked his chin, deep in thought. After a full minute, he said, 'I agree. Set everything in motion, Chief Inspector. Keep me informed every step of the way. Anything you need, let me know and I'll grease the wheels for you. We need to get this girl back to her family. Her safety is of paramount importance, understood?'

Danny nodded. 'Yes, sir. How soon can we get the cash sorted?'

The chief constable turned to his head of CID and waited for his response.

Potter blustered, 'I'll get straight onto it, sir.'

Jack Renshaw said, 'If there's nothing else, then, gentlemen? You've all got things to do.'

Danny and Rob left the office, quickly followed by Adrian Potter. As they walked along the corridor, Potter said, 'I'd like a word, Chief Inspector.'

Danny turned to Rob and said, 'Give me ten minutes. I'll see you back in our offices.'

As Rob walked on ahead, Potter hissed, 'In my office.'

Danny followed Adrian Potter into his office and said, 'Will this take long, sir? I've got things to get organised.'

'I don't appreciate being told what to do by a chief inspector, in front of the chief constable.'

'I'm sorry, sir, I didn't realise I'd done that. All I did was point out our individual responsibilities.'

'You need to appreciate that I'm not a man you should make an enemy of, Chief Inspector Flint.'

'And here's me thinking we're all on the same side. Will that be all, sir?'

'Get out!'

As Danny reached the door, Potter said, 'Tick-tock!'

Unable to contain his temper any longer, Danny rounded on Potter and said in a low growl, 'What's your problem? This isn't a fucking game. There's a young girl's life at stake here.'

'Do not take that tone with me. I suggest you leave while you've still got your pips, Chief Inspector.'

'I'm going. Don't forget that money needs to be available by nine pm on the fourteenth, sir. Tick-tock!'

Danny walked out and slammed the door behind him.

He was raging inside.

He knew he needed to calm down and try to remain rational.

He was angry at himself for allowing Potter to get under his skin.

By the time he'd walked across to the huts used by the Special Operations Unit, he had calmed down again. He was ready to brief Chief Inspector Chambers and his covert observations teams.

53

6.00pm, 13 October 1986
Foxhall Road, Forest Fields, Nottingham

Sam Jamieson was enjoying his fish and chips. As far as he was concerned, you couldn't beat eating them straight out of the paper, with lashings of salt and vinegar. He was a fit man who ran four or five miles every day, so he never felt the need to watch what he ate.

Once a week, he would walk from his little flat on Foxhall Road to the fish and chip shop on Bobbers Mill Road. He always ordered the same thing. Cod and chips, covered in a thick layer of green, mushy peas.

He enjoyed the slow walk back to his flat, eating the feel-good comfort food.

This evening had finally brought a welcome break in the continuous rain that had been falling for the last fortnight. As he approached Foxhall Road, he could feel the first spots of rain on his face. He glanced up at the nearest streetlight and could see that, once again, the rain was starting to fall.

Sam cursed under his breath and quickened his stride.

It was only as he quickened his own stride that he heard the footsteps behind him. He glanced over his shoulder and could see three men walking purposefully towards him. The street here was dark and poorly lit. Sam knew instinctively that these men were looking at him as a target.

Street robbery was rife in this part of the city. He cursed himself for not being more aware. He screwed up what was left of his fish-and-chip supper and tossed the paper into the gutter.

Seconds later, the men had caught up with him.

Sam stopped with his back against the wall of a terraced house and faced the men as they surrounded him.

The man standing directly in front of him was a young West Indian with short dreadlocks. He was very muscular and looked to be in his early twenties. He was wearing the mugger's uniform: a dark-coloured hooded top and jeans. His hands were thrust deep into the pockets of the hoodie.

He glared at Sam, with real hatred in his eyes. 'Give us your wallet, man! Or we're going to fuck you up!'

Sam said nothing. He adjusted his weight slightly, so he was now on the balls of his feet. He kept his hands open and by his sides. He glanced quickly to his left and saw that the second mugger was white and a similar age to the first. He was wearing a denim jacket and jeans. A quick glance to the right and he saw that the third man was also white. He had long, dark hair and a goatee beard.

Having assessed the threat, Sam held his hands up in a gesture of appeasement. He smiled and said, 'I don't have a wallet, and I've just spent the last of my cash on a fish supper. I'm sorry, lads, you're out of luck this time.'

Sam didn't possess a wallet, but he did have about thirty

quid in his jeans pocket. He didn't think for one second that the three muggers would take his word for having no cash. The West Indian took his right hand out from his jacket pocket. Sam saw immediately he was holding a black-handled kitchen knife. The blade looked to be about three inches in length. Long enough to do some serious damage.

The youth growled in his laconic West Indian drawl, 'I'm not going to tell you again, mister. Just hand over your cash, and you won't get hurt.'

Something inside Sam snapped.

Without saying another word, he smashed his right fist into the face of the West Indian. He felt his clenched fist drive into the soft, fleshy part of his attacker's nose. He could feel the cartilage and bone crunching beneath his fist. The force of the single punch, delivered so rapidly and effectively, sent the West Indian youth sprawling backwards. As he fell, the knife slipped from his grasp and clattered along the road.

Sam ducked and turned to his left. As he ducked, a punch from the denim-clad attacker whistled over his head. Sam hammered a right-handed punch into the ribs of his attacker, causing him to bend double. As the denim-clad youth doubled over, Sam smashed his knee into his face. The force from his knee was enough to knock the man backwards onto the ground.

The third attacker grabbed Sam from behind, pinning his arms.

Instantly, Sam used his head as a weapon, smashing it backward into the face of the final attacker. Again, he felt some satisfaction as his head connected with the front teeth of his attacker. There was a yelp of pain, and Sam felt the grip on his arms slacken. He squirmed out of the weakening grip and turned to face his attacker. He then delivered a heavy kick to the man's groin, sending him to his knees, doubled up in pain.

There was no rage or anger within Sam. Very deliberately, he walked across to each of the downed assailants and rained several heavy kicks into each of their faces. By the time he stopped, the three men were left battered and bleeding on the floor.

Finally, he bent down and picked up the knife dropped by the West Indian.

He slipped the knife into his pocket and was about to walk away when he heard a woman's voice from an upstairs window. 'Are you okay, love? I saw everything from my window. I've called the police; they're on the way.'

Sam said nothing.

The last thing he needed was for the police to know where he was. He ran off down the street, into the darkness.

The woman shouted after him: 'It's okay, love! The police are coming.'

Sam sprinted around the corner and kept running. The rain was falling heavier now, and he wanted to get back to his flat. He would need to make a small detour so he could get into his flat through the back gate. He dropped the kitchen knife down the first drain he passed and kept running.

He had to avoid the police at all costs.

Now that he was so close to achieving his revenge, being questioned by them was the last thing he needed.

54

9.00pm, 13 October 1986
Nottingham

Emily Whitchurch had no idea where she was. She had lost all sense of time and didn't know how long she had been held captive. She felt disoriented, sitting in the pitch-black darkness.

She felt constantly tearful and cried out for help on a regular basis. The shouts were born more out of frustration than hope of a rescue.

Her abductor had never spoken a word to her. Despite her pleadings to engage with her. He brought her food and fresh water every day and took away her waste in the bucket. Still, he never said a word.

Every time he came, she had tried to look at her surroundings in the torchlight. When he wasn't there, it was pitch black. There wasn't a single source of natural light. She literally couldn't see her hand in front of her face.

When she had first woken up, she found that her wrists were bound together by a nylon rope. She had followed this rope and found that it had been screwed into a wooden stake that was buried deep in the ground. She had initially panicked, screaming at the top of her voice to be let out. Eventually her voice grew hoarse, and her throat parched. Her shouts had soon become nothing more than a croaky whisper.

She had pulled hard at the ropes that bound her to the wooden stake. They were covered in a slippery, hard resin, so she couldn't attack the knots. The screws held the rope fast to the stake. She had tried to loosen the stake in the floor, but it was in too deep; she couldn't shift it. At least there was enough rope for her to move around and stand up. She could even raise her arms above her head.

As the days had gone by, she had become weaker. Eventually, she gave up and stopped trying to escape.

Her days were now spent in anticipation of her captor's next visit. She was literally starving; he had brought her very little food every day. Sandwiches, fruit sometimes, and water to drink.

The first time he came, she had been terrified. It had soon become obvious to her that he wasn't interested in her sexually. She was just being held captive. On that first occasion, he had brought the bucket. She had realised immediately what it was for. Although urinating and defecating in the bucket was base and abhorrent to her, it was better than soiling herself. At least he took her waste away with him every time he came. Every visit, he exchanged the dirty bucket for a clean bucket.

She knew she was starting to stink. She hadn't washed or cleaned herself after using the toilet bucket since she had been brought there. Her long, blonde hair was now lank and matted.

After looking at her surroundings, when he came with the torch, Emily had quickly realised she was being held underground, in some sort of excavation.

Recently, she had noticed that the ground she sat on and the walls surrounding her were getting wetter and wetter. The walls were now glistening wet in the torchlight.

Sometimes, when she sat alone in the darkness, she could hear bits of the roof falling. Small bits at first, but they sounded like they were getting bigger.

More alarmingly, she had often heard scurrying noises in the darkness. On a couple of occasions, she had felt coarse, stiff fur brush against the bare flesh of her legs. She knew what was making the scurrying sounds. Her mind wasn't yet ready to acknowledge the fact that she was sharing the small cave with big rats.

When he had come to feed her, she told him that she was constantly getting wet and that the roof was falling in. Once more, she had pleaded with him to let her go. She feared the roof caving in and burying her alive. She also told him about the vermin in the caves.

He had said nothing, but shone the torch at the walls and the ceiling. The next time he came, he brought with him a plastic sheet for her to sit on, so she was no longer constantly sitting in the mud.

When illuminated by the torchlight, the walls of her makeshift dungeon were a strange, honey-coloured hue. It was very small, no bigger than the average garden shed. The wooden stake she had been tied to was in the centre of the floor. The floor of the cave was about four feet below the level of the tunnel her captor came along. It meant he had to climb down into her cave. The ropes that bound her made it impossible for her to reach the entrance to the tunnel.

When she stood, the roof of the cave was only a foot above her head. She had tried to reach up and touch the wet stone above her head. The weight of the wet ropes was too much, and she had only managed it once. The stone above her felt sodden and wet to the touch.

She knew her captor would be arriving soon, so she sat cross-legged on the plastic sheet, patiently waiting for him to arrive. The sooner he got here, the better. She was starving hungry and very thirsty.

Hopefully, he would speak to her this time. She was desperate for him to say something. Anything.

The tears started to well in her eyes. She wondered just what the future held, and just how long he intended to keep her hidden away.

55

7.30am, 14 October 1986
Mansfield, Nottinghamshire

Danny poured cold milk on the cornflakes in the bowl before sprinkling a dusting of sugar on them. He carried the bowl from the work surface to the kitchen table and sat down opposite Sue.

Sue looked up from the magazine she was skim reading and said, 'Do you want another coffee?'

'Yes, please. I could murder one.'

'Is that all you're having? I can cook bacon and eggs if you like?'

'I haven't got time, sweetheart. I've got to be in the office for eight o'clock. I've got a hectic day today. I probably won't be home until the early hours of tomorrow morning, at the earliest.'

Sue looked concerned. 'Why? What the hell's going on?'

In between mouthfuls of cornflakes, Danny said, 'It's a

case we're currently working on that's really sensitive. There's a total media blackout, so I can't talk about it. Hopefully, it will all go to plan tonight, and I'll be able to tell you about it tomorrow.'

'Is it going to be dangerous?'

'It's not dangerous as such, but it could be a matter of life and death. If that makes any sense.'

'Oh my God, Danny. Please be careful.'

Danny realised he had said too much. The last thing he wanted to do was worry his heavily pregnant wife.

He smiled and said, 'Don't worry about me, sweetheart. I'll be fine. I've just got the worry of it all. I don't want you fretting about me all day. Okay?'

Sue handed him the mug of fresh coffee and nodded. 'Okay.'

'I've changed my mind, Sue. Would you mind making me a couple of slices of toast, please? These cornflakes haven't even filled a small hole.'

Sue smiled. She put two slices of thick white bread in the toaster and said, 'Butter and marmalade?'

'Perfect.'

As she buttered the hot toast, Sue said, 'So, apart from this case, how are things at work?'

'Do you mean, how are things with Adrian Potter?'

'Yeah, that's what I mean.'

'I just can't get on with him at all. We're like chalk and cheese. We clashed again the other day over this job. I just don't think I can work with him for very much longer. His attitude is so infantile. It drives me mad.'

'This isn't like you, darling. Where's your fight? The Danny Flint I know would be going out of his way to prove Potter wrong.'

'I hear what you're saying. I just don't know if I've got that fight in me anymore.'

'Of course you have. Go and prove Potter wrong; show him just how good the MCIU really is.'

Danny winked at his wife, smiled and took a huge bite of the sweet buttery toast before washing it all down with hot coffee.

He grabbed his jacket and car keys, kissed his wife and said, 'I've really got to dash, sweetheart. Thanks for the pep talk.'

As soon as he had put on his jacket, he grabbed the other slice of toast and raced out the front door.

56

11.50pm, 14 October 1986
Forest Road Cemetery, Nottingham

The midnight hour was fast approaching. The incessant heavy rain battered noisily onto the car roof.

Danny sat in the front passenger seat of Rob's Volkswagen Golf parked in the small yard at the rear of the Lincolnshire Poacher pub. Rob was in the driver's seat, and sitting in the back was Detective Chief Superintendent Adrian Potter.

When he had brought the black leather holdall containing the ransom cash to the MCIU offices, Potter had then insisted on staying for the duration of the operation.

The marked notes had been meticulously counted at the bank before Potter had signed for them. If any of the money went missing during the operation, the chief superintendent would have a lot of explaining to do. A point he had forcefully made to Danny when demanding to stay for the operation.

For anybody else, being squashed into the back of a Volkswagen Golf would have been uncomfortable. For the diminutive Potter, it felt spacious.

Danny and Rob had spent hours briefing Dominic Whitchurch at Richmond Drive, giving him full instructions for every scenario they could think of. Danny was satisfied that everything had been covered.

Whitchurch was to drive to the cemetery in his Range Rover. He would park at the main gates near Mansfield Road and walk in on his own. He was to carry the leather holdall in his right hand and keep his left hand free. If anyone approached him for the bag, he was to just hand it over. If nobody approached him, he was instructed to leave the bag at the base of the headstone that marked Benjamin Fosdyke's grave.

Danny had stressed to Whitchurch that the bag must be left on the grave side of the headstone. This was so that it could be observed by the teams of Special Operations Unit officers carrying out the covert observations within the cemetery.

As time went by, Dominic Whitchurch became more and more nervous. Danny had reassured him that he would be watched every step of the way, and to try not to worry.

Throughout the entire briefing, Potter had looked on. He never once made a comment.

As midnight approached, the radio in Rob's car crackled into life. 'DC Pope to all units. Delta Whiskey is now approaching the main entrance in his vehicle.'

Delta Whiskey was the radio code name given for Dominic Whitchurch.

DC Pope continued with the commentary. 'Delta Whiskey now out of vehicle, bag in right hand. On foot into the cemetery. He will be out of view in five, four, three, two, one.'

A new voice now came over the radio. 'PC Naylor to all units. I now have the eyeball. Delta Whiskey is on foot towards Position Alpha.'

The grave of Benjamin Fosdyke had been designated as Position Alpha.

PC Naylor from the Special Operations Unit gave a commentary from his hide near the main entrance: 'Delta Whiskey is alone. He's now at Position Alpha. Bag dropped in correct location; I have eyes on the bag. Delta Whiskey walking back to main entrance.'

DC Pope's voice took over the commentary. 'From DC Pope, Delta Whiskey now back into his vehicle. Away from plot. We will maintain eyes on Delta Whiskey. Over.'

Danny let out a huge sigh of relief.

One of his biggest fears was that Dominic Whitchurch could be injured during the ransom drop. The bag containing the cash had been left in the perfect place. It was now under observation by the Special Ops team, and Whitchurch was on his way home, unharmed.

Danny spoke on the radio: 'I want an update every five minutes.'

From PC Naylor: 'Received that, boss. Will do.'

It was now a waiting game.

Every five minutes, PC Naylor gave a concise update on the radio. 'No change. No change.'

As the time approached twelve thirty in the morning, Danny glanced at his watch. Just as he did so, the radio sparked into life again. 'From PC Naylor. We have movement at the main entrance. Stand by.'

The entire team waited.

PC Naylor said, 'There's a single figure, dressed entirely in black, with a full-face ski mask. He's loitering near the main entrance. He's now in the cemetery and approaching Position Alpha.'

PC Steve Grey was one of the two Special Ops officers manning the observation post nearest to Fosdyke's grave.

He took over the commentary: 'From PC Grey, I've now got the eyeball. Suspect now at Position Alpha. He's seen the bag but isn't approaching it. Stand by.'

Silence again.

Two minutes passed by. PC Grey said, 'He's definitely clocking points, but has still made no move for the bag. Stand by.'

Another minute ticked slowly by, then PC Grey said, 'Suspect now moving back towards the main entrance. Bag is still in situ, at Position Alpha.'

Danny said, 'Nobody move. Hold your positions. I don't want anybody following this person. The last thing we need is for them to get spooked now. Stand fast.'

PC Naylor said, 'Suspect has now left the cemetery. Direction of travel, towards Mapperley Road.'

Danny said, 'To PC Naylor, I want five-minute updates again, please.'

The Special Ops team all acknowledged the instruction.

Another hour passed slowly by, with updates being provided every five minutes.

Suddenly, radio silence was broken. A sense of urgency in his voice, PC Naylor said, 'PC Naylor to team. Motorcycle now approaching cemetery gates, at speed. Motorcycle into cemetery and approaching Position Alpha. Single rider, dressed entirely in black, no crash helmet visible.'

PC Grey said, 'I have eyeball. Motorcycle now at Position Alpha, the suspect has picked up the bag. Repeat! The suspect is now in possession of the bag. Motorcycle now at speed, towards main entrance.'

Danny was horrified. This was one scenario that hadn't

been foreseen. He just prayed that the regional crime squad surveillance team were alert and in position to effectively follow a motorcycle.

PC Naylor's voice came on the radio again. 'Motorcycle now approaching main entrance at speed. Through the gates and ... Fuck me!'

Danny shouted over the radio: 'What's happening?

PC Naylor said, 'The motorcycle's down! Repeat. The motorcycle's down. It's been totalled by a white van at the crossroads. The van has stopped the other side of the junction. Stand by. Suspect isn't moving at all; bag is now in the road and unattended.'

Danny had a decision to make.

He made it instantly. 'PC Naylor, you and your partner move in. Secure the cash and arrest the rider. Move!'

PC Naylor said, 'Roger that!'

Danny turned to Rob and said, 'Get up there sharpish!'

Rob started the car, and within seconds, they were skidding to a stop at the junction of Mansfield Road and Forest Road East.

Danny could see the two Special Ops men on the scene. He and Rob sprinted across to the unmoving motorcyclist, who was lying on his back.

Danny stood in the pouring rain and asked, 'Is he dead?'

PC Naylor replied, 'No, boss, he's alive. His left leg's well and truly fucked, though.'

The young driver of the van then approached warily. He was staring wide-eyed at the stricken motorcyclist and said, 'Is he okay? He pulled out straight in front of me. I didn't even have a chance to brake.'

Danny said, 'He's going to be fine. Don't worry, just give your details to PC Naylor here. The police will come and see you later today. Are you okay?'

'Yeah. I'm fine, just a bit shook up. It's a works van. I was just on my way in.'

'As soon as you've given all your details, you can get off to work. There were witnesses to the crash, so don't worry. Okay?'

'Okay.'

PC Naylor then walked over and began taking the details of the van driver.

Danny looked down at the motorcyclist's left leg. He could see white shinbone sticking through black jeans.

As other officers approached the scene, PC Jarvis continued to administer first aid to the stricken motorcyclist. Danny reached down and removed the black ski mask worn by the motorcyclist.

Just as the face mask came off, Brian Hopkirk and Rachel Moore arrived. Brian took one look at the motorcyclist's face and said, 'That's Florin Chirilov. He's the Whitchurch au pair's boyfriend.'

Danny gripped Chirilov by the front of his black jacket, pulled his face close to his own and growled, 'Where's the girl?'

Chirilov grimaced with the pain from his leg. 'I don't have her. I never had her. I just saw a way to make some quick money.'

Danny turned to Brian and said, 'You and Rachel go straight to his flat and talk to the au pair. I want her brought in for questioning, and I want that flat thoroughly searched. Understood?'

'Right you are, boss.'

Hearing Danny's instructions, Chirilov shouted, 'Alina knows nothing about this! This was all my idea. When she told me about the missing girl and how the parents had blamed her, I got angry. I thought I could get some money out of them.'

Danny said under his breath, 'For fuck's sake', then shouted, 'Rob, is there an ambulance travelling?'

'Yes.'

'Good. I want you to travel with Chirilov. Give me your car keys, and I'll send DC Lorimar over to the hospital. I want this piece of shit interviewed as soon as the doctors say he's well enough. I need to know if he's telling the truth, got it?'

Rob nodded.

Blue lights appeared in the distance. Danny could hear sirens as the ambulance approached, speeding up Mansfield Road, from the city centre.

Danny suddenly became aware of a presence standing behind him. He spun around and saw Adrian Potter clutching the black grip bag to his chest.

Potter said sarcastically, 'I suppose the one small mercy in this complete fuck-up is that we haven't lost a quarter of a million pounds as well. I'll get a lift back to headquarters with the Special Operations Unit. I'll expect a full debrief tomorrow afternoon, Chief Inspector.'

Potter walked across to one of the plain white Ford Transit vans, spoke to the driver and got inside.

Danny stood in the pouring rain and watched as the ambulance crew now attended to the injured Florin Chirilov.

He walked over and said to the nearest paramedic, 'Which hospital are you taking him to?'

'It'll be the Queen's Medical Centre. We need to stabilise that leg before we try to move him. It might be a while yet.'

'Okay, thanks.' Danny pointed to Rob and said to the paramedic, 'This officer will be travelling with you when you leave. Your patient is under arrest. Is that clear?'

The paramedic nodded.

Danny turned to Rob and said, 'I'll be in the CID office at

Central Police Station. Update me as soon as you can. I'm going to speak to the au pair as soon as Brian and Rachel bring her in.'

'Okay, boss.'

Danny walked slowly back to the Volkswagen and got in.

He shook his head and rubbed his temple. His mind was in turmoil. If what Chirilov had said was true, the entire enquiry was back to square one.

Danny felt totally frustrated. He still had no idea what had happened to Emily Whitchurch.

Where *was* that girl?

57

2.15am, 15 October 1986
Central Police Station, Nottingham

Danny walked into the interview room and sat down facing Alina Moraru. Rachel was already seated, and Brian stood by the door.

Rachel said, 'Alina, this is Chief Inspector Flint. He's the detective leading the search for Emily.'

The young woman nodded.

Rachel said, 'Sir, this is Alina Moraru. Until recently, she was the au pair for the Whitchurch family. She isn't under arrest; she's decided to come to the police station voluntarily to help with our enquiries. She understands her rights, including that she could have a solicitor here if she wanted to. She has declined legal advice. She wants to help us.'

Danny nodded, then said, 'Alina, do you really want to help us?'

The young woman nodded. Danny could see that she was already close to tears.

He said, 'I want you to tell me about this evening. Was Florin at home?'

'He was at home. We had a pizza earlier and watched the TV. He was very quiet, in a strange mood.'

'Go on.'

'We went to bed around eleven o'clock, but I read for a while. Florin was lying wide awake. At around a quarter to twelve, he got out of bed and got dressed. He said he had to go out. I protested, because it was raining so hard. I asked him what was so important.'

'And what did he say?'

'He just said he had some business to attend to.'

'Did you ask what?'

'Of course. He just told me to read my book, and that he wouldn't be long.'

'Then what?'

'A little later, I heard him come back into the flat. He didn't say anything. He just picked something up from the sideboard cupboard and walked straight out again.'

'How long is a little later?'

'I don't know. Maybe twenty minutes.'

'Are you sure he didn't say anything?'

'He said nothing.'

'Is this normal behaviour? You don't sound too surprised by his actions.'

'I wasn't surprised at all, Chief Inspector. Florin comes and goes at all hours of the night. I never ask where he's been, or he gets angry.'

Rachel said, 'Is he ever violent towards you?'

'No, never. He just gets angry and tells me to mind my own bloody business.'

Danny said, 'Does Florin own a motorcycle?'

'No.'

'When he was arrested tonight, he was riding a small black Suzuki motorcycle, but there were no registration plates on it.'

'That motorcycle belongs to old George; he lives in the flat opposite ours. He can't ride the bike anymore, so he told Florin if he ever needed to borrow it, he could. He even gave Florin a key. If he was on the motorcycle, I bet it was the key that he came back for.'

'Have you and Florin ever discussed Emily Whitchurch?'

'Only when she first went missing. He hasn't talked to me about her since then. He was really angry when Mrs Whitchurch fired me.'

'Has he ever taken an interest in Emily before she went missing?'

Alina looked at Rachel. 'I told this detective that Emily wanted me to ask Florin to get her drugs. Florin was upset because he doesn't do drugs. The only other time he showed any interest was when I bragged about the Whitchurch house. I would tell him how beautiful it was and all the expensive things they had. Florin would make comments about how rich they were. He would say things like "they must be loaded", but that's all. What's he done, Chief Inspector?'

'You really don't know, do you?'

'No, I don't, and I'm scared.'

Danny turned to Rachel. 'Has the flat been searched properly?'

Rachel nodded and said, 'Yes, boss.'

'Anything?'

'Nothing at all.'

'Okay, I want you to take Alina home. Check out the story about the motorcycle with this neighbour, George.'

Rachel nodded.

Danny turned to Alina and said, 'Thank you for talking to us. We may want to speak to you again later today, okay?'

'Okay. You still haven't told me what Florin has done. Will he be home later?'

'Florin is still at the hospital. He's under arrest, and we'll be speaking to him a lot more today. I'm sorry, but he won't be home anytime soon.'

A single tear trickled slowly down Alina's cheek.

Danny stood up and walked out of the interview room.

He went back upstairs to the CID office, picked up his radio and said, 'DCI Flint to DI Buxton.'

Rob Buxton replied, 'I've got an update, boss. Are you near a landline?'

'Central CID.'

Within seconds, the telephone began to ring. Danny snatched up the handset and said, 'Danny Flint.'

'Boss, it's Rob. We've been speaking to Chirilov for the last half hour, with the doctor's consent. This all seems like some hare-brained scheme he's dreamed up to extort money from the Whitchurch family. He says he always knew they were very wealthy, and that they would pay good money to get their daughter back. He made up the kidnap story to demand money from them. He's a blackmailer, not a kidnapper. He's got no idea where the girl is. On the day she went missing, he was at his flat screwing Alina. When she was abducted, he was naked in bed at home. There's no way he's involved.'

'Did you ask about the motorcycle?'

'Yeah. It belongs to an elderly neighbour who lets him use it. He took the plates off it tonight. He's not a very competent rider; that's why he crashed the bloody thing tonight. He was the figure in black who walked into the cemetery and looked at the bag. He didn't want to just take it there and then, because he thought it would be a trap. So he cooked this plan up on the spur of the moment, to ride in on the motorbike and lift it. He just didn't see the van at the junction as he accelerated out of the gates.'

'Does he realise how much shit he's in?'

'Yeah. He's been a petty criminal all his life. He just saw an opportunity to make some easy money.'

'What about the letters?'

'He's admitted sending them. He hand-delivered the first one and posted the second one, because Mrs Whitchurch nearly saw him when he delivered the first one. He says he cut up old copies of the *Sun* newspaper to make the letters.'

'Okay, Rob, thanks. I'm going to see Dominic Whitchurch first; then I'll drive over and pick you up from the hospital. You can drop me home on the way back.'

Danny put the phone down and exclaimed, 'Shit!'

He felt dreadful. His suit was still soaking wet, and his head was pounding. He wasn't looking forward to telling Dominic and Rebecca Whitchurch that he was no nearer finding their daughter.

58

10.30am, 15 October 1986
MCIU Offices, Mansfield, Nottinghamshire

After the debacle of the night before, Danny had assembled the entire MCIU staff and all the Special Operations Unit officers involved. He wanted to review the operation to learn from any mistakes that had been made.

Prior to starting the debrief, Danny sat in his office, talking to Mattie Carlisle and Rob Buxton.

Mattie Carlisle said, 'If you want my honest opinion, we got lucky when that van wiped out Chirilov on his motorbike. There would have been no way we could have kept up surveillance on a motorcycle. We could easily have lost that bag of cash.'

Danny said, 'I still can't believe I didn't consider it. I never dreamt a motorcycle would be used inside the cemetery.'

'Nor did I, Danny. That's definitely one I'll take away for the future.'

'Rob, as soon as you've briefed everyone about the interviews with Chirilov and what charges he's going to face, I want you to get back to the hospital, ready for when they release him.'

Rob nodded as he tried to stifle a yawn. 'Will do. Sorry for yawning; my eldest was up all night, throwing up.'

Danny grinned and said, 'The joys of parenthood, eh?'

Rob said, 'Yeah, something like that. Wait 'til it's your turn.'

Danny turned to Mattie and said, 'Thanks for coming over this morning. Did you want to have any input on this debrief?'

'No, thanks. It's best kept in-house. I just wanted to come over for an update this morning. I'll leave you to it. Don't forget if there are any new developments, I'm always available.'

'Thanks, Mattie, I'll keep you informed. Thank your staff for their efforts yesterday. I know it was a long day.'

Mattie nodded and left.

Danny said, 'You ready, Rob?'

'The sooner it's done, the sooner I can get back to the hospital. Let's go.'

The two senior detectives walked into the briefing room. Rob gave the details of the interviews he'd conducted with Alina Moraru and Florin Chirilov. He outlined how the kidnap plot had all been an elaborate fabrication, made up by Chirilov, in order to extort cash from the Whitchurch family.

The general mood in the office was sombre. Danny brought the debrief to a close by asking for any suggestions or ideas to move the enquiry forward.

The lone voice to speak up was DS Lyn Harris, who

asked, 'Now that it's no longer a kidnap enquiry, should we consider lifting the media blackout and holding a full press release?'

'That's a good idea, Lyn. It's definitely on the agenda for later today. I'm meeting with the chief constable at headquarters this afternoon; I'll have a meeting with our press liaison officer while I'm there and set the wheels in motion. A full press appeal is something that could easily generate fresh lines of enquiry.'

'Okay, you've all still got tasks to get through. Let's remember it might not be a kidnapping enquiry any longer, but there's still a young girl out there somewhere. Let's find her.'

Danny tried to sound upbeat, but he was struggling. He walked back into his office, closed the door and sat down heavily in his chair. He was dreading the meeting later with Jack Renshaw and Potter.

He just wished he had something new to say to them.

There was a knock on his office door. Danny shouted, 'Come in.'

Andy Wills walked in, saying, 'Have you got a minute, boss?'

'Grab a seat. How are you getting on with tracing Sam Jamieson?'

'That's what I've come to see you about. Yesterday, I made a call to HMP Leeds. I wanted to speak to the prison officer on the gate the day Jamieson was released. It occurred to me that sometimes a released prisoner is in such good spirits that they disclose snippets of information to the prison officer during the release process.'

'Go on.'

'Late yesterday, I had a call back from Prison Officer Armstrong, who was the gate officer when Jamieson was released. He told me that although Jamieson didn't really say anything on the day of his release, he did recall a conversation with him a few days prior to his release date. During that chat, Jamieson had told him that he intended to try to gain his master's degree in psychology when he was released.'

'How does that help us?'

'After talking to Prison Officer Armstrong, I've spent this morning ringing universities and colleges in this area. Nottingham Trent University currently have students working towards their master's in psychology. One of those students is Sam Jamieson.'

'Does the university have a current address for Jamieson?'

'The address they have is a one-bedroomed flat at 34 Foxhall Road, Forest Fields, Nottingham. He's renting Flat 3.'

'I want you to do all the enquiries you can on the address and do any digging necessary at Nottingham Trent University. I want you to be in position to get a warrant to search that address by the end of the day. That's brilliant work, Andy.'

Andy walked out of the office, leaving Danny feeling much more positive. At least he now had something fresh to talk about during the meeting at headquarters.

59

**3.30pm, 15 October 1986
Nottinghamshire Police Headquarters**

Danny had been kept waiting for fifteen minutes outside the chief constable's office. Finally, he was asked to go in and join the chief and Adrian Potter.

By the time Danny walked in, Potter had already given his version of the disastrous events at the ransom drop. Jack Renshaw had a face like thunder. He said gruffly, 'Sit down, Chief Inspector.'

Danny sat down and waited for the explosion.

It didn't come.

Jack Renshaw looked Danny in the eye and said quietly, 'I want to hear what happened last night, Chief Inspector.'

Danny took a deep breath and explained exactly what had happened. He admitted that there had been a hole in the planning of the operation. He had not foreseen the possibility that a motorcycle could be used within the cemetery. He admitted that it had been very fortunate the suspect had not made good his escape.

Potter interjected, with heavy sarcasm, 'You mean his escape with a quarter of a million pounds.'

Renshaw did not acknowledge Potter's remark. He held eye contact with Danny.

Danny continued: 'The chief superintendent's right, sir. We were very fortunate that the motorcycle collided with another vehicle, or we may well have lost the ransom money, as well.'

Renshaw said, 'Did you have a contingency in place for vehicle surveillance?'

'Yes, sir. The Regional Crime Squad were in attendance. They would have attempted to follow the motorcyclist away from the plot.'

Again, Potter butted in. 'Until they lost it!'

Renshaw turned to Potter and said sharply, 'That's enough!'

Once again, the chief looked at Danny. 'I take it you've done a full debrief this morning, along with the Special Operations Unit and the Regional Crime Squad.'

'Yes, sir.'

'Lessons learned?'

'Yes, sir. All the departments involved have taken things away from last night's operation.'

'That's good. Let's just all be thankful that no real harm was done. How were the Whitchurches when you broke the news afterwards?'

'Very upset, and understandably still worried. After all, their only daughter's still missing, sir.'

Renshaw nodded and said, 'Now that the kidnap plot has been shown to be a load of rubbish, what other enquiries have you got on the go?'

'While most of my staff were investigating the possible kidnap and preparing for the ransom drop, I kept some back to carry out other enquiries at the same time. I didn't want to put all my eggs in one basket, so to speak.'

'Just as well, Chief Inspector. What other enquiries?'

Danny suddenly felt very grateful to Andy Wills, who had managed to trace Sam Jamieson that morning.

He said, 'I've had staff researching every trial that Dominic and Rebecca Whitchurch have been involved in, to try to find someone holding a serious grudge.'

'Any joy?'

'There's one man who fits that criteria. He holds a serious grudge against Rebecca Whitchurch. He blames her for the death of his own daughter while he was serving seven years in prison. He was released from HMP Leeds a short time before Emily Whitchurch went missing.'

'Name?'

'His name's Sam Jamieson. He had been off the radar since his release, but my staff have finally located a current address for him. I'm expecting to execute a search warrant in the very near future.'

Adrian Potter said dismissively, 'Anything else?'

Danny said, 'Now there's no longer a media blackout, I want to hold a press conference as soon as possible. When I leave here, I'm going to see the press liaison officer and make the arrangements for tomorrow morning. I'll speak to the family this evening. I want to involve Rebecca and Dominic Whitchurch if they're willing.'

The chief nodded. 'That's good. We need actions that will keep this enquiry active. What's happened with the bloody idiot would-be kidnapper?'

'Florin Chirilov's a Romanian national. After making full admissions, he was charged earlier today with several offences. He remains in police custody at the Queen's

Medical Centre while he recovers from a compound fracture of his left leg sustained in the accident. Either tomorrow or the day after, he will appear before Nottingham Magistrates. Obviously, we'll be pushing for him to be remanded in custody.'

'Are you satisfied he was working alone and that there's no link from him to the missing girl?'

'I'm positive, sir. Chirilov's nothing more than a petty criminal. A handler of stolen goods who saw an opportunity to make a lot of money quickly. Nobody else was involved.'

Potter said, 'What about his girlfriend, the au pair?'

'She's been interviewed at length, sir; she knew nothing about Chirilov's plans.'

The chief said, 'What happened last night was unfortunate and could have ended a lot worse for us than it did. Police work has never been an exact science. Sometimes events happen that no one could have foreseen. The main thing is that lessons are learned for the future. Chief Inspector Flint, keep your team motivated, and I'm sure you'll trace this girl. Get the television appeal out as soon as possible. I want you to keep me personally informed of the outcome when you execute this warrant for Jamieson. That will be all, gents.'

Danny and Adrian Potter stood up and left the office together.

Just before Potter walked into his office, he said to Danny, 'You got lucky this time, Chief Inspector.'

Danny didn't rise to the bait. He just smiled and carried on walking.

He felt a little better as he walked down the corridors to see the press liaison officer. He felt like the chief constable still had his back. He had witnessed the way Potter had criticised his operational planning and subsequent actions.

The chief was having none of it.

Maybe there was a glimmer of hope for the MCIU after all.

60

**8.00am, 16 October 1986
Cavendish Vale, Sherwood, Nottingham**

Felicity Spencer was almost ready for work. Another day of mind-numbingly boring office work at Mulberry Chambers. No doubt when she arrived, there would be a mountain of filing waiting to be done. The filing would be followed by dozens of statements that needed typing, and finally any letters that needed to be typed up and posted.

Every day was identical.

Every day was boring.

Working at Mulberry wasn't all bad, though. The pay was excellent, the offices she worked in were modern and comfortable, and the other secretaries were all friendly. The car park at the rear of the offices was spacious enough for even lowly secretaries to park their cars in.

Then there were the perks that hadn't appeared on the

job description.

Very well-paid, handsome young barristers, most of whom had an eye for a pretty girl, even the married ones.

Felicity knew she was attractive to the opposite sex. She always wore just the right amount of make-up so that she looked stunning, without being tarty. It was a difficult trick to pull off every day. She spent most of her wages on smart clothes and was always immaculately dressed.

As far as she was concerned, it was an investment.

Felicity Spencer had a plan.

Within the next three years, she would have moved out of her parents' home in Sherwood and be married to a successful barrister. She planned to be living in a beautiful house in Woodborough, eating out every night and having the most wonderful foreign holidays.

The latest of those eligible barristers to fall for her charms had been Freddie Fletcher.

She had noticed the slim, handsome barrister checking out her curves whenever he was in the admin office. This attention had culminated in him asking her out on a date ten days ago.

It had been a wonderful night at Champagne Charlie's Bar, in the fashionable Hockley area of the city. Freddie had been extremely generous, buying bottle after bottle of the most expensive champagne, as he was celebrating landing a high-profile brief. The night had been a champagne-fuelled, fun-filled night with lots of laughter. They had both ended up at Freddie's stylish flat at Cavendish Road East, in the centre of The Park.

When Felicity had woken up the next morning, she was dressed only in her underwear. She was lying on the top of a huge double bed.

Her mouth felt dry, and her head was pounding. She had quickly got dressed, slipping on the tight leather trousers and mohair jumper from the night before. Once dressed, she had explored the spacious luxury flat. She had found Freddie lying fully dressed and comatose on the sofa in the lounge. He was on his back, his mouth was open, and he was snoring loudly.

Felicity had chuckled and said under her breath, 'Very attractive.'

She was already reasonably happy that nothing had happened between them the night before. Seeing Freddie in his current state had confirmed that.

Her memories of that recent alcohol-fuelled night made her smile as she ate her toast and sipped her coffee before leaving for work. The television was on in the kitchen of her parents' house, and she suddenly stopped chewing as she recognised Rebecca Whitchurch on the screen.

Felicity had never seen Rebecca Whitchurch looking like this. Her hair wasn't styled or brushed. She had no make-up on, and her eyes were bloodshot and teary. She wore a plain grey trouser suit that looked crumpled and creased, as though she had been wearing it for days.

She took another sip of coffee and turned up the volume on the television.

Rebecca was sitting next to a man and a woman, who were obviously from the police. Rebecca began speaking, and Felicity concentrated fully on the television.

The normally assured barrister said, in a shaky voice that was almost breaking with emotion, 'All I want is for my beautiful daughter to come home. If anyone has seen her, or heard from her, please contact the police. My husband and I are going out of our minds with worry. Emily, if you're watching, please come home.'

It was obvious that the woman was close to breaking down, and the camera zoomed in for a close-up shot. One of the police officers started speaking, and then a photograph of

Emily, with her big blue eyes and blonde hair, filled the TV screen.

Felicity switched the television off.

She was shocked by what she had just seen. The image of Emily looking so young and the pain of Rebecca had brought another memory of that night out with Freddie Fletcher crashing into her brain.

She now vividly recalled he had said something very strange about Emily Whitchurch that night. It had been so bizarre that it had stuck in her mind.

He had proposed a toast to Emily for being missing, which was strange in itself. But it was his second comment that had been so menacing.

He had said, 'May she remain hidden in the shadows for ever.'

It had troubled her at the time. After watching the press appeal this morning, it now troubled her even more. She knew she would have to talk to somebody about it, but she didn't really want to contact the police.

As she locked the door of her parents' house and walked to her tiny Fiat car, she decided to share her concerns with Mr Dawson at work.

He was always very friendly and polite to all the girls in the office. He would know what best to do.

There was another, more selfish reason why Felicity felt compelled to tell someone about Freddie's comment. She was more than a little annoyed with the handsome young barrister. Since their night out at Champagne Charlie's, Freddie hadn't once found the time to pick up a telephone and call her.

Felicity didn't feel she owed Freddie Fletcher anything. It was obvious to her that he wouldn't be the one who would fulfil her dreams and buy her the beautiful house in Woodborough.

61

10.30am, 16 October 1986
Mulberry Chambers, The Ropewalk, Nottingham

Felicity Spencer knocked politely on the office door of Sebastien Dawson. She felt comfortable around one of the most senior figures in Mulberry Chambers. She had worked at Mulberry for two years and had often done work for Sebastien Dawson in his office, under his personal supervision.

For his part, Sebastien Dawson enjoyed the company of the very attractive, vivacious young secretary. He was an extremely polite man, always behaving impeccably around the young female staff.

Felicity Spencer was treated no differently.

He was delighted when the office door opened and Felicity said, 'Have you got a minute, sir? I need your advice on a matter that may concern chambers.'

Sebastien smiled and said, 'I've always got a minute for you, Miss Spencer. Come in and close the door behind you.'

He waited until she had sat down on one of the two chairs in front of his desk, and then said, 'Well? What is it I can help you with?'

In a confident voice, Felicity said, 'Have you seen the press appeal with Mrs Whitchurch on the television this morning, sir?'

Sebastien had indeed seen the dreadful press conference. He had been shocked by Rebecca's appearance. He had never seen her in such a sorry state.

He was now feeling more than a little worried as to why one of the firm's young secretaries would want to speak to him about that.

He kept his voice level. 'Yes. I saw it this morning before I came to work. Why do you ask?'

Now it was Felicity's turn to look slightly worried. 'Sir, I need to tell you something in confidence about one of the barristers.'

'Okay. Whatever the problem is, I want you to speak freely, Miss Spencer. Which of the barristers are you referring to?'

'Mr Fletcher.'

'What has Mr Fletcher got to do with this morning's press appeal and Rebecca Whitchurch?'

'Well, sir, when you gave Freddie – sorry, Mr Fletcher – the Manchester brief, he invited me out to celebrate with him that evening.'

She paused because she knew that old man Dawson frowned upon social interaction between the staff.

He leaned back in his chair and placed his hands on his large stomach. It was a habit he had developed when he was thinking. He would drum his fingers on his rotund belly as he thought.

Eventually, he stopped and said, 'Is it something that happened when you were out that evening? Is that what's got you worried, Miss Spencer?'

'Nothing happened. Not like that. It was just something Mr Fletcher said, that's all. It was a bit strange.'

'Strange enough for you to remember it, obviously.'

'We had drunk rather a lot of champagne that night, and we were both a little tipsy.'

'What did he say?'

'We had talked about the reasons he had been given the brief in Manchester.'

'And?'

'He told me that he wasn't just celebrating because he'd been given the brief, but mostly because Mrs Whitchurch was no longer doing it. Then he wanted to drink a toast to Emily Whitchurch for being missing. At the end of the toast, he said, "May she stay hidden in the shadows forever." I just thought it was all a bit too weird, that's all. I thought you should know what he'd said, sir.'

Sebastien Dawson was now deep in thought.

His thoughts had turned to his own rather disturbing conversation with Fletcher when he had allocated him the Manchester brief. He racked his brains for the particular comment that had troubled him at the time.

The words rushed into his head: "I do hope the young Whitchurch girl decides to extend her vacation away from home".

On its own, it was a crass, insensitive comment. Tied together with the comment Fletcher had made to the young secretary when in drink, it took on a far more sinister tone.

He said, 'How did Mr Fletcher seem to you when he made that comment about the shadows? Was he joking?'

'No, sir, he wasn't. That's what made it so strange. It was like he really meant it.'

'Okay, Miss Spencer, thank you for bringing this to my attention. I'll give the matter some thought, but I'm leaning towards contacting the police.'

Felicity Spencer was now extremely worried.

How would the police getting involved affect her standing at chambers? Could she lose her job over this?

As if reading the young secretary's mind, Sebastien said, 'Don't worry, Miss Spencer. Whatever action I decide to take, it will not affect you or your role with this firm in the slightest. Is that understood?'

'Thank you, sir.'

'Was that everything?'

'Yes, sir. Thank you for listening.'

'No problem. I'll let you know what I decide to do later today, okay?'

She stood up. 'Thanks, Mr Dawson.'

She closed the door on her way out, leaving Sebastien Dawson with a huge headache. Difficult questions raced into his mind.

Should he involve the police?

What would be the fallout from the head of chambers if the police spoke to one of the firm's brightest young barristers about the disappearance of the daughter of one of the chambers' other barristers?

What would happen if Freddie Fletcher were involved in the young girl's disappearance?

He sat quietly in his office for well over an hour, mulling over all the pros and cons, before finally making his decision.

He reached across his desk and picked up the telephone.

When the phone was answered, he said, 'I'd like to speak to Detective Inspector Rob Buxton at the Major Crime Investigation Unit, please.'

62

**10.30am, 16 October 1986
Nottingham**

He was coming.

Emily could hear the man's footsteps before she saw the flash of torchlight in the tunnel that led to the cave she was in. She focussed on the light at the mouth of the cave, and finally, she saw his boots and legs.

The man lowered himself down into the cave. Instinctively, she moved back as far as she could.

He picked up the half-full bucket and replaced it with a clean one. He turned and placed the dirty bucket back out into the tunnel, ready to take it away when he left.

Without saying a word, he then placed a pack of tuna and mayonnaise sandwiches, an apple and a litre bottle of water on the plastic sheeting next to her.

She pleaded, 'How long are you going to keep me here like this?'

No response.

'Why are you doing this to me? Please, you've got to let me go.'

Nothing.

She started to sob.

Suddenly, the man spoke to her. 'Have you heard any more rats?'

Emily was shocked at hearing his voice. She spluttered, 'Yes. Big ones. They're getting bolder all the time. I woke up with one on my legs. It felt huge.'

From his pocket, the man took out a pencil-sized Mini Maglite torch and placed it on the sheeting.

'The light from the torch is very bright; it will scare them away. Don't keep it on all the time. When the batteries are dead, they're dead. You won't be getting any more. Understood?'

She couldn't believe he was speaking to her. She nodded her head and said quickly, 'I understand. How long are you going to keep me here?'

He growled his response. 'As long as I have to. There are people who need to learn what loss feels like. You won't be here forever. Just do what I tell you when I tell you, and everything will be fine.'

She started to say something in response, but the man barked, 'No more questions!'

She could detect the fury in his voice. As desperate as she was for conversation, she decided to remain silent and not antagonise the man further.

He then shone the torch above his head, as though inspecting the roof above her.

He said quietly, 'You must be silent down here. No loud noises. No screaming if you see the rats. There has been a lot of wet weather, and it's still raining heavily. The roof and the walls are very wet now. You must be very quiet and still.'

Emily was terrified. 'Please don't leave me here to die! I'm begging you!'

'Do as you're told. Just sit quietly. I'll be back tomorrow.'

He climbed up and out of the cave without another word.

She saw his torchlight disappearing along the main tunnel and waited until she was sitting in complete darkness again.

After a long wait, she grabbed the Mini Maglite torch and switched it on. For such a small torch, it produced a bright, powerful beam.

She shone the torch above her head to illuminate the entire cave. For the first time, she got a good look at her surroundings. She inspected the ropes and the stake she was secured to. Very quickly, she realised there was no way she could escape. The walls and the roof were glistening and extremely wet. The cave had been hollowed out of sandstone rock and looked man-made. She could clearly see individual tool marks on the walls.

She wondered exactly where she was.

She picked up the packet of sandwiches and flicked the torch off. She ate the tuna sandwiches in the dark, savouring every mouthful. It was amazing how much better food tasted now that she was starving.

It was essential to save the batteries of the torch. She knew the rats would soon smell the food and come scurrying along the tunnel.

As frightening as it had been listening to them in the dark, Emily was equally terrified about seeing the vermin for the first time.

She mouthed a silent prayer that the light from the torch would scare them off.

63

11.00am, 16 October 1986
MCIU Offices, Mansfield, Nottinghamshire

Danny sat alone in his office. He was using this quiet time to evaluate everything he knew so far. It was something he did on a regular basis. Going over everything that had happened during the enquiry. Desperately seeking something he might have missed, something that would unlock the mystery of the missing girl.

There was a knock on the door, shattering his thought process. Slightly annoyed, he shouted, 'Come in!'

Brian Hopkirk walked into the office. 'Sorry to disturb you, boss. I've got an idea I want to run by you.'

Danny placed his pen on the notebook in front of him and said, 'Grab a seat, Brian. What's on your mind?'

Brian said, 'Before we found Theresa Stanhope, you told me that you wanted me to investigate the missing person side of things rather than the kidnap angle. Does that still hold?'

'What do you mean?'

'I've got an idea that I want to follow up. The problem is, it's not really based on anything other than a hunch.'

'Tell you what. Why don't you just tell me what's on your mind?'

'Okay. After the ransom drop went all pear-shaped the other night, I was chatting to two of the Special Operations Unit officers who had spent days hidden in the cemetery. They had used the catacombs and natural caves to remain hidden throughout the time they were in there. It just got me thinking about those catacombs. Emily Whitchurch disappeared somewhere between Nottingham High School for Girls and Alpha Terrace. We're all agreed that the most likely site for her abduction was somewhere along Forest Road East, correct?'

Danny nodded. 'It seems the most likely.'

'What if the girl was never taken from Forest Road East? What if she's being held somewhere nearby?'

Danny could see what the experienced detective inspector was thinking. 'So your theory is that the girl has been hidden somewhere in the catacombs?'

'I know it sounds mad, but we haven't been able to find a single witness anywhere. It's as if that girl literally vanished into thin air.'

'So what are you proposing?'

'I want to make some enquiries into the possibility of her being snatched off the street and immediately hidden in one of the nearby catacombs along Forest Road East.'

'We can't search that entire area. It's impossible.'

'I appreciate that, boss. I know the catacombs and natural caves are extensive. To be honest, I wouldn't know where to start looking.'

'I sense a "but" coming.'

Brian grinned. 'But I know someone who will have all that information. I've done a little research into the feasibility of my theory. There's a guy called Brandon Temple, who's the Professor of Geology at Nottingham Trent University. He's currently researching all the caves beneath the city, with a view to compiling a definitive map of the entire system.'

Danny thought for a second, then said, 'Run with your idea. We've got nothing to lose. Take Rachel and go and see Professor Temple. Keep me informed, and don't spend days on it. If it's not feasible, you'll know quickly. I don't want you and Rachel chasing shadows, okay?'

'Thanks, boss.'

Danny picked up his pen again. He loved the way his team were always thinking outside the box.

He had read two more lines of notes when there was another, far more urgent knock on the door.

Rob Buxton walked in and said, 'The television appeal that was aired last night and this morning has turned something up. I thought you'd want to hear it.'

Danny sat back in his chair. 'Go on.'

Rob said, 'I've just taken a call from Sebastien Dawson at Mulberry Chambers. He's been approached by one of his secretarial staff this morning, who has concerns about one of the barristers at chambers. Apparently, this woman was with the barrister when he made some rather strange remarks about the disappearance of Emily Whitchurch.'

'Who's the barrister?'

'His name's Freddie Fletcher.'

'What sort of remarks?'

'Something along the lines of "the longer Emily Whitchurch stays hidden, the better". It's the use of the word "hidden" instead of "missing" that has raised alarm bells.'

'Where's Fletcher now?'

'Freddie Fletcher is currently in Manchester. He replaced Rebecca Whitchurch as defence counsel in the Denton Post Office robbery trial.'

Danny said, 'So, we've got very disparaging and strange remarks being made by one of Rebecca Whitchurch's colleagues. That same colleague then gains massively by the disappearance of Rebecca's daughter, when he replaces her as counsel for the defence at Manchester Crown Court.'

'That's it in a nutshell.'

'Take DC Lorimar and go talk to Sebastien Dawson and the secretary who reported the remarks. Get them both fully statemented, then drive up to Manchester. I want you to have a serious conversation with Freddie Fletcher tonight. I want you to establish exactly what he meant by those remarks.'

'Is he now a suspect?'

'Everyone's a suspect. Let's treat this enquiry as a trace, interview, eliminate situation to start with. See what Fletcher's like. If he's co-operating, then fine. If he doesn't want to be reasonable, you'll have a judgement call to make about whether you feel you've got enough to arrest him. From what I've heard so far, that would be pushing it. You'll know better what evidence you've got after you've spoken to Dawson and the secretary.'

'Okay.'

'I don't care what the time is when you get up to Manchester. I want to be kept informed, okay?'

Rob nodded and left.

Before Danny even had the chance to look at his notes, there was another knock on the door.

In exasperation, Danny shouted, 'Come in!'

Detective Sergeant Andy Wills walked into the office and said, 'I've just come back from the Magistrates Court. They've granted a warrant under the Police and Criminal Evidence

Act to search Sam Jamieson's home address for evidence of a serious arrestable offence.'

Danny grabbed his jacket from the back of his seat. 'That's great. Let's go.'

64

5.00pm, 16 October 1986
Foxhall Road, Forest Fields, Nottingham

The briefing at the MCIU offices had been short but very detailed.

There had been four other detectives working in the main office when Danny had emerged from his office with Andy Wills.

Ordinarily, the MCIU would have utilised the services of the Special Operations Unit to execute a search warrant. There was no time for that; this needed to be done urgently.

Together with his detective sergeant, Danny had briefed DC Simon Paine, DC Fran Jefferies, DC Phil Baxter and DC Martin Harper on the detail of the premises and what they would be searching for.

Andy Wills had earlier made enquiries with Nottingham Trent University. He had established that Sam Jamieson was working from home today. That meant there was a good chance their suspect would be at the one-bedroomed flat when they executed the warrant.

Danny had made a judgement call that six detectives would be enough to carry out a detailed search of the premises and to successfully detain Jamieson, if necessary.

Now, as he sat with Andy Wills on the street in the CID car and listened to the rain battering onto the roof of the car, he wondered if he was doing the right thing. The rain made him think of the ransom drop and of the debacle that had ensued.

It was now or never.

He reached onto the dashboard of the car and picked up his radio. 'DCI Flint to DC Baxter and DC Harper: Are you in position at the rear of the premises?'

DC Baxter replied, 'Yes, boss. We're in the alleyway directly behind number thirty-four. We can see the target flat. There's a light on inside.'

'Okay. Stand by. I'll give you the word when we're going in.'

Danny then continued: 'DC Paine, DC Jefferies, are you ready?'

DC Paine said, 'Ready. I've got the door opener.'

'Okay. Let's move.'

Danny and Andy got out of the car and walked across the street to the target premises. The research Andy had carried out in order to obtain the search warrant meant that he was aware that the front door of the property was always left unlocked. Once inside that door, there were two ground-floor flats and three more flats upstairs.

Sam Jamieson was renting Flat 3. This flat was on the first floor of the premises, up one flight of stairs. The door was on the right of the landing.

After walking in through the unlocked front door, followed closely by Simon Paine and Fran Jefferies, Danny said, 'Me and Andy will knock on the door first. Hopefully, it will be answered, and we won't need the sledgehammer to get in. I want you two to stay down here until we call you up.'

The two detectives nodded, just glad that they were waiting in the hallway and not standing outside at the rear of the property, getting soaked by the heavy rain.

Danny and Andy walked up the stairs and quickly located the door to Flat 3. There was a light shining from below the door.

Danny pointed to it and whispered, 'Looks like he's home.'

Andy nodded.

Danny knocked loudly on the door with the balled-up fist of his right hand, shouting, 'Police! Open the door!'

65

5.05pm, 16 October 1986
Foxhall Road, Forest Fields, Nottingham

Inside the flat, Sam Jamieson had been sitting on the settee in the lounge, reading a magazine. Hearing the knock and the shout, he instantly looked at the pinboard. It was covered in photographs of Crown Court buildings, various prisons and the interiors of cells. There were two photos that he needed to destroy before allowing the police to enter his flat.

The first was a photograph of the Whitchurch family, including Emily, standing outside Debenhams on Long Row. The second photograph was of Rebecca Whitchurch, in her robes at Crown Court.

Sam had seen the press appeals that had been put out about the missing schoolgirl, so he knew that the photograph of Emily could be incriminating. He also knew that taking photos within the confines of any Crown Court building was illegal. The photograph of Rebecca in her robes had been taken as she emerged from court number one at Nottingham Crown Court.

Both the photographs had been taken without the knowledge of the subjects.

He ripped the two incriminating photos from the pinboard and shouted, 'I'm coming. Just a minute!'

He heard more loud knocking, accompanied by threats from the police outside that unless he opened the door, they would smash it down.

Ignoring the shouts, Sam used his lighter to burn the two photos. He dropped the blackened remains into the sink in the tiny kitchenette. Turned on the tap and flushed the burned scraps down the plughole. There was a slight smell of burning, but it wasn't too bad.

He walked calmly to the front door, shouting, 'I'm coming!'

He pulled back the two deadbolts before unlocking the Yale lock.

As he opened the door, he could see two detectives standing in the hallway. He said, 'What's this all about, Detectives?'

66

5.10pm, 16 October 1986
Foxhall Road, Forest Fields, Nottingham

Danny said, 'Sam Jamieson? We've got a warrant to search these premises.'

'I'm Sam Jamieson, but there must be some mistake. I've never used drugs in my life. Please come inside. I don't want my neighbours to hear all this shit. I haven't been here long. I don't want that lot tittle-tattling to the landlord.'

Andy signalled for Simon and Fran to join them inside the flat; then he spoke into the radio, saying, 'Phil, Martin, we're inside the flat. Come back round to the front and wait inside the main entrance.'

The soaked detectives at the rear of the property said gratefully, 'Received, Sarge. On our way.'

Danny followed Sam into the lounge of the flat and said, 'Is something burning?'

Sam smiled. 'I'm a lousy cook. I put a pizza in the oven a

little while ago and forgot to take off the plastic wrapper. It stunk the flat out. Who are you, and what's this all about? Like I said before, I don't touch drugs. I don't understand why you've got a warrant to search my flat.'

Danny said, 'My name's Detective Chief Inspector Flint. I'm from the Major Crime Investigation Unit. We're not here under a Misuse of Drugs Act warrant. We're making enquiries into the disappearance of Emily Whitchurch, and we have reason to believe that you may be involved. I have a warrant issued by magistrates, under the Police and Criminal Evidence Act, to search for evidence linked to her abduction.'

'That's ridiculous. I know I've spent time in prison, but I'm a reformed character. I'm living here now because I'm studying for a master's degree at university, and it's easier to get to the university every day. I'm done with all that shit from the past. It's exactly that – the past.'

'Have you heard of Emily Whitchurch?'

'Of course I have. I saw the press appeal on the television.'

'So you're aware who her parents are?'

'You know I am. I can see that you've already clocked the pictures on the pinboard, Detective.'

Danny walked over to the board. He could see the two gaps where the photographs had been hastily removed. 'There appears to be a couple of photos missing. Does that account for the smell of burning?'

'I don't know what you're talking about.'

'You're going to need to accompany me to the police station so I can question you fully.'

'Are you arresting me?'

'Do I need to arrest you? If you're the reformed character you say you are, and you've got nothing to hide, surely you'd want to come with us voluntarily and assist with our enquiries. What's it to be?'

'Chief Inspector, you've obviously done your homework

on me, or you wouldn't be here. You must know I don't trust the police.'

'If you attend voluntarily, you'll be afforded the same rights as if you were under arrest. It's the new law.'

Jamieson was thoughtful, weighing up his options. He said, 'I know all about the Police and Criminal Evidence Act, Detective. I do want to help you. This is a young girl we're talking about, after all. I'll come with you voluntarily. There's no need for any handcuffs. I don't mind assisting you with your enquiries, but I'm not going anywhere until you've finished searching my flat. It's that trust issue again. I don't want to hear later that you've suddenly found the Whitchurch girl's clothes here. Can you understand that?'

'Your fears are unfounded, but I can understand them. The search won't take long; then we'll go to Central Police Station and have a conversation.'

'Will you bring me back here afterwards?'

'I'm sure that can be arranged, as and when it becomes necessary.'

'Well, then, just do what you've got to do, and let's get this over with. I thought I'd seen the last of the police.'

67

7.00pm, 16 October 1986
Central Police Station, Nottingham

Danny sat in the CID office at Central Police Station. He and Detective Sergeant Andy Wills were reviewing the items found during the search of Sam Jamieson's small flat.

Danny said, 'Who's sitting with Jamieson?'

Andy replied, 'Simon Paine's with him in the interview room. I've told the other three to get a cuppa and get warmed up in the canteen.'

'Has Jamieson been offered any refreshments while he's waiting?'

'He's been offered a drink but declined. He just wants to know how long this is going to take.'

As Danny looked at the items spread out over the desk in front of him, he said, 'So there's no paperwork for any separate rental premises anywhere, and nothing whatsoever to connect him with Emily Whitchurch?'

'No. This is all we have that's of any interest. We've got the pinboard that's covered in pictures and articles about Rebecca and Dominic Whitchurch, Mulberry Chambers, and the property on Richmond Drive. Street plans of Mapperley Park and the lime green running shoes very like those used by the serial jogger that was mentioned in the Special Operations Unit observation logs for the Whitchurch property.'

'It's not a lot, is it? I'm glad I didn't arrest him on this evidence. Flimsy doesn't really describe it, but it's bloody close.'

'Don't forget the threatening letter he sent to Rebecca Whitchurch at Mulberry Chambers.'

'You mean the letter we don't have and have never gotten sight of?'

Andy nodded. 'Jamieson doesn't know we haven't got the letter.'

'That's very true. We'll leave that until last. I want to see his reaction when we start talking about the threats he made.'

'I know it's not much to go on. Your hand was forced a little because we needed to get in that flat; the girl could have been hidden in there. If nothing else, we can at least finalise this line of enquiry.'

'I'm not criticising you, Andy. It was good work to find the connection in the first place, and even better work to track Jamieson down to an address. Grab all this stuff, and let's go and hear what he's got to say, shall we?'

68

7.00pm, 16 October 1986
Hilton Manchester, Deansgate, Manchester

Rob Buxton and Glen Lorimar approached the reception desk in the luxurious foyer of the Hilton Hotel, in the centre of Manchester. Sebastien Dawson had provided them with details of the reservations, made by Mulberry Chambers, for Freddie Fletcher's stay in the north west city.

The two detectives had waited for the reception area to be empty. Now, there was just the young woman working behind the desk and no guests waiting to be seen. It was the right time to speak to the receptionist.

As they approached, the young woman looked up. She beamed a laser smile in their direction and asked, 'Good evening, gentlemen. How can I help you?'

Rob Buxton produced the small leather wallet that held his warrant card from his jacket pocket. He opened it and discreetly showed it to the receptionist. 'My name's Detective Inspector Rob Buxton from the Nottinghamshire Police. I understand that you have a guest staying with you all this week by the name of Mr Frederick Fletcher. I think the booking was made by Mulberry Chambers in Nottingham. It's very important that we speak privately with Mr Fletcher immediately.'

The smile dropped instantly from the face of the young woman, and her brow frowned with concern. 'Oh, I hope it isn't bad news. Mr Fletcher's such a bubbly, fun person. Just a minute, please.'

The receptionist flicked through one of the books on the huge walnut surface of the desk. Eventually, she stopped and quickly ran her manicured fingernail down the page.

When the finger stopped, she exclaimed, 'Here he is. Mr Fletcher booked his evening meal for six thirty tonight in our award-winning Leander's Restaurant. He'll be eating in there right now.'

'I'm sorry. I know it's an imposition, but this is very important. Would it be possible for you to let Mr Fletcher know we're here and that we need to speak to him as a matter of urgency? Thank you.'

She nodded and reached for the telephone on the desk. Before she could dial, Rob said, 'I'm sorry. Is there somewhere we could talk privately with Mr Fletcher?'

'Yes, of course. The conference room across the foyer isn't being used. I'll contact the maître d' at the restaurant and then unlock the conference room for you.'

Rob smiled. 'That's great. Thanks for all your help.'

After making the call, the receptionist walked with the two detectives across the spacious foyer to the conference room. She unlocked the door and stepped inside. After flicking on the lights, she said, 'Can I get you any refreshments? Perhaps a tea or coffee?'

Rob replied, 'No, thanks. This room is great. Thank you.'

She smiled the same laser-beam smile, all white teeth and red lipstick. 'Okay, gentlemen. If you need anything else, I'll be at the desk.'

'Thank you; you've been very helpful.'

The conference room was quite small. It had one large table down the centre of the room. The table was made from a very light oak. It was surrounded by fourteen blue leather office chairs. In front of each chair there was a blue, leather-bound blotter and individual water carafes and glasses.

Glen Lorimar looked around the room and let out a low whistle. 'Very nice. We need one of these for our briefing room.'

Before Rob could respond, there was a tap on the door. It was immediately opened by the receptionist, who stepped inside, followed by the slim, blonde-haired Freddie Fletcher. The receptionist announced, 'Mr Fletcher, these are the two gentlemen from the police.'

Rob said, 'Thank you, miss.'

The receptionist understood Rob's tone and immediately left the room, closing the door behind her.

Fletcher said, 'Firstly, I'll need to see some identification. Secondly, what the hell is this all about?'

There was clearly a note of irritation in the young barrister's voice. Not quite anger, but getting close.

The two detectives showed Fletcher their individual warrant cards, which he inspected closely.

Rob said, 'Shall we sit down?'

Fletcher pulled out the nearest chair and sat. 'Is this going to take long, Detectives? I was literally about to start my main course. A beautiful rack of lamb.'

Rob and Glen sat down opposite Fletcher.

Rob said, 'I apologise for the inconvenience, Mr Fletcher, but this needed to be cleared up tonight.'

'Please call me Freddie. You still haven't told me what is so bloody urgent that you've driven up here from Nottingham to see me tonight.'

Rob said, 'We're investigating the disappearance of Emily Whitchurch. Your colleague's daughter.'

'I see. What has that got to do with me, exactly?'

'How do you get on with Rebecca Whitchurch?'

'Like every other young barrister at Mulberry Chambers, I don't get on with her at all. Rebecca Whitchurch is one of the most arrogant, condescending cows ever to walk this earth. You described us as "colleagues", but nothing could be further from the truth. Every barrister is a rival. Don't be fooled by all this "my learned friend" bollocks you hear in court; that's just tradition. Basically, we're all mercenaries. Our futures rely on the quality of briefs we're given. Without good-quality briefs, a career will soon flounder, as you have no way of building a reputation. The problem with Mulberry Chambers is that Dominic and Rebecca Whitchurch cherry-pick the best briefs all the time. I'm afraid it's notorious for it. Our clerk, Sebastien Dawson, sees to it that they're always given first refusal on all quality briefs.'

'So how come you're here leading the defence for this trial?'

'Oh, come on, Inspector; don't play games. You're probably already well aware that I was only asked to lead this trial because Rebecca cried off.'

'And the reason she cried off?'

'Because her precious daughter is missing. Again, this is information you already know.'

'It's obvious there's no love lost between you and Mrs Whitchurch?'

'And as I've just told you, that doesn't make me unique. If you're asking me did I have any involvement in the disappearance of her child? Of course I didn't. What do you take me for?'

The young barrister then switched into inquisitor mode. 'Exactly why have you come to see me? What have you been told? And by whom?'

Before Rob could speak, Fletcher exclaimed, 'Fliss! This has got to have come from young Felicity, hasn't it?'

Rob said, 'What makes you say that?'

'I took her out to celebrate getting this trial. Spent a bloody fortune on champagne, trying to get in her knickers, and failed miserably. I can remember, after the second or third bottle of bubbly, I proposed some ridiculous toast about the missing Whitchurch girl.'

'Why would you do that?'

'Because I was pissed and showing off. It was crass and in very poor taste, but that's all it was. I could never harm a child.'

'What were you doing on the evening of the second of October? Exactly two weeks ago tonight?'

'That's easy. I was playing cards. I'm a member of the Nottingham Bridge Club. We meet every Thursday evening at a different player's house. It's something I got into at Cambridge. I never miss a session unless, like tonight, I'm away on business. Two weeks ago, the meeting was at Virginia Drew's house. Generally, we all arrive at four o'clock for prematch drinks. The first hand is dealt at five. We play until eight o'clock. I do recall that I arrived early that afternoon, at three o'clock. Ms Drew lives alone, and she'd asked me to help her set all the tables and chairs up.'

'How many players were there?'

'Three tables, so a dozen.'

'Do you have their names?'

'There were a couple of new faces that night. I'm sure Ms Drew will still have the list.'

Glen asked, 'Where does Virginia Drew live?'

'She has the most stunning house at Fiskerton. It's right next to the river and is absolutely beautiful in the summer.'

He chuckled and said, 'She's seventy-five next year, bless her. I'm seriously thinking of proposing marriage just so I can get my grubby little paws on her wonderful house when she pops her clogs! Will that be all, gentlemen? That delicious rack of lamb will be getting cold.'

Rob looked at Glen, who shook his head; he had nothing else to ask Fletcher.

Rob said, 'Note down Virginia's full name and address so we can check out your story, please, Mr Fletcher. Then that will be all, and thank you for your cooperation this evening.'

Fletcher tore a piece of paper from one of the blotters. He took a pen from his jacket pocket and scribbled down the name and address of Virginia Drew.

He stood up, handed the scrap of paper to Rob and said, 'Seriously, gentlemen, I hope you find the girl soon. Good night.'

Fletcher closed the door behind him, leaving the two detectives sitting in the conference room.

Rob said, 'What do you think?'

'I think this will all check out. He's just one of those people who has no filter. Did you hear the comment about marrying the old lady to get her house? He thinks he's being hilarious, but he just comes over as being a charmless twat.'

'Succinctly summarised as always, mate.'

Glen just shrugged.

Rob said, 'We'll drive back tonight and check out his alibi tomorrow. I don't think this enquiry is taking us anywhere.'

Glen nodded. 'Looks that way.'

As the two detectives left the conference room, Rob said, 'I'll just find a phone and let the boss know that this is probably another dead end.'

69

7.30pm, 16 October 1986
Central Police Station, Nottingham

Danny Flint and Andy Wills walked into the small interview room.

Andy placed the items recovered from the search of the flat on the floor. Danny turned to DC Paine and said, 'Go and grab a cuppa, Simon.'

Simon Paine left the room. Danny and Andy sat down opposite Sam Jamieson.

The only furniture in the small room was a desk and four chairs.

The room was lit by a single fluorescent strip light that was housed behind a wire grille on the ceiling. There was a red plastic strip on the wall around the entire room that was an alarm. If it were pressed by the interviewing officers, other police would rush to render assistance.

Sam Jamieson looked calm and at ease with the situation.

He was sitting back on his chair, his arms folded loosely across his chest. He had glanced at the items carried into the room, but his face registered no emotion about them.

Danny leaned forward on his chair and rested his elbows on the desk. 'Thanks for being patient, Mr Jamieson. Would you like a drink of water or a cup of tea?'

'I'm fine. I just want to crack on so I can go home. I want to help you, but I don't want to be here all night, either.'

'Before we talk, I have to tell you that you're not under arrest and that you're technically free to leave whenever you wish. If at any time you feel you want legal representation while we ask you questions, tell me, and a solicitor will be provided for you. Are you happy for us to continue?'

'I understand the new provisions of the Police and Criminal Evidence legislation. The Codes of Practice under that Act was just one of the many books I studied during my degree course. Yes, I'm happy. So, let's get on, shall we?'

'I want to go back to the beginning. Tell me why you were sent to prison for seven years.'

'I was wrongly accused and wrongly convicted of being the getaway driver during an armed robbery of a post office at Mansfield Woodhouse. This is all well documented.'

'I've read the court file. I just wanted to hear your version.'

'It's funny how nobody was interested in my version back then, Chief Inspector. If they had been, there's every likelihood we wouldn't be sitting here having this conversation.'

'Why do you say that?'

'If you've read the court file, you already know the answer to that question. I was a convenience, a patsy, a stooge, whatever you want to call it. I'd driven that bloody car the evening before the robbery. I was nowhere near the post office when the robbery took place. I was at home with my sick daughter.'

Andy said, 'Could anybody corroborate that?'

'No, my wife was out all day. My daughter had a high temperature and was delirious with a fever.'

'What about the forensic evidence that linked you to the robbery?'

'Sergeant, your question is flawed. The forensic evidence was a single thumbprint found on the rear-view mirror of the car. It linked me to the car, not the robbery. None of the eyewitnesses at the robbery identified me.'

'There were two other men on trial for the robbery, one of them your own cousin. Why didn't they speak up for you? Especially your own cousin?'

'I can't speak for our Dave. I don't know why he didn't say anything. The last time I spoke to him was to ask if I could use his car the night before the robbery. I still can't believe that my own cousin let me go to prison, knowing I wasn't involved.'

Danny said, 'So you still maintain your innocence?'

'Yes. And there's a simple reason for that, Chief Inspector. I was innocent then, so consequently, I'm still innocent now. Being sent down and incarcerated within those bloody walls cost me everything I ever held dear.'

'I take it you're referring to your daughter?'

A flash of anger passed momentarily across Jamieson's eyes. 'Don't beat around the bush, Detective. What you mean is the death of my daughter.'

Danny spoke softly. 'How did that tragedy happen?'

'I never speak about this, and I don't want to now. Move on, or I'm out of here.'

Danny said, 'I can't imagine the pain of losing a child. I'm genuinely sorry for your loss. Without going into the details of what happened to your daughter, what I need to know is, how did it affect you personally?'

Sam Jamieson leaned forward and stared at the surface of the desk. Without making eye contact, he said quietly, 'I was crushed. Broken. I felt like I'd been snapped in half, like a dry twig. On the day I was told the news, I could barely breathe. I couldn't move from my bunk. It was as though a heavy weight was crushing down on my chest.'

'What stopped that intensity of pain?'

'I had to be strong for the funeral. The prison chaplain visited me every day and helped me through the blackest of days.'

'And after the funeral, how were you then?'

'Raging.'

'Explain what you mean, Sam. How did that rage manifest itself?'

Hearing Danny refer to him by his Christian name, Sam Jamieson looked up from the desk and made eye contact with Danny. He stared into his eyes for a full minute, the silence gradually enveloping the room, causing an oppressive atmosphere.

Danny held his gaze.

Finally, Jamieson said, 'Honest answer, I wanted to kill somebody. Anybody. I didn't care who. Anybody who crossed me, be it screw or con, I would lash out and cause as much damage and pain as I could.'

'How long did that rage and anger last?'

'Six long months.'

'Then what happened?'

'I suddenly realised that I could either spend my life raging against the system or use it to my advantage. I know it's a cliché, but I had reached a crossroads. One road would lead me to a painful destruction; the other to a brighter future. I used education to ease my pain. I achieved a degree; I'm now doing my master's, and I'll easily find work when I qualify. I've moved on. Well, if you bastards ever let me, I'll have moved on.'

Danny picked up the pinboard from the floor. 'Tell me

about this. Why the obsession over Mulberry Chambers and Rebecca Whitchurch?'

'I'm writing a thesis on wrongful convictions. Specifically, what the driving forces are within the legal system that make them possible.'

'Why Mulberry?'

'It's a Nottingham-based law firm, and I'm studying at Nottingham Trent University.'

'Rebecca Whitchurch?'

'She's the main subject of my thesis. I'm writing from my own experiences. I was railroaded into a long custodial sentence by a barrister using the legal system for her own advancement and not for justice.'

'Is that what you think Rebecca Whitchurch did?'

'It's what I know she did.'

'And her actions cost you everything?'

'Yes.'

'Including the life of your only child.'

Jamieson's eyes betrayed that flash of anger again. 'Yes!'

'Do you blame Rebecca Whitchurch for the death of your daughter?'

There was a long silence.

Jamieson was struggling to both control his temper and find the right response.

His eyes narrowed. He hissed, 'That woman was responsible for sending an innocent man to prison. By doing that, she ensured that man wasn't there to safeguard his only child when he needed to be. Do I blame her? Yes, I do.'

'Is it hatred, Sam?'

'Yes, I suppose it is.'

'Do you want revenge for your daughter?'

'Revenge is a strange word to use, Detective. How about justice?'

'Have you ever threatened Rebecca Whitchurch?'

Danny saw the slight change of expression on Sam Jamieson's face, and he knew he had struck a chord.

He could see Jamieson was thinking carefully. His answer when it came was obviously considered. He said quietly, 'My feelings towards Rebecca Whitchurch have changed over time. When my daughter died, I wasn't thinking straight or behaving rationally. My prison record at that time illustrates this. I was in a very dark place. I lashed out verbally as well as physically.'

'Did you ever threaten to physically harm Rebecca Whitchurch?'

'I wrote to her at Mulberry Chambers, I remember that. I can't remember making any specific threats.'

A silence filled the interview room.

70

7.35pm, 16 October 1986
Central Police Station, Nottingham

Sam knew the letter had contained some very explicit references to the physical violence he wanted to mete out to Rebecca Whitchurch. He waited for the next question, knowing those specific threats would now be raised.

The detective asked, 'Why did you write to Whitchurch at all?'

Sam was shocked at the ambiguous, weak question. He quickly realised that the only reason the detective hadn't gone into detail was because he hadn't seen the content of the letter. In fact, where *was* the letter? Why wasn't the detective proudly waving it around to prove his theory?

He asked, 'If you can show me the letter, I'm sure it will jog my memory. It'll help me understand what I was thinking at the time.'

'I don't have the letter with me.'

Sam thought to himself, *You haven't got it at all, have you?*

Feeling more confident, he decided to test the detective. He said, 'I don't recall there being anything in the letter that was specifically aimed at Rebecca Whitchurch. I was just ranting about barristers in general. It was all part of my behavioural problems back then. I don't feel anything like that now. I'm using my personal experiences to get on in life, that's all.'

Having said his piece, he sat back. He would soon know if the detectives had the letter or not.

After a pause, the frustrated detective picked up the fluorescent green training shoes. 'I take it these are yours?'

Sam allowed a small smile to form on his lips; he now knew for certain that they didn't have the letter.

'Yes, they're mine.'

'Are you a keen runner?'

'I run whenever I can. After being locked up in a cell for seven years, I find the freedom running brings both exhilarating and therapeutic.'

'Where do you run?'

'I generally run through Mapperley Park. It's quiet, not too much traffic, and I like the hills.'

'Do you run in Mapperley Park because you know that's where Rebecca Whitchurch lives?'

Sam remembered he had pictures of the Whitchurch house on the pinboard. He could see where the detective's questions were leading. He said, 'I knew she had a house up there, but that's not the reason I run there.'

'Where were you on the afternoon of October the second?'

'I would have been travelling home from the university.'

'What time did you leave?'

'My last lecture finished at three thirty in the afternoon. It was raining heavily, so I would have got home about three-quarters of an hour later, at four fifteen, give or take five minutes.'

'Can anyone verify what time you got home?'

'No. I didn't see any of the other tenants when I got home.'

'What transport do you have?'

'I've got a Suzuki 125cc motorcycle at the moment. It's all I can afford. It's rained every day since I bought it. I hate the bloody thing.'

'Can you drive a car?'

'Yes, I can drive.'

'Do you have access to a car?'

'No, or I wouldn't have been getting soaked every day. Are we nearly done?'

'Are you in any way involved in the disappearance of Emily Whitchurch?'

'Of course I'm not. Whatever I feel about Rebecca Whitchurch, I would never harm a child. After what happened to my own little girl, could you ever see me harming a child?'

The detective sergeant said, 'Even the child of the person who, in your mind, is responsible for the death of your own?'

Sam almost spat his reply. 'I'm sorry, Sergeant. I'm not even going to dignify that question with an answer. It's a disgusting suggestion. What I will say is this: Maybe you should be looking closer to home for this girl.'

The sergeant sat back, allowing the other detective to take over. 'Go on.'

'Look, as you know, I'm a keen runner. I run whenever I get the chance, day or night.'

The detective leaned back in his chair and allowed the silence to urge him to say more.

Sam knew what the detective was doing, but continued

anyway. 'The other night, I was running through Mapperley Park near to where the Whitchurches live. It was quite late, and the roads were empty. Anyway, I saw a car pull up on Richmond Drive. There were two people in the car, a man and a woman. As soon as the car stopped, they began kissing. Proper snogging, not just a peck on the cheek.'

The sergeant interrupted again. 'So now you're a peeping Tom?'

Sam retorted angrily, 'Do you want to hear this or not?'

The other detective said calmly, 'What's so special about a couple kissing in a car?'

'The man in the passenger seat was Dominic Whitchurch, and the woman driving the car was definitely not his wife.'

'What sort of car was it?'

'It was a dark-coloured Volvo. I did make a mental note of the number plate, but I'd forgotten it by the time I got home. It was quite a new model, though. So, you see, Detective. Everything isn't perfect in the Whitchurch house.'

The detective was thoughtful for a minute; then he said, 'Thanks for your cooperation today, Sam. I'll arrange a ride home for you. We may need to speak to you again soon, so don't go anywhere.'

Sam said, 'I'm halfway through my master's; I'm not going anywhere.'

'One last thing, Sam. I truly am very sorry for your loss.'

'Me too, Chief Inspector. Me too.'

71

8.00am, 17 October 1986
MCIU Offices, Mansfield, Nottinghamshire

Danny walked into the MCIU offices and was pleased to see both his detective inspectors already there. They were drinking coffee and holding an animated conversation with Andy Wills, Glen Lorimar and Rachel Moore. They were robustly discussing various aspects of their enquiries.

Danny grabbed a coffee himself, then sat down in the main office with his staff.

He turned to Rob Buxton and said, 'I know you told me last night it was a dead end, but how exactly did the Fletcher enquiry pan out?'

Rob put his coffee down. 'I went with Glen to Mulberry Chambers and obtained statements from Sebastien Dawson and Felicity Spencer. We found out from Dawson which hotel Fletcher is staying in while he's working the case at

Manchester Crown Court. We drove up there and spoke to Fletcher at his hotel in the evening. He was extremely cooperative. He has given us a strong alibi for the afternoon and evening of the second of October, the day Emily Whitchurch went missing. We intend driving over to Fiskerton this morning to check his alibi and make sure it's legit. He admitted making the comments about the Whitchurch girl to the secretary. He said he was pissed and just trying to impress her. He admitted it was crass and a stupid thing to do. He definitely doesn't like Rebecca Whitchurch, though. He told us that there's blatant favouritism shown to Rebecca and Dominic when it comes to allocation of briefs. From what he was telling us last night, it seems that the Whitchurches are despised by most of the other barristers working at Mulberry Chambers.'

Rob glanced at Glen Lorimar and continued. 'We spoke at length about Fletcher and what he'd said on the drive back from Manchester. We were of the same opinion, and that hasn't changed after sleeping on it. As I said last night, we both think it's another dead-end, boss.'

'Okay, Rob. Good work tracking him down so quickly. I still want his alibi checked out this morning, though.'

'We're on it.'

'While you're all here, Andy and I can tell you how we got on with Sam Jamieson yesterday. I made the decision not to arrest him. He came to the nick with us voluntarily and cooperated fully, answering all questions. He spoke openly about how he still thinks he was stitched up by Rebecca Whitchurch when he was convicted of the robbery offence. It's plain to see that he loathes the woman, and that despite what he told us last night, he still blames her for his daughter's death. He's an intelligent man and was very switched on during the interview. He very quickly picked up on the fact that we didn't have the threatening letter that he'd written to Whitchurch from the Armley jail. He's definitely no stranger to police procedures and tactics. He was very careful how he chose the words of his responses to our questions.'

Andy said, 'I totally agree. It was obvious he knew we hadn't seen the content of that letter for ourselves. He was almost grinning. His reaction makes me think that there would have been a lot of incriminating stuff in that letter.'

Danny said, 'I agree with that assessment. Anyway, we haven't got the evidence to connect Jamieson in any way to Emily Whitchurch's disappearance. I still think he's one to watch. We shouldn't rule him out completely. He needs to remain on our radar.'

Rob said, 'Didn't you find anything from the search of the flat?'

Danny replied, 'Nothing of any note. There was a lot of stuff in there about Rebecca Whitchurch. The problem is, he's currently working on a thesis about her, so he could easily explain that away. The only positive thing that came out of the interview was something he told us about Dominic Whitchurch. He claims to have seen Dominic locked in a passionate embrace with a woman in a dark-coloured Volvo while it was parked up just down the road from the Whitchurch house in Mapperley Park. According to him, that woman was definitely not Rebecca Whitchurch. Andy, I need you to follow that up today.'

Andy said, 'I'm putting a call into the Special Operations Unit this morning. I want them to check all the observation logs they have from Richmond Drive. Hopefully, if what Jamieson is telling us is true, they will have seen this Volvo. I'm also hopeful they'll have a full registration number for the vehicle. So we should be able to locate this mystery woman pretty quickly.'

Danny said, 'Keep me posted.'

He then turned to Brian. 'Have you made any inroads on that other enquiry we spoke about?'

Brian said, 'I'm going with Rachel to Nottingham Trent University this morning. We've got an appointment with the professor who's currently mapping the cave systems beneath Nottingham. I'm hoping he's already completed the area around Forest Road East.'

'That's good. Again, keep me posted, please. I'll be interested to hear what he's got to say. I'm having an admin day today. I've got a stack of paperwork to catch up on, so I'll speak to you when you get back from your enquiries.'

72

11.00am, 17 October 1986
Nottingham Trent University, Goldsmith Street,
Nottingham

There was nowhere to park outside the Newton Building on Goldsmith Street. Brian and Rachel left the CID car in the rear car park at Central Police Station and made the short walk to Goldsmith Street.

Brian had brought an old golf umbrella with him, and the two detectives huddled together beneath it, trying to shield themselves from the heavy rain that continued to fall.

As they walked, they discussed what they hoped to get from the meeting with the professor.

Rachel said, 'Did Professor Temple say much on the telephone yesterday?'

'Only that he was an extremely busy man, and that the only window he had was for this morning at eleven o'clock.'

'What did he sound like?'

'Honestly? He sounded arrogant and a little too full of his own self-importance for my liking. He's a world-renowned expert on caves and all things subterranean, so I suppose he should feel important.'

Brian winked at Rachel, and she laughed. 'What are you like, boss?'

Brian grinned and said, 'Seriously, I always knew there were caves beneath this city, but I've got no idea where they are, what they're like, how big they are. I just want to find out everything I can this morning, and see if my theory is feasible, that's all.'

'Your theory being that Emily wasn't snatched and taken away; she was just hidden from view? That she's still somewhere in the area where she went missing?'

'Do you think I'm mad, Rachel? I can take the truth.'

Rachel laughed. 'I think you're barking at the moon, boss.'

She paused, stopped smiling and said, 'Of course not. I think we'll both know more in about an hour. That's the Newton Building over there.'

The two detectives walked into the white stone monolith that was the Newton Building. It towered above the surrounding buildings, an enduring testament to the art deco style so popular in the mid-1950s.

Brian approached the main reception area and spoke to the elderly woman behind the desk. 'My name's Hopkirk. I've an appointment with Professor Temple at eleven o'clock.'

The receptionist smiled and glanced at the huge notepad in front of her. 'Ah, yes. Here you are.' She indicated an area of seating near the entrance doors and said, 'Take a seat over there, please. His assistant will be down to collect you presently.'

Brian smiled and said, 'Thank you.'

As they walked across the foyer to the seats, Brian said, 'I think I'll introduce you as my assistant. It's only fair, if the professor's got one.'

Rachel chuckled and said, 'You bloody well needn't bother.'

They were both still laughing as they sat down.

A few minutes passed by, then the brushed stainless-steel lift doors on the other side of the foyer opened, and a young woman stepped out. She was dressed in baggy blue denim jeans and an old navy-blue sweatshirt with the words Oxford University Rowing Club on the front. Although the clothes were loose-fitting, it was obvious that beneath the baggy clothes, the woman was actually lean and quite tall. She had short, spiky, dark brown hair and large brown eyes. She wore no make-up and looked rosy cheeked, as though she had just scrubbed her face.

The woman spoke to the receptionist, who pointed across to the two detectives. The woman walked over, smiling as she got closer. It was a generous smile that was genuine and warm.

Brian and Rachel stood as the woman approached.

She held out her hand towards Brian and said, 'Good morning. You must be Detective Inspector Hopkirk. My name's Stacey Bloom. I'm Professor Temple's assistant; pleased to meet you.'

As they shook hands, Stacey Bloom glanced at Rachel. Brian said, 'Ms Bloom, this is my colleague Detective Constable Rachel Moore.'

Stacey shook hands with Rachel and said, 'Pleased to meet you.'

Introductions completed, Stacey said, 'Follow me, please. The professor's waiting in his office.'

They walked back over to the lifts, and Stacey pressed the button for the fourth floor.

As the lift ascended, she said, 'I'm really sorry, but

Professor Temple has another appointment he can't put off this morning. So you've only got fifteen minutes with him. If that isn't long enough, hopefully I'll be able to fill in any gaps. I'm sorry, but he's a very busy man.'

Brian looked at Rachel before saying, 'That's fine. As you say, I'm sure you'll be more than capable of answering any questions we may have. We appreciate Professor Temple taking the time to see us at all.'

Standing immediately behind Stacey Bloom, Rachel mouthed the word *creep* towards Brian, who stifled the urge to grin.

Stepping out of the lift, Stacey walked down a long corridor, followed by the two detectives. When they were almost at the end, she knocked on a door.

The door was opened from inside by Professor Brandon Temple. There was no smile or courteous greeting this time. It was just a very curt, 'Come in.'

Brian and Rachel walked in and sat in the chairs offered.

Brandon Temple said, 'Detective Inspector, how can I help you?'

Brian said, 'Thank you for taking the time to see us today. I appreciate you're a very busy man, so I'll get straight to it. I'm interested in the cave systems around the Mansfield Road, Forest Road East area of the city. I want to know the extent of the cave systems and where the entrances are.'

Brandon Temple stared at the detective and said one word, 'Why?'

Brian was a little taken aback. He said, 'Excuse me?'

'Why? Why do you want to know this?'

His composure recovered, Brian said, 'I'm sorry, Professor Temple; I didn't explain on the telephone yesterday. We're currently investigating the disappearance of a young girl. I have a theory that she may have been abducted and hidden in the caves. She disappeared on her way home from the

Nottingham High School for Girls, on the second of October. That's why.'

'I see.'

The professor was deep in thought for a couple of minutes. Then he turned to his assistant and said, 'Stacey, can you grab a copy of the survey map? It will make it easier for me to show the inspector.'

Stacey said, 'Of course.'

She went to a wall unit, opened a large drawer and took out an A2 size sheet of paper. On the paper was a diagram that showed the cave system beneath the city. Street names had been superimposed to show the locations of the caves. Large swathes of the map were coloured red.

Professor Temple placed the map on his desk. 'Inspector Hopkirk, come and have a look. It will make things simpler. You'll be able to see where the caves are located.'

Brian and Rachel both stood next to Temple as he looked down at the map.

He placed his index finger on the chart. 'This is Mansfield Road at its junction with Forest Road East. You can see there's a vast cave network that runs from Mansfield Road towards Peel Street, beneath the length of North Sherwood Street. This cave system is what remains of Rouse's Sand Mine. It's vast. What you can see on the map is just what we've managed to explore and document so far. There's a school of thought that suggests these mine workings extend all the way up to Forest Road East and beyond, into the cemetery. The catacomb caves are well known within the cemetery. It's believed that these workings also extend beyond Forest Road East, back towards the city. Where, eventually, they would join up with the Rouse Sand Mine system.'

Brian said, 'I see. I had no idea they were so vast.'

'Not many people do. We walk these streets every day, and nobody really knows what lies a few metres below their feet.'

'What about entrances to the caves? How do people get access?'

'There are known entrances into Rouse's Sand Mine on Peel Street and Mansfield Road. The problem is, there are likely to be many other entrances. You see, although Rouse instigated the main development in this area, historians believe that many people excavated the sand from this area. A myriad of private enterprise mines, creating a veritable honeycomb of old mine workings, if you will.'

'I know this sounds a silly question, but what were they mining for?'

'It's not a silly question at all, Detective. Some parts of the caves underneath Nottingham were mined for the sandstone itself. It would be quarried in building-block size. Around the Mansfield Road area that I've pointed out to you, the sandstone is much more friable. It's far too fragile to be mined like that, but it was perfect for sand. They mined for sand.'

'Wasn't that dangerous?'

'Extremely dangerous. The old miners used a technique known as "pillar and stall".'

'What's that?'

'The miners would excavate the sand, leaving rounded pillars to support the cave ceiling. These were shaped like a huge egg timer. The pillars supported the roof, while everything else was excavated around them. The friable sandstone was then removed as sand. Although a dangerous enterprise, it was very profitable. The sand was very clean and used by the numerous glass makers in the city.'

'So, if I've got this right, although these workings are only marked on the map this far, you believe they could extend much further. All the way up to Forest Road East?'

'That's correct. It's a labyrinth down there. Hundreds of caves we haven't fully discovered yet.'

Rachel asked, 'Why are these areas you've shown us all marked in red?'

'Red for danger, Detective. Shall we say the caves in this area are notoriously delicate. Time and erosion have damaged some of the pillar and stall caves. This entire area is now extremely prone to roof falls and cave-ins. That's one of the reasons our survey hasn't progressed as far as I was hoping. It's extremely dangerous down there.'

Brian asked, 'What if I wanted to search the caves in that area?'

Temple looked horrified. 'That's totally out of the question!'

'Why?'

'Detective Inspector, I need you to understand how dangerous it is in those caves. We only ever work in pairs because the slightest noise or vibration can cause a roof fall. We know exactly what we're doing down there, and we haven't been into the cave system for almost a month now. Due to the torrential rain we've experienced over the last few weeks, it's just far too risky. As I've already said, the sandstone in that area is extremely friable, and water affects it very badly. The wetter the sandstone gets, the more unpredictable and fragile it becomes. A search party in those caves, at this time, would be a suicide mission. It's utterly preposterous and out of the question. People would be killed. It's as simple as that.'

Brandon Temple glanced at his watch. 'I'm very sorry, Inspector Hopkirk, but I need to leave for my next appointment. I'm meeting members of Bassetlaw Council at Creswell Crags. I hope this meeting has been useful. If you don't mind, I'll leave you in the very capable hands of Stacey. Stay out of those caves, Detective!'

Temple grabbed his coat and hurried out of the room, as

though his life depended on making that next appointment on time.

When he had left, Brian smiled at Stacey Bloom and said, 'Is he always in that much of a hurry?'

'Not really. He's usually quite laid-back about things.'

'Must be a very important meeting he's going to?'

Stacey shrugged. 'I don't know. He just said he had another appointment when he came in this morning.'

Brian said, 'He seemed pretty adamant that I shouldn't put men into the caves.'

Stacey said, 'He's right about that. The caves are very dangerous, especially with the amount of rain we've had lately. It can be extremely disorienting down there. I've been down in the caves dozens of times, and I still get lost. I can't tell you how frightening it is to be down there and not be sure of where you are. Or more importantly, how you get out.'

Rachel shuddered and said, 'The professor mentioned the possibility of other entrances. Where are they likely to be?'

'They literally could be anywhere. There was one found six months ago, by a young couple who had bought a house in The Park. When they explored the garden of their new home, they found an entrance into the cave system. New entrances are being found all the time.'

Brian said, 'Is there anything else you can tell us?'

'The only thing that hasn't been mentioned is the different types of cave in that area. The professor told you about the pillar and stall caves, but there are also long tunnels dotted with "pot" caves. These were used as storage by the miners. The pot caves are generally very small and round. They were excavated below the level of the main tunnels; some of the bigger ones even have steps down into them. Rouse's Sand Mine is actually on two levels, as well. As Professor Temple said, it really is a labyrinth down there, and most of it is still unexplored. Which is a very exciting prospect for me.'

Rachel said, 'And an absolutely terrifying one for me. I prefer to see the sky above my head.'

Stacey laughed. 'Each to their own, I suppose. Let me give you my card. Then, if you need anything else, you can contact me direct. I've generally got more free time than the professor.'

Rachel took the card and said, 'Thanks, Stacey.'

'If that's everything, Detectives, I'll show you out.'

After exiting the Newton Building, the two detectives walked back to Central Police Station in silence.

The heavy rain was still falling.

Brian broke the silence. 'What do you think of my theory now?'

Rachel replied, 'It's possible, I suppose. I hope to God you're wrong, though.'

'How come?'

'If that young girl's being held somewhere down in those caves, she must be absolutely terrified. The thought of her being down there in the darkness, all alone for two weeks, is horrifying.'

Brian remained tight-lipped and silent.

When they got back to the car and got in, Brian said, 'I know it's a red area on the map, and I get that it's dangerous ... but did Professor Temple seem a little *too* keen to keep us out of his precious bloody caves?'

'I know what you mean. He left the room like his clothes were on fire, as well. He's a strange one, alright. Stacey was great, though.'

'Yeah, she was,' Brian said. Then, 'As soon as it's stopped raining for a day or two, I'm getting in those caves. Whatever the bloody professor says.'

73

11.00am, 17 October 1986
Fiskerton, Nottinghamshire

The house on the banks of the River Trent was stunning.

Rob Buxton and Glen Lorimar had left their car outside the Bromley Arms public house in the village of Fiskerton. They had then walked along the path at the side of the river until they came to the house owned by Virginia Drew.

The house was built entirely of sandstone. The heavy rain had given the stone a mustard-coloured sheen. The dark grey slate roof contrasted beautifully with the orange hue of the walls. The house sat in a large, mature garden, clearly well cared for, with manicured lawns and colourful trees and shrubs.

As they approached the house along the riverside path,

Glen let out a low whistle and said, 'Bloody hell, this place is beautiful. I think I'll ask Virginia Drew to marry me, too.'

Rob nodded. 'Can you imagine what it's like in the summer? The weather's awful today, and it still looks gorgeous. Let's go talk to Mrs Drew and get out of this bloody rain.'

Having knocked on the front door, the two detectives waited under the overhanging porch. Eventually, there was a voice from inside: 'Just a minute. I'm coming.'

The heavy wooden door was slowly opened, and a diminutive, elderly lady stood in the doorway. She was dressed impeccably in a dark green tweed suit; her hair was grey and tied back in a tight bun. She wore wire-rimmed spectacles that magnified her bright blue eyes.

She said, 'Can I help you, gentlemen?'

Rob took out his warrant card, showed it to the woman and said, 'My name's Detective Inspector Rob Buxton. I'm from the Major Crime Unit. I was hoping to speak to Mrs Virginia Drew.'

'It's Ms Drew, and you're speaking to her. What does a detective inspector want to speak to me about?'

'I'd like a quick chat about a friend of yours, Frederick Fletcher.'

'Oh, young Freddie. You'd better come inside out of the rain. Can I get you both a drink? Perhaps a tea or coffee?'

'No, thank you, Ms Drew. I don't think this will take long at all. It's just a few questions.'

Virginia Drew directed the detectives into a sitting room that overlooked the river. She said, 'Please take a seat. Is Freddie in any trouble?'

Ignoring the question, Rob said, 'How well do you know Mr Fletcher?'

Sharp as a tack, the elderly Ms Drew said, 'Inspector, you

didn't answer my question. Now, is young Freddie in any trouble or not?'

'My apologies. The answer to your question is that we don't think he is. Hopefully, you'll be able to confirm that for us.'

'Very well. What do you want to know?'

'When we spoke to Mr Fletcher, he told us about the Nottingham Bridge Club. I understand that you're both members?'

'Yes, that's right, we are. Forgive me, Inspector, but the last time I checked, playing cards in one's own home wasn't illegal.'

Rob smiled, 'And it still isn't, Ms Drew. I'm particularly interested in the evening you hosted the club here. I believe it was on October 2?'

'That's correct. That's the last time I hosted.'

'How many people were here for that meeting?'

'It was a particularly good turnout that evening. There were twelve players here.'

'Was Mr Fletcher one of them?'

'Yes, he was. I've got to tell you, I was a little miffed with young Freddie that evening.'

'Why was that?'

'I'd asked him to come over early, to help me set the tables up. I live here on my own, and although I have a cleaner and a gardener who come in and help, neither of them were available for that week. So I asked Freddie to help me.'

'Was there a problem?'

'Yes, Inspector, there was. The first hand of the first rubber is always dealt at precisely five o'clock. Freddie didn't arrive here until four thirty. He came bursting into the house, full of apologies for being late. He was waffling on that something or other had come up.'

'Was he too late, or did he manage to get the tables set up before five?'

'Yes, he did. But that's not the point, is it? He should have arrived at three o'clock, as promised.'

'Did he tell you why he was so late?'

'No. He just fobbed me off with some story that he'd been forced to deal with something in the city first.'

'And he didn't say what, exactly?'

'No, he didn't. I won't be asking him for any more favours. He's a thoughtless airhead at times.'

'Do you have a list of the names of the people who attended that night?'

'I've got one somewhere. Do you really need it?'

'I'm sorry to be a bother, Ms Drew, but it could be extremely useful, thanks.'

'Just a minute. I'll go and find it.'

As soon as she left the room, Glen said, 'Well, well, well, sounds like Freddie was telling us a few lies in Manchester.'

Rob said, 'Emily Whitchurch left school at three twenty, Freddie didn't arrive here until four thirty. That would give him ample time to abduct her, hide her away somewhere, and then drive here.'

Ms Drew came back into the room clutching a piece of paper. 'Here you are, Inspector. All the telephone numbers are on the list, as well. I hope it helps.'

Rob said, 'Thank you so much, Ms Drew, that's great. Just a couple more questions and we'll leave you in peace. How did Mr Fletcher seem when he arrived that day?'

The old lady was thoughtful for a minute; then she said firmly, 'He seemed different to normal. He appeared agitated about something. He was excitable and seemed full of energy. I was just too annoyed with him to take much notice at the time. But thinking back, he looked scruffy, too. Freddie's normally impeccably groomed and very well dressed. He turned up at my house that evening wearing clothes that I would only deem suitable for gardening or some other menial task. I went off him big style that night, I can tell you.'

'One last question. What time did he leave the card game?'

'We play four rubbers every meeting. That's a maximum of twelve games. Freddie shot off like a scalded cat as soon as the final rubber finished. He didn't stay to help clear away the tables or say goodbye. I recall that I had to ask a few of the other gentlemen players to assist me in putting everything away. It was most embarrassing; I wasn't happy at all.'

'Thank you, Ms Drew. You've been very helpful.'

'I know I've criticised him today, but I do hope young Freddie isn't in any trouble. He's very mischievous and humorous, usually. I think he just let himself down that evening. He'd probably been working too hard or something.'

'Very likely, Ms Drew. We may need to speak to you again in the future; would that be okay?'

'Of course. Make a note of my telephone number so I know you're coming next time.'

The two detectives were both deep in thought as they walked back to the pub car park.

Rob said, 'It just goes to show, you always need to check everything.'

Glen replied, 'Doesn't it just. Fletcher was so plausible when he gave us that alibi. Did he think we wouldn't check it?'

'I honestly don't know. One thing's for sure, he was definitely up to something before he came here on October 2.'

'And why leave so urgently at the end of the night? What was the big rush?'

'Let's get back to Mansfield and start going through the

names on this list. I want to know if anybody else thought Fletcher's behaviour was strange that evening, or if he said something weird to anyone. We need to establish who else was on his particular table that night. Once we've done all that, then I think we'll need to revisit Freddie Fletcher and have another chat.'

74

12.30pm, 17 October 1986
Nottingham Trent University, Clifton, Nottingham

Sam Jamieson walked into the vast library at Nottingham Trent University. He had some free time between lectures, and he needed somewhere quiet to take stock of his situation and to think.

The warrant executed at his flat and his subsequent questioning by the police had rattled him. It hadn't deterred him from his path or his long-term goal, but it had most definitely rattled him.

He sat down in a quiet corner of the library and took out a notepad, pen and a random book from his rucksack. He placed them on the table in front of him. He opened the book and placed his pen along the spine.

It was a prop. He wasn't reading the text. He didn't want to be disturbed, and if other students thought he was hard at work, then he wouldn't be approached.

What he needed was a quiet space. He needed time to think things through.

He was pleased he'd offered the line of least resistance to the police when they had called. It had gone against the grain. He had no love for the police, and his overriding instinct had been to fight, to resist. He knew that his decision to cooperate had been the right one.

There was nothing in his flat that could incriminate him. Everything they had seized could easily be explained away. The thesis he was writing *was* on the subject he had spoken about when they questioned him. So if that crafty cop checked up on him and spoke with his tutors and professors, everything he had said would all ring true.

He smiled as he thought about the little gem he had dropped out to the detectives at the end of the interview. It had been a master stroke to tell them about seeing Dominic Whitchurch kissing the woman in the car. He knew the police would fixate on that and disregard most of his other answers. He had known the registration number of the Volvo, but giving that to the detectives would have made the enquiry too easy. He needed them to waste precious time trying to trace the vehicle.

That cunning detective had worried him though.

Flint by name; flint by nature.

He was like the ancient stone, hard and uncompromising. With his phoney show of compassion at the end of the questioning ... he wasn't fooling anyone.

As far as Sam was concerned, the detective had tried to con him. He had treated him like some juvenile delinquent arrested for the first time. Making the clumsy attempt at questioning him about that letter, like they had it with them.

Now, as Sam thought carefully about the questioning and how he had responded, he was proud of the way he had quickly seen through the detective's little game. He was even more pleased about the way he had maintained control.

He bitterly regretted ever sending that letter to Mulberry Chambers. The one bonus about the questioning was that he now knew the letter was no longer in existence. If it had been, they would have questioned him a lot harder. It must have been destroyed.

The letter had been a massive mistake. It had been written at a time when his emotions were raw. He had always known it could resurface and cause him problems in the future. Now it no longer existed, he could disregard it.

He pondered on his next move. There was no way he could go ahead as planned. He knew he would still be watched closely by Flint and his cronies. No, he needed a major rethink.

As he sat quietly in the hushed halls of the library, he thought to himself that even if his plans had to change drastically, the outcome would always be the same. He realised that patience was the key. He could easily abandon everything he had done so far. There would be consequences for people he had no concern for, so it could be done.

He picked up his pen and began to scribble on a scrap piece of paper.

Studying for his master's would take another eighteen months. He could start applying for jobs after another year. Time was the one thing on his side. He had no dependents and only had himself to think about. He scribbled down the names of countries: New Zealand, Australia, America, Canada.

He screwed the paper up and thrust it in his pocket. He closed his book and put it in his rucksack. His next lecture started in fifteen minutes, and he still had to walk across campus to the hall.

He had made his decision.

He would abort the current plan. Whatever the dire consequences of that decision might be for some. He was beyond caring about others. He would complete his master's first and then resume his quest for revenge. By the time he graduated in eighteen months' time, that cunning, deceitful bastard Flint would have forgotten all about him.

The very thing that had been his worst enemy when he was wrongfully incarcerated in Leeds prison was now his best friend.

Time.

75

1.00pm, 17 October 1986
MCIU Offices, Mansfield, Nottinghamshire

The sudden noise in the main office made Danny look up from his paperwork. Brian Hopkirk and Rob Buxton were having a loud discussion. Glen Lorimar and Rachel Moore were both chipping in, adding to the general din.

Danny stepped out of his office, saying sternly, 'What's all the racket?'

Rob said, 'Sorry. We're just discussing work.'

Pleased of an excuse to have a break from the paperwork, Danny grinned. 'I'm only joking. Somebody put the kettle on. You can tell me how you all got on this morning.'

Glen said, 'I'll make the drinks. Everybody want one?'

They all nodded, and Andy Wills shouted from his desk, 'Coffee for me, Glen, cheers.'

A few minutes later, Glen returned with a tray of coffees. 'I haven't sugared any of them. You'll have to help yourselves.'

Danny took a mug from the tray, sat down and said, 'Right, let's get cracking. Rob, how did you get on at Fiskerton?'

'We've had a very interesting conversation with Ms Virginia Drew. She highlighted some major discrepancies in the version of events given to us by Freddie Fletcher. Basically, the little shitbag has lied through his teeth.'

'How come?'

'He lied about the time he arrived at Fiskerton on the second. He told us he arrived at three o'clock in the afternoon. That would have made it impossible for him to be in Nottingham when Emily Whitchurch went missing. Ms Drew informed us that Fletcher didn't actually arrive at Fiskerton until four thirty that afternoon. That would have given him ample time to grab the girl and hide her away. There are other things Ms Drew told us that also raise concerns.'

'Such as?'

'He was in a strange mood when he did finally arrive, and was scruffily dressed, as though he had been doing some kind of manual labour.'

'That's very interesting. So, what plans do you have to follow up on her little bombshell?'

'We've got a list of everyone who was at Fiskerton for the card school that afternoon and evening.'

Brian interjected, 'Rob, it's a bridge club. Not a card school, you heathen.'

Rob grinned. 'Sorry to hurt your refined sensibilities, Brian. As I was saying, we've got a list of all the players at the bridge club that evening. We're going to speak to them all and see if we find anyone who can corroborate what Ms Drew told us. I've made a phone call to Mulberry Chambers; they're expecting Fletcher to be back in his office tomorrow. The trial in Manchester should be concluded today. The jury are expected to return their verdict later this afternoon. As soon as we've spoken to everyone on the list, we'll be seeing Fletcher again.'

Danny said, 'Like I always say, it pays to check everything. Good work. Let me know how you get on with the other card players. Brian, how did you and Rachel get on with the professor?'

Brian said, 'It was extremely informative, boss. The cave system in the area where the girl went missing is vast, and a lot of it remains uncharted. There are a couple of known entrances to the cave system in that area. There's one on Peel Street and one on Mansfield Road, but the professor believes there could be numerous other unknown entrances. Apparently, the whole area is a honeycomb of old sand mine workings.'

'So, what's your plan?'

'I want to put search teams down into the caves and look for the girl.'

'Okay. When can you get that organised?'

'It's not possible at the moment. It's too dangerous.'

'How come?'

'Because of all the heavy rain we've had over the last few weeks. When the sandstone gets wet, the cave system in that area becomes prone to roof falls. The professor and his assistant were adamant that nobody should enter the caves until the rain stops. They'll need a couple of days of dry weather then, to be safe enough to enter.'

'So, for now, you can't really progress your theory?'

'Not right now. But as soon as it's safe, I'd like to press on with the search.'

Danny nodded and then turned to Andy. 'Any joy on that Volvo enquiry?'

'I've been speaking to the Special Operations Unit observations teams; there is mention on their logs of a dark-coloured Volvo that dropped off Dominic Whitchurch. They had no view of the driver or the registration number of the car. They can't confirm any activity within the car before Dominic got out.'

'So, we know nothing more than what Jamieson told us.'

'No, we don't. It just confirms that there was a dark Volvo in the area and that Dominic Whitchurch was in it.'

'Thanks. I want you to give me a hand in the office this afternoon, Andy. These figures for Potter are a bloody nightmare.'

'Okay, boss.'

'Brian and Rachel, as soon as you've finished your coffee, I want you to go to Richmond Drive and speak to Dominic Whitchurch. We need to know who this woman is who was driving the Volvo. The information from Sam Jamieson is that Whitchurch and this woman were locked in a passionate embrace when she dropped him off on Richmond Drive on the tenth. I want to know who she is and her connection to Whitchurch. Okay?'

'No problem.'

76

3.00pm, 17 October 1986
Nottingham

Emily Whitchurch sat cross-legged on the floor of the cave, in total darkness. She gripped the Mini Maglite torch in her right hand so tightly that her hand was starting to ache.

There was no way she was going to drop it.

Her hearing, sense of smell, and sense of touch had all become far more acute after living in total darkness for days. She desperately wanted to flick on the torch and illuminate the small cave she was being held in. She resisted the temptation. She realised the life of the batteries needed to be preserved for as long as possible. She knew the torch would be needed soon, when the rats returned.

Shortly after her captor had left yesterday, she had hungrily started to eat the food he had left. The strong smell of the tuna sandwich had obviously attracted the vermin. In no time at all, the voracious rodents had appeared in the main tunnel. She had heard their scurrying first. The sound of their stiff, bristle-like fur rubbing against the walls of the tunnel as they raced to find the food.

When she had flicked on the bright white light, she had been startled by the sheer size of the rats. Some of them were huge, with evil-looking, slanted eyes that shone yellow in the light of the torch.

The rats had retreated from the stark white light, and she quickly devoured the remainder of her food.

Since then, the sound of dripping water in the cave had intensified. It was getting wetter by the minute. The plastic sheet she was sitting on was almost floating on the amount of water building up on the floor of the cave. The small pot cave, in which she had been tethered to a stake, was slowly filling with ice-cold water seeping from the porous walls and roof.

Emily hated water. She felt panic begin to surge within her. As a young girl, she had been left unattended for a minute at a holiday hotel's swimming pool. She had fallen in and almost drowned before her anxious father had pulled her from the bottom of the pool. As a result of that dreadful incident, she now suffered from an overwhelming fear of drowning. Just the feeling of the inch or so of water beneath her was enough to make her experience feelings of anxiety. If the water got any deeper, those feelings of panic would quickly escalate to ones of sheer terror.

The water was also freezing cold, and she could feel herself gradually succumbing to her body's drop in temperature.

Her mind was asking searching questions. *What if she passed out with the cold and fell face down, in the dirty water? Could she drown in that much water? If she passed out, would the rats return and devour her while she was unconscious?*

The thought about the rats caused a far more urgent question to smash into her brain. Where were the rats?

They had been constant visitors to the pot cave ever since she had been incarcerated there. She hadn't heard any of them for hours. Why weren't they in the tunnel?

The reason for their absence hit her like a hammer blow. She let out a low mournful cry: 'Nooooo!'

Almost immediately, large chunks of rock began to fall from the roof, splashing loudly in the water at the base of the pot cave.

She had suddenly realised the reason for the rats' disappearance. Using some kind of animal sixth sense, the rats knew that very soon the entire roof of the pot cave would collapse. It would be filled forever, with lumps of sandstone and soft sand, burying her alive in the process.

She had heard of rats deserting a sinking ship.

The pot cave was her ship, and the rats had left her to it.

Eventually, the pieces of rock stopped falling, and she was left sobbing quietly in the dark. The only sound was that of incessant dripping water slowly filling the pot cave.

Emily now understood that nobody was going to find her. Nobody would rescue her. She was going to die alone in this cave.

77

6.00pm, 17 October 1986
Richmond Drive, Mapperley Park, Nottinghamshire

It was getting dark by the time Brian and Rachel parked outside De Montfort House on Richmond Drive.

As they got out of the car, Rachel said, 'So, where has he been all day? Why couldn't he see us until now?'

'When I spoke to Dominic earlier, he said he was taking Rebecca to Burntstump Park, to have a walk in the fresh air. He said she needed to get out of the house for an hour or so.'

'Brian, it's been raining all day.'

Brian shrugged. 'Well, the lights are on. Let's go and have a chat with him now.'

Dominic opened the front door of the house and said, 'Oh, it's you. Is this urgent? It's getting late. Rebecca's taken a sleeping tablet and has gone to bed; she needs to rest.'

Brian said, 'It's you we want to speak to, Mr Whitchurch. May we come in, please?'

'Is this going to take long?'

'Five minutes, max.'

With a resigned air, Dominic opened the door wide and gestured for the two detectives to come in. He said wearily, 'Go through to the lounge; you both know where it is. I'm going to get myself a drink. I won't be a second.'

Brian and Rachel remained standing in the lounge until Dominic returned with a tumbler full of ice and whiskey. He indicated for the detectives to take a seat on the large settee. He sat down in an armchair opposite, took a sip of the fiery spirit and said, 'You said it was me you wanted to speak to. How can I help?'

Rachel said, 'After your wife received the ransom demand, you came back from Leicester that night. How did you get back?'

'I was driven back by a colleague. I hadn't taken my own car.'

'What time was it when you arrived here?'

'It was late. It must have been gone ten.'

'What's the name of the colleague who drove you home?'

'Why is this relevant?'

Brian said, 'We're just trying to work our way through all the vehicle sightings that have been logged by the observations team that have been looking out for you. We're particularly interested in a dark-coloured Volvo that was seen on Richmond Drive the night you returned home.'

'That would be the colleague who drove me home. Angela drives a dark-blue-coloured Volvo.'

Rachel said, 'Angela?'

'Angela Temple. She's a junior barrister at Mulberry. She was my second chair for the trial in Leicester. She very kindly drove me home and then returned to Leicester for the trial.'

'That was extremely accommodating of her. It's a long drive there and back. Did you invite her inside the house for a tea or coffee before she drove all the way back to Leicester?'

'At that time, I wasn't fully aware of what was happening. I didn't think it would be appropriate to invite her in. So, the answer to your question is, no, I didn't. She dropped me off outside the gates and left immediately.'

'Right outside the gates?'

'Yes, outside the gates. Why?'

'Have you worked with Ms Temple for long?'

'I think she's been at Mulberry for a year or so. I've worked with her on a few occasions now. She has a very bright future ahead of her.'

Brian said, 'Do you have an address for her?'

Dominic swirled the ice in his glass. 'I'm sure the office will have her home address on file. I can't think of it off the top of my head.'

A drowsy-looking Rebecca walked into the lounge and said, 'Come along, Dom, you *do* know where she lives. Don't you remember? We went there for drinks in August. She lives in Papplewick; the Temples have that charming little cottage. The address will be on the calendar in the kitchen. Be a dear and go and get it for the detectives, please.'

Dominic slammed his drink down on the coffee table and stalked out of the room. As soon as he had left, Rebecca said, 'Why do you want to know about Angela Temple?'

Brian told her the same story about checking vehicle sightings.

Rebecca smiled and said, 'Angela's such a pretty woman and so very ambitious. She reminds me of how I was at that age.'

Dominic walked back into the lounge and handed a scrap of paper, containing the scribbled address for Angela Temple, to Rachel.

He then turned to Brian and said sarcastically, 'Who

knows, Inspector, one of these days you might knock on my door and return my daughter to me. Any chance of that happening anytime soon? Or are you too busy chasing around like headless chickens, following up ridiculous dead ends?'

Brian flushed at the unexpected angry outburst. 'We're all working around the clock to try to find your little girl. I've got a daughter myself who's the same age as Emily. Believe me, nothing would give me greater pleasure than to return your daughter safely to you. We'll find her, Mr Whitchurch.'

Dominic picked up his glass of whiskey, took a mouthful and hissed, 'Well, don't let me detain you any longer, Detective.'

Rebecca walked the detectives to the front door and said, 'Please excuse my husband's tirade. This is all really getting to us now. The longer it goes on, the more it's affecting him. Please do what you say and find our daughter soon.'

The front door was closed behind them, and Rachel said, 'Are you okay?'

Brian rubbed his eyes and nodded. 'I'm fine. I was just thinking of my Laura for a second, that's all.'

'Your little girl?'

'Not so little anymore. She's thirteen now. I love her to bits; she's such a great kid. Now, where does Angela Temple live?'

7.00pm, 17 October 1986
Honeysuckle Cottage, Papplewick, Nottinghamshire

Rachel sighed as the car came to a halt and she saw Honeysuckle Cottage for the first time.

She said wistfully, 'Rebecca Whitchurch wasn't wrong; this cottage is charming. I don't know about you, boss, but I can't wait to meet Angela Temple.'

'That must be her Volvo on the driveway. Let's hope she's at home as well.'

The two detectives got out of their car and walked along the gravel driveway, to the front door of the cottage. Brian knocked loudly, then waited for a response. He didn't have to wait long.

The front door was suddenly flung open. Both detectives were surprised when they saw who'd done so. Standing in front of them was Professor Brandon Temple.

Brian said, 'Hello again, Professor. We're here to speak to

Angela Temple. It's about the Volvo car, nothing to worry about. Is she home?'

'Angela's my wife. She's in the shower. Is it urgent?'

Rachel smiled and said softly, 'It's something we do need to clear up tonight. Would you mind if we came inside to wait? It's just a few questions. I promise it won't take long.'

Brandon Temple tutted loudly and said, 'Very well, you'd better come in. I'll let Angela know you're here.'

He directed the detectives into the small but comfortable lounge and said, 'Please take a seat. I won't be a minute.'

Temple left the room and ran up the narrow flight of stairs.

Five minutes later, he returned to the lounge, followed by his wife.

Angela was wearing a white towelling robe; her long wet hair was hidden by another towel she had fashioned around her head like a turban.

She flashed a perfect smile when she walked in the room and said, 'Please excuse me, I was in the shower. Brandon said it's something important about my car?'

Rachel said, 'We're sorry to intrude at this late hour; it's just a few things we need to clear up about your car. Is that your Volvo on the driveway?'

'Yes, it is.'

'Does anyone else drive it?'

'No, just me. Brandon doesn't drive; he's got a motorcycle that he uses to commute into the city. What's this all about?'

'We've just come from Dominic Whitchurch's house. He informed us that you recently worked a trial with him at Leicester Crown Court. Is that right?'

'Yes, it is, but Dominic had to return home shortly after the trial started. I had to complete it on my own.'

'When Dominic returned home from Leicester, did you drive him?'

'Yes, I did. He had to get home urgently, and he hadn't taken his own car. It would have cost him a fortune in taxi fare.'

Brandon interrupted, 'You never told me you'd driven back from Leicester. Why didn't you come home and stay the night?'

Angela rounded on him and hissed, 'Not now, Brandon!'

Picking up on the tension between the couple, Brian said, 'It's a fair question, Mrs Temple. It's a long drive from Leicester. Why go straight back when you only live fifteen minutes away from Mapperley Park?'

Angela flashed a resentful look at Brian. 'I had just had a complex rape trial dumped on my lap. I had prepared to be a second chair, not to be the lead defence counsel. If I was going to be ready for trial the next day, I had a lot of prep work to do that night. Does that answer your "fair" question, detective?'

Rachel said, 'Have you worked with Dominic Whitchurch much?'

'On a few occasions.'

Again, Brandon interrupted, 'It's much more than a few times, darling. Dominic has taken quite a shine to his star pupil. He always wants you as his second chair.'

Rachel said nothing, but looked quizzically at Angela. The silence became too much, and eventually Angela said, 'Alright! It's more than a few times, okay? We make a good team.'

Rachel had seen the weakness. She said, 'So, how would you describe your relationship with Dominic Whitchurch?'

'Excuse me?'

'I said, how would you—'

Angela interrupted angrily, 'I heard what you bloody well said! I just don't understand exactly what it is you're inferring? My relationship with Dominic Whitchurch is strictly professional. In case it had escaped your notice, Detective, I'm a married woman, and Dominic's a happily married man. We have to work closely together, that's all. With the emphasis on the word "work" and not closely. Now, will that be all?'

Rachel turned to Brandon Temple and said, 'Mr Temple, do you mind leaving us for a moment? I need to ask your wife a couple of questions in private.'

Brandon replied, 'Of course not, but we have no secrets in this house, Detective.' He turned to walk away, but not before Brian had seen the cruel smirk that crossed his features.

When he had walked upstairs and was out of earshot, Rachel said, 'We aren't here to cause problems in your marriage. What is the truth about your relationship with Dominic Whitchurch?'

With real anger in her voice Angela whispered, 'I've told you, it's purely professional.'

'I don't think your husband sees it that way?'

'What does he know about anything? I work very closely with Dominic and that's it.'

Rachel allowed a silence to descend on the room for a few minutes, then said, 'That's all for now, Mrs Temple. I'm sorry to have interrupted your evening, and thanks for being so frank with us.'

Angela shouted upstairs, 'Brandon, we're finished down here. Can you show them out?'

The two detectives were escorted to the front door by Brandon, who smiled and said, 'Good night,' as he closed the door behind them.

Brian and Rachel remained standing outside the door for a few seconds. As soon as the door had been closed, the two detectives overheard Angela Temple shout at her husband, 'Why the fuck did you let them into our house without finding out what they wanted first? You fucking idiot!'

As they walked back to their car, Brian said, 'She's got some anger management issues, that one. Do you believe her?'

'Do I believe her relationship with Dominic Whitchurch is purely professional? Not a chance. A woman can sense these things. Angela Temple and Dominic Whitchurch are bang at it, trust me.'

'There's something else, Rachel. I think Brandon knows his wife is having an affair with Dominic.'

'Why do you think that?'

'When you hit that raw nerve with the question about their working relationship, and she began to lose it, he was almost smirking. He was enjoying watching her squirm in front of you.'

'Here's a troublesome thought. How keen was the professor to keep us out of those caves?'

'Very keen. We need to run all this by the boss. I think we need to keep a very close eye on Professor Temple.'

'Do you think he's capable of snatching the girl?'

'Who knows? Does he have a motive to hurt Dominic Whitchurch? If he knows about the affair, which I think he does, then I would say yes, definitely. It's just a matter of whether he hates Dominic Whitchurch enough to harm his young daughter.'

Rachel said, 'We need to speak to Angela again, somewhere we can apply more pressure. That's the only way we'll find out the real state of her marriage.'

'We can do that first thing in the morning at Mulberry Chambers. In the meantime, let's talk to Danny and see if he'll sanction a full surveillance on Brandon Temple.'

79

8.15pm, 17 October 1986
MCIU Offices, Mansfield, Nottinghamshire

Brian wasn't surprised to find Danny and Andy still in the office, working on the numbers and figures demanded by Adrian Potter.

He stuck his head around the door, knocked politely and said, 'Have you got a minute?'

Danny looked up wearily and said, 'Of course. We're almost done here.'

He then glanced at his watch and said, 'Jesus! Is that the time? What did you want, Brian?'

'I think Rachel and I may have just stumbled across something important.'

Intrigued, Danny said, 'Why? What did Dominic say to you?'

'We spoke with Dominic alone. He told us that the car he was in when he was dropped off that night belongs to another barrister at Mulberry Chambers. She was acting as his second chair at Leicester Crown Court, for the rape trial. The barrister's a woman by the name of Angela Temple. She's married to Professor Brandon Temple.'

'The geology professor at Nottingham Trent University?'

'The very same. It would appear, reading between the lines, that Dominic Whitchurch and Angela Temple are having some sort of extramarital affair. This is unconfirmed, but all the signs are there.'

'Go on.'

'Do you remember how keen the professor was to keep us out of those caves? What if it's because he knows the Whitchurch girl's down there?'

'That's a huge leap, Brian. I know you're dead keen on your cave theory, but didn't you say the professor's assistant was also advising against you entering the caves?'

'Stacey Bloom did echo what the professor said, that's true. To be fair to her, she's hardly going to say anything different while her boss is standing there, is she?'

Danny was thoughtful for a minute. 'What are you thinking?'

'I'm wondering if we can arrange a full surveillance team to watch Brandon Temple for a few days. That's all.'

'Bloody hell! You don't want much, do you?'

Again, Danny paused, deep in thought. He grabbed the telephone and dialled a number from memory. After a few rings, the phone was answered.

Danny said, 'Hello, Mattie, sorry to call you at home. Does the regional crime squad have any capability to run a full surveillance on a single target for the next three days?'

There was a long pause; then Danny said, 'How many officers is there in half a team?'

Another pause. 'Eight should be fine. The target won't suspect that he's being followed, and I doubt very much that he'll be tactically aware. Can your half team be in this office for seven o'clock tomorrow morning for a briefing? The target lives at an address at Papplewick. I'll put two of my officers out at five-thirty tomorrow morning to observe the cottage. This will give us some cover until we can get your team briefed and on the plot.'

There was a shorter pause; then Danny said, 'By the way, does any of your half team ride a motorcycle? This target's only means of transport is a small 125 cc motorbike, so a motorcyclist is essential ... Two, that's great. I'll be in at seven o'clock to brief your officers. Cheers, mate.'

Danny put the phone down and said, 'It's on. Mattie Carlisle is sending over a skeleton surveillance crew tomorrow morning. Brian, I want you and Rachel here at seven o'clock to brief them, okay? Andy, I want you to designate two officers to work an early turn tomorrow morning. I want them to be on duty here at five o'clock tomorrow morning, and on plot at Papplewick no later than five thirty. Can you organise that now?'

Andy walked out of the office, saying, 'I'm on it, boss.'

Brian grinned. 'Thanks, Danny. I'll go and give Rachel the good news.'

Danny grinned back and said, 'I don't know if all this will turn anything up, but what have we got to lose?'

'At this moment in time? Fuck all!'

80

9.15am, 18 October 1986
Mulberry Chambers, The Ropewalk, Nottingham

Angela Temple had been surprised when she walked into the offices of Mulberry Chambers that morning. The surprise had been that Sebastien Dawson wanted to see her in his office straight away. The young receptionist had smiled when she had given Angela the message. When asked why Sebastien wanted to see her so urgently, the young girl had shrugged her shoulders benignly.

With a growing sense of unease, Angela had walked through chambers until she found herself outside Dawson's office door. She knocked politely and waited until she heard the barrister's clerk shout, 'Enter!'

Angela walked in and was surprised to see the same two detectives who had been at her cottage the night before.

Sebastien Dawson said pompously, 'Mrs Temple, these good people are detectives, who wish to ask you a few questions. You need to understand that here at Mulberry Chambers, we always cooperate fully with the police. Understood?'

She nodded meekly.

Dawson raised his huge frame out of his seat and said, 'Detective Inspector Hopkirk, I'll leave you and your colleague to ask your questions in private.'

Brian said, 'Thank you, Mr Dawson. We appreciate all your help.'

As soon as Dawson closed the door behind him, Brian said, 'Take a seat, Mrs Temple.'

Angela Temple sat down. 'What's this all about?'

Rachel said, 'As you know, we're investigating the disappearance of Emily Whitchurch. Part of our investigation is to find anybody with a motive to abduct that young girl.'

'I understand that, but what's that got to do with me?'

'We have a witness who was on Richmond Drive when you dropped Dominic Whitchurch off outside his home.'

Angela Temple said nothing.

Rachel continued, 'Our witness has described how they saw Dominic Whitchurch passionately kissing the driver of a dark Volvo before getting out and walking along Richmond Drive towards his home. Dominic was kissing you, wasn't he, Angela?'

Angela looked at the floor for a moment, then lifted her head to face the detectives. Her eyes were blazing. 'Yes, it was me Dominic was kissing! So what?'

'Let me ask you the same question I asked last night. What is your relationship with Dominic Whitchurch?'

'We love each other. He's going to leave his wife, and we're going to set up home together. If his daughter hadn't gone missing, we would have been together already.'

'You seem pretty certain about that, Angela. How long have you been having this affair?'

'It's not an affair. We're in love.'

'Whatever it is, how long has it been going on?'

'Ever since I met him. A few days after I started at Mulberry.'

Brian said, 'Does Brandon know what's going on?'

Angela was becoming indignant. She said haughtily, 'I really don't know, and to be perfectly honest, I stopped caring months ago.'

'Do you think he knows?'

'He's not a stupid man, Detective. I'm sure he has a pretty good idea. Ever since I started working at Mulberry, our marriage has effectively been over.'

Rachel said softly, 'Your private life really is none of our concern, Angela. What we do need to know is this: If your husband's aware of what's been going on, is he capable of exacting some sort of revenge against Dominic Whitchurch?'

'I've no idea what that cold, unloving excuse for a man is capable of anymore.'

'Is he capable of harming a child?'

'You mean Dominic's daughter, don't you?'

'Yes, that's exactly what I mean.'

'Detective, I'd love to sit here, be outraged and say, "Don't be ridiculous, of course he isn't!" The truth is, Brandon does possess a very cruel streak. I've been unfortunate enough to be on the receiving end of his cruelty on a number of occasions during our marriage.'

'Has he been violent towards you?'

'Never physically. But he enjoys playing cruel mind games all the time. He constantly tries to make me feel small and insignificant. He genuinely believes that nobody can compare to his own soaring intellect. My husband possesses an ego the size of a small country.'

'What's your husband doing today, Angela?'

'As far as I know, he's working from home. He was just having his breakfast when I left for work this morning. Why?'

Brian said, 'We may wish to speak to him later today. It's vitally important that you don't contact him. He mustn't know that we've had this conversation. Is that understood?'

'As far as I'm concerned, Brandon and I are already finished. I won't be going back to that bloody awful, draughty cottage. I'm done with all of that. As soon as Dominic leaves his wife, we'll be spending the rest of our lives together.'

'Thanks, Angela, that will be all for now. Could you ask Mr Dawson to come back to his office, please?'

Angela Temple looked teary-eyed and tired. With a resigned air, she nodded her head, stood up and left the office. She always knew the affair would have to be revealed one day. Now that day had finally arrived, and she desperately needed to be with Dominic, it wasn't possible. She felt angry and frustrated. She just needed to spend some time on her own.

As they waited for Dawson to return to his office, Brian said, 'What did you make of that?'

Rachel replied, 'I'll bet my house and everything in it that Dominic Whitchurch has absolutely no intention of leaving his wife. That love story is definitely only felt one-way. In a strange way, I feel sorry for her.'

'And what about Brandon Temple?'

'He doesn't sound capable of hurting someone physically, but who knows? At least we know he's still at home. That means the regional crime squad surveillance team will be able to pick him up if and when he leaves the cottage.'

Brian spoke into his radio. 'DI Hopkirk to DS Travers. Over.'

DS Travers, who was leading the regional crime squad surveillance team, quickly answered, 'DS Travers. Go ahead. Over.'

'We have confirmation that the suspect is now alone at the target premises.'

'Received that, thanks. Will let you know the moment we have any movement. Over.'

Brian replaced the radio back inside his jacket pocket, turned to Rachel and said, 'I think we should go and see Stacey Bloom at the university. Can you call her and see if she's available for a chat at the university this morning?'

Rachel reached inside her handbag and retrieved the card given to her by Stacey Bloom. She picked up the telephone on Sebastien Dawson's desk and dialled the number. After a brief conversation with Stacey, Rachel replaced the telephone on its cradle just as Sebastien Dawson entered the room.

He ignored the fact that his telephone had been used and said, 'Productive conversation?'

Brian said, 'Very. Thanks again for the use of your office, Mr Dawson.'

'Anything you need to share with me, Detective Inspector?'

'Not now. When the time's right, I'll be in touch. Thanks again, Mr Dawson.'

As the detectives walked out the door and closed it behind them, Dawson muttered to himself, 'Don't mention it, I'm sure.'

81

10.00am, 18 October 1986
Nottingham Midland Station, Nottingham

The announcement over the tannoy system on the train was surprisingly clear: 'Your next stop is Nottingham Midland Station, repeat, Nottingham Midland Station. The service from Manchester Piccadilly terminates at this station. Please ensure you have all your belongings before leaving the train. Thank you.'

Freddie Fletcher started placing documents back into his briefcase. He retrieved his black Crombie coat from the overhead rack.

He made his way along the first-class carriage to the door. As the train pulled into the station, he scanned the platform. He couldn't see any sign of police activity. No uniforms, no detectives in ill-fitting suits waiting to pounce.

He allowed a smile to form on his face. His plan had worked.

He had needed time to get rid of the incriminating items from his luxury flat in The Park. That was why he had lied so blatantly, and so effectively, to the two detectives in Manchester. He knew his lie would be found out as soon as the detectives spoke to Virginia Drew. He was fully aware that the old lady would remember exactly what time he'd arrived at her house on the afternoon of the second of October. He also knew that she would quickly inform the police of that fact.

He didn't care.

It had provided him with a window of opportunity to do what he needed to do.

As soon as all the incriminating evidence had been squirrelled away, he would go to the police and offer up some other spurious reason why he had lied in the first place. The police were stupid. They would swallow his plausible lies. Even if they didn't, without any evidence there would be nothing they could do. Telling lies wasn't against the law. One thing Freddie Fletcher knew everything about was the law. He knew all the limitations and restraints it placed upon the police when dealing with individuals.

With a confident air, he stepped off the train and sauntered along the platform. He was feeling very pleased with himself. Not only had he just successfully defended his client at the trial in Manchester – the jury had only taken five and a half hours to return a not guilty verdict – but by the look of the deserted platform, he had also managed to outwit the police.

The telephone call made to Mulberry Chambers late afternoon yesterday had formed the final part of his elaborate cover story. He had called to inform Sebastien Dawson of the verdict at Manchester Crown Court. During the conversation with the barrister's clerk, he had let slip that he intended to remain at the hotel in Manchester for another day. He wanted to properly relax and recharge before returning to the office on the nineteenth.

Fletcher was convinced that if the police discovered the discrepancy in his account, the first thing they would do would be to contact Mulberry Chambers to see when he was due to be back in the office. As soon as they had made that telephone call to the office, they could then plan when they would come and speak to him about his untruthful alibi. If they thought he would be back in Nottingham on the nineteenth, they would come and question him then.

He walked slowly up the stairs of the railway station to the taxi rank. He hailed the nearest cab and directed the driver to take him to his apartment in The Park.

The journey from the railway station to the upmarket suburb of the city only took five minutes. He paid the driver and walked towards the front door of the stylish apartment. He retrieved the door keys from his coat pocket, walked in and closed the door behind him.

82

10.00am, 18 October 1986
The Park, Nottingham

Freddie Fletcher had been totally oblivious to the nondescript Ford Escort that had followed the taxi from the railway station. He never noticed the car as it came to a stop behind the van that was parked twenty yards from his front door. He had also been completely unaware of the two men who watched him leave the train, walk along the platform and up the stairs to the taxi rank.

Those two men were now sitting inside the Escort parked outside his apartment.

Seated in the passenger seat, Rob Buxton grinned and said to the driver, Glen Lorimar, 'What did I tell you, Glen? I knew that slippery bastard would be back today.'

'It's a good job you checked the Hilton in Manchester to see when Fletcher was booking out. He really does have a low opinion of us, boss.'

Rob said, 'He's not nearly as smart as he thinks he is. After I spoke with Sebastien Dawson last night, it was obvious that something wasn't right. He wasn't due back until the nineteenth anyway, so why make such a fuss about telling Dawson he was staying another night? He didn't have to say anything. A quick telephone call to the hotel confirmed that he was booking out at eight o'clock this morning, and that he'd ordered a taxi to take him to the railway station in Manchester. You didn't have to be a brain surgeon to find that out.'

Glen laughed. 'Are we going to have a word with him now?'

'No, not yet. Let's give it a minute or two. He's obviously up to something; let's hang fire and see where it takes us. We know the missing girl isn't in his flat, because the secretary spent the night there four days after the girl went missing. We've got nothing to lose, and everything to gain, by playing things slowly.'

Glen Lorimar removed his seat belt and got comfortable for the possibility of a long wait. He said, 'That sounds like a plan.'

83

**10.30am, 18 October 1986
Honeysuckle Cottage, Papplewick, Nottinghamshire**

The regional crime squad surveillance team had been in position outside Honeysuckle Cottage since seven thirty that morning.

The briefing at the MCIU office at seven o'clock had been concise.

Maps had been produced, and a plan quickly formulated to cover all possible routes away from Honeysuckle Cottage. Lessons had obviously been learned from the ransom drop debacle, as there were now two officers riding motorcycles attached to the surveillance team. The team would be using the two motorcycles and three other vehicles. The three cars were all double crewed. This would allow for the passenger of each vehicle to do foot surveillance if it became necessary.

Each car had been designated a different radio call sign:

Charlie One, Charlie Two and Charlie Three. The two motorcycles were Mike One and Mike Two.

The message relayed to the team from Brian Hopkirk earlier that morning, confirming that the suspect was definitely still inside Honeysuckle Cottage, had raised everyone's morale.

DS Travers, coordinating the surveillance, was the passenger in Charlie One. He glanced at his watch; the time was now almost ten thirty. He would need to change the vehicle parked nearest to the cottage in the next few minutes. He had changed the vehicles every thirty minutes so the same car wasn't seen parked outside the address for too long. He was just about to give the order to change when his radio crackled into life. 'Charlie Two to Charlie One. We have an off, repeat we have an off, from the target premises. Suzuki motorcycle, one rider no pillion, has just left the target premises towards the junction at Griffin. Over.'

Everyone in the team now knew that the motorcycle was heading towards the junction where the Griffins Head pub was located.

DS Travers said, 'Charlie One has the eyeball. Suspect has turned left at the junction and is heading towards the A60. Mike One, can you take the eyeball as soon as possible, please?'

'From Mike One, fifteen seconds before I pass you.'

The powerful motorcycle roared past the surveillance car.

'Mike One has the eyeball, staying back, no vehicles for cover. Speed is four zero, traffic lights ahead.'

The surveillance team then carried out a convoy check on the radio so everyone in the team knew their position in relation to the target vehicle.

The two motorcycles maintained the eyeball, alternating as they sped along the main A60 towards the city.

DS Travers monitored the radio, coordinating the surveillance.

The rider of Mike Two spoke over the radio: 'At Redhill roundabout. Target vehicle has indicated and is into the service station. Repeat, into the service station. I'm going past. Mike Two no longer has the eyeball.'

Immediately, Charlie Two came on the radio. 'From Charlie Two, we've got the eyeball. We've pulled in for petrol. Not blocked at the pumps. Footman down into services, following target. Over.'

There was silence for a few minutes.

The surveillance team quickly got into position to cover all exits from the services.

Charlie Two spoke: 'From Charlie Two, target is now out of service station. It's definitely our man. He took his crash helmet off inside the services. He's purchased a couple of two-litre bottles of water and several packs of sandwiches. Target has placed all the purchased items in a plain white carrier bag, which is now inside the top box of the target motorcycle. Helmet now back on, starting motorcycle. It's an off off, and it's the first exit, towards the city. Over.'

'Charlie Three, we have the eyeball. Mike One, take it when you can, please.'

'From Mike One, will do.'

The two motorcycles alternated the surveillance as they sped first through Arnold and then Sherwood. The motorcyclists kept pace with the target easily as he weaved in and out of the traffic. The three cars kept up as best they could.

DS Travers picked up another radio, which was on the channel being used by the MCIU. He said, 'DS Travers to DI Hopkirk.'

Brian was walking into the Newton Building when he heard the message. He grabbed the radio from his jacket pocket. 'DS Travers, go ahead.'

'From DS Travers: We're following the target into the city. We are currently going through Sherwood, approaching Carrington.'

'From DI Hopkirk, keep me informed. I want to know if you have a stop.'

'Will do. Over.'

At the MCIU offices, Danny Flint was also monitoring the radios for both the surveillance channel and the MCIU channel.

He was in the office with Andy Wills, finalising the figures for the crunch meeting with Detective Chief Superintendent Adrian Potter that would determine the future of the MCIU.

Danny turned to Andy and said, 'I wonder why Temple's bought all that food and water. Still, it sounds like things are moving. Have you got car keys?'

Andy nodded. 'Yes, boss.'

'Good. I think we might be going to the city very soon.'

'What about your eleven-thirty meeting with Potter?'

'That might have to wait.'

84

10.30am, 18 October 1986
Nottingham Trent University, Goldsmith Street, Nottingham

Brian and Rachel walked into the Newton Building. Rachel could see Stacey Bloom waiting in the reception area for them. She approached Stacey while Brian spoke to the surveillance team on the radio.

Rachel said, 'Hi, Stacey. Thanks for taking the time to see us again today.'

'No problem. What's up?'

Brian had finished speaking on the radio. He joined the two women as they made their way to Bloom's office. He said, 'Hello, Stacey. I just want to run a few matters by you again so I'm clear about things.'

'Happy to help, Inspector.'

'It hasn't rained for almost eighteen hours now. How dangerous will those caves be right now?'

'Sandstone does dry out fairly quickly. I would think it's still going to be pretty treacherous down there. Why?'

Rachel said, 'Stacey, has Professor Temple been okay lately? He seemed extremely stressed when he was talking to us yesterday.'

Stacey was thoughtful for a second; then she said, 'Professor Temple's normally really laid-back. In fact, he's so laid-back, he's almost horizontal. Just lately though, he's been a bit uptight and snappy.'

'Can you think of any reason why?'

'I suppose it could be frustration.'

'About what exactly?

'We normally go down into the cave system every other day, to monitor things. He hasn't allowed anyone underground for just over a fortnight now.'

'Why is that?'

'Because they're so dangerous.'

Brian said, 'How do you know?'

'Excuse me?'

'If you haven't been in the caves for over a fortnight, how do you know they're dangerous?'

Stacey was silent.

Rachel asked, 'Is there anything else about him, or his behaviour, that you've found a little odd recently?'

Stacey was again deep in thought, as though wrestling with a decision. She looked at Rachel and said, 'Yesterday, when Professor Temple said he had to rush off to another meeting.'

'Go on?'

'It was a lie. He told you that he had an urgent meeting with members of Bassetlaw Council, at Creswell Crags. I telephoned the council later that day, to discover what the outcome of that meeting was. Nobody at the council knew what I was talking about. There was no meeting.'

'Why would he do that?'

Stacey shrugged. 'I've got no idea. He's done it a lot lately. Made an excuse to leave the office and then not come back for the rest of the day. It's all been a bit weird and not like him.'

As they walked into Bloom's office, Brian said, 'Stacey, I'm going to be straight with you. I genuinely believe that a young girl could be being held against her will in the caves around the Forest Road East area. I'd like you to take us down into the caves so we can have a look.'

'I can't do that without obtaining permission from Professor Temple first. I don't think you understand the situation. I could lose my job here.'

'And there could be a young girl in those caves, who may be in serious danger. At least take us down into the Peel Street entrance. If the caves are still too dangerous, I'll accept what you're saying, and we won't go any further. Would you consider doing that?'

Stacey looked troubled for a minute. Then she grabbed two heavy bags from the floor of the office and said, 'These bags contain all the equipment we'll need. Let's go.'

85

10.30am, 18 October 1986
Cavendish Road East, The Park, Nottingham

Thirty minutes had ticked slowly by before a taxi pulled up outside Freddie Fletcher's flat.

As the front door opened, Glen Lorimar said, 'Here we go. Looks like our man's on the move.'

Fletcher had changed his clothes. He was now wearing dirty jeans and an old maroon-coloured sweatshirt. A navy-blue baseball cap covered his blonde hair. He was carrying a brown leather grip bag with the word ADIDAS emblazoned on the side in gold letters.

Rob said, 'Start the car. Let's see where he's going.'

As the dark green city taxi pulled away from the kerb, Glen eased the CID car behind it. He deliberately hung back a little, in case Fletcher was looking around him.

Rob said, 'Take it easy; don't get too close. I don't want him to see us.'

A brief five-minute ride across the city ended when the taxi's nearside indicator came on, and it was driven to a stop on Cranmer Street, not far from the Forest Road cemetery.

Rob said, 'Pull in here.'

Glen manoeuvred the CID car behind another parked vehicle.

Cranmer Street was a tree-lined road, with large houses that had been mainly converted into flats. At one time, it would have been a very salubrious area of the city to live in. Now it was a dump. At night, the street became a regular haunt for girls working the vice trade.

The taxi had stopped outside a large house that was in a sorry state of neglect and disrepair. The gardens had been left to run wild and were now so overgrown that it was difficult to see the front of the house. The parts of the house that could be seen were a total mess. Glass in the windows had long since disappeared. What paint there had been on the window frames had peeled away, and the frames were now rotting. The roof was missing all the lead flashing, a target for thieves soon after the house became empty. Many of the grey slate roof tiles were also missing, exposing the bare wood of the roof trusses.

Fletcher got out of the taxi. He leaned back in through the front window and paid the driver. The taxi drove away, leaving Fletcher on the quiet street, holding the brown leather bag.

Twenty-five yards away, the two detectives slunk down in the seats of their vehicle as Fletcher looked around him.

Rob whispered, 'What's he doing in this shithole?'

Glen replied, 'And what's in that bag?'

The street was empty. As soon as the young barrister was satisfied he wasn't being watched from the neighbouring houses, he opened the rusting gate into the garden of the derelict house and walked in.

Rob and Glen immediately got out of their vehicle and followed Fletcher. They watched him walk to the rear of the property. They followed, being careful not to disturb any of the overgrown vegetation and make a noise.

At the back of the house, Fletcher stopped in front of a wooden cover that protected the cellar. There was a gleaming new padlock securing the cellar cover. From behind bushes in the rear garden, the two detectives looked on as Fletcher removed a key from his jeans pocket and opened the padlock. He took one last look around him, then flung back the two wooden covers and climbed down into the cellar.

Rob whispered, 'Let's get closer. I want to get hold of him when he comes back out. What the hell's down that cellar?'

Both detectives were already daring to think the missing girl could be being held captive in that cellar.

86

10.45am, 18 October 1986
Forest Road East, Nottingham

The regional crime squad surveillance team were still doggedly following Brandon Temple as he raced through the city streets on his Suzuki motorcycle.

Mike One was directly behind Temple. He spoke over the radio using the usual surveillance technique of repeating directions. 'Target has now turned right onto Gregory Boulevard, at the goose fair island. Repeat, it's a right right onto Gregory Boulevard. Mike Two, are you in a position to take the eyeball?'

'From Mike Two, I'll be behind you in twenty seconds. I'm just turning onto Gregory Boulevard now.'

Listening to the commentary in his own vehicle, DS Travers said on the radio, 'Charlie One to team, close in. Let's all close up now.'

'From Mike Two, I now have the eyeball. It's a left left on to Noel Street, stand by.'

There was a pause.

'From Mike Two, target vehicle is now through the traffic lights and onto Mount Hooton Road, towards Forest Road East. It's a left left onto Forest Road East. Target vehicle is slowing, I'm going past. Can anybody behind me take the eyeball?'

'From Charlie Two, we're behind you and in position to slow with the target vehicle. Stand by.'

Another pause.

'From Charlie Two, target vehicle slowed opposite a row of derelict garages on Forest Road East. Rider was clocking the garages. Target vehicle didn't stop, just slowed right down. I now have an offside indication on the target vehicle. It's a right right onto Addison Street and a right right again onto Baker Street. Going past. Baker Street's a dead end, putting a footman down. Stand by.'

There was a pause as the passenger in Charlie Two got out of the car and sprinted back to the junction of Addison Street and Baker Street.

'From DC Ryan, I've now got eyeball on the target. He's parked his motorbike and is removing the white bag of groceries from the top box. Helmet off and into top box. He's secured the top box and applied the steering lock on the bike. He's on foot and walking back towards Addison Street. Any other foot officers down?'

DS Travers had already got out of Charlie One and was waiting at a bus stop on the junction of Addison Street and Forest Road East.

'From DS Travers, I'm out and have the eyeball. Suspect is walking back towards Forest Road East. He's in possession of the white carrier bag containing the water and sandwiches he bought at the services. All units, stand by.'

There was a longer pause.

'From DS Travers, suspect has entered one of the garages on Forest Road East. Maintain your positions. I've got eyeball on the garage and will give the off when he comes out again. Stand by.'

While he maintained observations on the derelict garage, DS Travers used the other radio to contact DI Hopkirk.

Speaking clearly, he quickly informed Brian of his location and informed him that Brandon Temple had disappeared into a derelict garage, carrying food and water.

Brian was with Rachel and Stacey Bloom, about to enter the Peel Street entrance to the caves. He stopped at the entrance and said to Stacey, 'Is it possible there are other entrances to the cave system from Forest Road East itself?'

Stacey Bloom nodded. 'Yes, it's possible. The mine workings were accessed from lots of places in this area. Over the years, most of these entrances have become hidden.'

Brian said, 'I think we should travel to Forest Road East; officers have followed a suspect into a derelict garage on that road. There's no real reason why anybody would want to go in those garages. Will you come with us, Stacey?'

'Yes, of course.'

Back at the MCIU offices in Mansfield, Danny was also listening intently to the radio signals. He'd heard enough. Turning to Andy, he said, 'Come on, Andy, grab your car keys. We're going to the city. The meeting with Potter will just have to wait. Something's developing down there.'

87

10.45am, 18 October 1986
Cranmer Street, Nottingham

Rob and Glen had moved in closer and now had a clear view of the cellar cover as they waited for Freddie Fletcher to re-emerge. After a five-minute wait, Fletcher climbed out of the cellar. He was no longer in possession of the brown leather Adidas bag.

Rob waited for him to secure the padlock, then stepped forward. 'Hello, Mr Fletcher. What's down the cellar?'

Totally surprised at the sudden appearance of the detectives, Fletcher blustered, 'What? I don't understand. Why are you here?'

Glen said, 'We thought you might be home today, and we wanted to find out why you lied to us when we spoke to you in Manchester.'

Fletcher smiled. 'Oh, that. Don't worry, I can explain everything.'

Rob said, 'Start by explaining what's in the cellar.'

The smile disappeared. Fletcher said, 'There's nothing down there. The house belongs to a mate. I'm just keeping an eye on it.'

Glen growled, 'Give me the padlock key. Now!'

Surprised by the venom in the detective's voice, Fletcher handed over the key for the padlock.

As Glen bent down to unlock the cellar cover, Rob said, 'Let's all go and have a look, shall we? Is the Whitchurch girl down here, Fletcher?'

Fletcher said, 'What? No, of course she isn't. You're wasting your time, Detective. There's nothing in the cellar.'

'In that case, it won't take us long to have a look, will it?'

The three men stepped back down into the cellar. The only light was the sunlight filtering down through the open hatch. In the corner of the cellar, there was a large hole in the wall.

Glen walked over and inspected the hole in the wall. He said, 'Bloody hell! There's a small cave through here.'

Rob gripped Fletcher's arm and walked him towards the hole in the wall.

Fletcher blurted out, 'I didn't know that was there.'

As his eyes became accustomed to the low light in the cave, Rob could see the brown leather holdall just inside the cave entrance.

'How did that bag get in there, then?'

Fletcher smiled a sly grin. 'I've never seen that bag before.'

Glen snarled, 'Don't be a dickhead, Fletcher. You're not wearing gloves; your fingerprints will be all over the bag. The taxi driver who brought you here will have remembered you and the bag. Not to mention the two well-respected and honest detectives who have watched you carry it out of your flat, into the taxi and then into here.'

Rob said, 'What's inside the bag, Fletcher?'

Realising he had been backed into a corner, the young barrister started a damage-limitation strategy. 'Look, it's not much. It's for personal use. I knew at some stage you would want to search my flat. So I moved it here.'

Rob indicated for Glen to look in the bag. The burly detective took out a pair of white latex gloves from his pocket and carefully picked up the bag, avoiding the handles.

The three men walked out of the cave, through the cellar, and back outside into the garden. Glen placed the bag on the floor and carefully eased the zip open.

Looking inside, he saw three medium-sized, clear plastic bags full of white powder.

He turned to Fletcher and said, 'That's a lot of personal use. Quite a habit you've got.'

Fletcher didn't answer.

Rob indicated the bags of powder and said, 'Exactly what's your poison?'

A crestfallen Fletcher said, 'You'll find out anyway. It's cocaine. I got hooked on the stuff while I was studying at Cambridge. I had to lie to you about the time I arrived at Fiskerton for the bridge club. I was late because my dealer hadn't arrived on time. I didn't have time to change my clothes after I'd met him at Hyson Green to take delivery. I drove to my flat, dumped the gear under my bed and drove straight to Fiskerton. What you see there will keep me going for almost six months. I promise you I'm not a dealer. I need it to function properly.'

'You must have known that we would check your alibi, and that lying to us would make us suspect you even more.'

'I knew that. I just needed time to get rid of the drugs before you came to search the flat. I knew you would want to search after what that ditzy secretary from Mulberry told you. I knew if you found the gear beneath my bed, it would be the end of my career.'

Rob shook his head and said, 'Frederick Fletcher, I'm arresting you on suspicion of possession of a Class A drug, namely cocaine.'

He cautioned the barrister as he placed him in handcuffs, then said, 'Come on, let's get you to Central Police Station.'

Rob held onto Fletcher's arm as they walked back through the overgrown garden. Glen followed behind, carrying the brown leather grip bag.

As they reached the CID car, Freddie Fletcher began to weep.

88

10.55am, 18 October 1986
Caves below Forest Road East, Nottingham

Emily heard him coming and shone her Maglite torch up at the ceiling. She watched him as he arrived at the entrance to the pot cave. He would normally get down into the pot cave, but today he remained in the tunnel. From where she was sitting, she couldn't see his face, just the lower half of his body, as he squatted down.

He threw the food and water down into the pot cave and said, 'Make it last. It's the last you'll be getting from me.'

A shocked Emily said, 'What do you mean? Are you letting me go?'

'Things have changed. They didn't learn their lesson. So, now you'll have to stay here.'

'I don't understand; what lesson? Who didn't?'

'Your father and my wife.'

'I don't know you or your wife. What's this got to do with me?'

'This isn't a debate! You're staying here to die. That's the only way your feckless father will understand true loss.'

'You can't leave me here. I'm begging you. Please.'

The man had already started to walk away.

Emily shouted, 'Come back! Please!'

There were loud splashes as lumps of the sandstone roof began to fall into the water she was sitting in.

Realising it was her shouting causing the unstable roof to fall, she fell silent. A muted, wretched sobbing began emanating from her tightly pressed lips.

89

11.10am, 18 October 1986
Forest Road East, Nottingham

Rachel parked the car on Addison Street, near to its junction with Baker Street. As soon as they arrived, Brian got out of the car and walked over to DC Ryan. He was now listening intently to the surveillance officers' radio.

Suddenly, it crackled back into life. 'From DS Travers, suspect is now leaving the garage. He's walking along Forest Road East towards Addison Street. Everyone in position?'

Brian spoke on the radio: 'This is DI Hopkirk. Has the suspect still got the bag of food with him?'

DS Travers replied, 'Negative. He no longer has the bag of food and water.'

'Right. I'm going to intercept him at his vehicle. I'm going to detain him on suspicion of abduction. Over.'

'Received. Suspect's turning onto Addison Street. He should be in your view now.'

'Yeah, we've got him. Secure the garage, please.'

'Will do.'

DS Travers immediately left the bus stop and made his way to the disused garage. The wooden doors were closed, but not locked. The detective opened the door.

The garage was empty.

'DS Travers to DI Hopkirk. The garage is empty.'

'Any sign of the bag of food?'

'Negative.'

Brandon Temple was now already back at his motorcycle, and Brian had a huge decision to make.

He walked across the road towards Temple, cautioned him and said, 'Brandon Temple, I'm arresting you on suspicion of the abduction of Emily Whitchurch.'

At first, Temple was shocked. He quickly recovered and said, 'That's preposterous! What utter nonsense.'

Brian wasn't fazed by the university professor's bluster. He said calmly, 'Where have you just been?'

'I went for a walk on the recreation ground. I needed some fresh air.'

'Been there long?'

'I don't know, about half an hour or so. Why?'

'What's in the garage, Professor?'

Abruptly, the mask of normality slipped from Temple's face. His lip curled, and he snarled, 'It doesn't matter what's in the fucking garage anymore!'

Brian placed handcuffs on Temple, grabbed his arm and said, 'Come on. Let's go and see, shall we?'

As Brian began to walk Temple back along Addison Street, towards Forest Road East, Rachel jumped out of the car and said to Stacey Bloom, 'Follow me, but try not to let Professor Temple see you, okay?'

Stacey nodded and said, 'Bloody hell! I didn't think your suspect would be my boss.'

Rachel quickly caught up with Brian, who said, 'DC Moore, Professor Temple's going to show us what's inside the derelict garage he's just visited.'

Temple snarled and tried to break Brian's grip on his arm. Brian gripped him even tighter and whispered in his ear, 'Don't fucking bother, Temple. There are cops everywhere.'

As Brian, Rachel and Brandon Temple approached the garages, DS Travers opened the door.

Brian looked inside; the garage was empty except for several sheets of hardboard that were propped against the far wall.

Brian turned to Rachel. 'Shift those boards.'

With help from DS Travers, Rachel moved the boards away from the back wall. Secreted behind the boards was a small hole in the brick wall. Rachel looked inside and could see that beyond it was an entrance into the cave system. Anybody entering the caves via this entrance would need to get down on their hands and knees. The hole was tiny.

Brian turned to Brandon Temple and, for the first time, noticed the dust on the knees of his trousers. He said, 'Is the girl down there?'

Temple said nothing, but allowed a cruel smile to play on his lips.

Brian turned to DS Travers and said, 'Take him back to my car and keep him there. I need to clarify something.'

DS Travers spoke quietly, out of earshot of Temple. 'Sir, the new guidelines of the Police and Criminal Evidence Act say we should take him straight to a designated police station, to get him booked into custody, now that you've nicked him.'

'I only need five minutes, Sergeant; a young girl's life could be at stake here.'

Travers nodded. 'Okay, boss.'

As soon as Travers had removed Brandon Temple from the garage, Brian said, 'Where's Stacey?'

'She's outside.'

'Fetch her in here.'

Rachel returned a minute later with Stacey Bloom. The geology student was carrying a bag of equipment.

Brian said, 'Stacey, will you have a quick look in there, please? I've looked as far as I can, but it's very dark. We need torches. Do you think this entrance could lead into the main cave system?'

Stacey grabbed a torch and a hard hat from the bag and crawled through the small hole. She was only gone for a few minutes before she re-emerged and said, 'This entrance leads into the main mine workings, alright. He's definitely been down here today as well. I can see his footprints in the soft, damp sand. It's still very wet inside the caves, Inspector. I don't think we should go in any further at this time.'

'Okay, Stacey. I need to go and speak to the professor.'

Brian jogged back round to Addison Street, where he saw DS Travers standing outside his car. Temple was sitting in handcuffs on the back seat.

Brian opened the rear door of the car and said, 'Professor, I know that the entrance in the garage leads into the mine workings below. It's not too late to stop people getting hurt. Is Emily hidden in those mine workings?'

'She's down there alright, but you'll never find her. Don't even think about putting search teams down there. It's so wet the whole system could collapse at any moment. I'd be surprised if the roof hasn't collapsed already.'

'Come on, man. Tell us where the girl is; none of this is her fault. Nobody needs to get hurt. We can go down there quietly and get her out.'

'You really don't get it, do you? Why can't you understand that I don't want you to find her? I want her to die down there. Her father took away the only person I've ever truly loved, so now he needs to know what real loss feels like.'

'Professor, I'm begging you. This has nothing to do with that young girl. Whatever's been happening between her father and your wife, it's not Emily's fault. Can't you see that? Why should she pay the price for their betrayal?'

Temple scoffed. 'Somebody has to pay.'

Brian said angrily, 'So you're too much of a coward to physically harm the girl, but you're quite happy for nature to take its course, and allow that young girl to die a slow death underground?'

Temple smiled malevolently. 'You're wasting your breath, Detective. I've said all I'm going to say.'

Brian shook his head in frustration. He turned to DS Travers and said, 'I need somebody to secure the garage while we search that cave for the girl.'

Travers turned to DC Ryan and said, 'Stevie, take Temple to Central, and get him booked in. Inspector, I'll come back with you and secure the garage.'

The young detective nodded. 'Okay, Sarge.'

Brian stared at Temple and said to the young detective, 'Get this piece of shit out of my sight.'

As Temple was driven away to Central Police Station, Brian and DS Travers ran back around to the garage. Brian said, 'I want you to make sure nobody comes in the caves after we've gone in to look for the girl. It's very unstable down there. If too many people go in at once, the roof's likely to collapse. DCI Flint's on his way. I want you to fully update him when he arrives. Remember, the most important thing is that nobody else enters the cave. Understood?'

'Understood.'

90

11.15am, 18 October 1986
Forest Road East, Nottingham

Brian walked back inside the garage and spoke to Rachel and Stacey. 'Professor Temple's just told me that the girl's hidden down there somewhere.'

Stacey said, 'Did he say how far down into the system?'

Brian shook his head. 'The only thing he said was that we'd never find her.'

DS Travers said, 'Temple was only down there about twenty-five minutes. How far could he get in that time?'

Stacey said, 'That's good. He couldn't have gone too far.'

Rachel said, 'We don't even know if she's still alive.'

Brian replied, 'She's alive, alright. He wouldn't have bothered coming here, bringing food and water, if the girl were already dead. It's obviously not for him, is it?'

Stacey looked worried; then she said, 'Any second now,

you're going to ask me to go with you to look for her, aren't you?'

Brian replied, 'I'm going down there anyway. I can't leave the girl down there alone in the dark, when the roof could fall in on her at any moment. I've got to try to get her out of there. Stacey, I can't ask you to go into the caves if you think it's too dangerous.'

Stacey smiled. 'It would be far more dangerous for everybody if I *didn't* go with you. I'm coming. Look in the equipment bags. You'll find hard hats and utility belts. Find ones that fit you and put them on. Understand this though, when we're down in the caves, what I say goes. I'm in charge. If at any time I tell you to get out, just do it. There won't be time to have a debate; just get out as fast as you can. These caves can be treacherous and deadly. I know the signs before a roof fall, so you must listen to me.'

Rachel started to open the bags, searching for kit.

Brian said, 'What are you doing?'

'I'm getting kitted up as well. I'm coming with you.'

'I don't think that's a good idea.'

'Are you ordering me to stay here? You may need an extra pair of hands when we eventually find her. We have no idea how she's being held, or what state she's going to be in after spending a fortnight down here.'

Stacey interrupted, 'It doesn't really matter if you both go. As long as you're extremely quiet while we're underground. Noise is going to be our enemy. Loud noises from above or below ground can suddenly cause an unstable cave roof to collapse completely.'

The detectives nodded and both began rooting around inside the bags for equipment.

Brian removed his suit jacket, rolled his sleeves up and clipped on the belt. The belt contained a torch, first aid kit, spare batteries and a bone-handled sheath knife.

'What's the knife for?'

'We use it to scrape lumps of rock off the walls. Sometimes we need to take samples to determine the age of workings. The point of the knife will be blunt, but the blade is still razor sharp, so be careful with it.'

Stacey finished adjusting her own equipment. She looked at the two detectives, who were now fully kitted out, and said, 'Ready?'

Brian said, 'Realistically, what are our chances of finding the girl?'

Stacey said, 'It's extremely wet – saturated, really. This means the rock is in a very unpredictable state. It's friable at the best of times, but when it's soaked like it is now, it's bloody dangerous. The plus side to it being so wet is that I'll easily be able to see the footprints left by the professor when he was down here earlier. I'm hoping those footprints lead us straight to the girl. If you're both ready, let's go.'

91

11.30am, 18 October 1986
Forest Road East, Nottingham

Andy Wills drove the CID car at speed along Forest Road East. The derelict garages were on the right-hand side of the road, directly opposite the cemetery.

Suddenly, Danny shouted, 'That's DS Travers outside the garages! Pull in!'

Andy braked hard and brought the car to a juddering, screeching halt. Danny jumped out of the car and ran across the road, towards Travers.

He said, 'Where's DI Hopkirk?'

DS Travers said, 'The DI's gone down into the caves to look for the girl.'

'What?'

'We followed Professor Temple from his house to here.

He left his motorcycle just around the corner and walked back to this garage. Your DI made the decision to arrest him.'

'Why did he arrest him?'

'I think it was the bag of food. We watched Temple purchase food and water from the services at Redhill when we were following him into the city. After he left his motorcycle, he walked back around to this garage. When he went in, he was carrying the food and water. When he came out again, he was minus the food and water. It was a good call by your DI, I reckon.'

'So why has he gone straight in the caves?'

'Brandon Temple admitted to us that the girl's down there somewhere. He wouldn't say where, so both your officers have gone looking.'

'Officers?'

'Yes, sir. The DI and the DC he was working with have both gone down with the cave expert they brought with them.'

Danny turned to Andy and said, 'We need to get a full search party organised. We need to get in and search the caves fully. I don't know what Brian was thinking, rushing straight in there like that.'

DS Travers said, 'That's out of the question, sir. The cave expert said a big search party would be far too dangerous because of the state of the rock. She said a large search team would be too noisy. Apparently, noise can be enough to cause the roof of the caves to collapse. That's why your detectives have gone down now. It's the best chance of getting the girl out alive.'

'Bloody hell!' Danny looked at Andy and said, 'Who is this cave expert?'

Travers spoke before Andy could. 'The cave expert is a young woman; I didn't hear her name though.'

Andy said, 'It sounds like it could be the professor's

assistant, Stacey Bloom. Rachel was telling me yesterday how impressed she was with her.'

Danny turned back to DS Travers. 'How long have they been down there?'

Travers glanced at his watch. 'About ten minutes.'

'How long was Temple in the garage alone?'

'From going inside the garage to coming out again, about twenty-five minutes to half an hour.'

Danny said to Andy, 'This is going to be a long fifteen minutes.'

92

11.35am, 18 October 1986
Nottinghamshire Police Headquarters

Chief Superintendent Adrian Potter was drumming his fountain pen on the blotter on his desk. He looked up at the clock. Snatching the telephone off its cradle, he punched the button for his secretary. The call was answered immediately: 'Yes, sir.'

Potter growled, 'Amanda, you can send in Detective Chief Inspector Flint now.'

'I'm sorry, sir, the chief inspector hasn't arrived yet.'

'Has his office called to say that he's going to be late?'

'No, sir. I haven't had any messages from the MCIU.'

'Very well. Can you put me through to the chief constable, please?'

'Of course, sir.'

The next voice Potter heard was that of the chief constable. 'Jack Renshaw.'

In a queasy, servile voice, Potter said, 'I'm sorry to bother you, sir. I really need to speak with you about Chief Inspector Flint and the MCIU. The whole department are a disgrace. They appear to have no respect for authority at all. It stems right from the top, all the way down.'

'I don't understand, Adrian. What lack of respect?'

'I had scheduled a meeting with Chief Inspector Flint this morning, to discuss the organisation and cost-effectiveness of the MCIU. He just hasn't bothered to show up. I'm totally disgusted by his lack of professionalism and courtesy.'

'Have you phoned his office to see where he is?'

'I don't think I should be running after him to attend a prearranged meeting, sir. That would send out all the wrong signals. He should have the common courtesy to attend. I really think something needs to be done about this department, sir.'

Jack Renshaw was surprised by what he was hearing. He had always considered Danny Flint to be the consummate professional. He could tell there was no love lost between Detective Chief Inspector Flint and the new head of CID.

The chief constable was all too aware of Potter's talent for alienating his staff. That lack of management skills always had to be weighed against the excellent administrative brain he possessed.

Renshaw decided to intervene personally. 'Thank you for bringing this to my attention, Adrian,' he said. 'I'll contact Chief Inspector Flint myself and see what the hell he's playing at.'

Potter allowed a satisfied, smug grin to form before saying, 'Thank you, sir. I knew you would understand.'

Renshaw hung up the phone and said to himself, 'Oh, I understand alright, Adrian.'

He picked up the telephone and dialled the direct line number for Danny Flint's office. There was no reply.

With growing frustration, he put the telephone down.

He thought that maybe Flint was on his way and had been delayed in traffic.

Jack Renshaw decided that he would wait thirty minutes and try his office again.

93

**11.35am, 18 October 1986
Caves below Forest Road East, Nottingham**

Stacey Bloom shone her torch along the floor of the narrow tunnel. She ignored the sound of water constantly dripping from the roof and concentrated fully on following the footprints left by Brandon Temple. There was one set of footprints leading further into the cave system and another set returning.

Brian and Rachel crept quietly along behind the young student, hardly daring to breathe. They made painfully slow progress. Every so often, without warning, a piece of the tunnel roof dropped to the floor with a wet thud. Each time it happened, all three of them stopped and crouched down for a minute, fearing the worst.

Brian whispered, 'Do you think it's much further, Stacey?'
Stacey shrugged and whispered, 'No talking.'
They were deep into the cave system now and had walked

past countless examples of the old hourglass-shaped pillars carved out by the sand miners.

The footprints illuminated by Stacey's torch suddenly veered off to the right and into yet another narrow tunnel.

Suddenly, from out of the darkness came a solitary shout. 'Help me!'

The sound of the young girl's mournful voice instantly caused large pieces of the roof to start dropping into the tunnel.

Once again, the three would-be rescuers crouched down and waited for the inevitable.

Eventually, the lumps of rock stopped falling, and the only sound to be heard was that of water constantly dripping into the tunnel.

Stacey turned back to face Brian and Rachel.

She had a worried expression on her face and said in a voice that was barely a whisper, 'It's really bad here. If she shouts again, we could all be buried. I think we need to get out while we still can.'

Brian whispered, 'She didn't sound that far away. You two wait here. I'll go on for another twenty or so yards and see if I can find her.'

Stacey breathed, 'It's too risky. We need to leave now.'

'I'm not leaving that young girl down here to die. I'm sorry, Stacey. I won't be long.'

Brian squeezed by Stacey and began making his way along the narrow tunnel, shining his torch on the footprints left by Temple.

Twenty yards along the tunnel, the footprints suddenly stopped.

Shining his torch right and left, Brian saw the entrance to the pot cave.

Suddenly, he heard a voice that was little more than a breathy whisper. 'Please don't leave me here to die.'

Brian shone his torch directly into the pot cave, and for the first time he saw the girl. As he climbed down into the pot cave, he said quietly, 'Don't worry, Laura.' He didn't even notice he'd used his own beloved daughter's name. 'I'm going to get you out of here.'

The girl answered with a sob.

Brian shone his torch onto the roof, illuminating the entire pot cave. He could see that the girl's hands were bound with thick rope, and that the rope was attached to a large stake at the centre of the cave. Grabbing the rope around the girl's wrists, he could feel that the knots had been covered in a resin-type substance. He realised that he would be unable to untie the knots that secured her wrists.

He turned his attention to the stake and found that the knots securing the rope to the stake were also covered in the same type of resin.

Grabbing the sheath knife from his belt, he felt his way along the rope until he found an area that hadn't been smothered in the hard resin. He quickly set to work with the knife, trying to saw his way through the thick nylon rope. The blade of the knife was as razor sharp as Stacey had said it was, and Brian was able to sever the rope near to the clump of knots that bound the girl's wrists.

Now that she was finally freed from the stake, he was able to help the terrified young girl to her feet.

He said in a whisper, 'As soon as you're in the tunnel, walk to your left. There are people waiting there to help you get out. You'll see their torches. I'm going to be right behind you.'

The girl simply stared back before nodding.

Brian physically lifted her up and out of the pot cave, placing her into the main tunnel.

Emily looked to her left and began to sob when she could see the light of the torches held by Stacey and Rachel along the narrow tunnel.

Brian stood below her in the pot cave. He said, 'Get going, Laura. I'm right behind you.'

As Emily staggered along the tunnel, Brian started to climb out of the pot cave. He was almost out when his right foot slipped on the wet sandstone and he fell backwards. He landed heavily onto the wet floor of the pot cave, narrowly missing the wooden stake in the centre of the floor.

Just as Emily reached Stacey and Rachel, there was a low rumbling noise above their heads, followed by a loud cracking sound.

Stacey said, 'All of you, move now. Run!'

Brian had almost made it out of the pot cave when he heard the crack. Suddenly, the entire roof of the pot cave fell, burying him beneath tons of wet sandstone.

In the tunnel, more of the roof continued to fall as Stacey, Rachel and Emily staggered along, trying to follow Temple's footprints on the wet, slippery floor.

As they progressed along the narrow tunnels, gradually the roof falls lessened. Eventually, the only noise they could hear was their own laboured breathing.

Rachel grabbed Stacey and stopped her. 'I've got to go back and look for Brian.'

'Rachel, you saw the same thing as me. That entire tunnel near the entrance to the pot cave fell in. I think he was still in the pot cave when it came down.'

'I've got to go and look.'

Stacey shook her head. 'You stay here with the girl; I'll go and have a look.'

Rachel nodded and put her arm around the frightened young girl. As they watched Stacey disappear back into the gloom of the tunnel, illuminated in silhouette by her torch, Emily said quietly, 'Who was that man? Is he going to be okay?'

Rachel nodded. 'He's a policeman who's been looking for you, Emily. Don't worry; he'll be fine.'

Slowly, Stacey retraced her steps back through the tunnels, carefully stepping over the debris from the recent roof falls. When she reached the point where the tunnel had veered off to the right, she stopped in her tracks. There was a wall of wet, sludgy rock that completely blocked the narrow tunnel to the pot cave.

She said a silent prayer, turned and walked back through the maze of tunnels until she found Rachel still holding Emily tightly.

Rachel said, 'Well? Did you find him?'

Stacey shook her head and whispered, 'There's a major roof fall back there. The tunnel where the pot cave was is entirely blocked from floor to roof. We're going to need expert help to get him out.'

Rachel stifled a cry and wiped her eyes before setting off behind Stacey and Emily. The two women and the young girl were now only five minutes away from the exit that led into the garage.

94

11.45am, 18 October 1986
Forest Road East, Nottingham

The low rumbling noise that emanated from the hole at the back of the garage made Danny spin round and stare into the black void. The low gravelly sound had rolled on, like some distant thunderstorm approaching.

The sound was ominous; it filled him with dread.

He waited anxiously for another five minutes before he heard coughing coming from within the cave system.

Stacey Bloom crawled out of the small hole first, followed by Emily Whitchurch, then finally Rachel.

Danny continued staring at the hole as the two women and the young girl stood up.

Still staring at the small entrance to the caves, Danny said, 'Rachel, where's Brian?'

'He's still down there, boss. There was a roof fall, and Brian got separated from the rest of us.'

'How did that happen?'

'He rescued Emily from a small pot cave. He had to climb down into the cave, cut her free from the ropes that held her, and push her up and out. He had lifted her out and was just coming out himself when the roof came down.'

'So is he trapped or buried?'

Rachel shook her head and said tearfully, 'I don't know.'

Stacey said, 'I went back to look for him, and the tunnel where the pot cave is located is now completely blocked. There's a chance the pot cave roof may have held, and he's trapped behind the roof fall in the tunnel. Either way, we're going to need specialist help to try to get him out of there.'

'I see. Are you Stacey?'

'Stacey Bloom. I'm a geology student studying this cave system.'

'Thank you for going back to look for Brian. That took a lot of guts. I need to start getting things organised here. Are you three okay? Have you got any injuries?'

'Rachel and I are fine, but I don't know about this young lady.'

Stacey indicated Emily, who was now sitting cross-legged on the floor of the garage. The young girl was shattered by her exertions to get out of the caves.

Danny turned to Andy Wills and said, 'Get an ambulance for Emily. I also want enough uniformed staff here to establish cordons. We're going to need to block Forest Road East entirely, so we'll need to get diversions organised. It sounds like it's going to be a long job getting Brian out of there.'

Andy said, 'How are we going to get him out?'

'I'm going to put a call into the Mines Rescue Station at Mansfield Woodhouse. They train for this sort of thing every day. I know their gaffer, Ray Machin. Hopefully, they'll be able to get here quickly and get him out.'

There was a brief pause as Danny thought about his options. 'While I'm organising that, I'll need you to remain on scene here to co-ordinate the cordons and the road closures. Rachel, I want you to go with Emily to the hospital. Don't worry about getting a first disclosure unless she volunteers something. That will keep. I'm going to try to contact Rob, to establish where he is and what he's doing. I'll get him to pick up Emily's parents from Richmond Drive and take them to the hospital with DC Bailey. As their family liaison officer, it's better if Helen remains at the hospital with them. As soon as they arrive, I want you and Rob to come straight back here. Okay – does everyone know what they need to do?'

Andy said, 'I'll get onto it.'

Rachel said, 'Should we contact Brian's wife, Maggie?'

Danny shook his head. 'Not yet. Let's see how things develop for now. There's no point dragging her down here and frightening her to death.'

Rachel nodded.

Stacey said, 'Would you like me to do anything, Chief Inspector?'

'Stacey, I'm going to ask the Mines Rescue teams to help get my colleague out. Would you mind staying and speaking with their boss, Ray Machin? I'm sure he'll appreciate your expert knowledge of the type of rock he's going to have to get through.'

'No problem. I'm happy to help in any way I can.'

'Thanks, Stacey.'

Danny walked out of the garage and saw DS Travers, who said, 'Everything okay?'

'Not really. My DI's still trapped down there. He's got the girl out, but then the roof caved in on him.'

'Bloody hell! Is he going to make it?'

'I don't know. As soon as uniforms start arriving, you and your staff can resume.'

'We'll stay if there's anything we can do.'

'Thanks for the offer, but there isn't. It's going to take an expertise far beyond our skills to get him out of there. I appreciate all you've done today. Please tell DCI Carlisle that I'll call him first thing tomorrow.'

'Okay, boss.'

Danny then spoke into his radio: 'DCI Flint to DI Buxton.'

Rob was in the cell block at Central Police Station, preparing to interview Freddie Fletcher. He picked up his radio. 'Go ahead.'

'Where are you, Rob?'

'Central cells. I'm just about to interview Freddie Fletcher with Glen Lorimar. We found Fletcher earlier in possession of a substantial amount of Class A drugs.'

'Can you leave Glen to do the interview? I need you, as a matter of urgency, to travel to Richmond Drive and pick up Dominic and Rebecca Whitchurch. Take them and DC Bailey to the QMC. We've located their daughter in the caves near Forest Road East. Tell them she's okay, and hospital is just a precaution. Rachel's travelling with Emily to the hospital by ambulance. When you've delivered the parents, leave DC Bailey at the hospital with them. I want you and Rachel back here on Forest Road East.'

'That's great news.'

'It's great news, but it's come at a high price. Brian's still trapped in the caves. Rachel will fill you in on what's happened. I need to get to a telephone and make some calls to the Mines Rescue people now.'

A much more sombre Rob replied, 'Okay. I'm on my way. Glen's more than capable of interviewing Fletcher on his own. Tell Rachel I'll see her at the hospital.'

'Thanks, Rob.'

Danny then got in the car and drove to Central Police Station. He abandoned the car in the rear yard and ran inside. He sprinted upstairs to the CID office and picked up the nearest telephone.

DC Fran Jefferies answered the telephone on the second ring. Danny said, 'Fran, I want you to look at the records for the Jimmy Wade enquiry. I need the telephone number for Ray Machin. He's the man in charge at the Mansfield Woodhouse Mines Rescue Station. I need his telephone number urgently.'

Fran said, 'Just a second,' then quickly scanned the computer records for the Wade enquiry. As soon as she had found Ray Machin's details, she picked the telephone back up and gave Danny the number he had requested.

'Thanks, Fran. I'll make this call; then I'm going to call you straight back. Don't go anywhere. I'm going to need you to co-ordinate things over there.'

A puzzled Fran said, 'Okay, boss.'

Danny hung up and then quickly dialled the number Fran had just given him.

There was a long delay before the telephone was answered. 'Hello, Mines Rescue.'

Danny said, 'Could I speak to Ray Machin, please?'

'Speaking.'

Danny breathed a sigh of relief and said, 'Ray, I don't know if you remember me, it's Chief Inspector Danny Flint. I came to see you about the death of Albie Jones at Warsop Main pit. It was a couple of years ago, during the strike?'

'I remember you, Chief Inspector. That was a bad business. What can I do for you?'

'Ray, one of my officers has just rescued a young girl who'd been abducted and held in the caves below Nottingham. Unfortunately, before he could get out himself, there was a roof fall, and he's trapped. I need your expertise to try to get him out. Can you help me?'

'Is he trapped and alive, or buried?'

'I don't know.'

'But there's a chance he's still alive?'

'Yes, there's a chance. I've got an expert on the caves here with me, who says it's possible that he was trapped behind rock as the tunnel collapsed. He was still in a small pot cave, so he may still be alive and in an air pocket.'

'I'll scramble my team. If there's a chance he's still alive, we'll do our best to get him out. Is your expert still on-site? I'll want to talk to him as soon as we arrive.'

'He's a she, Ray. Her name's Stacey Bloom. She's a very gutsy lady and is quite prepared to go back down into the caves if you need her to.'

'Keep her there, please, Danny. Where exactly is the entrance to the cave system?'

'It's on Forest Road East, near to the Goose Fair site. By the time you get here, the roads will be closed. I'll let the officers manning the roadblocks know that you're on your way. Thanks for this.'

'No problem. We'll be with you in thirty minutes.'

Danny hung up and dialled the MCIU number again. This time, he explained to Fran exactly what was happening on Forest Road East. He instructed her to send all available MCIU officers to Central Police Station, to await further instruction.

95

12.05pm, 18 October 1986
Nottinghamshire Police Headquarters

Jack Renshaw was thoughtful as he sat alone in his plush office. He had only been the chief constable for a few weeks and already he had a major conflict between two of his senior officers to try to resolve.

He reflected on the appointment of Adrian Potter as his head of CID. Was the newly appointed detective chief superintendent out of his depth?

Renshaw knew that in a force the size of Nottinghamshire, finance was the key. It was imperative that all departments were cost-effective. He knew the intelligent Yorkshireman would see to it that the CID remained on budget.

He had to weigh that particular talent against his obvious lack of interpersonal skills. Jack Renshaw had been with the Nottinghamshire force long enough to know what a talented detective Danny Flint was, and what a great asset the MCIU was.

It was his first real test of leadership, and he hadn't expected it to come so soon.

He had formulated a strategy that he hoped would satisfy both men. He took a deep breath and dialled the number for the MCIU office.

It was answered on the first ring. 'MCIU, DC Jefferies. How can I help you?'

'DC Jefferies, it's the chief constable. Is your chief inspector in his office?'

'No, sir, he's at the incident on Forest Road East.'

'What incident's that?'

'I'm sorry, sir, I thought you would have heard by now.' She quickly explained the situation at Forest Road East.

'Is DI Hopkirk alive?'

'We don't know, sir. DCI Flint is on scene, coordinating the attempted rescue. He's mobilised the Mines Rescue Service from Mansfield Woodhouse to try to get DI Hopkirk out.'

Jack Renshaw had instantly forgotten all about the petty squabble between his senior officers. One of his men was now in grave danger, and he knew where he had to be.

He said calmly, 'Exactly where is Chief Inspector Flint, and when did this happen?'

'It happened about forty minutes ago; the rendezvous point is on Forest Road East, at its junction with Addison Street.'

'Thank you, Detective.'

Renshaw placed the telephone on the receiver, picked it straight back up and spoke to his secretary. 'Caroline, I need to be in the city immediately. Contact my driver and have him outside the front doors in five minutes, please.'

'Yes, sir.'

He hung up the telephone and grabbed his tunic from the coat stand. He buttoned up the tunic and grabbed his hat and an overcoat, then strode along the corridor.

When he reached the office of Adrian Potter, he banged on the door with his balled-up fist. He opened the door and said, 'Get your coat, Adrian. We're going to the city. I'm going to show you exactly why Danny Flint never made the meeting this morning, and you and I are going to have a serious conversation on the way there.'

Potter looked up from behind his desk, nonplussed.

He could tell the change in attitude of the chief constable was not in his favour, and he wondered what had happened to cause that change.

He grabbed his overcoat, and the two men made their way to the front of the headquarters building.

PC Dave Pepper, the chief's driver, was already waiting with the rear doors of the powerful Jaguar saloon open.

As the chief constable was in full uniform, PC Pepper saluted as he got into the vehicle. Jack Renshaw acknowledged the salute and said, 'Forest Road East, at its junction with Addison Street. Quick as you can, please, Dave.'

The instruction was music to the ears of the experienced traffic officer. As soon as the rear doors were closed, he gunned the powerful engine and said, 'Seat belts on, please.'

The dark blue Jaguar raced down the lane from headquarters and approached the traffic lights at the Seven Mile House junction. PC Pepper activated the two tones and the blue lights that were beneath the grille to safely negotiate the junction. As soon as he had turned the vehicle left onto the A60, he accelerated the powerful car.

In the back of the vehicle, Jack Renshaw said, 'The reason Danny Flint didn't make your meeting this morning is because one of his men is trapped in a cave beneath the city.

There's no way of telling whether the officer is still alive, or if he's dead.'

Potter said, 'What on earth was he doing in the caves?'

'Rescuing the Whitchurch girl, by all accounts. By some miracle, he managed to get her out before the roof of the cave collapsed, trapping him.'

'So the Whitchurch girl's okay? That's great news.'

'Yes, the Whitchurch girl's okay, and that *is* good news, Adrian. Don't you see that comments like that are the reason I have a problem with you?'

'I don't understand, sir. What problem?'

'You never think about the consequences of what you're saying. Yes, it's great that the young girl is safe and well. Right now, that is scant consolation to Danny Flint, when the life of his friend and colleague is still at risk. Of course, we'll all rejoice in the fact that the young girl is safe and well, but let's get our man out as well. Do you understand what I'm saying?'

Potter nodded. In reality, he hadn't a clue what the chief constable was talking about.

Renshaw went on, 'You and Danny Flint need to bury the hatchet. I don't know why you've got this bee in your bonnet about the MCIU. I know you're a stickler for the cost of everything, but I'm telling you here and now, the MCIU is staying whatever the cost. They're far too valuable a resource to be disbanded. Is that understood?'

'But, sir ...'

'No buts, Adrian. Is that understood?'

'Yes, sir.'

'Let's get this mess sorted today. Then I'll arrange a proper clear-the-air meeting with you and Danny Flint. You're both very valuable to me and to the future of this force. I need you to be able to work together in the future.'

Potter knew when to acquiesce. He said simply, 'Of course, sir. No problem.'

From the front of the vehicle, Dave Pepper waited for the two senior officers to finish speaking, then said, 'We should be there in fifteen minutes, sir.'

'Thanks, Dave.' Then he reiterated, 'Quick as you can, please.'

96

12.15pm, 18 October 1986
Forest Road East, Nottingham

Danny breathed a sigh of relief as he watched the convoy of bright yellow vehicles turn into Forest Road East and drive towards the row of derelict garages. Two Ford Transit vans, full of experienced mines rescue personnel, were immediately followed by the large equipment trailer that had the appearance of a converted horse transporter. The last vehicle was an articulated lorry that towed the large mobile generator on a trailer.

The first Ford Transit came to a stop beside Danny. As the door of the vehicle opened, he recognised Ray Machin.

Ray Machin smiled grimly as he got out of the vehicle. 'Hello again, Chief Inspector. Where's the entrance to this cave?'

The two men shook hands. Danny said, 'Hello, Ray.

Please call me Danny, okay? Thank you so much for getting here so quickly. The entrance is inside one of these garages.'

'No problem, Danny. We shouldn't really be here, as technically we're only supposed to operate in old mine workings or on National Coal Board property. When there's a life at stake, though, all that procedure malarkey goes out the window, right? My men are getting their equipment together. They'll be ready to enter the cave system in ten minutes.'

Danny nodded grimly.

A woman's voice said, 'If we're talking technicalities, these are very old mine workings, not caves. They're not coal, though. They're sand.'

Ray looked beyond Danny and saw the young woman in the hard hat, standing about a yard away. He smiled and said, 'Well, that's good to know, young lady. And you are?'

Danny said, 'Ray, this is Stacey Bloom, the geology student I told you about.'

'I see, so you're the cave expert. It's good to meet you, Miss Bloom. What can you tell me about the conditions down there?'

Stacey said, 'All of these tunnels and workings were originally excavated by hand. The system used was the pillar and stall method, so the workings themselves supported the roof structure. Normally, although the sandstone is friable, they're a lot less volatile. It's the constant heavy rain we've experienced lately that has made the mine workings so dangerous and unpredictable at the moment.'

Ray nodded and got straight to the point. 'You went back and saw where the officer was buried. Do you think it's possible he's still alive down there?'

Unfazed by the hard question, Stacey replied, 'The entire roof of the tunnel leading to the pot cave has come down. There's a wall of sludgy sandstone filling the entire tunnel, floor to ceiling. It's possible that it was just the roof of the tunnel that collapsed, and that the roof of the pot cave remained intact. If that's the case, then there's a good chance the detective is trapped within the cave. He could be in an air pocket, but the air won't last very long. A maximum of three to four hours is my best guess.'

Ray was deep in thought. 'How far is the pot cave from where the cave-in ends? I need to know how much roof fall we need to get through.'

'I would estimate somewhere between ten to fifteen yards.'

Danny said, 'That's a hell of a lot of dirt and rock to shift.'

Ray said, 'Stacey, are you prepared to direct us to the roof fall? It will save us valuable time.'

'Of course. Anything I can do to help get him out of there.'

Danny marvelled at the young woman's selfless courage. He said, 'Thank you, Stacey.'

He turned back to Ray. 'How long will it take your men to dig their way through the roof fall?'

'I'll let you know better when I've been down and had a look. My intention is to dig a crawl space through the roof fall in the tunnel until we reach the pot cave. From what Miss Bloom says, we won't have time to dig it all out. I won't know if digging out a crawl space is even feasible until I've had a good look.'

'Isn't that method dangerous?'

'There isn't a safe method. All our work is dangerous, Danny. We'll endeavour to shore up the crawl space as we go along. It won't be until we get through to the cave that we'll know if your man has survived the roof fall. I need to get my equipment and recce the situation. Are you ready to go, Miss Bloom?'

Stacey nodded and said, 'I'm ready, but please just call me Stacey, okay?'

The experienced miner smiled and said, 'Stacey it is.'

He turned back to Danny. 'One last thing, I need you to arrange for a couple of ambulances to be here on standby for the duration of the rescue operation. If anything goes wrong, I don't want my staff to be waiting for medical assistance.'

'Of course. I'll get that sorted, Ray. Anything else you need?'

'No, we're all good. We've got our own lights for when it gets dark later.'

Danny nodded and watched as the powerful, squat mines rescue chief made his way towards the equipment trailer. Several of his men were already standing outside the trailer, fully kitted up and ready to go.

Danny looked at the serious expressions on the men's faces. He felt humbled by the miners' willingness to put their own lives at risk to try to rescue a complete stranger.

He felt a lump form in his throat and quickly brushed away the single tear that ran down his cheek.

97

12.15pm, 18 October 1986
Queen's Medical Centre, Nottingham

Emily Whitchurch had been taken to a private room behind the main accident and emergency department at the Queen's Medical Centre.

Doctors had quickly assessed the young girl and found little physically wrong with her. She was malnourished, dehydrated and suffering from sleep deprivation. She was also slightly disoriented after being held in pitch-black darkness for the best part of two weeks.

What the damage to her mental health would be could not yet be determined. Only time would reveal the answer to that question.

Rachel sat at the side of Emily's bed, holding the young girl's hand, while they waited for her parents to arrive. The doctors had advised Emily to keep her eyes closed for a few hours until she got used to the surrounding light. Rachel kept hold of the young girl's hand so that she knew she wasn't alone.

In a voice barely a whisper, Emily said, 'Can I ask you something?'

Rachel said gently, 'Of course you can.'

'You know the policeman who got me out? Why did he keep calling me Laura?'

Rachel said, 'Laura's the name of his own daughter. She's about your age. He must have got confused because of the stressful situation, that's all.'

'He saved my life. If he hadn't got me out of that cave, I'd be dead now. Is he going to be okay?'

'I really don't know, Emily; people are trying to get him out now. You need to try to get some rest now.'

Emily began to sob quietly. 'I hope he's going to be okay.'

Rachel thought to herself, *So do I, sweetheart; so do I.*

The door to the room opened, and a young nurse stuck her head around the door. She said, 'Your mum and dad are here now, Emily. We want you to stay here and rest for a couple more hours while we keep an eye on you. I'll send them in to see you, okay?'

Emily stopped sobbing and nodded.

Rebecca and Dominic walked into the hospital room, followed by DC Helen Baxter. Rebecca sat on her daughter's bed and held her hand tightly. Tears were rolling down her cheeks, and she said quietly, 'Hello, sweetheart, it's Mum. It's so good to see you again. We're going to take you home soon.'

Emily started to cry and said, 'Give me a hug, Mum.'

Rebecca started to cry as well, leaned forward and hugged her daughter.

A hard-faced Rachel stood and asked Dominic, 'Is my inspector here? I need to get back to Forest Road East. DC Baxter's going to stay here with you to make sure you're okay.'

'Detective Inspector Buxton's outside, waiting for you.

Can I ask you a quick question before you go? How did you find her?'

Rachel said, 'We followed a suspect who led us to the caves.'

'A suspect? Who?'

Rachel made eye contact with Dominic and hissed, 'Brandon Temple, Angela's husband.'

Rachel walked out of the room and saw Rob Buxton waiting in the corridor. She said, 'Can we get back to Forest Road East? I can't stand to be around these people any longer.'

98

12.35pm, 18 October 1986
Forest Road East, Nottingham

Rob Buxton parked the CID car next to the Mobile Incident Room that had been driven into position alongside the bright yellow Mines Rescue vehicles, opposite the garage that housed the entrance to the caves.

A tent had been erected in front of the garage doors to prevent the prying lenses of the press from seeing events unfold within the garage.

Rachel got out of the car and saw Danny standing next to the Mobile Incident Room. He was staring into the white tent that led to the garage. Powerful floodlights had been erected inside the garage, causing the tent to shine brilliant white.

Rachel and Rob walked across to Danny. She said, 'Any news, boss?'

Danny shook his head. 'Nothing yet. I'm expecting Ray

Machin to come back with a sitrep any minute now. How were Emily's parents?'

Rob said, 'Obviously overjoyed to have their daughter back safe and sound, but also understandably concerned about the situation here. They've both sent their sincere gratitude to Brian and want to thank him for what he's done.'

Rachel said, 'Yeah, well, let's hope they get the chance to do that in person.'

Danny looked at Rachel and said, 'Something on your mind?'

Rachel was fighting back tears. 'Yes, sir, something's on my mind. This is all down to them. They send us their "sincere gratitude", but it's their selfish behaviour that's led to my friend being trapped underground, fighting for his life.'

Danny put a comforting arm around her shoulder. 'You've every right to be angry. And there's more than a grain of truth in what you say, but we can't afford to think like that. Brian wouldn't have cared how he came to be in that situation. All he would have cared about was that there was a young girl's life to save.'

'Emily told me at the hospital that when Brian was freeing her and getting her out of the pot cave, he kept referring to her as Laura. That's his own daughter's name, boss.'

'I know it is. Brian cares deeply for his own daughter. So it's no surprise to me that he acted so courageously if he was thinking about his own daughter when he freed Emily. Go inside and get a hot drink. I'll keep you informed of any progress, okay?'

Rachel nodded and walked into the Mobile Incident Room.

Rob said, 'She's feeling it, boss.'

'I know. This isn't exactly the easing back into police work I'd envisaged for her. I hope she can cope with this.'

'Rachel's a tough cookie. She'll be fine. It's strange about Brian referring to the Whitchurch girl as Laura, though.'

Danny stared at the ethereal white light emanating from inside the tent and kept his thoughts to himself.

He and Rob were the only people who knew that Brian believed he was about to lose his own daughter, when she flew to America with her mother to start a new life.

Danny understood completely why Brian had been so desperate to get that young girl out of the cave. He now realised that his friend and colleague had seen saving Emily Whitchurch as a substitute for being unable to prevent his own daughter from leaving.

Suddenly, there was movement at the cave entrance, which ripped Danny from his thoughts. He stepped inside the garage, followed by Rob.

A dirty-faced Ray Machin emerged from the entrance. He saw Danny waiting and said, 'It's good news. Things down there aren't as bad as I feared. Now that Stacey's had another look, she thinks we're probably only ten yards from the entrance to the pot cave. The soil and sandstone that's come down from the roof is still very wet, but that means it's easy to shift. I just need to get more props organised, and then we can start digging the crawl space in earnest.'

'How long before your men can reach the cave?'

'If we work flat out, we should make it within the three hours. I just hope Stacey's right about how much air will be available in the cave. I'm sorry, Danny; I need to get cracking.'

'Sorry, don't let me stop you.'

Ray Machin started barking orders to his men in the supply truck. They immediately began unloading more of the white props and sheets of corrugated metal that would form the support for the crawlspace.

Rob looked at the flimsy sheets of metal and said, 'Jesus Christ, rather them than me.'

Danny said, 'I just hope it's all going to be worth it.'

Rob said, 'It'll take more than a few rocks and a bit of mud to finish off Brian. He's tough as old boots.'

Danny began to walk back towards the Mobile Incident Room. He couldn't stand to look at the entrance to the cave any longer. He had suddenly felt a real sense of loss and doubted that Rob's assessment was going to be right this time.

Just as he reached the door, Danny heard a voice behind him. 'Any updates, Chief Inspector?'

Danny spun around and saw Chief Constable Jack Renshaw and Chief Superintendent Adrian Potter walking towards him.

Danny said, 'Hello, sir. How much do you know already?'

'I know that one of your men is trapped underground, Danny. Any updates on when they can get him out of there?'

'I've just spoken to Ray Machin, the Mines Rescue supervisor. He thinks they should be able to get him out within the next three hours.'

'That's very time specific.'

'That's the estimation of how much air he might have in the pot cave. That's if he's still alive.'

'I see. What are the odds on him still being alive?'

Danny shrugged. 'I've really no idea, sir. I wouldn't like to guess. What I do know is that these men from the Mines Rescue Service are risking their own lives to get a complete stranger out of a hole.'

'As did your detective inspector for a vulnerable young girl,' said Adrian Potter. The chief superintendent continued, 'We're all very proud of him, Danny.'

Danny was taken aback. It was the first time Adrian Potter had ever used his first name.

Danny mumbled, 'Thank you, sir. It's just a waiting game now, I'm afraid.'

Jack Renshaw said, 'I'm going to stay here for the duration. It's where I should be. Do we need any other resources?'

'No, sir, everything's in hand. As I said before, all we can do is wait and let these men do their work.'

Adrian Potter added, 'And say a quiet prayer while we do.'

Jack Renshaw looked at Potter and nodded in agreement. He had noted the two comments Potter had made to Danny Flint about Detective Inspector Hopkirk's situation. He hoped that his brief conversation in the car had got through to the acerbic Yorkshireman.

99

2.30pm, 18 October 1986
Richmond Drive, Mapperley Park, Nottinghamshire

Rebecca Whitchurch walked into the lounge of her beautiful home, carrying a single suitcase.

She placed the suitcase on the floor and said, 'Emily's fast asleep.'

She turned to DC Helen Baxter and said, 'Thank you for everything you've done for us, Helen. These have been extremely difficult times, and you've been extremely supportive, but I think you can leave now.'

Helen said, 'Are you sure, Rebecca?'

'Yes, I'm sure. We've got our precious daughter back now, so everything will be fine. Thanks again for everything you've done.'

Helen stood up and grabbed her coat from the back of the settee. As she put her coat on, she took a card from her pocket and said, 'Here's my card. You can still contact me any time day or night. I fully understand if you want to be left alone, to have some precious family time. I'm just so pleased that we got Emily back for you both.'

Rebecca walked with the detective to the front door.

At the door, Rebecca embraced Helen and said, 'Precious family time, exactly. Thanks, Helen.'

The detective was a little surprised by Rebecca's comment, but she nodded and walked down the driveway to her car.

Rebecca closed the door and walked back into the lounge.

Dominic had already poured himself a large tumbler full of whiskey.

He looked at the suitcase and said, 'Are you going somewhere?'

Rebecca snatched the glass of whiskey from her husband's hand, walked into the kitchen and poured the drink down the sink.

Dominic said, 'What the hell's wrong with you? What are you doing?'

She turned round sharply. With real venom in her voice, she said, 'Am I going somewhere? No, Dom, you are! Get your clothes packed and get the fuck out of this house!'

'What? You've got to be kidding.'

'I heard what that bloody detective said to you at the hospital. Brandon Temple, Angela's wife. I'm not stupid, and I'm not blind. Your sordid little affair almost cost our daughter her life. If having sex with Angela Temple was that important to you, you can have it for good. Now get your stuff packed and get out!'

'It wasn't important to me. Sex with her meant nothing, Rebecca! This is where I belong.'

'Well, it obviously meant something to Brandon Temple. You don't belong here. You're nothing but a user! Now get out, or have I got to call the police to throw you out?'

Dominic became angry. 'You'll regret this, you cold-hearted bitch! I'll make sure you're finished in chambers.'

'That's all you're bothered about, isn't it? Your precious career,' she sneered.

He snarled back, 'Well, you're as bad. If you'd been a better mother, Emily wouldn't have gone off the rails the way she did.'

'I'm sure your pretty little airhead mistress will be waiting with open arms for you, Dominic. Now, for the last time, get the fuck out of this house!'

Dominic grabbed the Range Rover keys and a bottle of whiskey. Ignoring the suitcase, he stormed out of the house, slamming the door behind him.

Rebecca smiled and walked into the hallway.

She picked up the telephone and dialled a number.

She said, 'Hello, Sebastien. I just wanted to let you know that the police have found Emily, and that she's back home safe and well.'

Sebastien Dawson gushed, 'That's wonderful news, Rebecca. You and Dominic must be so relieved. How on earth did they find her?'

'Apparently, the police followed a man by the name of Brandon Temple to some caves where she was being held captive. Temple was arrested, and Emily was brought home to me.'

'That's brilliant. I'm so happy for you.'

'Don't you recognise the man's surname?'

Dawson mused, 'Hmm, Temple. Should I?'

Rebecca said, 'I'll help you out. Brandon Temple is married to Angela Temple. Junior barrister at Mulberry Chambers, and the woman my wonderful husband has been fucking for months. It appears that Mr Temple was less than happy about this arrangement. He decided to exact his revenge against my errant husband by abducting our daughter. I've no doubt that eventually this monster would have let her die in those fucking caves.'

Sebastien Dawson was trying to process what he had just heard. He mumbled, 'I'm so sorry, Rebecca.'

'I just wanted to let you know that I'll be leaving Mulberry just as soon as I can find a job elsewhere. Obviously, Dominic and I can no longer be together. I really hope that the policeman who is still trapped underground makes it out alive, or the publicity for Mulberry Chambers could be disastrous.'

Dawson blustered, 'What trapped policeman? What are you talking about?'

'I'm sorry; didn't I mention that? The police detective who found our daughter is still trapped in the caves where she was being held by Brandon Temple. If the officer dies, I'll make damn sure the press knows the full story. I'll give them the true reason why my daughter was abducted and hidden in the caves that eventually claimed the life of the hero detective.'

'But if you do that, it will ruin Dominic's legal career.'

'Yes, it will, won't it? At least he'll always have the beautiful Angela Temple to keep him warm. Goodbye, Sebastien.'

100

3.00pm, 18 October 1986
Caves below Forest Road East, Nottingham

Ray Machin was lying on his stomach, immediately behind Pete Millership. Both men were in the claustrophobic confines of the crawl space they had excavated by hand. They were both attached by a lifeline to other members of the team, who were waiting at the entrance to the crawl space. It was a precaution against further roof falls. The only light in the small passageway was provided by the helmet lights of the two experienced miners.

The Mines Rescue supervisor grabbed hold of Pete Millership's boot and shook it. He whispered, 'We're ten yards in now, Pete. You should be at the entrance to the pot cave by now.'

Using a small hand shovel to move the loose sandstone that had fallen into the tunnel, Pete Millership scraped back another load of soil. Reaching forward, he grabbed at what he thought was loose soil immediately in front of his face.

Suddenly, he froze.

Ray Machin sensed his colleague had found something. 'What is it?'

'It's his hand, Ray.'

'Can you feel a pulse?'

Pete Millership carefully wiped the soil away from the exposed wrist and felt for a pulse.

There was nothing.

The skin felt cold and clammy to the touch. Pete Millership said grimly, 'There's nothing, Ray. He's gone.'

The miner began to scrape more soil away from the hand, exposing the dead man's arm and chest. He said, 'It looks like his top half is lying on the floor of the tunnel, and his bottom half is still in the pot cave. Poor sod must have almost made it before the roof came down.'

Ray said, 'Can we get him out?'

'It's going to take a while, but yes, I'm sure we can. We'll need to dig right past him and shore the crawl space up properly before we dig down to free his bottom half. Be another hour or so of digging, I reckon.'

'Are you alright to keep going?'

'Yeah, I'm fine. Let's get this poor bugger out of here.'

'I'm going to send Stan in to help you. I need to let everyone up top know what we've found.'

'Okay. Sorry it's bad news, mate. At least he would have been killed instantly. He hasn't suffocated down here.'

Ray backed out of the crawl space and said, 'We've found him, lads. It's a recovery job, not a rescue. Stan, get in and give Pete a hand to complete the recovery.'

Stacey Bloom had remained in the tunnel while the miners searched. She said, 'Is he dead?'

'Yes, lass, I'm afraid he is. I need to go up top and tell

Danny. There's really no need for you to stay down here now. You might as well come up top with me.'

A sad Stacey Bloom just nodded and followed Ray Machin towards the entrance.

As she trudged along, Stacey thought to herself that this was now a journey that Detective Inspector Brian Hopkirk would only be able to make with the assistance of the Mines Rescue Service, as they carried his crushed body out.

101

3.20pm, 18 October 1986
Forest Road East, Nottingham

Danny saw the lamps approaching from within the entrance to the cave system. He saw Ray Machin emerge first, followed by Stacey Bloom. The grim expression on the face of the Mines Rescue supervisor told Danny all he needed to know.

As soon as Ray took off his helmet, Danny said, 'You've found him, haven't you?'

'We have, Danny. I'm sorry. It's not good news, I'm afraid.'

'Was there no air pocket in the pot cave?'

'There was nothing. The whole lot had collapsed. We found your colleague right on the edge of the pot cave. It looks like he'd made a last desperate attempt to get out just before the lot came down.'

'Can you get him out?'

'Yes, we can. We're in the process of recovering his body now. I'm sorry it's such shit news.'

A clearly upset Danny said, 'So am I, Ray. I really appreciate the courage and the efforts of you and your staff, trying to rescue him.'

Ray said nothing and just gripped the shoulders of the man standing in front of him.

The tough miner made eye contact with Danny and said, 'To get that young lass out of there took real guts, Danny. All my lads have said so. My men appreciate courage, and your man had it in bucketloads. It's the least we can do to get him out of there.'

'Thanks, Ray. How long do you think it will take to get him out?'

'Probably another hour, I reckon. I'll get back down there now and make sure there are no hitches. I'm really sorry.'

Danny nodded and watched as Ray Machin put his helmet back on and crawled back through the hole in the wall and into the cave system.

Stacey Bloom said, 'Are you okay?'

Danny brushed the tears from his face. 'Yeah. I'll be okay. Thanks for all your help today, Stacey.'

He walked out of the tent and into bright sunlight. It had finally stopped bloody raining. He could see Jack Renshaw in his full uniform, standing next to Adrian Potter outside the Mobile Incident Room.

The chief constable saw Danny approaching and took his hat off. He knew instantly from the expression on Danny's face what had happened. He said, 'It's bad news, isn't it?'

'Yes, sir, the worst. Detective Inspector Brian Hopkirk's dead. They're recovering his body now. It's going to take at least another hour to get him out of there.'

Jack Renshaw gripped his cap tightly and said angrily, 'Bloody hell!'

The three men stood quietly on the street, taking a moment to remember their fallen colleague.

It was Danny who broke the silence. 'Sir, I need to go and talk to his next of kin. Brian was divorced from his wife, Maggie, but he also has a thirteen-year-old daughter, Laura. Sorry, he *had* a thirteen-year-old daughter.'

Jack Renshaw said, 'We'll go in my car. Adrian, you hold the fort here?' Adrian nodded. Then Danny said, 'Can you give me a minute, please, sir?'

'Take as long as you need.'

He walked into the Mobile Incident Room, where Rachel and Rob Buxton were waiting.

Danny broke the sad news and then said, 'Rachel, I'm going with the chief constable to tell Brian's ex-wife and daughter what's happened. Are you okay to come with me? Maggie may need your support.'

Rachel brushed away her tears and nodded. 'Yes, sir.'

102

11.00am, 25 October 1986
Wilford Hill Cemetery, Nottingham

The weather matched the sombre mood of the day. The sky was a grey leaden colour, and more rain was a distinct possibility. A strong wind buffeted across the open spaces of the cemetery, making it feel very cold.

Danny raised the collar on his overcoat in a futile attempt to keep the frigid wind at bay. At the specific request of Maggie Hopkirk, the police presence at the graveside for her estranged husband's burial was minimal.

Only Danny and Rob Buxton had been invited to stand and pay their respects with the family.

The service of remembrance earlier that morning had been a different matter. The small, picturesque St Wilfrid's church in Wilford had been packed inside and out as officers of all ranks attended to pay their own final respects to a friend, colleague and fallen hero.

After the service, as Danny and Rob had walked to their car to make the short drive to the cemetery, Chief Constable Jack Renshaw had approached.

He had taken Danny to one side and said, 'Obviously not today, Danny, but we need to get things sorted out between you and Adrian.'

Danny replied, 'You're right, sir. Now is definitely not the time, but we do need to straighten things out. I don't know if I can, or if I even want to, continue working for that man.'

'I'll see you both in my office at ten o'clock on the twenty-seventh, okay?'

Danny nodded, caught up with Rob and continued walking to the car.

In the car, as they drove slowly behind the hearse and the funeral cars, Rob had said, 'What was all that about?'

Danny had brushed off the question. 'Nothing for you to worry about, Rob.'

Now, standing at the graveside, as Danny watched the coffin that contained his good friend being slowly lowered into the cold earth, he glanced over at Maggie and her daughter, Laura.

His thoughts turned to the recent conversation he'd had with Brian. About his concerns over losing touch with his precious daughter when she moved to the United States of America with her mother and her new husband.

How cruel life could be, thought Danny. That unique, loving relationship between a father and his daughter had now been ripped apart for ever.

As the priest began the interment service, Danny's thoughts turned to his own impending fatherhood. He wondered what the future held in store for him and his child.

The thought of it made him shudder and rejoice all at the

same time.

The short service over, Danny waited in turn to take soil from the box held by the clergyman. He stood at the side of the grave and bade his own silent goodbye before dropping the handful of soil onto his friend's coffin.

Danny had been surprised when Maggie had chosen burial for Brian, bearing in mind the circumstances of his colleague's tragic death.

He was torn away from his melancholy thoughts when Maggie approached him and said, 'Thank you for coming, Danny. Brian thought the world of you.'

'I feel honoured that you asked me to attend, Maggie. It was important to be able to pay my respects. Brian was a great detective, a good man, and he still thought the world of you and Laura.'

'We always loved each other, Danny; we just couldn't live together. I couldn't have wished for a better father for Laura.'

'When do you leave for the States?'

'Brian told you?'

'Yes, he told me. He was concerned about losing touch with Laura.'

Tears formed in Maggie's eyes. 'I would never have let that happen.'

Danny put his arms around her, hugged her and said, 'I know, Maggie, I know. And more importantly, so did he.'

She found her inner strength and resolve, stepped back from Danny, smiled and said, 'I hear you're going to be a father soon?'

'It won't be long now. I can't wait.'

'Be a good father, Danny. Always make the time to be part of your child's life.'

'I will, Maggie.'

Maggie nodded and walked on. Her young daughter, Laura, ashen-faced, walked behind her.

103

10.00am, 27 October 1986
Nottinghamshire Police Headquarters

Danny Flint and Adrian Potter sat stern-faced opposite an equally stern-faced Jack Renshaw.

Renshaw said, 'I've asked you both here this morning to clear the air and start again. I'm willing to go on record right now and say that, as far as I'm concerned, the MCIU is an integral part of this police force's ability to investigate and detect major and serious crime, and will remain so. Is that understood?'

Danny said, 'That's always been my point of view, sir. I don't think the chief superintendent shares that opinion.'

Adrian Potter said, 'I've never doubted the abilities of the MCIU. My only concern was that it was never going to be cost-effective.'

Danny said, 'Everything isn't about pounds and pence. The day that happens, we can forget about police work and giving good service to the public. Our role is to protect people and detect crime. We're coppers, for Christ's sake, not bank managers!'

Jack Renshaw said, 'I applaud your passion, Danny, but you must temper that passion with a sense of realism. Unfortunately, it's a fact of life that we operate on fixed budgets. The work that Adrian does is just as vital to the well-being of this force as good detection rates. I think you both need to accept that you have very different approaches to police work, but that basically, you're on the same side.'

Danny said, 'I do appreciate the need to run on tight budgets, and I've always strived to keep the costs of my department to a minimum. Nobody on my team takes liberties with the overtime and expenses budget.'

Adrian said, 'I never really got the chance to say, one way or another, whether I had found your department to be cost-effective.'

Danny scoffed, 'You made it abundantly clear to me on several occasions, with your barbed asides and snide comments, that you wanted the MCIU disbanded. You can't deny that?'

'When I first arrived here, and from the outside looking in, the MCIU did seem to be a very expensive luxury. I've since had the opportunity to have in-depth meetings with all the detective chief inspectors on the various divisions across the county. They were all adamant that the MCIU is a wonderful idea, because it stops major crime enquiries impacting on their own meagre budgets. I'm always open to change, Chief Inspector. I've never been so blinkered in my approach that I cannot admit when I may have been wrong about something.'

Danny said, 'I appreciate that, and accept that I am a little overprotective towards my department. Every single one of my staff are bloody good detectives, who always give one hundred per cent on whatever case they're working on. I just want you to acknowledge that fact from time to time.'

Potter said, 'I'm willing to wipe the slate clean and start our working relationship afresh, if you are. I think we can both accept that we'll never be bosom buddies, and I'm sure there'll be times in the future when we clash again. Let's take the personalities out of this and work together in a professional manner.'

'That will suit me down to the ground. I don't want any more cheap stunts like the Emily Whitchurch case. That should never have been given to the MCIU to investigate.'

Potter held his hands up and said, 'Understood. You need to know that request didn't actually come from me.'

Danny looked at Jack Renshaw, who said, 'That was my decision. I was getting a lot of heat from various sources, and it was my first week in post. In hindsight, I should have played it differently. The bottom line is, I made the wrong decision then, and I can't change it. What I can say is that I wouldn't make the same decision today. We all have to learn from experience.'

There was a pause. Nobody spoke.

Jack Renshaw broke the heavy silence. 'Do I take it that I haven't got to advertise for a new head of CID or a new detective chief inspector for the MCIU?'

Danny said, 'I'm staying put, sir.'

Potter squirmed a little in his seat and said, 'I've got unfinished business here, sir.'

Renshaw said, 'Good. In that case, let's all get back to work, shall we?'

EPILOGUE

3.30am, 3 May 1988
Sevenoaks, Kent

Sam Jamieson was parked in a secluded layby on the country lane that led to Sandford Manor, the luxury barn conversion that was now the home of Rebecca Whitchurch. She shared the house with her teenage daughter, Emily, but whenever Emily was away at Roedean School in Brighton, she lived there alone.

Sam Jamieson had carefully studied all the newspaper reports about the abduction of Emily Whitchurch by Professor Brandon Temple. He had been as shocked as everyone else when the motive behind the abduction had been revealed. Rebecca Whitchurch had delighted in telling the whole sordid story to the media. She had divorced Dominic Whitchurch, obtained custody of her daughter and left her job at Mulberry Chambers. She then relocated and started work in London. It had been a simple task for Jamieson to locate her at a firm of barristers that were located on King's Bench Walk, in the city.

He had spent days watching her and had been overjoyed when she completed on the purchase of the secluded Sandford Manor, just outside Sevenoaks in Kent.

He felt that everything was coming together at the right time.

Sam Jamieson had recently completed his master's in psychology and had been successful in applying for a job at the University of Alberta, in Edmonton, Canada.

His life was about to take a complete change of direction, but there was still unfinished business to attend to.

He had purchased the old second-hand car he now sat in from a newspaper advertisement in the *Sheffield Star*. He had caught the train to Sheffield to pick the vehicle up. The battered Ford Escort had cost the grand sum of one hundred pounds. He had paid cash. Yesterday, he had packed up all his belongings into the two large suitcases that now sat in the boot of the car.

In the glove compartment was a one-way ticket from Heathrow International Airport to Edmonton International Airport. The flight was due to leave at five o'clock that evening.

Yesterday had been an emotional day, as he bade a sad farewell to his daughter at Mansfield Woodhouse cemetery. He had sworn at her graveside that he would fulfil the promise he had made before he left for Canada.

It had been a long road. He had never wavered in his conviction that he would one day achieve justice for his dead daughter.

He glanced down at the clear plastic bag and the plastic tie wraps on the car seat beside him.

He had spent hours studying the forensic techniques employed by murder squad detectives at crime scenes.

He was now dressed in a light blue, fibreless overall. He had overshoes made from the same material, ready to put on his soft-soled shoes. Two pairs of latex gloves on his hands, and a mask to cover his face.

He had selected suffocation as the means to exact his final revenge, as it left the least trace of forensic evidence. He had cleaned the plastic bag and the tie wraps in bleach and had only ever handled them wearing gloves. They had been purchased with cash, along with several other items, from a hardware store in Cambridge that had no CCTV.

He had carefully selected the route from Nottingham to Sevenoaks, avoiding the motorways and their hidden cameras. The final precaution he had taken was to disguise the registration plate on the Ford Escort.

At the airport, he would abandon the car in one of the long-stay car parks, where it would be left to rot and rust.

He glanced at his watch. It was time. He picked up the bag and the tie wraps.

He had no plans for a sophisticated entrance to the property. He knew that the nearest police response was over half an hour away. He would disable the alarm system by severing the electricity supply cables, force entry through a French door at the rear of the property, then go to her bedroom.

Once inside the bedroom, he planned to overpower her, place the bag over her head and secure it with tie wraps. He would stand over her and watch until she gasped her last breath. Only then would his long wait for justice be over. He would be long gone before Rebecca Whitchurch was ever found.

He climbed over the five-bar gate and began walking down the hill, across the moonlit field, towards the secluded house.

After all the years of waiting and preparation, he knew that justice for his beloved Vanessa was now only five minutes away.

WE HOPE YOU ENJOYED THIS BOOK

If you could spend a moment to write an honest review on Amazon, no matter how short, we would be extremely grateful. They really do help readers discover new authors.

ALSO BY TREVOR NEGUS

EVIL IN MIND
(Book 1 in the DCI Flint series)

DEAD AND GONE
(Book 2 in the DCI Flint series)

A COLD GRAVE
(Book 3 in the DCI Flint series)

TAKEN TO DIE
(Book 4 in the DCI Flint series)

Published by Inkubator Books
www.inkubatorbooks.com

Copyright © 2021 by Trevor Negus

Trevor Negus has asserted his right to be identified as the author of this work.

TAKEN TO DIE is a work of fiction. People, places, events, and situations are the product of the author's imagination. Any resemblance to actual persons, living or dead is entirely coincidental.

No part of this book may be reproduced, stored in any retrieval system, or transmitted by any means without the prior written permission of the publisher.

Printed in Great Britain
by Amazon